LOVER BETRAYED

WINDSTORM
PRESS

Praise for Lover Betrayed

In this riveting recast of events that took place in Secret Sky, *the viewpoint shifts to that of Emelynn Taylor's first love, the darkly handsome Jackson. He may possess the same mysterious, life-altering gift as Emelynn does, but he has a very different perspective – especially when it comes to affairs of the heart. Author JP McLean possesses her own unique gift: the ability to bewitch her readers with her boundless imagination.*

—Elinor Florence, Globe and Mail bestselling author of
Bird's Eye View

JP McLean has a style and immediacy of detail that pulls the reader into a complex tale set with all-too-human characters ruled by their extraordinary capabilities. Exciting action and conflict of loyalties make this a fantastic page-turner.

—Kristina Stanley, bestselling author of
the Stone Mountain Mystery Series

Praise for The Gift Legacy

A profoundly intelligent story of a captivating young woman whose victories and struggles with a unique gift will grab your every emotion.
—Jennifer Manuel, award-winning author of
The Heaviness of Things That Float

A deftly crafted, impressively original and inherently compelling read from first page to last.
—Midwest Book Review

Danger, suspense, and mystery all bundled into one perfect read.
—Urban Lit Magazine

A gripping read you won't want to put down.
—Debra Purdy Kong, award-winning author of
The Casey Holland Mystery series

McLean's expertly drawn world is filled with intriguing characters and near-familiar settings that draw you into this compelling read.
—Katherine Prairie, author of
the Alex Graham thriller series

A compelling journey into a unique world that supernatural suspense fans will adore!
—Lisa Voisin, author of The Watcher Saga

The author swept me into a world that's unique in fiction. A "can't put it down" read.
—Diana Stevan, author of *A Cry from the Deep*

Fun, exciting and addictive.
—Annie Siegel, author, lyricist and jazz musician

JP McLean's adventure fantasy series, while full of tense and dangerous moments, is also playful and expansive.
—Bill Engleson, author of *Like a Child to Home*

Titles by JP McLean

The Thorne Witch Novels
The Never Witch

Hexborn

The Dark Dreams Novels
Blood Mark

Ghost Mark

Scorch Mark

The Gift Legacy
Secret Sky

Hidden Enemy

Burning Lies

Lethal Waters

Deadly Deception

Wings of Prey

The Gift Legacy Companion
Lover Betrayed (Secret Sky Redux)

Novellas
Crimson Frost (A Supernatural Noel)

LOVER BETRAYED

THE GIFT LEGACY COMPANION
BOOK 1

JP MCLEAN

Lover Betrayed
The Gift Legacy Companion ~ Book 1
First Canadian Edition

Copyright © 2019 by JP McLean
All rights reserved.

Previously published as *The Gift: Betrayal*

ISBN
978-1-988125-49-7 (Paperback)
978-1-988125-50-3 (MOBI)
978-1-988125-51-0 (EPUB)
978-1-988125-52-7 (PDF)

Edited by Nina Munteanu
Copy edit by Rachel Small
Book cover designed by JD&J with stock imagery
provided by Steve Estvanik & elwynn © 123RF.com
Author photograph by Crystal Clear Photography

Excerpt from *Secret Sky* copyright © 2018 by JP McLean

Cataloguing in Publication information available
from Library and Archives Canada

For Molly and Soozie—you were the best writing companions.
I miss you every day.

Oh what a tangled web we weave,
When first we practise to deceive!

—Sir Walter Scott
Marmion

Chapter One

The oppressive heat was unavoidable, omnipotent, like the man in the casket. We followed dutifully behind, our steps out of time with the rhythmic clops of the black hearse horses. White lilies hugged the casket, quivering to the drum roll of a jazz band's lively rendition of "When the Saints Go Marching In," an absurd funeral favourite. Tourists in waist pouches and flip-flops, unsure of the show, whispered behind finger curtains and stole glances under furrowed brows and baseball caps. I understood their uncertainty. The father I'd loved and loathed died without warning, too soon to recognize his mistakes, let alone fix them.

"This is a goddamn freak show," I said. "I'd never have agreed to it if it wasn't spelled out in his will."

"But it was," Sandra said. "You and your father may have had your differences, but you're a good son, Jackson."

"Was. I *was* a good son."

"You always will be," Sandra said. My wife's fingers felt cool in my hand, despite the heat. She looked up at me, her blue eyes hidden behind sunglasses and a loop of black netting that covered her face. I eased the pressure off her hand with an apology, ignoring the bead of sweat that crawled down my spine.

It took thirty minutes for my father's slow funeral procession, wafting the cloying scent of flowers, to wind through the streets of New Orleans. We'd walked an unpleasant mile behind the coffin before passing under the iron arch of the cemetery. Like a shrimp trawler with its net out, our parade snagged tourists and curiosity-seekers in its wake.

The music took on a sombre tenor only when we mounted the slight rise, which housed the Delaney tomb. The last time I'd seen the tomb open was fifteen years ago when we'd laid my mother to rest. Following long tradition, her coffin had been discarded and her remains dumped into the bone heap below to make way for the new arrival. One day, my coffin would displace my father's in a similar ritual. Would I also succumb to a stroke before I'd finished living my life?

I was a teenager when my mother died. There were times now when I had to see her picture to remember her face, but I had no trouble remembering her love. She'd bathed me in it, cooking my favourite crawfish boil, which my father hated, and baking pecan pies he wouldn't touch. She liked that I'd inherited her hazel eyes. Dad had said she coddled me, or at least that's the excuse he used to justify his tough-love approach to parenting. I doubted I'd ever need a photograph of my father to remember him.

The priest raised his voice over the crowd while photojournalists captured video of the mourners. Tomorrow, they would justify the intrusion in the name of news. Equally unwelcome tourists snapped cell-phone photos they'd later show their friends at home in some macabre recollection of their good fortune in stumbling upon a genuine City of the Dead funeral.

I looked out over the perspiring faces. Tourists aside, my father would have been pleased to see the calibre of mourners who'd braved the August heat to pay their last respects. Top-echelon politicians and business people mopped their brows and donned sombre expressions, hopeful that the priest was nearing the end of the ritual. Half of the men gathered were better candidates for a casket. My father wasn't yet sixty. It shouldn't have been his time.

After the casket was laid in place, I bid him a final farewell and then nodded to the cemetery workmen, who kept their wheelbarrows at a respectful distance. As soon as they moved in to seal the tomb, the mourners began to scatter.

Jimmy Marchant was the first to approach. Sweat was beading on his red face and dribbling down ample jowls that melted into a thick neck. His jacket was soaked through, but he hadn't loosened his tie. He'd be a proper southern gentleman for my father one last time if it killed him.

He pecked Sandra on the cheek before offering me his hand. "Sorry for your loss, buddy. Your father's left a big hole on half the boards in

Louisiana." Jimmy was born and raised in New Orleans. He spoke with a Yat accent, pronouncing "boards" with a barely perceptible *r* and "Louisiana" as "Loo-ziana."

"Thanks, Jimmy." In his younger years, Jimmy could have passed for John Goodman's brother. My father respected Jimmy Marchant for his legal counsel and even more for his discretion. Jimmy understood my father's definition of doing business. It entertained him, and earned his firm a lot of money, especially when my father bent the law. I was in Jimmy's debt for making sure no one knew how often that had happened. "I hope you'll join us at the Omni tonight. Let Dad buy you one last drink."

"Wouldn't miss it. Matthew Delaney knew how to throw a party and I intend to honour my promise: your father's wake will be one to remember." He leaned close. "And well lubricated," he added with a conspiratorial wink.

I forced a smile and shook Jimmy's hand. One final spectacle to endure.

Dad had made a good and loyal friend in Jimmy. I'd known Jimmy all my life and had my own reasons for liking the man. It was through him that I'd met my wife, Alexandra, or Sandra, as she preferred to be called. Like Jimmy, her father was a lawyer, and Redmond Moss was well connected. After Katrina, Redmond used those connections to generate funds to help rebuild. Sandra Moss distributed her father's funding out of Jimmy's donated office space. When Jimmy recruited my father's development expertise, I was the lucky son of a bitch who got to work with her.

I took Sandra's elbow and turned toward the first in a long line of idling limos.

"Kyle, Anthony, you'll ride with us, of course," Sandra said, addressing my old Stanford classmates who'd flown in for the funeral. Kyle Murphy lived in Dallas so knew enough to wear a light coloured suit. Anthony Dimarco was New York through and through. His navy Brooks Brothers was a choice I suspected he now regretted.

The driver opened Sandra's door, and we followed her into the blessed air conditioning.

"Jackman—how the hell do you live in this heat?" Anthony said, using my college nickname as he mopped the sweat from his brow with a limp pocket square. He tugged his tie loose.

"Northerners," Kyle quipped.

The driver pulled out, leading the train of limos to the hotel.

"I'm serious," Anthony said, supplementing his pocket square with several tissues he'd yanked from the limo's complimentary supply.

"You get used to it," I said, sparing a glance at Sandra. She'd smoothed her hair into some complicated knot the heat didn't seem to touch.

"Will you be staying long?" Sandra asked.

"Only if you dump that lousy husband of yours," Kyle said with a lecherous smile. Anthony swatted him. "What? We all know she's out of his league."

"Oh, and you think she's in yours?" Anthony said, raising his eyebrows.

Sandra looked down at her folded hands, fighting a smile. They'd met her on our wedding day. The last-minute introduction had been unavoidable, but Kyle and Anthony had taken the piss out of me about it. They insisted she would have chosen either of them over me if they'd been introduced earlier. The truth was, if Sandra and I hadn't wed quickly, and quietly, her family would have tried to stop us. It wasn't just that she came from old money and I came from new—it was that her father didn't approve of the way my father had amassed his fortune. Redmond Moss was not a religious man, but he was a judgmental bastard who held firmly to the belief that the sins of the father should be visited upon the son. Thankfully, Sandra had a mind of her own.

The driver pulled up in front of the Omni hotel, where a black-capped doorman hurried to open Sandra's door. The limo's cool air dissipated in a suffocating wave of heat. We hurried inside.

"We're going to freshen up," Sandra said, removing her sunglasses. "We'll see you in an hour or so?"

"For sure," Kyle said. Anthony already had his jacket off and his tie in hand.

Sandra took my arm and we headed to the elevators. Back in our suite, she kicked off her shoes. "That went well, don't you think?" she said.

I removed my jacket and flopped on the sofa. "A few more hours and it'll be over."

"Don't wish it away too fast." She stood in front of a mirror untangling the netted hat from her hair. "After all, the Delaney board will be there and so will most of the city's politicians, not to mention the governor."

"And your father?"

"He'll be there. Mom as well. Etiquette dictates, as you know." Etiquette and old money went hand in hand. Sandra should know; she'd been raised on both.

"Have you told them about my plans for Delaney & Son?"

She dropped her hat on the coffee table and sat beside me. "No. I want them to hear it from you."

After the initial shock of Dad's death had worn off, Sandra and I talked through the night about what came next. I didn't keep secrets from Sandra—her discretion was impeccable, so she knew about Dad's *strategic donations*, as he'd referred to them, and his propensity to *eavesdrop* when he thought it would win him an advantage. I was ashamed of that. I told her I wanted to be a better man, to behave respectably and with honour. To do things right.

"Cleaning up Delaney's reputation will take a long time. Years probably."

She turned in her seat. "The fact that you want to is what matters. And soon you'll be the one making the decisions, not your father. Dad will see the difference. He'll come around."

I took her hand and brushed my thumb against her wedding band. "I hope it's not a mistake. My father may have been short on scruples, but he knew how to make money."

"And so do you, but you know how to do it without compromising your integrity."

I lifted my head in a flash of annoyance. "My father had plenty of integrity."

She stiffened. "Of course. That was careless of me to say."

I dropped her hand and stood. "I'm going to shower."

"I'm sorry."

"I know. It's been a tough week." I squeezed her shoulder in passing. "We'll get through it."

After changing into fresh clothes, we took the elevator back down to the ballroom. The scent of flowers nearly knocked me over. I doubted there was a lily in Louisiana outside of this room. Was this the measure of a man? Personally, I'd never understood the flowers. A man had died. He'd lived and breathed business, not flowers. Flowers were something his guilt trotted out on Valentine's Day. Why not a genuine tribute to the man when he was still alive? A fine bottle of bourbon? Midfield seats at a Saints game? A favour he didn't have to pay for?

My arrival dimmed the raucous laughter. Jimmy, finally free of his jacket, raised his glass in a silent toast from across the room, and held it aloft. One by one, everyone in the ballroom did the same. Say what you want about my old man, he made an impression. A rocks glass landed in my hand. I stared at the amber liquid and fought the lump at the back of my throat.

Slowly, I raised my glass. "To Matthew Delaney," I said. "A formidable businessman, a generous benefactor, and my father. May he rest in peace." A collective shout rang out and then bubbled away.

Conversations resumed, backs were turned and bursts of laughter rose above the ambient noise. Sandra stroked the back of my arm. "That was lovely."

Lovely? Anger crawled up my chest, prickling my neck. I scanned the crowd. Every gluttonous supplier, every slippery politician, every Barbie Doll wife, and every major charity bold enough to send a representative had benefited from my father's acumen and generosity. They still were, sloshing back the best the bar had to offer. What had Dad gotten? Flowers he would hate and a toast from a son who couldn't even say he loved him. He'd taught me everything he knew, and it wasn't enough. My love for him was rough around the edges. In time, it may have softened, but we had no more time.

I quaffed my drink and another magically appeared. Condolences flowed, abundant as the liquor, and one after another, Dad's impressive circle of influencers, friends and rivals approached me to pay their respects. Marcel Cadieu, a Louisiana senator and early convert to my father's way of doing business, was one of the first to slither up.

"My wife, Claudette," he said, making an unnecessary introduction. "Please accept our sympathies, Jackson. Louisiana has lost a great man." Marcel hid his animosity behind a politician's smile. He'd never figured out how my father had learned of his affair with a sandy-haired gentleman half his age. Marcel had been so careful; he and his lover had never acknowledged one another in public, not so much as a wayward glance. They'd checked into separate but adjoining rooms on the forty-second floor of the Sheraton in New Orleans. Yet my father knew the sandy-haired gentleman had spilled his flute of Cristal out on the balcony that fateful night. Dad had a photograph to prove it. And if he knew that detail, then he knew everything.

Marcel immediately became a staunch supporter of Delaney & Son. But while he championed Dad's development projects, he quietly initiated and then backed the strongest anti-drone legislation in the country. If only he knew that a drone had not been necessary.

Carl Prudhomme, also a convert, waddled up with a hearty handshake. He was head of Industrial Rod and Steel in Lafayette. My father had ensured his loyalty and a favourable pricing structure after Carl heard a recording my father played for him. Apparently Carl and two other major steel suppliers had taken a midnight trail ride into the wilds of Carl's eight-hundred-acre ranch outside of Vidalia in Concordia Parish to discuss their new pricing scheme. My father had been eager to point out that collusion in any form would likely be frowned upon in Louisiana's legislative circles. Carl had had little choice but to tip his hat, but soon afterwards, he fired his ranch hands and hired new security. Not that any of that would be an obstacle to one of our kind.

With Sandra on one side and Jimmy on the other, we received the mourners. They dropped their smiles to shake my hand, and offer condolences. Sandra's father, Redmond, and her mother, Diana made their obligatory appearance and soon after disappeared. But not all the guests wore fake smiles. My father was a generous man who loved a good party and treated his friends well.

The line of grievers marched on and my father's acquaintances crawled by, kissing my wife and patting me on the shoulder. I grew tired of repeating what felt like my mantra: "Yes, I am proud of my father's legacy." And to those few who needed to hear it, I added, "Yes, I look forward to taking Delaney & Son in a fresh, new direction."

After the handshakes and back pats subsided, Jimmy headed to the bar and Sandra excused herself. I searched the room for Kyle and Anthony. They had been welcomed into Jimmy's clutch of insiders at the bar, many of whom were Dad's closest friends. I joined them and we put a dent or two in some of the finer bottles on offer and listened to my father's friends tell ribald stories of Dad's exploits.

My father had chosen to lead a public life, and some of the tales were ones he'd leaked himself. He'd manipulated the media as handily as the men he'd kept markers on, cashing them in when it suited his game. And it didn't suit his game to have the public know his other persona: the man who grieved when my mother died; the man who stayed by my side until I conquered my deadly fear of heights; the man who helped me bury Razz, short for Razzmatazz, the crazy black lab he'd bought me for my fifth birthday. Sadly, his tender moments had been as rare and fleeting as a *loup-garou* sighting in the bayou.

This game he played ensured that, to his face at least, people referred to him as a maverick, a shrewd negotiator, a visionary. But in the backrooms and bars, they called him manipulative, contemptible and crooked. That was my legacy. I was the *& Son* of Delaney & Son, and now I had to clean up the mess.

Standing in the midst of the huddle of men at the end of the bar, I watched Sandra work her way through the mourners. She clasped a hand here, stroked a shoulder there, smiled a blessing with a nod of her head. She charmed every man in the room and befriended every woman, and she was mine, my oasis in the quagmire of grief and guilt my father's death had stirred.

A little after midnight, Sandra approached the table where Jimmy had been reminiscing about Dad and the early days, when it was still just Delaney Developments. He'd been developing strip malls back then and married to his first wife. I loved those stories best. Dad hadn't yet felt the sting of betrayal or learned to like the feel of dirt on his hands.

The wake was just warming up and wouldn't end until dawn. Sandra offered the men a shy smile and then leaned down to my ear. "I think we've done our part, Jackson. Let's go."

Her sweet vanilla scent pulled me out of my chair. It always put me in mind of my mother's bread pudding, something else I could never resist. My father once told me Sandra was too good for me. His callous comment had angered me at the time, but not because he was right. He considered her a feather in the Delaney cap, but he never once acknowledged it was me, the *& Son*, who'd won her.

I excused myself and followed her to our suite, freeing the mourners to drain the bar and speculate about what would happen to the dirt Dad had on most of them.

CHAPTER TWO

The next day, Dad's funeral was front-page news. Sandra emerged from the bathroom wrapped in a white robe, blotting her hair with a towel. "Don't let those newspapers get under your collar, Jackson. You know how much your father would have enjoyed the coverage."

I sighed in resignation. Indeed, my father would have been pleased. "Coffee?" I asked, and poured her a cup. I examined a grainy photo in the *Times-Picayune*. "Is that Cole Des Roche?"

Sandra glanced at the photo. "Could be. You'd best get dressed," she said, taking the cup from my hand. "Mustn't keep the pit bulls and sharks waiting too long."

I stared at the image of Dad's first wife's son. "What the hell was Cole doing at my father's funeral?"

"Jackson, please. Go shower. Get dressed."

"Of all times to show his ugly face."

She pressed her fingers to her forehead. "Let it go, darling. It's over."

She was right. Today was going to be hard enough. No need to add Cole and his daddy issues to our schedule. Hell, maybe Dad would have enjoyed having Cole there—one last chance to thumb his nose at the bastard's mother.

I discarded the papers and stood. "Come here." Sandra stepped into my embrace and I tucked her damp head under my chin. She smelled fresh, like a new day. "I don't think I'd have made it through this charade without you. Thank you for keeping me sane."

"I love you. Now get ready or we won't make it to the *Symphony* before dark."

After showering, I dressed in the navy Armani she'd laid out for me and paused in the bedroom doorway to admire her. She exuded a calm confidence that affected everything she touched, including me. She'd pulled her soft brown hair into a ponytail at the nape of her neck, and clutched a wide-brimmed hat and oversized sunglasses. We'd been married four years and despite my father's best efforts, she'd managed to keep her face out of the press. Sandra Moss was one of the most private women I'd ever known. I loved that about her. It was a refreshing change from the public life my father favoured. *Used to favour*, I reminded myself, once again correcting the tense.

The limo drove us around the curve of the Mississippi, from the Omni in the French Quarter through the Katrina-pruned live oaks of the Garden District and to the air-conditioned offices of Montgomery, Kean and Marchant in the Central Business District on St. Charles Avenue. My father's passing had triggered a tidal wave of paperwork that would flood Jimmy's legal team for weeks. Today, I would dip my toes in the murky water and put my faith in the same man my father had trusted for thirty years.

Air conditioning agreed with Jimmy. His colouring had returned to normal, but his rotund physique was a walking billboard for his love of Cajun cooking and an impending heart attack.

"Alexandra," Jimmy said, addressing my wife formally. He kissed her left cheek, and then her right. He offered me his hand. "How you doing, buddy?" If he'd overimbibed last night, he was hiding it well this morning.

"It doesn't seem real yet."

He reached a big paw to my shoulder and gave it a reassuring squeeze. "I know just what you mean. We're set up in the boardroom. This way." He gestured with a sweep of his hand.

Two hours later, the preliminaries for transferring Dad's personal and corporate assets were complete, and paralegals scurried to file papers with half a dozen authorities. The resulting legal fees and inheritance taxes could fund a small country. Leave it to politicians to tax the dead, the crooked bastards.

Sandra, having endured the complex legal maze, excused herself. Jimmy and I walked her to the elevators and then retreated to his office.

He poured two healthy shots of bourbon and handed me a glass.

"Matt was one of a kind. We're going to miss him." We raised our glasses in a toast. Jimmy swallowed, and dipped his head to the side, appreciating the whisky's burn.

"There's one more thing I'd like you to take care of," I said.

Jimmy cocked his head.

"The Dixon deal. I want you to kill it."

Jimmy frowned. "There's nothing to kill, bud. It was just a twinkle in your father's eye."

"It was more than that."

"A few discussions with the mayor and some preliminary correspondence with the Dixon people. Nothing more."

"He started a file."

"A little information gathering, that's all," Jimmy said, dismissing my remarks with a wave of his hand.

"A little?" I said with a chuckle. The leather creaked as I settled on the sofa. "He already had the mayor in the bag. What's he got on the Dixon stakeholders?"

Jimmy took a seat opposite. "Not much, though he did dig up a nice little tax evasion nugget on Jeremiah Dixon. Seems his socialite wife, Amelia, owns some property in Zurich that no one knows about." He settled back on the sofa. "Might be useless, though. Dixon hasn't even decided where their new headquarters will be located. Could be here, could be Baton Rouge."

"It's here," I said, feeling my jaw tighten. "Dad shined up that five-acre parcel on the north side, and the mayor threw the taxpayers under the bus to seal the deal."

Jimmy took another appreciative sip of his bourbon. "I take it you and Matthew had your usual disagreement on strategy."

"Delaney doesn't need to stoop that low. We can be better than that."

Jimmy pursed his lips and then upended his drink. "I admire your intent, but this business has never been *better than that*."

"It's got to start somewhere. No disrespect to you or my father, but I meant what I said yesterday. Delaney & Son is on a new path." My love for my father was complicated, but I wanted my legacy to be one of integrity. When the time came, and I had an heir, I wanted to hand down a company he or she could be proud of. If I could accomplish that, then Sandra's family would come around. I leaned forward. "Shred the file. I won't use it."

He frowned in contemplation. "It's a bold move, but all right. I'll support you."

"I appreciate that."

Jimmy heaved his bulk off the sofa and walked our glasses back to the credenza and the bottle of bourbon. "Hadn't seen Kyle or Anthony since your wedding," he said, changing the subject. The bottle gurgled up two more shots.

"Yeah, wish we'd had more time, but Anthony had to fly back to New York this morning." I checked my watch. "And Kyle's on a commuter to Dallas as we speak."

He handed me my refilled glass. "It was good of them to come—"

"Did you know Cole Des Roche was at Dad's funeral yesterday?"

"Can't say as I did, but you don't need to worry about Cole. Your father's death may have been unexpected, but he took precautions a long time ago to protect his assets from his first wife and her son."

"Precautions? What do you mean?"

"How much did your father tell you about his marriage to Bronwyn?"

"Only that it was short and she'd been unfaithful. It wasn't his favourite topic."

"No, I don't imagine it was." He turned to the window and took a sip of his drink. "After your father learned of her indiscretion, he got the proof he needed to ensure a tidy parting of ways. The only concession he granted was allowing her to file for the divorce."

I raised my glass. "My father—such a gentleman." I rolled my eyes with a shake of my head.

Jimmy chuckled and turned back around. "Yes, well Matt was shrewd and Bronwyn knew him well enough not to contest the small settlement. Of course, at the time, Delaney Developments wasn't the success it is today. However, with your father out of the way, I wouldn't put it past her or her son to take a run at your fortune."

"Bronwyn? That would be a hell of a stretch, wouldn't it? They divorced more than thirty years ago. Before I was born."

"True enough, but you know the rumours. If they could prove that Matt was her son's father, they could keep us in court for years."

I knew all about the rumours; I'd grown up with them. Cole was four years older than me. He and I had measured one another across dance floors at more than one debutante ball. It didn't help that Cole and I shared the same tall frame and features, but as my father had pointed out many times, Cole took after Richard Des Roche with blond hair and blue eyes, whereas I favoured Dad with dark hair and I had Mom's hazel eyes. We were *not* brothers.

"Cole's father is Richard Des Roche."

Jimmy swirled the dregs in his glass. "Yes, through adoption."

"I understood that was merely a formality."

"It allowed Richard to change Cole's name, but your father's name is the one on Cole's birth certificate."

"Only because Bronwyn was married to Dad at the time."

"Assumption of paternity. Yes, amusing law that—assuming husbands to be the fathers of their wives' offspring." He shook his head and chuckled. "Bronwyn thought she was hurting Matt when she presented him with the papers to relinquish his parental rights. Your father never flinched."

"That was a long time ago. I'd just as soon bury that tired battle-axe with my father and move on."

Jimmy frowned thoughtfully and stroked his almost empty glass of bourbon. "If Cole was at your father's funeral, I'd question what they're up to."

"I don't give a damn. I've washed my hands of them. Whatever hostilities lay between them died with Dad."

Jimmy nodded, which was his way of agreeing to disagree.

After a late lunch, I returned to the Delaney building and addressed the board of directors for the first time as chairman. The board held court on the same floor as my father's office. Ten chairs surrounded an oblong cherry table; their occupants stood upon my arrival. I made my way around the table, shaking hands with each of them, and ended behind my father's empty chair at the head of the table.

Pierre LeDoux, who fancied himself the second chair, cleared his throat. "Jackson. Welcome."

His words were a shot across my bow. As if I needed a welcome. This chair was my birthright. "Pierre, glad you could make it," I said. Pierre's face reddened. He should have let Natalie Thorne take the lead. She was the one with the balls.

"Please, take your seats," I said, glancing around the table, but no one sat down.

Pierre shifted his weight and ignored the darting glances from Natalie to his left and Arliss Whiting a few seats to his right. Denton

Desbois was the only other voting member, and he stood studying his shoes. Standing behind four other seats were warm bodies; advisors to the voting members. The advisors had opinions but no clout, and were of little consequence. My former seat remained empty.

"All right," I said, smoothing my hand along the top edge of my father's chair. "Why don't you tell me what's on your mind, Pierre."

He puffed out his chest and adjusted his tie, inadvertently drawing attention to an unsightly barbecue stain. "Everyone around this table had great respect for your father. You have our deepest condolences."

"Thank you," I said, and dipped my head in acknowledgement.

"However," Pierre continued, "I speak for all of us when I say that we are concerned about the financial viability of this company going forward."

I straightened my spine, rising to every inch of my six-foot-two frame. "Oh?"

Pierre broke eye contact and tapped a finger to the conference table. "Your father built this company. He steered it clear of the rocks in '88 when a lot of other companies went under, and again in '08. His vision, his drive was what got us through and kept us profitable." He looked around the room for moral support. "We question whether you, at the age of twenty-nine, have the experience Delaney needs at the helm."

"Delaney *& Son*," I said, correcting him. I offered them a thoughtful gaze. "Do you know how old my father was when he founded this company?" I didn't give anyone time to answer. "Twenty-two, and he didn't have the eight years of experience I have. Experience, I might point out, I gained while working side by side with my father, the man you admired so much."

Natalie, finally out of patience with Pierre, rushed in. "You voted against your father on three of Delaney's last six developments. Those projects are some of Delaney's most profitable." She pointed her nose in my direction like an accusatory finger.

"Those projects also damaged Delaney's reputation," I reminded them. "And one earned us a lawsuit we're still fighting."

"Perhaps," Arliss Whiting said, cutting in, "you would consider co-chairing with Ted Worley. He's been your father's second-in-command longer than you've been with the company. The board would be happy to entertain a co-chair of Worley's stature." Arliss settled a benevolent smile on his cherubic face, but his angelic expression did little to hide his goal of breaking my majority hold on Delaney & Son.

"I appreciate that, Arliss," I said. "Yesterday, Ted Worley and I spoke at length. We reviewed Dad's targets and projections, and we're confident Delaney & Son is on track for another profitable year."

"That is—"

"I'm not finished," I said, interrupting him. "I've spent the better part of today in Jimmy Marchant's office. As you know, Montgomery, Kean and Marchant is Delaney & Son's chief legal counsel. We reviewed the structure of this company and this board. In 2008, when Dad restructured and sold 49 percent of Delaney & Son, he made certain the chairmanship was tied to the 51 percent majority owner. As of today, that's me.

"I intend to stay the course my father set, and grow Delaney & Son into a powerhouse infused with the integrity and respect that will ensure our future profitability. If any of you do not wish to take a chance on me in this chair then you are free to sell your stock and move on."

I walked around my father's chair and took my rightful seat. This time, they all sat down.

Chapter Three

A few hours later, my driver skirted the south shore of Lake Pontchartrain on our way to the Southern Yacht Club. My thoughts turned back to Jimmy and our earlier discussion about Cole. I'd never given serious consideration to the rumours that Dad was Cole's father. And Dad's feelings where Bronwyn was concerned were unequivocal. He'd abhorred the woman. His ego never recovered from her infidelity. She'd effectively tainted his opinion of the gender.

My mother seemed to understand that, and accepted his arms' length love, contenting herself with motherhood. I often wondered if she saw the same thing as I did when I looked at their wedding photos. Her resemblance to Dad's first wife was striking. Both she and Bronwyn were blonde, beautiful and of uncomplicated minor pedigree. When I came along, I imagined my father's *fuck you* to Bronwyn was complete.

After Mom died, Dad took me into his confidence and treated me like a man instead of the fifteen-year-old boy I was. He mourned her properly but when he moved on, he never allowed himself to love again. He devoured one woman after another, going through them like Popsicles on a hot summer's day. He encouraged me to do the same, instilling in me that women were playthings that shouldn't be trusted.

I have to admit, I gave that approach a good shot. But when a woman, whose last name I didn't even know, presented herself to me on campus at Stanford, pregnant, I reassessed my philandering ways. A tidy sum of money took care of changing her mind about an abortion, but not before she had a public meltdown. It wasn't just her tears and humiliating accusations that made me reassess; it was thoughts of my mother, and how disappointed in me she would have been.

After that, I sought out the uncomplicated solitude of one plaything at a time.

And then Sandra came along. She was strong-willed and independent and took shit from no one. If you wanted to play ball with her, you stepped up to the plate, and man, did I want to play. From the first day we worked together in Jimmy's office, we recognized that our interests aligned, and our priorities fell into step. She believed in our shared vision and supported it without reservation. Not once did she kowtow to my father. She never disrespected him, her upbringing wouldn't allow it, but she held her ground, opting to change the subject or leave the room when their wills collided. She had integrity. She also shared the peculiar gene we called the *gift*. It was a refreshing change to enjoy a relationship without the burden of that secret between us.

I stepped out of the limo and back into the thick heat. Fan palms rattled in a soft offshore breeze. My jacket came off before I hit the ramp to the docks and a few steps later, I unknotted my tie. I skirted the hose snaked across the path and nodded hello to one of the regular cleaning crew. At the far end of the dock, I slowed as I approached the gleaming white hull of the *Aerial Symphony*. How many times had I come down here to find Dad kicking back with his yacht club cronies? How many deals had come together over a bottle of Scotch on the foredeck? How many women had he escorted below deck?

"Permission to board?" I called, seeing Sandra through the window. She waved and came out to greet me.

"Careful," she said, indicating a stack of flattened moving boxes on the dock beside the steps.

"You've been busy."

"Just a few things to make the *Symphony* feel more like home," she said.

I mounted the steps, pulled her close and unwound in the scent of her. I gazed back at the shore-bound clubhouse, whose windows reflected the late afternoon sun. The original structure had been consumed by fire in the wake of Katrina, but the replacement mimicked her style and grace beautifully.

I pulled back, suddenly inspired. "Let's take the *Symphony* out for a spin."

Sandra furrowed her brow.

"Come on. She's ours now. I want to kick the tires and celebrate."

Half an hour later, I cut the engines and we settled into the loungers on the foredeck, watching the sun paint the sky over Lake Pontchartrain in shades of pink and gold.

Memories of my father, and the times we'd spent aboard, clouded my thoughts.

"You okay?" Sandra asked, reaching for my hand.

"Just thinking about Dad."

"You miss him?"

"He was a hard man to love, but he was the only father I had."

She squeezed my hand.

"Did you know I used to be afraid of heights?" I asked.

"Oh my god," she said, twisting in her seat. "You never mentioned it before."

"Dad took it as a personal affront to the Delaney gene set."

A smirk curled the corners of her mouth. "He would."

"He got me through it though. Nearly killed me in the process, but a Flier who's afraid of heights wouldn't have survived long."

"This ship is a minefield of memories. Are you sure you want to live aboard her?"

"Most of the memories are good. Dad taught me how to fly from this very deck."

"Matthew was quite proud of your gift. He liked to take credit for it."

"I remember," I said, laughing. "When I was eighteen, Dad and I were invited to the International Debutante Ball in New York. I heard some snippy little shit of a senator's son talking trash about Dad, so I took the opportunity to introduce myself. I shook his hand and accidentally knocked him out. The kid was taken out on a stretcher. We were lucky he wasn't one of us. I think that was one of Dad's proudest moments." I smiled at the memory.

When the sun faded, we headed back to our slip at the Southern Yacht Club. Later that night, after dinner and a cold bottle of Chardonnay, we toasted my father and walked every one of the *Symphony's* 102 feet and called her our own for the first time.

Grief had made me ravenous for Sandra. If she was within arm's reach, I needed to touch her, peel off her clothes and get inside her. She'd been accommodating but drew the line at my father's stateroom, the largest of the *Symphony's* three staterooms.

"I am not going to be the next notch on that bedpost," she'd said, and she was adamant. Sandra insisted we wait until the remodel was complete before we moved into it. She had plans for all the staterooms, the salon and even the two aft cabins. I would have agreed to anything that made her happy, and when she agreed to make the *Symphony* our home, I gave her carte blanche on the remodel. Besides which, thanks to Jimmy's tax-planning efforts, she was now the *Symphony's* owner, on paper anyway. But I was still the one with the captain's licence, so she wasn't going anywhere without me.

It was a month before the workmen cleared out. Sandra had been right to wait. The first night we made love in the new stateroom, it was our own, not my father's. We drank a bottle of champagne and rocked the yacht half the night. We made it our thing to christen each of the staterooms as their renovations were completed, and I do believe I made her blush the afternoon we claimed the salon.

Her sense of style breathed new life into the *Symphony*. She'd selected sleek modern furniture, replacing the heavy captain's chairs with slim white pneumatic swivels and installing twin sofas in both the salon and on the observation deck. The teak floors had been refinished and the carpets replaced. Stainless-steel appliances and granite counters now graced the galley, and each of the heads sported new marble counters.

She created a fresh, clean slate on which we scratched new memories. Her touch swept away my father's lingering shadow, and in doing so, she freed me of a weight I hadn't realized I carried. I found myself spending more and more time on board working from the *Symphony* rather than making the trip to the office.

In early November, Sandra told me that Cole had been in touch with her.

"He's curious about you," she said, rising from the table with our plates in hand.

"Then the bastard can call me. I don't want you talking to him."

She frowned and studied my face. "What if your father was wrong about him?"

"You think Cole's my big brother?" I laughed at the absurdity of it.

She shrugged. "There was a lot of animosity between your father and Bronwyn. You know that. Cole just wants to meet with you—to talk."

Visions of Jimmy shaking his head came to mind. "I suspect that what he wants is a piece of my portfolio."

"And what if all he wants is a brother? What harm could possibly come of that?"

"Dad would reach out from his grave and cane me if I gave that family the time of day."

"Not to be insensitive, darling, but your father is gone and I didn't see a cane in the tomb. That was his war. It doesn't need to be yours."

Yes, Dad was gone, so Cole knew damn well he had no business with me. That's why he'd tried his little snake-charming act on my wife instead. But the hurt Cole's mother inflicted on my father, and the public humiliation he endured because of her, robbed Dad of his dignity and his ability to love another woman properly. It changed him. Even entertaining the thought that that bastard Cole could be Dad's son felt like one more indignity, one Dad couldn't protect himself from.

"Let me think about it," I said.

CHAPTER FOUR

Two weeks later, I was back in Jimmy's office. The mayor had long since shined my father's halo and taken credit for securing the Dixon Financial Group's new head office. I'd ridden the wave of goodwill and sympathy to establish a relationship with the Dixon Financial Group's stakeholders. Our collaboration was refreshingly free of coercion or any other unsavoury incentives. We'd been hammering out the details of a development contract for the five-acre parcel that would lay the foundation for my reputation, and set Delaney & Son on the high road.

Jimmy had called me in to discuss a licensing issue on what we now called the Dixon Tower complex. It was a minor hiccup at best and didn't require a face-to-face meeting. I cocked my head at Jimmy, who'd folded his arms and moved to the window to stare across the city.

"It's not like you to pad your billable hours," I said, raising an eyebrow in jest.

He pressed his lips into a tight line, stuffed his hands in his pockets and turned, studying the carpet.

"Okay. I'll bite," I said. "What's on your mind?"

He smoothed his tie and settled on the sofa opposite me. "You told me that Cole Des Roche contacted Sandra a few weeks ago. Has she heard anything more from him?"

"Not that I'm aware of."

He pushed a file folder across the table toward me.

"What's that?"

"Sandra met with Cole day before yesterday."

I froze midreach.

Jimmy continued. "You remember Jean Benoit?"

"Indeed." Jean was a private investigator Jimmy's office hired regularly. A good one. My father had used him a time or two as well.

"I briefed Jean on the situation after you informed me that Cole had made an appearance at Matt's funeral. Asked him to keep his eyes open. Jean was meeting a client when he spotted Cole and your wife at another table."

I pulled the folder over and opened it to find a contact sheet of colour photos. They were perfectly focused shots of Cole, with an artfully windblown hairdo, having what looked like a pleasant conversation with Sandra. Did women really go for that model-wannabe look? Dirty lunch plates and two empty wine glasses stood on their table. My blood ran cold at the sight of her hand over his in the last shot.

Jimmy interrupted my thoughts. "It was just lunch," he said.

I closed the folder and pushed it back across the table. My legs trembled. I stood anyway and buttoned my jacket. "I appreciate you letting me know."

"They went their separate ways afterwards."

"Thank you. I'll deal with it," I said, and clamped my jaw closed.

"I know that look, Jackson. Your father had one just like it, but don't read more into this than it is. This is not history repeating itself." He hefted his bulk off the sofa and lumbered toward a long credenza. "Sandra is a good woman." He opened a drawer and extracted a thick envelope. "These are copies of the evidence your father kept of Bronwyn's affair. It'll go some way to counter whatever nonsense Cole is trying to feed your wife."

I took the envelope and left.

At the clubhouse, I ordered a Laphroaig and retreated to an empty corner. A gulp of the peaty liquid fortified me. Anger seethed out around my collar and I loosened my tie. Prior to today, I would never have accused my wife of being deceptive. I thought I knew her better. Jean Benoit's photographs were a slap in the face that said otherwise. Then I imagined my father telling me "I told you so," and that thought halted my ruminations. My father was not right about women. Sandra must have had a good reason for meeting with that cocky bastard behind my back. I'd find out why.

I downed the drink and opened the envelope. Elastic bands separated two sets of photos. The first set was sedate, the second graphic. I checked over my shoulder feeling every inch the sleazy voyeur with a stash of porn. Bronwyn had been a beautiful woman, full breasted, smooth thighs and firm ass: Playboy material right down to her shorn pussy.

My father might have been okay sharing these, but not me. I removed the worst of the photos and slid them in my pants pocket. The remainder I returned to the envelope and tucked inside my jacket.

Of all the men in New Orleans, Bronwyn had chosen Dad's biggest business rival to take to her bed. Her pillow talk had cost Dad more than his pride. Richard Des Roche owned Touchstone Developments, and before my father learned of their affair, Touchstone managed to outbid Delaney on more than one lucrative contract. Dad blamed Bronwyn. He'd shared details with her that with hindsight he shouldn't have.

After their divorce, everyone who was anyone in the south knew that Bronwyn had thrown Dad over for Richard. That Richard Des Roche was one of us made their betrayal worse. Over the years, their paths crossed frequently, and each time was like ripping off a scab. The painful reminders of Bronwyn's infidelity fanned my father's hatred for them, and his determination to get even.

My father bided his time. When he finally struck back, it was decisive. Touchstone was no longer in a position to compete with Delaney. They were back in the strip-mall business.

A second whisky chased the first, and then I headed down the dock to the *Symphony*. A lake breeze chilled the night air. On board, I tossed my jacket on a stool and waved at Sandra. She was reading on the foredeck with a blanket across her legs. She wore a black dress I was particularly fond of. It had a silver zipper conveniently located down the front. I envisioned her small breasts, the curve of her hips, and my mind wandered into a dark place I'd never considered before today. I pushed the image of Sandra's hand over Cole's out of my mind.

Now I understood better why my father had reacted so strongly to Bronwyn's infidelity. I had the bitter taste of something similar in my mouth right now and had no intention of letting it linger. I poured two glasses of Chardonnay and strode outside to join my wife.

"We need to talk," I said, handing her a glass.

The smile slipped from her face. "Oh?" She swung her legs off the lounger and set her book down.

"Why didn't you tell me you met with Cole?"

She took a slow, deep breath and exhaled. "Sometimes this town is far too small."

"Well?"

"I aimed to spare you having to deal with him."

The anger I'd reined in leaked out in my clipped tone. "I asked you not to speak with him."

She tipped her head and glared up at me, a warning I had no patience for, given her clandestine rendezvous with Cole.

"I'll assume that's the Scotch talking," she said. "I can smell it from here."

"I deserve an answer."

She took her time. "I was hoping that if I met Cole face-to-face, I'd be able to impart how difficult this situation has been for you so soon after Matthew's passing—perhaps delay his efforts to reach out to you." She set the wine down without tasting it.

I drew a line in the condensation on my glass. "And?"

She frowned. "It didn't work out as I had hoped."

Her disappointment was genuine and it unwound my anger. I picked up her glass and handed it to her again, a peace offering. She accepted. I took a seat beside her and stretched out.

She took a sip of her wine. "I know you don't want to hear this, but that man looks so much like you it's scary. He even taps his foot like you do when he's nervous."

"He is *not* my brother."

"What if he is?"

"Do you not think my father would have known his own son?"

"Wouldn't you like to know for sure?" she asked. "One way or the other?"

I swung my head around to meet her gaze. "What are you suggesting? A DNA test?"

"I think you should consider it. If Cole isn't your brother, the test would put an end to the rumours."

"Was that Cole's idea?"

"He wants answers. That's all."

"What he wants is to get his hands on a piece of Delaney."

"I honestly didn't get that impression. He feels like he's been a pawn in the war between Matt and Bronwyn. He doesn't know who to believe."

Twice now, that smarmy bastard had used Sandra to deliver his message. If he thought using her naïveté was the ticket to get to me, he was mistaken. "Well, I think I may have the answers he's looking for.

And it doesn't require a DNA test." I stood and held out my hand. "Come inside."

I retrieved the envelope from my jacket and sat beside her on the sleek leather sofa we'd christened not that long ago. I dealt the modest photos first, laying them out in a horizontal line. She leaned forward and picked one up.

"Bronwyn and Richard?" The photo showed them sitting on a park bench. She returned it to the table and picked up another, also of the happy couple, but different clothes, different day. They were walking in the second picture, holding hands. The other photos were similar, obviously taken without their knowledge.

"Help me out here," Sandra said, creasing her brow. "How are these photos proof?"

"Check the date. Bronwyn was married to my father when these photos were taken."

She tilted the shiny photo and squinted to see the date. "Matt must have been very hurt when he saw these." She set the photo back down. "But as a lawyer's daughter would tell you, it's not proof of paternity."

I removed the second set of photos and dealt another row. "Neither are these, but they're compelling."

Sandra's eyes grew wide and her mouth dropped open. She looked up at me. "Where did you get these?"

"Jimmy. Dad hired an investigator when he suspected Bronwyn had strayed. He used them to his advantage in their divorce."

"I've no doubt," she said, sitting back.

"How did you leave things with Cole?"

"I made no promises."

"But he's expecting to hear from you?"

She nodded, gazing back at the graphic photos. "You think he knows about these?"

I gathered the photos and returned them to the envelope. "I don't know. But I think it's time he did. When you see him, make sure he gets them." I held out the envelope to her. "They're copies. Tell him I'm prepared to expose them if he calls you again."

She didn't take them. "That's a bit heavy-handed, don't you think?"

Heavy-handed would be sharing the photos burning a hole in my pants pocket. "It's all I have to dissuade him from pursuing the absurd notion that we share a father."

"You could entertain the possibility that you do."

"And then what? Add an *s* to Delaney & Son and give him half of it?"

She searched my face, perhaps looking for a sign I'd back down. "I had hoped this animosity would fade when your father passed. There is room in the company . . . and room in your heart for Cole, if he is your half-brother."

"Goddamnit! He is *not*. And if Cole were looking for a brother, he would have come to me. I'm not even sure it's about the money, but one thing I do know, if I give in to a DNA test, I might as well tell the world I believe my father was a lowlife who'd abandon a son to exact revenge on an unfaithful wife. I won't do it. Dad had his faults, but he was my father, and he isn't here to defend himself. I owe him that much."

She pinched her lips and stood, swiping the envelope from my hand. "I will do your bidding, but don't fool yourself. We both know what your father was capable of. I doubt this will be the end of it." She turned on her heel and marched away.

My chest tightened as I watched her retreat. How the hell had I let Cole drive a wedge between Sandra and me? I'd have to tread lightly and make reparations after this. We'd been in a similar situation before. Her brother, James, had driven the wedge that time.

It was a few months after we'd married. James and I were two years older than Sandra. She and James had always been close, but the way she worried about him was unnatural. He was a grown man, ex-military and trained by the best, so it was ridiculous that she worried every time the asshole went AWOL. According to Sandra, he'd been doing it for years.

I let it slide until it started to impact our marriage. When he surfaced after a three-week disappearing act that had Sandra in tears every night, I paid him a visit, told him just what I thought of his self-centred behaviour. A simple phone call would have eased her mind, and he couldn't even do that.

Sandra was livid with me when she found out. For her own peace of mind, she needed to put some space between herself and James, but she wouldn't listen to reason. I soon learned that loving her to distraction didn't grant me a free pass to straighten out her brother. Her blind loyalty to her family, at my expense, was an irritant I worked hard to ignore. It took a while, but we got past that rough patch. How long would it take this time?

Chapter Five

Sandra and I rarely argued about the little stuff. Maybe we should have. Maybe arguing about the little stuff gives you practice for dealing with the big stuff. Sandra clammed up, gave me the silent treatment. She refused to discuss her meeting with Cole and found excuses to avoid me.

Weeks later, when Cole's lawyers tried, unsuccessfully, to force the DNA issue in court, she joined her parents on vacation in Spain. When she returned, she slept with her back to me. I would have apologized, but that would have been dishonest. Instead, I told her I wished I'd not asked her to deliver the photos. With the dreadful clarity of hindsight, I realized that it was something I should have done myself. Though there was one good thing that had come of it—Cole had slithered back into his hole.

Each day I chipped away at the iceberg between us. I brought her gardenias and made her breakfast. I tucked love notes in her handbag and collected the dry cleaning. Nothing worked.

Then, with New Year's almost upon us, the ice finally thawed, thanks in part to a carefully misplaced receipt—a necessary if somewhat distasteful ruse.

"You hate ballet," she'd said, laying aside the receipt for my substantial donation to the New Orleans Ballet Theatre.

"But *you* love it, and I love you," I'd said, as she'd come into my arms. It was a relief to hold her again, despite having stooped to my father's level to get her there.

By the end of January, the storm was a distant memory.

And then Cole contacted her again.

"I'll deal with him this time," I said, grateful that Sandra had come to me with it first. I folded the *Times-Picayune* and drained my coffee. "He needs to stop using you to get to me."

She stood behind me. "Good," she said, resting a hand on my shoulder. "Then you'll meet with him?"

I covered her hand with mine. "I was thinking more along the lines of a restraining order."

She freed her hand and walked around to stand in front of me. "Why won't you consider that he could be your brother?"

"I don't want to argue about this again. I know you think it's misplaced, but my father deserves my loyalty."

"Your father was a vindictive man who could win a grudge match against the Hatfields and McCoys."

"He had his reasons."

She inhaled as if it were her last breath. "You're exasperating, Jackson. Just meet with the man."

"To what end? He already failed to get my DNA through the courts."

"Then what do you have to lose?" She knit her brow the way she did when a migraine threatened. "Please, Jackson."

Watching the pain cross her face made me realize how trying this had become for her. Cole had thrown her into the middle of a vendetta she had nothing to do with. I reached for her hand. "How about we both meet with him?"

"Are you serious?"

"A united front will take you out of the equation."

She smiled. "Then you'll consider his position?"

"I'll think about it."

Her smile faded. "You wanted to be a better man than your father," she snapped, and dropped my hand. "Prove it."

She didn't even flinch as she stabbed me with my own words. She snatched her jacket and stormed out.

Hours later, she returned, once again calm and collected. I was on the foredeck nursing a bourbon. The night had grown cool. The bottle and Jimmy's empty glass sat on the table, his seat long since vacated.

"May I?" she asked, joining me with an empty tumbler in her hand. She took Jimmy's chair.

I tipped my head and poured her a shot. Neat.

"I'm sorry about earlier," she said. "I shouldn't have said those things about your father."

Her apology felt like salve on a wound. "He loved you."

"I know. Sometimes it's hard to see past the things I disliked about the man, but he was your father. For that, I'm grateful."

"Thank you," I said, and clinked her glass. We tasted our drinks, and then I said, "We're meeting Cole at his club tomorrow morning."

Her gaze darted to the empty glass. "We meaning you and I, or will Jimmy be joining us as well?" she asked.

"No. Whatever Cole has up his sleeve is for covey only."

"Covey?" she repeated, sounding alarmed. She pulled her jacket closed. "What's this have to do with the covey?" The New Orleans covey was an exclusive society of sorts, one whose membership shared the gene, and the secret of the gift.

"I don't know. Cole said it had to do with Dad. He didn't enlighten me with the details. I imagine that's what tomorrow is all about." But even as I said it, I had my suspicions. My father had never been above utilizing our gift to enhance a business opportunity, a practice that other Fliers considered dishonourable. But of more consequence was the fact the practice was prohibited by those who policed our kind.

Our covey numbered just over fifty people. We called our kind Fliers because the gift allowed us to shed gravity. The gene that made it possible was dominant, which meant offspring would inherit it, regardless of partner, but even so, we rarely brought outsiders into our ranks. Sandra's family had the gene as did mine . . . and Cole's. Jimmy did not have it. He was, therefore, not privy to the secret of the gift.

"Why did you agree to meet at the Pickwick?" she asked. "We could have met him here at our club instead."

New Orleans was very much a society town with firmly established cliques, and each clique had its own habitat. The Delaneys associated with the Southern Yacht Club, the Des Roches were well-established at the Pickwick Club.

"Could have, but I don't want him to embarrass us in our own backyard. If we go to him, we can end the meeting when it suits us. Besides, home club advantage will give him the illusion he's in control."

"You sound like Matthew when you talk like that," she said, her disappointment evident in her frown. The tone of her voice was an echo of my mother's when I'd done something she'd disapproved of.

"I'd like to think I learned a few useful things from the man. He taught me how to negotiate. That's all this is."

"You and I both know that's not true. Just the mention of Cole's name pushes your buttons. And now he's played the covey card. There's a lot more to this than a simple business negotiation."

"I know. It was a mistake to not meet with him before. I can see that now." I reached over and grasped her hand. It was an apology, and far too late, but I owed her that.

"I'm worried," Sandra said. "I know you loved your father, but you're not blind to what he's done. What do you think Cole has on him?"

"Good question. I have no idea." I rubbed my thumb over her knuckles. "Did he give you any hint when he contacted you?"

"None. But he seemed different. Smug."

That didn't sound promising. "Well, there's no point in making suppositions." I emptied my glass. "You and I have nothing to hide. If Cole has a beef about something Dad's done, he can take it up with him. He knows where to find him."

"I wish I felt your confidence."

I leaned over and kissed her, tasting bourbon on her lips. "Come to bed," I said. "I have just the thing to boost your confidence."

Later that night, as Sandra slept soundly, I stared at the teak ceiling wondering if my father had done something I would live to regret.

The next morning, our driver dropped us on St. Charles outside the Pickwick Club. The melancholy notes of a saxophone drifted down the street. Music was everywhere in New Orleans. Unrestrained by any clock, it leaked out of windows and doors throughout the city. We stood under the iron gallery that ran the length of the building. The ever-present aroma of barbecue hung in the air.

"You okay?" Sandra asked, pausing to smooth my lapels. I'd worn a sports jacket to keep the meeting casual.

"Indeed," I said. "My wife assures me I have nothing to lose."

"She sounds very smart, this wife of yours."

All I could see of her beautiful face beneath her oversized sunglasses was her smile. That smile had beguiled me from the moment I met her. She was the only woman I could remember, besides my mother, who accepted me and was proud of me despite knowing all the ugly parts.

I took her hand and opened the door, ushering her inside. The club had a stately presence with lofty ceilings and large gilded paintings perched high on wainscotted walls. The front desk staff checked our names against the guest list and arranged for our escort into the inner sanctum, where we were promptly delivered to a linen-covered table in a quiet corner. Cole hadn't arrived yet. Probably thought he'd push the home club advantage by having us wait for him. Classical music blended softly into the background. I seated Sandra to my right and sat with my back to the tall arched windows. Sunlight beamed over my shoulders and across our table, leaving my face in shadow.

Cole's absence made me wish I'd brought the paper or at least the crossword. Instead, we ordered coffee and Sandra distracted me with her father's retirement plans, which somehow didn't include Redmond Moss actually giving up his law practice.

An oversized clock high on the wall ticked off the minutes. The hostess appeared with two elderly gentlemen, looked in our direction, and then steered them away.

"Do you get the feeling they think we have the plague?" I said, looking at the empty tables that circled us.

"More like we're in the enemy's camp," she said, gazing around the room. "Be patient."

The big clock ticked off five more minutes. Sandra chirped in the background, but my ire dampened her words. Patience was one thing, but I was beginning to feel like a serf waiting for the lord of the manor to make his appearance. Fuck that shit.

"He's got three more minutes," I said, shifting in my seat.

A moment later, Sandra's cool hand closed over mine. "He's here," she said, without looking in his direction.

I held her gaze and ignored the approaching son of a bitch. Two could play this upper-hand game. I waited until he was upon us before I feigned surprise and acknowledged his arrival.

"Sandra," he said, extending his hand. "I hope I haven't kept you waiting."

"Not at all," she said, offering her fingertips. "Jackson and I were enjoying your club's hospitality."

"Jackson," Cole said, as I stood to shake his hand. "Glad you could make it."

Insincerity crept into my smile. "Happy to accommodate you, Cole." He'd polished his teeth for the occasion.

I took my seat as a waiter approached. Cole declined a beverage and sat to my left, across from Sandra. His linen suit was stylishly crumpled.

I would have told him Jay Gatsby wanted it back, but the suit wasn't good enough for Gatsby.

"So, you wanted to meet. Here I am. What's this about?"

"Same thing it's always been about, Jackson. Our father."

"*My* father."

He inhaled deliberately, flaring his nostrils. "Fine. *Your* father lied to you." He gazed at Sandra and paused, softening his features. "If it's easier for you to believe the lie than know the truth, then have at it." Sandra looked away, her expression neutral; her calm facade firmly in place.

I dragged his attention away from my wife. "Don't take this the wrong way, Cole, but if it comes down to believing my father versus believing your mother, whose morals are questionable, to say the least, then I'll stick with Dad's version of events."

"I'm so glad you brought up morals because that's what this conversation is about. Your father's morals in particular."

He hadn't known Dad well enough to question his morals, but I played along. "What would you know about my father, Cole?"

"I know that he got access to Touchstone's sealed bid on the West Lakeview Marina complex before the contract was awarded."

I interrupted, having heard this accusation before. "As I recall, Touchstone was awarded that contract. Perhaps you should have thanked him."

Cole leaned forward on his elbows and narrowed his eyes, catching my gaze. "Your father set us up. He used our bid to identify our major suppliers, and then he employed his usual corrupt tactics, which I'm sure you're familiar with, to convince those suppliers to not deal with us."

"Touchstone's lawyers already pursued that fairy tale in court and failed to convince anyone it had merit. We all use the same suppliers. If you'd locked them in, they would have been available when you needed them. Simple as that. There were other suppliers you could have used." Unfortunately for Touchstone, the foreign suppliers' prices tripled the costs. Touchstone had had to choose between completing the contract at a crippling loss, or backing out of the deal and paying the substantial non-performance penalties. They chose to pay the penalties, which decimated their reputation and nearly bankrupted them. Delaney then swooped in, picked up the contract and ran with it. To this day, the marina complex continued to be our most lucrative asset.

He sat back in his chair and glared at me, shaking his head in unrestrained disgust. "It's taken me years to get the proof I need to wipe that smile off your face, *brother*."

Such bravado, I thought, as Cole pulled an SD card from his pocket. His nostrils flared as he pursed his lips, turning the card in his fingers. "I've spent uncountable hours sifting through days of surveillance footage, identifying faces, tracking down strangers, and it's finally paid off. I found the man your father used to do his bidding—a man with a . . . let's say . . . unique skill." He leaned in and jutted his chin. "Your father made sure I had no claim on an inheritance that's as much mine as it is yours. He went to great lengths to ruin my family and damn near put us in the poorhouse. Now it's my turn." He stood and tossed the card with a careless flick of his wrist. It landed beside my coffee cup. "It may not be proof enough for a court of law, but it will be proof enough for the Tribunal Novem. You know who they are? Right?"

The name of the powerful body that policed our kind fell like a bomb. *Leniency* and *mercy* were not in their lexicon. Cole paused to let it take its intended effect. "I suggest you take a look at that and rethink your position on welcoming me to the family."

He turned and addressed my wife, whose colour had paled under a pinched brow. "I'm sorry, Sandra. As you know, I would have preferred to handle this differently." He then switched his attention to me. "I'll be expecting your call." Cocksure of himself, he turned and strode out of the room.

CHAPTER SIX

B astard!" I said, shoving my chair back. I stood and held out my hand for Sandra. "Let's go." She rose and fumbled with the strap of her purse.

We held hands on our way back to the yacht club but didn't exchange a word. She'd known my father as well as I had. There wasn't a rule or law he hadn't broken. He'd taken pride in the fact he'd gotten away with it, and more so if he'd done it with creativity and flair. He was a lot more than "shrewd," as Jimmy had so kindly put it.

I learned things from my father that would never find their way into the curriculum at Stanford. If you could look beyond the corporate espionage, bribery and antitrust violations, you'd recognize the gamesmanship and critical thinking of a genius.

On board the *Symphony,* I stared at the computer screen as it went through its start-up routine, and then inserted the SD card. Sandra stood behind me, still clutching her purse.

"It's probably got a fucking virus," I said, and clicked on the file Cole had prepared. Surveillance footage played. The film was identified as *East Entrance, Nordec Engineering.* I recognized the building where the West Lakeview Marina complex bids had been secured. The frame froze and the shot zoomed in on the figure of a man exiting the building. Thinning hair and a loose-fitting bomber jacket put him past his prime. Circles appeared around his gaunt face and the August 13, 2006, date and time stamp. I didn't recognize the man, but I'd bet good money the date was before the sealed bids were opened.

Another film clip began playing. The footage was from one of our own security cameras outside the Delaney & Son building. Whoever had given Cole our security footage would soon be looking for a new job. I leaned in. As a figure emerged, the frame froze and the camera zoomed in. The same man with the thinning hair and lean face was circled in red, as was the date and time stamp: thirty minutes later that same day, August 13, 2006.

"That's it? The same guy was at both buildings. So what? Hell, *I* was at both buildings. Doesn't prove that man got access to the sealed bids, and it doesn't prove my father knew him. Cole's got nothing," I said, leaning back in the chair. Relief flooded me. I reached behind and pulled Sandra's cold hand loose and gave it a reassuring squeeze.

She nodded to the screen. "It's not done yet."

A third film clip started to play. It was dated four days ago. Ghostly green-and-black night-vision footage zoomed in on a man. What little hair he had left was longer, but it was the same guy with the narrow face from the first two clips. The footage showed one location split between two vantage points, one at ground level from a distance, and one from a rooftop overhead. They played side by side. Both had time stamps running. Palm trees lined the street. Sandra and I leaned in as the film zoomed in on the man walking toward the ground-level camera, down a dumpster-lined laneway. The man paused at the mouth of the lane . . . and vanished.

"What the hell?" I said, and straightened. In the screen's reflection, I saw Sandra take a step back. Flier mythology whispered tales of Fliers who could disappear, but everyone knew those were just old myths.

The ground-level camera panned out revealing more of the street. The corner shop sold handbags. To its right was a nondescript door. The other side of the door housed a storefront displaying women's clothing. High-end by the look of the exterior. The ground-level camera zoomed in on the nondescript door. A small plaque in the centre of it read *DCI, 136 Ocean Drive*, and below the plaque, *Ring for Service*, with an arrow pointing to a doorbell.

"Do you know where this is?" I asked, watching Sandra's reflection.

She shook her head and kept her eyes trained on the screen.

The time stamps sped up, flipping through six minutes rapidly before slowing to real time again. I pressed in and watched as the gaunt-faced man reappeared from the ether into the mouth of the alley. "Oh, come on!" I said. He stuffed his hands in his pockets and scurried down the lane retracing his steps.

I shook my head at the absurdity of the disappearing act. "Looks like Cole got Photoshop for Christmas."

With my attention still on the screen, the night-vision footage blinked out and was replaced with a still shot of a *Miami Herald* clipping reporting a robbery at DCI, a gem wholesaler that specialized in diamonds. The address was 136 Ocean Drive.

The screen went black. We both stared at the computer in expectation of more, but when no further images appeared, I removed the SD card. I held its edge between my forefinger and thumb and teetered back in the chair. "Tell me if I've got this right. Cole's trying to sell the story that he's got a genuine *Ghost* on film at the site of a diamond robbery. The same man—or Ghost, if you believe in fairy tales—who showed up on security cameras years earlier at both Delaney and Nordec before the marina complex bids were opened?"

Sandra backed away, clutching her purse.

"Cole thinks that this is proof that Dad hired a 'Ghost,'" I said, putting *Ghost* in air quotes, "to get a look at Touchstone's sealed bid? That's absurd. The only thing the film proves is he's doctored that footage. What an idiot. No one's going to believe that's real."

I pushed away from the desk. "I could use a drink," I said, standing. "What about you?" I headed toward the bar, took out two tumblers and began pouring. "Darling? Drink?"

Sandra had moved to the sofa and seated herself as if the leather were covered in tacks. "The film isn't doctored," she said, cradling her purse. "Cole wouldn't be that stupid. He knows we'd have it analyzed."

"You bet your sweet ass I'm going to have it analyzed. If Cole thinks he can blackmail me with something as absurd as a Ghost in our employ, he's mistaken. What's next? Big Foot? Loch Ness? I'll take it to the Tribunal myself." I knew little about the Tribunal, other than that it was made up of delegates from the nine founding coveys, and that these delegates were the most powerful of our kind. Dad said they meted out justice and retribution without the burden of trials. He knew of a Flier who'd disappeared after being arrested for burglarizing penthouses in Seattle. Speculation in the press about how he'd pulled it off sealed his fate.

Sandra hadn't moved. I handed her a tumbler and sat beside her. "What's wrong? You know those stories of Ghosts among our kind are fables. They're no more real than Santa Claus or the Easter Bunny. We have nothing to worry about."

She stared at the drink in her hand. "Don't we? If that man is a Ghost and your father hired him to destroy Cole's family, the Tribunal will grant Cole his retribution."

"Sandra, what's gotten into you? There is no 'what if.' Do you really think something as big as the existence of Flier Ghosts could be kept secret?"

She looked up at me, her face drawn. "Why not? The gift has been kept secret for hundreds of years." She set her drink down and pulled her cellphone from her purse. "I need to call James."

"No," I said, and reached over to still her hand. I didn't need her brother up in my face, judging me. I plucked the phone away from her. "I know James has access to skilled computer techs, but so do I. There's no need to call your brother." I dropped her phone back in her purse. My tech team was just as good as James's, probably better. "We can handle this ourselves."

"I disagree. I know James rubs you the wrong way sometimes, but he's one of the best private investigators in the country. He can find the man in that video, and then we'll have our answers."

Yeah, James was a bloody star, but he could shine somewhere else. "Darling, we already have our answers: that man isn't a Ghost. There are no Ghosts. And regardless, even if James could find him, Cole's not going to wait."

Sandra lifted her hand and rubbed her forehead. I picked up her glass and handed it to her. She took a deep swallow. "Let my family help. Please."

"I thought we'd agreed to work together. Your family already thinks the worst of my father. This isn't going to help."

She cradled the glass in her hand. "Are you absolutely certain you don't recognize that man?" she asked.

"Yes. I'm certain."

"He must have met with someone in your office. Maybe his name is in the visitors' log?"

"That's good thinking. I'll get Jean Benoit on it right away. Meantime, I'll have that video footage analyzed." I started to rise, but Sandra grabbed my forearm.

"No!" Panic edged her voice. "It's too dangerous. We can't risk anyone seeing it."

I sat back down and studied Sandra's face. I'm not sure I'd ever seen her so shaken, and her reaction to the suggestion of a fabled Ghost in our midst was beyond uncharacteristic. "You're going to have to help me out here. Is there something you know that I don't? Because I'm sure that footage has been tampered with. It has to be, and once it's proven, Cole is out of ammunition. Isn't that what you want?"

"Without a doubt," she said. "But this accusation. It could get out of control."

I grasped her hand. "Then let me take care of it."

"Humour me, would you, Jackson? My family will think better of you for letting them in, trusting them to help. Matthew would never have done that. Let's keep this in the family. Send it to James. See if he recognizes the man. My father too. Between them, they know most of the Fliers on the west coast."

I reached up and cupped her face, smoothing my thumb over the worry lines etched in her forehead. I saw fear in her eyes and a steely determination in the set of her jaw. Damn it. "All right. If it'll put your mind at ease." Perhaps the ghost stories she'd heard as a child were more realistic than the hauntings I'd been told about. "Call them. I'll send the footage."

She stepped out on the deck to make the calls. After I'd forwarded the footage, I dialled Jean Benoit. He assured me he'd look at the visitors' logbook that afternoon.

"Dad says hello," Sandra said, returning to my side. "He looked at the film."

"Did he recognize the man?"

"No."

"And James?"

"He didn't answer. I sent him a text."

"Oh, great. He's AWOL again?"

"No." Her defiant tone threatened to open an old wound. "Dad says he'll be back tonight. Let's hold tight until we hear from him."

"We can't sit on this."

"I know that, but, please? It's only a few hours."

Her reaction baffled me. What was going on in that head of hers? "A few hours, then," I said. If a short delay was the price for her peace of mind, we could wait. "Maybe Jean will have a name to go with the face by then."

I pulled her into my arms and held her close, but she didn't relax. "Talk to me, sweetheart. Your reaction makes me think there's something going on here that I've missed."

"I'm sorry," she said, pulling away from me. "It's just the shock of it."

It sure as hell felt like more than that. "Are you keeping something from me?"

"Of course not, darling." She reached up and pressed her palm to my chest. "I'm going to change." She straightened her dress and collected her purse from the sofa. "Maybe I'll work on the grant proposal for the children's park. It's due next week. It'll keep my mind off Cole for a few hours."

Our hands clasped briefly as she passed, and then she was gone. I stared at the door she'd passed through. Times like this, I was glad Dad had never confided in me about the Touchstone bid. It meant I didn't have to lie. I never knew how he'd gotten his hands on it, but I knew. He vehemently denied it in public, but in private, you couldn't wipe the fucking smile off his face.

And he hadn't done it using some fairy-tale Ghost, though the possibility one might exist did intrigue me. No, if Dad hadn't pulled it off himself, he'd likely used the services of an amoral Flier named Desmond Cross. The little weasel had grown wealthy supplying Dad with a stash of compromising photos, evidence of bribery and a seemingly endless supply of dirty little secrets with which to bargain. After Dad died, Desmond turned up like a bad smell. I slapped him on the back, told him I'd call if I needed him and sent him on his way. You had to be careful not to piss off a degenerate like Desmond. You didn't want to be on the bad side of a man like that.

Dad knew exactly how to play the development game, and he'd taught me well. He approached every deal with an open mind, and never left money on the table. He knew when to walk away and when to play hardball, and he rarely lost.

With Touchstone, he had the added incentive of a personal vendetta. The set-up was a work of art. First, he ensured that Touchstone would be awarded the contract, and then he planted the bombs that would blow it up. I'd overheard him right outside on the foredeck of the *Symphony*. He and Jack Klein of Overland Concrete in Baton Rouge made a deal over a bottle of Scotch. Soon after, he struck a similar deal with Carl Prudhomme of Industrial Rod and Steel in Lafayette. No paperwork, just a smile and a handshake. It was Dad's biggest coup, his most elaborate scheme, and he'd shut me out of it. I was still new to the business back then and chalked it up to the *& Son* being too green. But after I'd learned the extent of the sting, and the threat the fallout posed, I understood he'd been protecting me.

I poured another shot and opened my laptop. Even if Jean Benoit found the name of the man in the surveillance footage and James was able to locate him, it wouldn't be enough to get Cole off my back. As Dad would have said—use everything at your disposal. That footage needed to be exposed for what it was—a fraud.

I fired off an email to Kerry Morris with a plausible cover story and attached the surveillance footage. Kerry was a little off-kilter, but an absolute IT whiz and a consummate gamer. She'd dated Anthony when we were at Stanford and was one of the few who still called me by my freshman nickname, Jackman. We shared a comradery forged under pressure of exams, bad dates and keg parties. I trusted her implicitly. She would have been at Dad's funeral if it weren't for her participating in an epic gaming lockdown in Los Angeles. She was the first out, after three gruelling days. Most importantly, she didn't share the gift so she'd have no preconceived notions of Ghosts when she saw the footage.

Half an hour later, the bank sent confirmation that Kerry had collected the fee I'd sent, which meant my job was now at the top of her queue.

Chapter Seven

At 6:00 p.m. I texted Jean for a progress report. He'd sifted through the logbook working backwards from the time stamp on the surveillance footage, and hadn't yet found a name he couldn't verify.

Sandra was clearing the dinner dishes when James called. She took the call outside, pacing the foredeck with one arm pressed into her stomach. I hated seeing her like that. At least now she knew what kind of a man Cole was. He'd undoubtedly snuffed out any sympathy she may have had for him.

I kept an eye on her while I finished cleaning the galley. Sandra and James's sibling bond remained abnormally strong despite James's thoughtless behaviour. But I could see this wasn't one of their happy conversations. She hadn't so much as smiled. I set the towel down when she returned.

"James doesn't know who the man in the film is, or what covey he belongs to," she said.

"And Jean doesn't have a name. So we're back to square one."

"Worse. James ran the footage through a digital scanner. He said it's going to be difficult to prove it isn't genuine."

"Come on. That footage is a sham."

"James agrees, as does my father, but you heard Cole: he's been planning this for years. He's poured all his pent-up anger into that footage and James said he's done a brilliant job of it."

"I don't believe that. I'm certainly not going to roll over on James's word."

"No one's asking you to roll over," she said in a huff. Her phone interrupted what I sensed was quickly disintegrating into an argument.

Unfortunately, the call was from her father. He asked her to put him on speakerphone. She set the phone on the counter and stepped away.

"Redmond," I said, feigning a cordiality I wasn't quite feeling at the moment.

"Jackson. Sandy tells me you're having some trouble over there with Cole Des Roche."

"*Trouble*? You do have a gift with words, Redmond. The son of a bitch is trying to blackmail me."

I heard the sneer in Redmond's voice. "I saw the film. Pure fiction."

Finally, a sensible opinion. "You got that right. And when I prove it, I'll have that lowlife right where I want him. Then we'll see who's worried about the Tribunal."

"How are you going to prove it, son? James says it's a top-notch piece of work."

James. I had to restrain myself from rolling my eyes. "I know IT people who can do the job." Sandra walked to the far side of the counter and perched on a bar stool.

"And what if your people get the same result as James?"

"You telling me you believe in Ghosts, Redmond?"

"No. I'm telling you that you need to be right careful. Even a rumour that a Ghost exists, let alone that he's for hire, will catch the Tribunal's attention."

"You needn't be concerned, Redmond. The right amount of money buys a lot of confidentiality. My people are solid." I wasn't worried. Kerry wouldn't blab and she certainly wouldn't sell me out.

"I'm sure they are. But if they are unable to prove the footage has been tampered with, they might believe it's real. It's tempting to tell a friend or two that you've seen a Ghost. Those ripples could prove difficult to stop. You risk the Tribunal's finding out."

Sandra's presence kept me civil in the face of Redmond's unfounded lack of faith in my judgment. "Yes sir, but that's a gamble I'm going to have to take. I'm not giving that extortionist a dime."

"Hold on. Don't be so hasty. Cole's behaviour is reprehensible, I'll give you that, but the wiser choice may be to throw him a bone."

"Why would I do that?" Sandra reached for my hand, but I waved her away. I didn't need to be soothed like a pet.

"Because it's probably the cheapest way to make that film disappear. And, you'll get to look like the good guy."

"I'll look like the guy who had my ass whipped. No thanks. I'll take my chances with the Tribunal."

"I wouldn't recommend that route."

Now he was being exasperating. "Even if the Tribunal gets wind of that film, and by some stretch of their sanity, believe it, do you really think they would reward a blackmailer, grant him his retribution? Since when is blackmailing any better than what he's accusing my father of?"

"That's not the kicker here. The Tribunal doesn't have to believe it. They just need to see it. And then they'll find that man, and before they kill him they'll find out exactly what he did and for whom. Are you so sure of your father's innocence that you're willing to risk the consequences?"

Redmond had never hidden how he felt about my father's reputation, but this was the most direct the arrogant bastard had ever been.

"Consequences? My father is dead."

"There are few rules in our world, Jackson. Secrecy is one of them, followed closely by not using the gift for financial gain. The Tribunal police them both quite heavily."

"And how do you know so much about the Tribunal, Redmond?" I ignored Sandra's glare. There were rumours about Redmond and even James. They knew more about the Tribunal than they ever let on.

"I know people too, Jackson, and I've been around longer than you. Money is a motivator, you said it yourself, and when enough of it is stolen, the wronged party is motivated to find out how, and by whom. The Tribunal won't risk a Flier exposing our kind like that."

"And how would the Tribunal feel about Cole's little blackmail scheme?"

"As distasteful as it is, Cole didn't abuse his gift. Your father, on the other hand, may have. You know what the penalty is for that offence."

And there it was again: Redmond's contempt for my father, and now he had something new to hang it on. "Even if that's true, what are they going to do? Kill him again?"

"No. But he has a son who's still alive."

It took me a moment to process his words. "You're not suggesting they would come after me?" I looked over to see Sandra's face darken.

"The horror stories you've heard about the Tribunal—they aren't just rumours," Redmond said.

"And you know this how?"

"They've wiped out families before. Retribution is a nasty business."

He hadn't answered my question.

Redmond continued. "There's always the possibility that Cole's crime may mitigate the situation. The Tribunal might spare you and offer him a portion of Delaney & Son instead."

"Instead? That's exactly what Cole wants. I'm not giving him a fucking dime! He has nothing without that footage and I'm going to expose it for what it is: a farce."

Sandra slapped her hand on the counter. "Don't you think Cole has already thought this through? He's just bet his life on that footage being foolproof."

Once again, Sandra had aligned herself with her family. "Just whose side are you on, Sandra?"

"Stop it!" Redmond bellowed in a tinny voice from the counter. "This isn't about sides, or who's right and who's wrong. This is damage control, something you and Matthew have done a thousand times, Jackson. Something he was quite good at, as I recall."

It wasn't a compliment.

"Please . . . listen to my father," Sandra pleaded.

I had listened, and I didn't like what I'd heard. He'd effectively turned a case of blackmail into a threat on my life to coerce me to give up the fight. Why? He wouldn't if he were in my position. Did he really believe my life was at risk? The possibility of ridding his family of the disreputable scourge his daughter married should have thrilled him.

Ah . . . but maybe he worried that the Tribunal wouldn't stop at me. It was Sandra he worried about. He didn't want her caught up in Cole's mess. That was motivation I understood completely, and it gave me the edge I needed. Cole's blackmail scheme was my hand to play, not his. For the first time since I married into the family, Redmond would have to trust me. What I needed to do now was consider my cards.

I leaned forward on the counter, my weight on my palms, and hung my head. I took a calming breath and regained my composure. "You're absolutely right, Redmond. It's damage control. Sandra, my apologies. Let me think about it. I'll come up with a plan. Redmond, I'll be in touch." I reached over and ended the call.

"Are we okay?" I asked, rounding the counter and stopping inches from Sandra. She had the grace to nod. We weren't okay yet, but we would be. "I'm sorry." I wrapped an arm around her shoulder and kissed her hair, inhaling that sweet vanilla fragrance. "I need some space to think. Don't wait up." I grabbed my keys and bustled out of there. The cool air felt like a soothing balm to my overheated skin.

The Porsche hadn't been driven in a month, but it fired up with a familiar throaty purr. I raced out of the marina and wound my way east toward the Bayou Wildlife Refuge on Lake Borgne. My father drifted into my thoughts. Redmond might not have approved of him, but at least Dad would know what to do in this situation. And it sure as hell wouldn't involve rewarding Cole for his treachery.

Twenty minutes later, I hit the gravel service road and cut the headlights. I marvelled at the miracle of a Flier's night vision as I always did out here away from the city lights. It was impossible to imagine what it would be like to suffer darkness.

I pulled over and killed the engine. Stars lay scattered across the clear night sky, and the fetid smell of the bayou hung thick in the air. I popped the trunk before I got out, and quickly changed into the dark clothes I kept there. A dozen trails led off to Lake Borgne along this road. The ink wasn't yet dry on my driver's licence the first time I stumbled upon it. I'd been driving an old Chevy pickup, and my sense of direction had failed me. Since that day, Lake Borgne had become my safety valve, a place for me to blow off steam.

I ducked down a trail I knew well, accompanied by a chorus of frogs. The moment I cleared the low shrubs, I broke free of gravity's hold and soared into the blackness. Relief was instantaneous. The wind blew the tension out of me as I punched a path over the lake. Exhilaration edged out the tightness in my chest and I finally felt like I could breathe again. I expanded my lungs with deep drafts of cool lake air and flew flat out until the worst of my anger had dissipated. When I slowed, I was once again thinking with a clear head.

Cole would not win this game. He'd thrown the first ball with that surveillance footage, gambling that I'd flinch. But he didn't know me. If he did, he'd have known that I'd been taught by the best—*my* father—a man who would not be challenged lightly. And I wasn't without a bat. It was time to play hardball.

CHAPTER EIGHT

Back at the car, a message from Kerry awaited. I got behind the wheel and dialled her number. "What'd you learn?"

"Whoever put that footage together is good."

"Good enough to make a believer out of you?"

"If I wasn't sane? Maybe. What I'm telling you is that there isn't a pixel out of place. Not one. I ran it through every program I have and eyeballed it myself. It would stand up in court if the subject matter wasn't so corny. I mean, really? They couldn't do better than the invisible man?"

She mistook my laughter for agreement.

"Seriously," she said, "if you're thinking of hiring whoever put that together, be prepared to pay top dollar. It's quality work. You won't find anyone better."

"Thank you, Kerry. That's exactly why I pay *you* top dollar. Don't forget to destroy that footage and any record of our discussion about it."

"I will. Pleasure doing business, Jackman."

I dropped the phone on the passenger seat and let my head fall back against the headrest. How had the bastard done it? I took some satisfaction in knowing it would have cost him a small fortune, but without proof that the footage was fake, I had one less course of action.

I started the car and spun it around, heading back toward the city. Cole might think he'd been clever, but I wasn't out of cards yet.

The underground parking garage at the Delaney building was deserted. I took the elevator to my office and went straight to the safe. I'd never wanted to use the lewd photos of Bronwyn and Richard that

I'd held back. Grossly indecent was an understatement. They made me want to take a shower. Now, thanks to Cole, I was snapping cellphone photos of them. I locked the originals away and sat in the glow of the computer screen until I found the information I needed on the Internet.

It was past midnight when I made my way back to the *Symphony*. The lights were dimmed, which meant Sandra had gone to bed. I walked to the bar and poured myself a Scotch then headed out to the foredeck and settled in a lounger. My father would have approved of my plan, but he would have cautioned me not to rush. Each potential ramification needed to be teased out and assessed. So far, the upsides outweighed any possible downsides.

It was Sandra's reaction that worried me the most. She'd be angry, no question, but at least I wasn't putting her in the middle this time. And she had to be disgusted with Cole right now. That would help.

Redmond would probably think I was stalling.

Jimmy, on the other hand, would have a shit-eating grin on his face and slap me on the back. Jimmy understood the criminal mind. He knew they couldn't be trusted. If I paid off Cole now, he'd be back for more. It was just a matter of time. I would have to make sure that Redmond and Sandra understood that.

I poured a second Scotch, returned to the lounger and pulled out my phone. The text to Cole was to the point: *It seems we're at an impasse. Perhaps your mother has an opinion?* I attached the photo of his mother, naked and on her knees in front of Richard Des Roche with her mouth full. I copied the email to Bronwyn. At the bottom, I typed out the email addresses for the *National Tattler* and a half-dozen trashy porn sites so there would be no mistaking my next move. I downed my drink, pressed send and then powered it off. He could stew in it for a while.

After checking the security alarms, I headed below. Sandra lay in bed. The sheet had fallen away from her shoulder to reveal the silk-clad curve of her hip. I undressed, crawled in behind her and pressed my lips to her bare shoulder. She woke from her slumber and turned in my arms. I brushed the hair from her face. God, she was beautiful.

"Where have you been?"

"Lake Borgne."

"I thought as much. What did you decide?"

"We should hear from Cole in the morning."

A smile lit her face and guilt elbowed me in the gut. "You contacted him?"

"I did." I would pay for misleading her in the morning, but right now I needed to bathe in her. "I love you," I said, and kissed her. She opened her mouth to me and I devoured her, pressing my growing arousal into her hip. I pushed the delicate silk of her camisole up over her breasts and caressed her warm, soft skin. Her breath hitched when I pinched her nipple, and her reaction made me smile. She was so bloody responsive. It hardened me to the point of distraction.

I rolled on top of her. "Do you see what you've done to me?"

She wrapped her hand around my shaft and drew a gasp out of me. "Umm, I do."

"You can stop that sometime next week," I said, pushing into her grip. She laughed and stroked me just the way I liked. I dropped my head to her shoulder, enjoying her touch a while longer. She slowed when she knew I couldn't take much more, and I dipped down and tongued her nipple, teasing it to a stiff point. I left it sopping wet and shifted my attention to the other one. A moan escaped her throat as I edged her shorts off, and trailed wet kisses down her stomach.

She parted her legs at the touch of my hand and I slid my fingers inside. "Always ready for me," I said, seeking her gaze. She had a lovely please-fuck-me look on her face. I let my fingers do the work and held her gaze as I crept lower and licked a lazy circle around her hardened clitoris. She'd taught me well, and I was rewarded when she arched her back and groaned, pushing her pelvis into my face, wanting more. I was happy to oblige.

"Enough," she finally pleaded. "I want you inside me."

I didn't need to be asked twice. Her heels pressed into my ass as I crawled into place and her hands guided me right where I wanted to be. I buried myself in her and stilled. This was nirvana. I pulled back until just the tip of me remained in her warmth, and then plunged in again. This time I couldn't stop, and she met me thrust for thrust. The moment I felt her insides contract against me, I let myself lose control and released my soul into her warm embrace.

"I will never get enough of you." I kissed her gently and rolled on my back, regaining my breath. She curled into my side with her head on my shoulder and her knee on my thigh. I pulled the sheet over us and we drifted off to sleep.

I awoke in the midst of a wet dream, squinting against the sun that peeked through the portholes. Sandra was awake and massaging my raging hard-on. God! What a way to start my day.

"Good morning," she said, sporting a come-hither grin. She stopped her ministrations and straddled me. Her hair was dishevelled and fell to the tops of her breasts. I reached up and cupped them. She purred, pressing into my hands, looking every bit like a sleepy sex goddess. She rose to her knees and rubbed the sensitive tip of my erection against her wet folds, teasing me. I couldn't take my eyes off her. How did I ever get so lucky? She kept her gaze locked on mine as she sank down onto my shaft, taking me back to nirvana. My breath escaped in a hiss. I held her hips and let her set the pace. She wanted a slow fuck this morning, and I was happy to go along for the ride. After she collapsed on me, sated, I rolled her over and finished with a few hard thrusts.

She looked content lying there with a smile on her face. I rose to my elbows. "You, my love, are the sexiest woman on the planet. And these," I said, kissing one breast and then the other, "are absolutely perfect. I plan on worshipping them for a very long time." I swung my legs off the bed. "I'm going to shower."

"So much for a very long time," she said with a pout.

"Care to join me?"

"Now you're just being greedy," she said. "How about I make a pot of coffee instead?"

"Your choice," I teased, enjoying our banter.

The bed was empty when I returned from my shower. With a towel around my hips, I headed barefoot upstairs to the galley. Sandra didn't hear me push open the door. She was on the phone with her back to me.

"No. He contacted Cole last night," she said, and paused to listen. "I don't know. I imagine he'll have to run the details past Jimmy." Another pause. "Don't! Dad, please. You're going to have to trust him. He knows what he's doing."

That's my girl, I thought, and backed away, slipping behind the door frame.

"I'll call you, okay?" she said. "Just as soon as I know the details."

When I was sure she'd disconnected, I banged the door open and sauntered in. She dropped the phone into her robe's pocket and turned around. "Coffee's ready," she said, schooling her face into a bright smile. She didn't mention the phone call, and we both gave the subject of Cole a wide berth.

I made pancakes and tried to coax her into staying home with me, but she'd made an appointment with the company that managed the wharf where the new children's park was planned. She kissed me goodbye after breakfast and I watched her sashay up the dock. When she was out of sight, I poured one more cup of coffee and turned on my phone. I'd missed a call from my assistant, Michael, but not a word from Cole.

I returned the call to Michael and told him I wouldn't be in. He said he'd send a courier with some papers from Jimmy for me to sign. The Dixon Tower deal was coming together nicely. Our margins were down, but it couldn't be helped. Steel prices were up and volume only went so far to beat down the price of concrete. The good news was that we'd found a hungry new architectural firm that hadn't been tainted by Dad's reputation. Through them, I had the opportunity to present Delaney & Son in a new light.

I couldn't wait to share the details with Sandra when she got home. We both knew it would take more than one deal to clean up Delaney's reputation, but it was a start.

Jean Benoit called when I was reviewing the Dixon Tower paperwork. The visitors' logbook was a dead end, so we wouldn't get a name to go with Cole's Ghost. It was disappointing, but in the absence of any word from Cole, I was betting the man's identity was already a moot point—that surveillance footage wouldn't see the light of day.

My next call was to Jimmy. We agreed to meet at LuLu's for lunch. I called my driver. After a brief ride past some of the finest antebellum architecture in the French Quarter, he dropped me in front of the small diner. Their smoker was out back, and mouth-watering barbecue aroma permeated the air. Jimmy sat at his usual table in the corner, his sleeves rolled up and a half-empty glass in front of him. The owner, Louie, a wiry man with full-sleeve tattoos, acknowledged my arrival with a nod. I shook Jimmy's hand and sat down, as a waitress in a short, cleavage-baring dress and an eyebrow ring slid a drink in front of me.

"Thanks, love," Jimmy said, and the waitress smiled sweetly and left. Jimmy's appreciative gaze followed her across the room.

When she slipped out of view, Jimmy returned to the here and now with a sigh. "Don't keep me waiting, buddy. What happened at your meeting with Cole yesterday?"

I'd already given my story some thought. Jimmy wasn't one of us. He wouldn't understand the significance of *the invisible man*, but he'd have no trouble comprehending the blackmail aspect.

"Just what you thought," I said, tasting the bourbon. "He wants a chunk of Delaney and he thinks he can blackmail me into giving it to him."

"What's he got?"

"He thinks he can prove Dad got his hands on Touchstone's sealed bid and sabotaged it."

"And how's the genius going to do that when his own lawyers couldn't?"

"He's got surveillance footage of a man at the Delaney building half an hour after leaving the engineering firm where the bids were locked up."

"So what?"

"He's made a lame attempt to connect the same man to a diamond robbery. In effect, he's trying to make it look like Dad hired a known criminal. It's speculation. Could sully Dad's reputation, that's all."

"Sully his reputation?" Jimmy chuckled. "He really didn't know your old man at all, did he?"

"I shut Cole down. Sent him a copy of one of those photos you gave me. I'd held back a few of the worst offenders and now I'm glad I did. And just so he knows I'm not playing around, I copied Bronwyn on the email and included some websites I'm sure she wouldn't want to be associated with."

Jimmy raised his glass in a toast. "Matthew taught you well, buddy."

I touched my glass to his and took a drink. "It had to be done, but I'm not proud of it. I feel like a shit using those photos."

"You had no choice. Don't beat yourself up about it."

I could only hope Sandra felt the same when I told her what I'd done. "I'll get over it. I just wish he hadn't made me do it. But damn it! He didn't even have the balls to come to me. He used my wife—tried to manipulate her into feeling sorry for him."

"He's a piece of work."

"You're right about that. Dad suffered enough with what Bronwyn did to him when he was alive. But that little shit waits until he's dead to go after him."

"He's a fucking coward. Let it go, bud. Let's order."

I got home in the early afternoon. Sandra was out and I still hadn't heard from Cole. A part of me was curious to know what Bronwyn's reaction had been, but Cole's silence said it all. I unpacked the groceries and placed the bottle of Veuve Clicquot in the fridge to cool. I'd prepare Sandra a special dinner tonight, and we'd celebrate the Dixon Tower deal. I set the shrimp out and got to work.

Everything was prepared when Sandra returned. I'd been at the computer and quickly rose to greet her, but my smile dropped at the sight of her troubled face. "What is it?" I asked, reaching for her.

She stepped away as if my touch repelled her. "How could you?" she said, her face a mask of horror.

Instantly I knew this was about Cole. "So the little coward went running to you again, did he?"

"Actually, it was Mrs. Des Roche. She sent me the photo you shared with her son. The one you threatened to share with the world." Her lip curled in a most unflattering way. "Your father would be proud of you."

Oh shit. I'd vastly underestimated her reaction. I softened my tone, appealing to her sense of pride. "They're using you, Sandra. They have nothing except your sympathies to play on and you're letting them." It astounded me that she could be so naive.

"I have never been so humiliated. So embarrassed. I thought this was beneath you. Apparently, I was wrong."

"Are you forgetting who's threatening whom? Cole's the one blackmailing us, not the other way around. That photo was a last resort, and I used it in self-defence. I'm sorry they pulled you into this, but I'm not going to let a punk like Cole drag my father through the mud and plunder his company without putting up a fight." I could tell by the scowl on her face that I wasn't reaching her.

She shook her head from side to side. "You could have stopped it. Hell, you could have prevented it if you'd only acknowledge what's right in front of your face. Cole is your goddamn brother."

"For fuck's sake. How many times do I have to tell you? *He isn't!* And since when do you take that bastard's word over mine?"

She clamped her mouth shut and took a moment. When she spoke, her voice was tight, controlled. "Your behaviour sickens me."

Her words hit like shrapnel. "I could say the same. Have you no loyalty to me, to my father?"

"What your father did to Cole was disgraceful. And you . . . I can't even look at you right now." She turned and stormed from the salon, leaving my ears ringing in her wake.

Chapter Nine

What the fuck! I dropped to the sofa. How could Sandra turn on me like that? She was my goddamn wife. I shouldn't have to beg for her support. Was she being willfully naive? Had her family's opinion of me finally taken root? An ache developed in my chest. I pressed my hand against my sternum with no relief. Sandra's reaction was off the charts. I'd never seen her so angry. She had no right. Fucking hell.

I got up and pulled a beer from the fridge and stormed upstairs to the observation deck. Cole, that fucking bastard, had once again driven a wedge between us, and I feared this one would leave scars.

Redmond called later that night. I'd been prepared for him to tear another strip off me, but he hadn't yet heard. I guess Sandra had been too angry to tell him what had happened. I didn't enlighten him about our argument, but I did tell him that I'd quashed Cole's blackmail scheme. I gave him the details and had little difficulty agreeing with his assessment that his daughter would not be happy with my choice. The righteous prick made it clear he felt the same way and for the first time in a long time, I didn't give a damn.

Sandra didn't come home that night or the next. Each time I returned to the *Symphony,* I checked to see if she'd been home. I expected she'd want to collect some clothes at least, but she hadn't been back. She was well and truly pissed. Which was okay—I felt the same.

The days lengthened to a week, and I caved in and called her cellphone. One of us had to be a grown-up about this. She didn't answer.

At the two-week mark, I called her again. She didn't pick up. I contacted Bernadette Schuller, the neighbourhood coordinator for the children's park Sandra had been so committed to. Bernadette was most embarrassed to tell me that Sandra had withdrawn from the project.

It felt like a sucker punch. How long was Sandra planning to drag on this fight? Her absence seasoned my growing anger. We were adults, not hotheaded teenagers, and this silent treatment of hers had passed its best-before date.

If she'd bothered to return my calls, she'd at least have known that my plan—the one she'd found so distasteful—had worked. I'd had no contact from Cole, and Jean Benoit confirmed that the bastard hadn't been to the Touchstone offices since the day I sent him that photo. It made me smile to think his mother had had something to do with that.

A few days later, I called Sandra again. "Would you please call me? I get that you're angry, and maybe you're not ready to talk, but at least tell me you're okay." I disconnected and tossed the phone across to the facing sofa. Almost three weeks, and not a word from her. It was bloody inconsiderate. I'd already checked the credit card statements for a clue as to where she was staying, but she hadn't used them. Instead, she'd made several large withdrawals from our bank account. It seemed she'd picked up a trick or two from her brother about how to go AWOL.

The Dixon Tower deal was finalized on the twenty-second day of her hissy fit. I checked my messages as I exited the boardroom. James had called and my hackles immediately came up. I played his message. "It's James. Would you please have Sandra call me? Her phone's acting up."

He wasn't angry, which was an odd but pleasant surprise. Immediately, I dialled Sandra and got a recording. "The number you are trying to reach is out of service."

It wasn't until that exact moment that I finally saw the light. Her resigning from the children's park project should have been a clue, but I'd missed it. I'd been so busy giving her space to come around, time to see the bigger picture, that I hadn't grasped the most important detail. I'd been the one who'd been naive. Sandra had no interest in talking to me. There would be no discussion, no getting past this.

She had left me. The certainty of it dropped me like a sledgehammer.

I didn't return to my office. A distraction was what I needed; one free of anything that reminded me of Sandra, including Fliers and covey and secrets. I called my college buddy, Kyle. When I told him about Sandra, he didn't hesitate. "I'm on my way, Jackman," he said.

I had my driver take me to Jimmy's. His assistant took one look at me and pulled Jimmy out of his meeting.

It was the start of a very long night, the bulk of which I wouldn't remember.

I awoke in my bed on the *Symphony* with the drummer from the Red Hot Chili Peppers playing a raucous solo inside my skull. I stumbled to the head, downed some extra-strength Tylenol, and then fell back into bed. Hours later I emerged, still feeling like a sack of shit.

Kyle was out cold in the starboard stateroom. Jimmy's snores erupted from the stateroom across the hall. The thought of coffee made me want to throw up. I grabbed some crackers and drank down a few more Tylenol with a glass of cola.

By the time Jimmy emerged, I was feeling somewhat human. There was an unhealthy pallor to his skin. "You look like hell, my man," I said, handing him the bottle of painkillers. He groped his way to the sofa.

"Coffee?" I asked, heading to the galley. I poured two cups. My hands shook under the strain of holding the carafe.

"I'm getting too old for this," Jimmy said, swallowing a mitt-full of pills with a slurp of coffee. "What happened to Kyle? Did we kill him last night?"

"Death would be an improvement," Kyle said, lumbering into the salon, his bare feet slapping the teak. The wrinkles in his clothes told me he'd slept in them. "I'll have some of those," he said, reaching for the Tylenol bottle.

I passed him a cup of coffee. "We need grease, and lots of it," I said, pulling out a frying pan. Between the three of us, we devoured a pound of bacon, nine eggs and a stack of toast.

Jimmy left shortly after breakfast and Kyle hit the shower. I tried Sandra's cellphone one more time, because I hadn't tortured myself enough, and got the same recording. I supposed the next contact I'd have with her would be through her lawyer. I poured another cola and walked out to the foredeck to let the fresh air blow out the cobwebs.

"I feel good," Kyle said, channelling James Brown as he joined me on the foredeck buttoning the shirt I'd given him. He glanced over at me and toned down his exuberance. "I'm really sorry about Sandra. You two were the real deal."

After I'd called him yesterday, Kyle had boarded a ninety-minute commuter flight without so much as a toothbrush. "Thanks. Never imagined I'd need that prenup."

"Wish I could say I had one," Kyle said. "Marilyn's hired herself a real hotshot. I'll be lucky to keep my tighty-whities."

I hadn't even realized he and Marilyn were divorcing until last night. He hadn't mentioned it when he was in town for Dad's funeral last summer.

I arranged a cab to take Kyle to the airport and then settled my overserved body back into the lounger.

James's voice woke me. "You look like hell, Jackson."

I squinted up at the long, lanky frame in silhouette against the sun. The drummer in my skull started up again. "What are you doing here?"

"Looking for Sandra. You didn't get my message?"

I rested my arm across my eyes. Now that he was here, there was no avoiding the inevitable. I decided to get it over with. "I got your message, but I can't help you. Your sister isn't speaking to me."

"What are you talking about?"

Did he really not know, or was he just getting his kicks by making me say it? I lifted my arm to see his face. He didn't know. "Sandra left me. Walked out three weeks ago and didn't look back. I thought that's why you were here."

"Three weeks ago? What the fuck happened?"

"Cole Des Roche is what happened. Sandra didn't approve of how I disarmed his blackmail scheme. She told me as much before she marched out of here."

"When exactly was that?"

"James, if you don't mind, you're interrupting an exquisite hangover and I really don't care to rehash it."

"Fine. Then tell me where she's staying."

"I don't know. She's not using her credit cards. Apparently she's on a cash diet, and a mighty healthy one."

"She hasn't been in touch with me or Mom and Dad."

I snickered. "Well, well. How does it feel to have someone you love go AWOL?"

"Don't be a jerk. Sandra would never leave without telling us."

"Yeah? That's what I thought too. And yet, look around. She's gone."

"You must have some idea where she went."

"I don't, but I'm not the hotshot PI, James. Why don't you go find her?"

He shook his head in disgust. "You need to sober up. I'll make a pot of coffee."

"Don't bother. I don't need a mother, James. Go home."

He ignored me and turned on his heel, his ponytail swinging behind him. He kept his hair long, tied in a style I'm sure he thought the ladies liked. I heard him banging around in the galley. If I hadn't felt like crap, I'd have taken a swing at the prick. Always wanted to do that. I must have drifted off again. When I woke, the sun had moved to the western horizon. James's voice drifted out to me, a one-sided conversation. Shit! He hadn't left. I swung my legs off the lounger and rested my forearms on my thighs until the dizzy feeling passed. I stood and strolled back into the salon.

James's gaze followed me to the galley, and he watched as I poured a glass of water. "I'll be in touch," he said into his phone and disconnected.

The water tasted like nectar from the hangover gods. "You're still here," I said, and poured a second glass. My laptop was open on the coffee table in front of him. "By all means, James, help yourself. *Mi casa es su casa.*"

"Yeah, well, I had to do something to pass the time. You've been out for five fucking hours. Feeling better?"

"Like you give a damn. Did you find her?"

"Not yet. Dad's on his way. We're meeting with Wells Fargo security at 9:00 a.m. The police will meet us there."

"Seriously? You reported her missing?"

"We had no choice. I can't get access to the bank's security cameras and they won't show us the ATM images of Sandra's withdrawals without a police report . . . and your consent."

I couldn't help but smile at the knowledge that needing my consent irritated him.

"Dad talked them into allowing us to view the images to make a visual ID."

"You're going a little overboard here, don't you think?"

He glared at me through narrowed blue eyes, the same shade of blue as his sister's.

"Fine," I said. "Do you know where she made the withdrawals?"

"Don't you look at your bank statements?" He nodded to the laptop, completely oblivious to the gross invasion of my privacy. "The bank sent the details to the police. They'll have the images for us tomorrow."

"What are you thinking, James?"

"As much as it pains me to say this, Jackson, I don't think Sandra left you."

"Why? Because she didn't tell you?"

He treated me to his glare again. "It's not like her to be out of touch this long."

"Hurts, doesn't it?"

James's nostrils flared. "She hasn't contacted you or her family in three weeks. What if someone snatched her? Did that possibility even cross your mind?"

"She's far too careful for that."

"Careful? Like the other Fliers who've gone missing? Like David Ashton?"

"That's a fucking low blow." We all lived with the knowledge that our gift could be stolen, which would in all likelihood be fatal, but David Ashton was a new horror. He'd been abducted and experimented on like a lab rat for months. He'd escaped, but not before they removed one of his eyes. We still didn't know who *they* were. "If I thought for one minute she was in danger, I'd have done something about it. That's not what happened. She left me; she didn't go running into the ever-loving arms of her family. Deal with it."

"How can you be so flippant about this?"

"You weren't here. I was. She's livid, not missing. There's a difference. After she left me, she had the wherewithal to remove herself from the children's park project at the wharf. Obviously, she planned to be angry for a while." A vein in James's forehead bulged. "It really goads you that I know Sandra better than you, doesn't it?"

James stood with a mouthful of words he didn't dare spit out. Not when he needed my cooperation. "Dad and I will come by to collect you at 8:30 tomorrow morning. Be ready."

"I don't think so. I'll meet you there."

He pressed his hands to his hips. "The meeting's at 9:00. The building's on Poydras. Don't be late," he said, and then he stormed out much like his sister had not that long ago.

I had to admit, Sandra's silent treatment didn't usually extend to her family, but I understood her reluctance to contact them. She'd defied them when she married me. Why would she give them the opportunity to rub an *I-told-you-so* in her face?

I took James's place on the sofa in front of the laptop. The browser history had been wiped. I looked for a trail of his activity, checking my

JP MCLEAN

sent mailbox and the search engine's drop-down box, and found nothing. Though I suspected it was futile, I changed my passwords.

In the morning, my hangover was a distant memory. I drove into town, turned off Poydras Street and parked in the shadow of the prominent, black-glass Wells Fargo building. It was still early, but an unmarked police vehicle already sat in the parking lot. James arrived at 8:45 a.m. behind the wheel of a piece-of-shit rental; the man had no taste. Redmond sat in the passenger seat. They pulled in beside me.

Redmond, in full lawyer mode, wore a perfectly fitted Gucci suit. He exited the car and looked down to check the shine on his brogues. James had two inches on him. He'd dressed down in slacks and a long-sleeved shirt.

We shook hands like wary opponents at a boxing match, and then turned and walked to the entrance in tense silence. We were escorted to a conference room on the executive floor and greeted by the balding manager, Cliff Honeycott. I introduced James and Redmond and then we were introduced to Mannering and Sims, the plainclothes police investigators with no first names, and the bank's lawyer, Delores Puente. Puente needed to buy better suits. The young technician manning a computer console didn't rate an introduction.

Ms. Puente started on a low note with cover-your-ass documents the bank needed me to sign before they'd disclose my banking details or the images of my wife. Next, she asked me to sign a document acknowledging that Sandra had full access to the funds in our joint account.

She whisked the documents away and advised the lead investigator, Mannering, that she had what she needed. Mannering then nodded to the technician at the console, who explained the details of the video he displayed on the wall screen. "This was taken February 2 in Biloxi, Mississippi." The video was shot at a downward angle without audio, but there was no doubt it was Sandra. She punched in her code and waited calmly until the machine rolled out the bills. After she removed her card, she neatly folded the bills. The video caught her movement as she turned, and then the screen went black.

Mannering asked, "Is that your wife, Mr. Delaney?"

I shook myself out of a minor state of shock. "Yes." Knowing she was out there was one thing, but seeing her was something else entirely.

"Let's see another one," Mannering said.

"This one was taken February 5 in Fairhope, Alabama," announced the nameless tech.

Once again, the video showed Sandra, calmly withdrawing money from our joint account. She might as well have buried an axe in my back.

"And that is also your wife, Mr. Delaney?"

"Yes."

"There are three other withdrawals by your wife on"—Mannering referred to his notes—"February ninth, the thirteenth and last Tuesday, the sixteenth. As you can see for yourself, there is no evidence to suggest that she is being coerced or threatened in any way. I've viewed the other digital files and I can assure you they offer no more detail than the two you have already viewed."

Redmond said, "The fact she hasn't contacted her family or her husband in three weeks tells me that something's wrong. It's completely out of character for her."

Mannering frowned. "I can appreciate how troubling that is for you and your family, but this isn't a police matter. Alexandra Delaney isn't missing. She's chosen to not communicate with her family. That may be difficult to accept, but she's an adult. It's her prerogative. There is nothing we can do for you."

He stood. "If the situation changes, we'll take another look. Good day," he said, and he and Sims excused themselves.

Mr. Honeycott cleared his throat. "Mr. Delaney, as you are aware, your wife has a Triple-A withdrawal limit. At the rate she's drawing from that account, you'll need a quarter million a year to fund it. Perhaps you should consider closing it."

Redmond interceded with a sharp, "No!" All eyes turned to him. "We'll keep it open. Sandy obviously needs the money for something. Until we figure out what it is, those withdrawals are our only access to her whereabouts."

Mr. Honeycott dragged his pointed attention from Redmond to me. "Mr. Delaney, perhaps you would like to consider reducing that account's daily withdrawal limit."

I could almost see the tendrils of smoke rising from Redmond in my peripheral vision. The perfect family had to deal with me, and this time it was their own flesh and blood behaving badly. My ego lingered over the much-deserved and long-awaited development.

"Thank you, Mr. Honeycott," I said. "I think that's a good idea—"

"Jackson—"

I cut Redmond off. "I'll consider it. I'll be in touch if I have further instructions."

James, who'd been quiet until then, spoke. "Mr. Honeycott, I wonder if we could make arrangements to have the digital files of my sister's past and future ATM withdrawals forwarded to us?"

Mr. Honeycott exhaled through puffed cheeks and considered the request for a moment. "That would be highly unusual, Mr. Moss."

Redmond stepped in without missing a beat. "I'm sure, given the amount of business Delaney & Son directs through your bank, you could see your way clear to making those arrangements."

"What do you think, Delores?" Mr. Honeycott asked.

She took a moment to consider her response. "I'm prepared to authorize the release of that information to the account holder, Mr. Delaney. Whether he chooses to share it is up to him." She then turned her attention to me. "But a word of advice, Mr. Delaney: get a lawyer. Discuss your options with her or him."

"Thank you, Ms. Puente. Mr. Honeycott, you have my contact information. Kindly use my personal email address."

"I'll send the files right away," Mr. Honeycott said.

I stood and shook his hand. "Thank you for your time."

We exited the building quickly. When we were clear of the front doors, Redmond said, "We need to talk."

"About what?" I asked without breaking my stride. I'd had about enough interference from the two of them for one day. When we crossed into the shade, I pulled out my keys.

"You know Sandy is close to her family. She would never intentionally worry us like this."

"You saw the video, Redmond. She's fine."

"Maybe, but looks can be deceiving." He quizzed me for information, centring on Sandra's actions, not mine, and it was that detail that conveyed the sincerity of his concerns.

"I'm sorry, Redmond. If I hear from her, I'll let you know, but I imagine you'll hear from her before I will."

Redmond offered his hand. "Stay in touch, son. And please send us those files from the bank."

"Of course," I said, and tipped my head goodbye to James, who was already at the driver's door of his car. I pulled out of the lot ahead of them and headed for Delaney to bury myself in work and put the images of Sandra withdrawing wads of our money out of my mind.

Chapter Ten

Plans for the groundbreaking ceremony at the Dixon Tower site were underway, and Delaney's office was hopping with activity as tender packages for construction were reviewed by the architects and engineers, and permits were put in place. Jimmy was at the office more frequently than not, and each time a new digital file arrived from the bank, I'd share it with him.

It had been almost six weeks with no word from Sandra, and she'd drained almost forty thousand from our account.

"I think it's time you considered closing that account, Jackson," Jimmy said during one of his visits.

"You're right. I should, but Redmond is still of the opinion Sandra is somehow being coerced into making the withdrawals. I'll hold on a little longer."

Jimmy offered me one of those you-poor-schmuck smiles. "Redmond is a friend of mine, but it's not his money, not his account."

Jimmy didn't mention the account again. The weeks stacked up, and the ripples of her absence lapped at the minutiae of my life. The cleaners had put away her cosmetics, and every morning my eyes were drawn to the empty space on the counter. Her clothes no longer accompanied mine when I collected the dry cleaning. Everything she had once touched—books, flower vases, jewellery—was slowly being put out of sight.

She was ebbing away.

We cut the ribbon at Dixon's groundbreaking ceremony, and after all the hand-shaking and Kodak smiles, I retreated to the *Symphony*.

I'd immersed myself in work to avoid thinking about Sandra, but the celebration brought home how hollow it all felt without her to share it with.

I grabbed a glass and the bottle of Veuve Clicquot that I'd put in the fridge the night she'd left me, and dropped to the sofa. I filled my glass and flipped on the TV. The Hornets were at home playing the Phoenix Suns.

With my feet on the table, I pulled out my phone. I was done with Sandra's bullshit. It was time for some fun, and I knew just the thing. I'd invite Kyle and Anthony out for a weekend of debauchery on the *Symphony*. Lord knows I needed some action and we were all single now, or close enough to it. We hadn't had a weekend like that since graduating from Stanford. I pulled up Kyle's number, but a shout from the dock interrupted me.

It was a courier with a box from Bernadette Schuller. She was returning some personal items that Sandra had left behind at the project office. I set the box on the coffee table and opened it. Inside was a diorama of Sandra's life: lipstick, pearl earrings, perfume, programs from the ballet and opera, and requests for donations from every charity in Louisiana; some of the envelopes weren't even opened.

I flipped through the stack of unopened mail, recognizing all of the senders' logos except for one. Universal Genetics. It was addressed to Alexandra Moss, Sandra's maiden name. A sense of dread chilled me. I slid my thumb under the flap and withdrew the folded contents. The subject line read *DNA Test Results*.

Sandra had gone behind my back and done the unthinkable. The test samples were named Father, Brother 1, Brother 2.

Fucking bitch! She knew I'd said no—hell, our lawyers had fought it in court—and she'd done it anyway. I tossed the report on the coffee table and lurched to my feet, raking my hands through my hair. Dad was right. Women couldn't be trusted. My loving wife had just proven it.

I traded the champagne for Scotch. I felt gutted, violated. As if leaving me weren't enough, Sandra had heaved one final kick in the balls.

I picked up the report and scanned the first page again. Regardless of the results, I'd learned enough from the lawyers to know the results would be non-binding without my consent to the sampling. I was tempted to tear it up, but a tiny piece of me was curious. I flipped the page and forged on, seeking out the plain-language test results. They were conclusive. There was a greater than 50 percent chance that Cole was my half-sibling.

I refolded the report and slid it back in its envelope. That piece of trash was my half-brother. And Sandra had done this for him. She'd betrayed me . . . for him.

I took the envelope to the sink and held it by a corner then set it on fire. When the flames forced me to drop it, I watched it fizzle out, and hosed the ashes down the drain.

I turned and gazed outside across the water. It was time to move on.

My phone buzzed. It was James. I declined the call and drained my Scotch. A few minutes later, the phone buzzed again. This time it was Redmond. Hmm, James and now Redmond? Maybe the bitch had finally surfaced.

"Hello, Redmond."

"Jackson. Have you viewed the latest Wells Fargo file?"

"Which one?"

"Came in this afternoon."

Goddamnit! I knew it. James had been hacking my emails. "Give me a minute," I growled. I strode across to the galley counter and opened the laptop. The email had come in two hours ago. "Okay, I'm looking at it now."

"Tell me what you see."

"Sandra, obviously." Her hair was loose around her shoulders. Her face looked drawn. Must have been the treachery wearing on her. She took the money, like always, and folded it before turning away from the ATM.

"Wait!" Just before the camera cut out, I caught a glimpse of someone standing behind her. I fumbled with the touchpad and inched the footage backwards, freezing it when the figure emerged from behind Sandra's shoulder. My chest felt too tight. "Well. I guess we know why she hasn't contacted me."

"So you agree? It's Cole Des Roche."

"Looks like him." I couldn't breathe. My blood ignited. Heat shot up my neck and burst through my skull. "I'm closing the bank account in the morning, Redmond."

"Jackson, please don't do that."

Anger swept through me like wildfire. "She's with my so-called brother. What do you think they're doing together? Writing a travel book? And you want me to foot the bill? Come on, Redmond!"

"She's wearing her wedding rings, Jackson. Don't you think she'd have taken them off if she was carrying on with someone else?"

"It looks like I didn't know your daughter at all, Redmond."

"Well, I do know her. She would not behave like this."

"It's right there in front of you, Redmond. On tape. No one's forcing her hand."

"Just wait another day or two. James is already working on it. Cole will lead us right to them."

"I'll give you a day. When you find them, offer my congratulations. The account will be closed day after tomorrow." With that, I hung up.

I closed the laptop. That fucking bastard! Cole had wormed his way into my wife's sympathies, then into her bed. Jimmy had been wrong. History *was* repeating itself. And I would never forgive her. I gritted my teeth against the pain radiating up my chest.

I barely slept. The shower helped revive me, but it wasn't until I arrived at the office that I realized I'd forgotten to shave. I sent Jimmy a text to come by my office and started clearing out my desk. My concentration was shot. I had to get away. I'd delegate as much as I could, and then I'd take the *Symphony* offshore for a few weeks to clear my head.

Jimmy looked at the video and didn't say a word. "I'll get the paperwork ready. Your prenup is ironclad in a case like this, but I can get Jean on it. I'm sure he can get better evidence of their affair."

"No. I don't think I could stand to see more proof than that. I already feel like an ass. I've been rehashing our falling-out for weeks, wondering if we'd ever be able to patch things up, move past this. And all along, she's been sleeping with Cole. At least now I know why she didn't call."

"I think it's good you're getting away. Ted Worley can take the reins for a while."

"I've called an emergency meeting of the board," I said. "After that, you can reach me on my cell. How long will it take to prepare the paperwork for the divorce?"

"A matter of hours. The prenup spells out the terms. She'll have to be served, certainly, but then we can file it with the New Orleans Parish. From there it's just a matter of the waiting period before it's final."

"Good. How about I come by your office after the board meeting?"

After Jimmy left, I pulled Ted Worley into my office and explained that I was going to be unavoidably absent for a number of weeks. We went over the notes for the properties Delaney had in its sights, and the contacts we hoped to develop in the coming months.

The board took my impending absence in stride. The Dixon Tower Project was on schedule and on budget, and with Worley at the helm, Delaney & Son was in competent hands. Ted and Michael would keep me apprised and I would be available by cell.

I phoned Kerry before I left the office and asked her to organize a new computer and cellphone. She assured me that James would have his work cut out getting through her encryption. She would have them delivered to me day after tomorrow.

I took one last look around the office. How long would it take for the news to leak out and set chins flapping around the water cooler? The endless speculation was just one more reason to get away for a while. I shook Michael's hand and headed over to Jimmy's to sign the paperwork that would put an end to my marriage.

Tomorrow I'd visit Mr. Honeycott and kill Sandra's cash cow. After that, I'd head offshore and toss everything Sandra once treasured into the sea.

Aboard the *Symphony* I opened an exquisite bottle of Scotch that was older than I, and coincidentally, also single. Old Pulteney was a thirty-five-year-old single malt worthy of tonight's celebration. Standing in the galley, I poured a generous shot and raised my glass. "Here's to dipping my wick wherever I please!" I savoured a taste, enjoying the complex flavours that lingered on my tongue.

Before I could fully appreciate the rare drink, a familiar and unwelcome voice called out from the dock, ruining my celebration. It was my favourite brother-in-law.

I strode to the door of the salon. "James? What are you doing here?"

"Nice to see you, too, Jackson. Where the hell did you learn your manners?"

Ah, Mr. Bloody Etiquette. Just like his sister. I turned away and headed inside. "I'm not feeling very cordial these days, James, but come aboard. I'll see what I can do. Beer?" I offered, not willing to waste eight-hundred-dollar Scotch on the likes of him.

"No thanks."

I picked up my tumbler. "What's that?" I asked, seeing James remove a sheaf of papers from his inside pocket. "Did you find the son of a bitch?"

"No. Something else." He walked to the sofa and spread the papers out on the coffee table. "Do you have a map of the southern states?"

"Sure. Why?" I located an atlas I kept on the bookshelf and handed it to him. He opened it to the double-page spread of the southern states.

"When Sandra first went missing, her ATM withdrawals were all over the place. Mississippi, Alabama . . . as far east as Pensacola." James waved his hands over the area in question. "They're all port cities. And these recent ATMs,"—he referenced his notes then pointed to the California coast—"are over here. Imperial Beach, San Diego, La Jolla. Again, port cities."

"And?"

"I think they're travelling by boat."

"How nice for them."

James threw his arms in the air. "Jesus, Jackson." He stood and resettled on the sofa opposite. "Can you set aside your wounded pride for a fucking minute and think about Sandra?"

A derisive laugh escaped my lips. "Sandra is all I've thought about since she walked out that door."

"Yeah, she walked out. So what? She was angry. You seem to have forgotten she had a good reason. But she loved you—god only knows why—and she's not a quitter. She would have come back, even if only for the satisfaction of confronting your sorry ass."

"You didn't see her. You didn't see how angry she was when she left."

"No, but I know how much it takes to get her to lose her temper. She must have been spitting fire. But she would have calmed down. Eventually. And after Cole's blackmail scheme, I can't believe she would have turned to him."

"If I hadn't seen that ATM footage, I wouldn't have either, but there you go. Wrong again."

"I am not wrong. Dad's not wrong. Sandra would not have walked away from her marriage without a fight. Do you not love her enough to give her the benefit of the doubt for just one minute?"

"Love her enough?" Anger licked up my spine and into my scalp. "I loved her with all my heart and soul." I scrubbed at my face and skull. "Where'd that get me? She didn't just walk away, she ran into the arms of a man she believes is my half-brother."

"Take another look, Jackson. You know this is not like her, and Cole is the last person she would take up with."

Cole's name stung like salt in a wound. "Did you know he'd been reaching out to her? She'd met him at least once without my knowledge. Now I have to wonder, how many other times?"

"She did that for you."

I shot a glance his way. Figures they'd discussed it. What else had they talked about? I stood and walked to the galley. It was difficult to tell if James was manipulating me, or if he believed what he said. I took a Corona from the fridge and snapped the cap. No need for me to drink alone.

"She felt sorry for him," I said, and handed him the beer. "She said she thought my dad behaved *disgracefully*. I'm sure that was in reference to his refusal to acknowledge paternity."

"And what do you think?"

"I don't believe my father would knowingly turn his back on a son." Dad had every right to believe Cole was the product of Bronwyn's affair, regardless of Sandra's illicit DNA results. "Unfortunately, I'm the only one left to stand up for him."

"I can understand that. Honour is important in our family too."

Honour? Sandra obviously had a different definition of the word.

James massaged the neck of his Corona. I actually felt sorry for him. He stared at the atlas with unfocused eyes. I took a breath and let my guard down. "You and I have had our differences over the years, James, but we both loved Sandra. I used to think I'd do anything for her, but seeing her with Cole? Man. That hurts." The anguish returned, squeezing my chest. "I'm not running after her. I don't want to know where they are."

"What if she's being held against her will?"

I had to give him credit for his stamina, but I was exhausted. "Come on. You've seen the ATM footage. Sandra isn't being strong-armed."

"We don't know that. Cole might be threatening her in some way."

I eyed James skeptically. "How?"

"She's my sister. It's repulsive for me to think about *how*. He's a man. Use your imagination."

I allowed the possibility temporary purchase in my mind then dismissed it. "Blackmail is a far cry from what you're suggesting."

"Is it? How about kidnapping? Everyone knows these ATMs have cameras. Maybe the withdrawals are punishment."

"Punishment?" I straightened and let the word settle. Images of Sandra raced through my mind.

"Don't you think Cole knows how much this would hurt you?"

I couldn't deny it had gotten my attention. "Then why isn't he lording it over me?"

"He doesn't need to. The ATM footage is doing it for him."

"You think he wants me to go after him?"

"No. I think he wants to torture you, and the longer he stays out of your reach, the worse your punishment."

I stood and headed for the relief of fresh air out on the foredeck. My thoughts scrambled. I rested my forearms on the rail and gazed at the small ripples on the surface of the water. Could it be true? Had I been so blinded by anger that I'd missed it? Hope nibbled at my heart.

But Sandra would know about the cameras. Everyone knew ATMs were monitored. She could have signalled any time if she'd been in trouble. Even without audio, she could have mouthed something, or gestured. Anything.

James approached and passed me my glass. "What if Cole isn't alone?" he said.

The thought grabbed hold and burrowed in. I met his frozen gaze. "Oh, shit."

Chapter Eleven

James had successfully planted a seed of doubt. In good conscience, I couldn't dismiss the possibility, however slight, that Cole might be holding Sandra against her will. I agreed to go along with James's assumption.

We returned to the map on the coffee table and roughed out some ideas to locate Sandra. Keeping the account open and her withdrawal limit unchanged was key. We didn't want Cole thinking we were on to him, and the withdrawals would help us track their movements. James would investigate Cole with an eye to finding out whom he might be working with. I'd have some confidential discussions with my yacht-club contacts to see if I could scare up info on a boat he may have had access to.

"We need to keep the police away from this," James said.

"That's not going to be a problem. They made it clear they weren't getting involved."

"Let's hope nothing happens to change their minds."

Was Cole unhinged enough to draw police attention? "Maybe we should involve the Tribunal?"

"No!" James visibly bristled. "It's too risky."

"Riskier than Cole?"

James skipped a beat. "Yes."

Well now, this was interesting. "Care to elaborate, James? Why would it be *risky*?"

He narrowed his gaze and studied my face as if he were weighing his options. I spread my hands, inviting him to proceed.

"I've met the Tribunal. I don't trust them."

"You've met them?" So the rumours were true. "How did that happen?"

"That's not something I can share."

"The Tribunal is there to help us. Isn't that what we're taught?"

"If it were just Cole, I'd call them myself. But not with Sandra involved."

"Sandra being involved is exactly why we need their help," I said.

"No! If the Tribunal learn she's been abducted, they're liable to destroy her along with Cole."

"That's insane. You're going to have to do better than that, James."

Muscles twitched along his jawline. He sprang from the sofa and paced a short line beside the galley, his gaze on the floor. Eventually, he looked up. "The Tribunal asked for our family's assistance a few years back. And I use the word *asked* loosely. We complied. Sandra knows about it. If they think she's passed that information along, they will eliminate the leak and its source."

His confession knocked the wind out of me. I flopped back against the sofa. "All this time? Why wouldn't she tell me?"

"She didn't want to put you at risk."

"What did they ask you to do? . . . Ah, shit, no. Don't tell me."

"What? You thought I would? It's bad enough I told you this much, and you'd better take it to your grave."

How many years, I wondered, had Sandra carried the weight of that threat? "All right, no Tribunal," I said. James's shoulders slumped and he tucked his hands in his pockets. "Sandra should make her next withdrawal in three or four days. We'll know then if they're still on the west coast."

"And by then I'll have more information about who Cole's cohorts might be."

We agreed to meet again when the next ATM footage came in.

The moment he was clear of the *Symphony*, I called Jimmy and had him put the divorce papers on hold. I was grateful he didn't question me when I told him I needed to think on it a while longer.

I poured another shot of Old Pulteney and took it out to the foredeck. Was Sandra playing me? If so, she and Cole were having a good chuckle at my expense. It seemed the more likely scenario, but still, I couldn't completely dismiss James's theory. After all, Cole had proven himself corrupt, and stooping to blackmail put him in the criminal class.

And now, thanks to Sandra, I knew something I'd never wanted to. The bastard was my half-brother.

I downed my drink and headed to bed. Sleep kept out of reach as I stared at the ceiling flipping between scenarios. I pulled the tablet from the bedside table and replayed the ATM footage. I studied Sandra's calm facade, her steady hands, and convinced myself anew that she'd made a fool of me. I pictured a lusty smirk on Cole's face as he gazed at Sandra out of camera range and her answering smile when she turned from the ATM. Then I imagined worse, and my stomach clenched as I pictured her on her knees in Bronwyn's pose, looking up at Cole with adoration in her eyes. Was Sandra a victim or a whore?

At some point in my sleepless night, I made a decision to believe the victim scenario. That option, at least, gave me hope, and a plan of action.

The following day I schmoozed with my dad's yachting cronies. They were most helpful, supplying me with boat rental contacts that took two days to follow up on. Keeping busy kept the negative voices out of my head. I emailed a picture of Cole I'd copied from the Internet to a number of the contacts, but came up empty.

On Tuesday, another email arrived from Mr. Honeycott with an ATM file attached. It gave me great satisfaction to know that James hadn't learned of it before I did. Kerry was a genius; I made a note to send her a bonus.

The map was already spread out on the coffee table when James arrived. I'd marked each withdrawal's location with a date. Today's was from another U.S. Bank in San Diego. The ATM footage contained no surprises, just Sandra, relaxed and wearing sunglasses this time.

James updated me while he studied the map. "I talked to a friend of Cole's. She thought he'd been in Mexico. I checked his credit cards. If he was there, he wasn't using them."

"Why would he? He doesn't need credit with Sandra feeding him cash."

James looked up, his annoyance barely concealed. "Did you get any leads on a boat?"

"No," I said. "No rentals or sales in his name or hers, and no one recognized his photo."

James referenced my notations on the map. "There are only four days between the ATMs in Alabama and California. That's not enough time to get through the Panama Canal. They must have flown to the coast. If they were in Mexico, that's probably where they got the boat."

"Or California. I can make some enquiries."

James traced a finger along their route. "Do you see a pattern here? Each time they hit an ATM, they retreat south, hit another, then head north again."

"It's not consistent." I pointed to San Diego. "There were two withdrawals south before they hit San Diego for the second time. He doesn't want us to be able to predict his next move."

"Yeah, but we know two things," James said. "One, they're not hitting the same ATMs twice, and two, they're heading north."

James sighed and sat back. "It feels like we're spinning our wheels. I know some people in San Diego. Maybe it's time I caught a flight out there and did some digging."

"If they're on a boat, you'll have a hard time tracking them."

"Got a better idea?"

"I do. Thought of it yesterday. I'll ship the *Symphony* to San Diego and use her as our home base."

James grudgingly nodded. "Not a bad idea, but a ship like this— he'd spot it a mile out."

We both leaned over the map. James said, "If they are headed north, we want to beat them there. Cut them off. How long would it take you to get the *Symphony* to the west coast?"

"I talked to Graham last night. He's the captain we keep on retainer. He can board in the morning and get her underway immediately. Shouldn't take more than ten or twelve days to get her through the Panama Canal and up to San Diego. Maybe budget a few more days for bad weather. He can cruise offshore. Won't draw attention."

"Two weeks? Cole could be in Alaska by then."

"Not at the rate he's going."

He looked back to the map. "You're probably right. Can you get her into Canada?"

"Don't see why not. Where are you thinking? Vancouver?"

"It's a big city. Lots of yachts like this. She won't draw attention."

"It'll add a few days to the trip, but once there we can bear down from the north."

James cracked a smile. "Exactly what I was thinking."

"Do you know anyone in the Vancouver covey?" It was customary for a Flier to arrange for an introduction to the local covey if he planned to stay in the area for any length of time.

"No," he said, shaking his head.

"Okay. I'll find someone. Learn what I can."

"Be careful," James said. "We don't want to spook them. Probably best you don't mention Sandra right away in case they get it into their heads to call in the Tribunal."

"I agree."

"And leave my name out of it for now," James said. "I want to lay low, put some feelers out along the coast before I head up there."

After James left, I called Graham and made the arrangements. The next morning, I packed a bag, left the *Symphony* in Graham's hands, and checked into the Omni. Three days later, Sandra made another uneventful withdrawal, a scant twenty-three miles north of the previous one. I studied her face looking for a sign, anything to give me some insight into her state of mind, but came up empty.

James's discreet enquiries to uncover Cole's contacts weren't producing results, but at least the *Symphony* was en route. If the weather held, she would arrive in Vancouver by month's end.

The next order of business was finding a trusted contact to introduce me to the Vancouver covey. It was a little like playing the game six degrees of Kevin Bacon. Eventually, I tracked down a Flier I knew in New York, who knew a Flier in Portland, who knew the man who ran the Vancouver covey. A doctor, as it turned out.

Dr. Avery Coulter was pleased about the introduction. We talked for thirty minutes on the phone. The Vancouver covey was small, just ten Fliers loosely organized around his practice by the sound of it. I imagined him as the father figure in *The Waltons*. I told him the television coverage of the 2010 Vancouver Olympics had sold me on Vancouver, and that I planned to relocate for a few months. My motivation seemed to satisfy him, and I agreed to update him after I arrived in Vancouver and settled in.

Afterwards, I got in touch with Josh Walford, a Flier and an information broker I knew, and asked him to compile a dossier on Dr. Coulter.

It arrived two days later and came with a big surprise. The man couldn't fly. He'd suffered some sort of accident as a child and had been grounded as a result. What kind of accident, I wondered? A gifting gone wrong? As I understood it, the Tribunal Novem were the only ones who knew how to transfer the gift, and they approved very few of them. I hoped he didn't have any lingering connection to them, and more than ever, I was glad I hadn't mentioned Sandra's predicament.

I skimmed the rest of the report: born in Arizona, moved to Canada in the eighties to complete a medical residency, and never returned to the States. He'd not married, had no children and his parents were deceased. How strange that this Flier with clipped wings should be the one leading the Vancouver covey.

It took sixteen days for the *Symphony* to arrive in British Columbia. Graham cleared her through customs and delivered her to Coal Harbour in downtown Vancouver. I flew in and met him there. He assured me that if I needed it, he could have the yacht crewed with a few days' notice. He then left for home.

The pace of Sandra's withdrawals slowed somewhat; the gaps between cash infusions grew to five days rather than three or four. She'd made eighteen trips to the ATM and through all those withdrawals there had been only the one slip-up where we'd caught a glimpse of Cole. She wore sunglasses more often than not, but her demeanour was pure Sandra, poised and calm. Seeing her reminded me of better times. I missed her, but it was becoming increasingly difficult to remain committed to the kidnapping scenario. I kept those thoughts to myself when James arrived in Vancouver a few days later.

I replayed the latest Wells Fargo instalment for him. The withdrawals were continuing to inch northward. Sandra had pushed her sunglasses into her hair.

"Damn it, Sandra! Look at the camera." James slammed his fist on the counter.

I'd been standing beside him and felt a twinge of comradery in his frustration. "We'll find her."

"She's been gone more than two months, and all we know is she's in a boat heading north. We need a break or we're going to lose her."

"No luck on Cole's acquaintances?"

"I have one name. No confirmation."

"What about his mother, Bronwyn? You said you had a trace on her phone. Has Cole called her?"

"He's being very careful. Using burner phones and reassuring her that he's fine. Just 'needs more time,' he tells her. I don't think she knows what's going on."

"He'll screw up."

James walked to the fridge and helped himself to a beer. "Want one?"

"Sure."

"How's it going with the local covey? You making any headway?" he asked.

"I spoke with the man in charge, Dr. Avery Coulter."

"A doctor? Hmm, what did you think?"

"He manages the covey like a social circle instead of the trained protection it ought to be. And get this: the man can't fly." I explained what I'd learned.

"Interesting."

"That's it? Interesting?"

"Yeah. I'm sure there's a story there, but I'm a little more concerned about the covey. Why aren't they trained?"

"Not much trouble up here I'd guess. The good news is, if the covey isn't trained, they won't get in the way."

"But not good if we need their assistance."

"Yes, there is that. I'll have a better idea after I meet them. Dr. Coulter is waiting to hear from me. You still want your name left out of it?" I asked.

"Yeah. I'm not staying. I've got a contact in Seattle I need to see."

"What? You're some jet-setter now? Fly in for a few hours, fly out?"

"I drove up. Had some business in Bellingham. It's not that far."

The next morning, I called Dr. Coulter. He lived in a suburb called St. George but he had an afternoon meeting at a hospital in Vancouver. He accepted my invitation to dinner.

I spotted him thirty yards out. He had straight, straw-coloured hair and the squint of a sailor, but his gait told me he was uncomfortable on the docks, even these sturdy ones in Coal Harbour, and his clothing was all wrong. Definitely not *The Waltons*, unless they'd moved to the city and started shopping at Bergdorf Goodman.

"Dr. Coulter?" I asked, seeing him searching for the name of the ship.

He looked up. "Yes, and it's Avery, please."

"Of course. Come aboard," I said, indicating the ramp twenty feet farther along on the dock. The man looked young for fifty-two, which I knew was his age.

"This is one hell of a ship," he said, offering me his hand. "Avery Coulter."

"Jackson Delaney. Welcome, and thank you. I'm rather fond of her. It's chilly out here. Let's go inside."

He gawked with the awe of someone who'd never been on a yacht before. I relieved him of the jacket he'd forgotten was folded over his arm. "Would you like a tour?"

"Yes, I would," he answered with an enthusiasm belying his years.

We started below; I toured him around the engine room, guest cabins and staterooms, and then we made a quick trip up top to the outdoor observation deck before returning to the warmth of the main deck, where I showed him the crew quarters and chart room. He was a curious man and wanted to know how things worked: the water systems and holding tanks, fuel storage and engine thrust. He asked about docking and manoeuvring such a large ship. I laughed, reassuring him I had the necessary captain's licence. It had been a long time since someone had shown such interest.

"Would you like a drink?" I asked when he'd exhausted his questions. "I have wine or beer. Maybe you'd like something stronger?"

"I wouldn't say no to a Scotch with a drop of water."

While I prepared our drinks, I asked about the covey.

"We're too small a group to bother much with formalities. When we get together, it's to celebrate a new job or a birth. However, most people get their news through the secure online message boards these days, but if something important comes up, I'll coordinate a meet, or pass on the news myself. Thank you," he said, as I handed him his drink. "How are you enjoying Vancouver?"

"Every bit as beautiful as what I saw during the Olympics." I raised my glass in a toast.

"That it is," Avery replied. "Early April is often wet. A couple more weeks and it'll be warm and dry."

Our dinner arrived from Cardero's, a restaurant on the quay within walking distance. I'd ordered cedar plank salmon, which seemed to be a specialty of theirs. While I set it out on the table, Avery asked about Delaney & Son.

"I understand your firm is one of the biggest developers in Louisiana."

"Yes. It's a credit to my father. He built the company from nothing and grew it to what it is today."

"I read that he passed away last year. My condolences."

"Thank you. You've done your homework."

"No more than you, I'm sure. Since it looks like you're going to be here awhile, how about I set up a meet and greet with the covey?"

"Sounds good."

"Great. I'll make the arrangements for Saturday afternoon. We meet at an old bar called Clam Diggers. It's in Seaside, a small suburb south of here. I'll email you the details."

He left after dinner without confessing that he couldn't fly.

Chapter Twelve

Clam Diggers operated out of an old house with more add-ons than a midnight infomercial. Its décor was cliché nautical, complete with Maine-style lobster traps and rafters draped in fishnet. The place smelled of stale beer and fried food. I crossed the worn wood floor of the main bar area and turned into a smaller, carpeted room to the right. The lively chatter in Avery's group subsided when he stood and came over to greet me.

"Glad you could make it. Let me introduce you."

He walked me to the side of the room, where four tables had been pushed together. They'd been there awhile gauging by the empty glasses . . . discussing me, I had no doubt.

"Jackson Delaney," he announced, then went around the table. "Eden Effrome," he said, indicating a slight, redheaded woman with spiky hair.

"Her husband, Alex Klause." Alex stood to shake my hand. "If you need your Harley painted, he's the man to see." A biker then. He had the solid build of one, but no visible tats.

"Victoria Lang," Avery said, introducing a blonde goddess who could have been a cover model. She offered her hand and a hint of a smile. She didn't wear a wedding band.

A grey-haired gentleman stood next to her. "Gabe Aucoin," he said. "Pleased to meet you."

"He's our resident ambulance chaser," Avery said in good humour, and Gabe shook his head and smiled as though he'd heard the line a thousand times.

"Kate Dennison and Deidra Lewis," Avery said, moving on to the soccer moms, who tipped their heads like twins in greeting.

"Danny Thornton." A young black man with dreads past his shoulders popped up and shook my hand. "And Steve Elliott," Avery said, introducing the last man at the table. Steve did a half-lift out of his seat and offered his hand.

A waitress came up behind and reached past me to drop two draft jugs on the table.

"And this is Sydney Davenport," Avery said, introducing the woman I'd mistaken for a waitress. The dark-eyed woman of Japanese heritage offered a firm handshake.

Avery poured beers all around, and we raised our glasses in a toast to new friends. The next hour passed as time usually does among new acquaintances, with polite probing questions to unearth what I did for a living, where home was, what had brought me here, and so on.

As I looked around the table, I wondered if any of them were fit enough to help us when we found Sandra. The women I eliminated immediately; Kate and Deidra were not in shape; Eden was feisty but too small; and both Sydney and Victoria were mere wisps. Gabe and Avery were probably past their prime, which left Danny, Steve and Alex. Later, I'd see what I could find out about them.

Our gathering broke up in time for everyone to get home for dinner. It had been a pleasant afternoon, and a relief to get the formalities out of the way. I promised to keep in touch with Avery and caught a cab back to Coal Harbour.

Waiting for me was the latest Wells Fargo digital file. Sandra's sunglasses were pushed back into her hair. The image was black and white, making it difficult to assess her well-being. Were those dark circles under her eyes, or was it just the camera's angle? Why aren't you helping us out here, Sandra? Are you in trouble, or just stringing me along?

This one had been taken in Santa Barbara, so they were once again headed north. I sent it on to James, along with the names Danny Thornton, Steve Elliott and Alex Klause. I then sent those names to Josh Walford and asked him to do some more digging.

A few days later, I had dossiers on all three and forwarded them to James.

Thornton was Canadian, twenty-two. No record. Owed money on a student loan. Earned a BA from Simon Fraser University, where he also competed in tae kwon do. Danny Thornton would definitely be an asset.

Elliott was twenty-five. Born in Saskatoon. Completed grade ten and had a juvie record for assault. A Flier who resorted to fisticuffs was unusual, but he'd been young at the time, and it meant he'd likely be of use.

Klause held dual citizenship in Canada and the US. He was thirty, originally from Seattle. He completed high school and went directly to trade school for auto body tech. No record, good credit, a few speeding tickets. He looked solid. Another good prospect.

I grew restless as the first week of April drifted past. Heavy clouds lined the skies most days, but when the sun peeked out it was glorious. My mind wandered between two equally unsettling scenarios: either Sandra was desperately waiting for me to free her, or she was willfully twisting a knife in my gut.

To fill the empty days, I wandered Vancouver's downtown and explored the seawall that looped around the downtown land mass. One day I rented an SUV and crossed over the Lions Gate Bridge to learn the layout of the north shore, from Horseshoe Bay to Deep Cove. It was beautiful country with no shortage of secluded areas and potential flight paths. After dusk, I parked my rental outside the gates to the Deep Cove Marina and hiked in. Cameras were mounted high on poles in the marina parking lot and along the docks. I lifted off, keeping outside of their range, and flew east until I was past the lights that signalled habitation. My early fear of heights had curbed my enthusiasm for flying, and Sandra was so wary of being caught that she rarely flew. I could count on one hand the number of times we'd flown together. I flew Lake Borgne when I needed to clear my head. Tonight, boredom and frustration fuelled my flight. An hour later, I felt better and slept soundly that night.

The next day, Sandra made another withdrawal, this one from Morro Bay, which I located on the map. They were still in the lower half of California, crawling north. Sandra's hair looked wet. Had she been swimming? Is this a holiday for you, Sandra? I wondered, trying to see her eyes, which were hidden behind sunglasses.

Ted Worley forwarded me Delaney's first-quarter financials, and I was glad for the distraction. I was reviewing the spreadsheets when James called.

"Cole talked to his mom today and let a name slip. It was one I'd hoped I was wrong about."

"Who?"

"Johnny, as in Johnny Lorenzo. His real name is Juan."

"I don't know him."

"He's not a Flier. He's an ex-con. Six five, three hundred pounds. Hires himself and a bunch of his ex-con buddies out for security. They work the bar circuit, concerts, that sort of thing. Cole's old man's company, Touchstone, hires them to guard their construction sites."

"What's his reputation?"

"His only loyalty is to the greenback. For the right price, he'd break a puppy's legs."

"And you know for sure he's travelling with them?"

"If I thought all he was doing was travelling with them, I wouldn't be worried," James said. "Johnny's being paid. Therefore, Cole has something to guard, and my guess is it's Sandra."

"Could be he's guarding their boat."

"Is that your commitment I hear wavering?"

Good question, I thought, and inhaled my indecision.

James said, "Ask yourself this: why would you choose an ex-con like Johnny for simple security when you could hire someone much more pleasant?"

"You've got a point." Johnny would be unavoidable company in the close quarters of a boat. "So how do you know he's being paid?"

"An educated guess. I was told he got a 'sweet gig' and wouldn't be available for security for a few weeks. That was a few days after Cole disappeared from the radar, and neither one has been seen since."

"Then Johnny is a serious complication."

"Yeah. We're going to need help. The people I'm using for surveillance aren't Fliers. It's time we tell the Vancouver covey about Sandra."

"That could be a problem. They think I'm here as a tourist. I blew smoke about the 2010 Olympics and what a beautiful city Vancouver is. If they learn I've been lying to them, I'll lose their trust. Doubt they'd stick their necks out for me after that. They might even bring in the Tribunal."

The line went quiet, but I could hear him breathing. Moments later James said, "All right. Let's stay with the tourist angle. They don't need to know our connection to Sandra. She's a covey mate, nothing more, and you've just learned she's gone missing. Her family has asked for your help to locate her. That's not even a lie. Tell them about Johnny Lorenzo. Anything that gets them to throw some manpower our way."

"I can sell that."

"Good. Those names you sent me from the covey look like possibilities. What do you think?"

"They're completely untrained. And against an ex-con the size of Johnny? Hard to say. If we're restricted from flying, the martial arts guy might stand a chance. I don't know about the others. If they can deliver a powerful *jolt*, we could be in business. Otherwise, we'll need to get our hands on some guns." The strength of a Flier's gift determined the range of jolt he was able to deliver. Weak gifts produced *sparks* similar to static electricity. Strong gifts could deliver jolts like those of a stun gun. Extraordinary gifts could cause a fatal brain hemorrhage.

"These are Canadians, remember; don't mention the gun option. Work on the doctor. Get his support and he'll bring the others around."

"I hope you're right. I may need to make it personal to shake them out of their complacency."

"Sounds like they could use a push in that direction anyway."

"Yeah. Let's hope I can convince a few of them to join us."

"Good luck."

The next morning I contacted Avery and asked for a meeting. He invited me to his home, which was also his office. The cab driver dropped me in front of a large Tudor-style two-storey and agreed to come back in an hour. The leaves on the old maple and chestnut trees that lined the street were still the bright green of spring. A sign at his front door directed patients to the converted garage at the side. I rang the bell.

"Come in," Avery said, and held the door open. He led the way to the back of the house and into a den, where Alex Klause stood waiting by a fireplace. So Alex was his second in command. I'd pegged Gabe Aucoin for that position. Bookshelves lined the walls and an old wood desk stood in front of patio doors.

Alex stepped away from the fireplace to greet me. There was a closed door to his left. "Good to see you again, Jackson."

"You too."

"I trust you don't mind my including Alex in our meeting," Avery said.

"Not at all. I hope I'm not taking you away from business."

"Nah," Alex said. "Slow morning at the shop."

"Thank you for seeing me." Avery and I sat in the two wingback chairs and Alex leaned against the mantle again. A verdant back garden was evident through the patio doors. "I may need your help. I've learned that a covey mate of mine has gone missing. Her name is Sandra. She's twenty-eight years old and her family hasn't heard from her in weeks. She was last seen with a man named Cole Des Roche. Yesterday the family learned some disturbing news. An ex-con named Johnny Lorenzo, a known associate of Cole's, went missing around the same time. They think he had a hand in her disappearance, and he's not the sort she'd voluntarily chum around with. She could be in trouble."

"Is he one of us?" Alex asked.

"Johnny isn't, but there could be others."

"Others?" Avery asked.

"Johnny doesn't work alone. He's been known to associate with some low-lifes from Baton Rouge. After Sandra dropped off the radar, she began making substantial cash withdrawals from ATMs in port cities. That spending pattern is new for her. Naturally, the family thinks she's being coerced. They also suspect she's travelling by boat."

"What can we do to help?" Avery said.

"We need manpower—Fliers ready to move in and extract her the moment we locate her."

"A physical confrontation?" He shook his head. "Our covey doesn't have the skills. We'd be more of a hindrance, I'm sorry to say."

That much, I knew, but I wasn't looking for the whole covey. "Perhaps just two or three of you, then?"

"We'd be cannon fodder. What you need are trained fighters."

"Surely some of you must be trained to protect the covey?"

"Not in the way you need. We have medical and legal expertise, electronics and mechanical know-how and excellent IT support. That's how we protect our covey."

He couldn't be serious. "I'm surprised, Avery. Surely you know about the other Fliers who have gone missing?"

"Yes, but statistically speaking, the risk is very low."

"Statistically?" No wonder they thought they were immune. "I would have thought that eighteen Fliers in the past three years would have had more of an impact on the stats." The number was much lower, but these folks needed a push.

"Eighteen? We'd heard the number was six?"

"Of course," I said, acknowledging his numbers. "I hadn't realized only six were made public, and you wouldn't know about the others. Families of the missing don't report them for fear they'll draw attention to others in their coveys. A friend of mine is an investigator who's been hired by a few of the families. He thinks there are even more than the eighteen he's aware of."

"I'm sorry to hear that," Avery said, furrowing his brow.

"There's talk that our own government is responsible. Some even think organized crime may be involved."

"These disappearances are bad omens for our kind. We had so much more freedom before security cameras and cellphones, and now this. We may have to re-evaluate the risk." He looked over to Alex. "Perhaps it's time to look into proper training."

I'd have taken Danny, Alex and Steve even without the training, but I could see that Avery wasn't prepared to put his people at risk. Perhaps he'd be more amenable with a quid pro quo arrangement, and I had something valuable to offer. "I can help you set up some training."

"Oh?"

"I was trained in the New Orleans covey. They've had a program in place for years. Everyone who comes into the covey, men and women, old and young alike, spends time in a boot camp. When the instructor deems them fit, they're assigned to teams and go into field training. After that, they serve for five years. I completed my service two years ago."

"That's impressive," Alex said. "You must have a lot of trouble in Louisiana."

"We have our share. But thankfully, because of our training, we don't need to involve the Tribunal in our business."

A glance passed between Alex and Avery. My mistake. I shouldn't have mentioned the Tribunal before I knew how they felt about them. Avery rose and walked behind the desk. "I'll discuss the situation with the covey and let you know."

"By all means," I said, hoping I hadn't blown it. "I expect I'll be in Vancouver for a few weeks yet."

"You told me you think this woman is travelling by boat. Do you have any idea of her whereabouts?"

"The last ATM withdrawal put them just south of San Francisco. They're heading this way."

"Then we don't have much time."

"No, but I'm confident I can put suitable training in place quickly."

Avery and Alex were already discussing training options when my cab arrived. It was a good indicator that they'd take me up on my offer. Once they did, they'd cough up some manpower to help us out.

When I got back to the *Symphony*, I set to work. My new focus kept my mind off Cole. The Internet was rife with fitness training options, including boot camps, but they lacked the team and tactical training components we needed to rescue Sandra. We also needed access to a large arena where we could practice our moves, including flying.

I changed the search criteria to suss out suitable facilities and found my answer: the perfect venue for our needs. I phoned the proprietor, Jerry, who was happy to negotiate a deal.

Chapter Thirteen

very called two days later. The push I'd given him had worked.

"The covey's in agreement," he said. "As much as we don't like what's happening, we need to pull off the blinders. We have to be prepared to defend ourselves."

"I agree."

"Is your offer still on the table?"

"Absolutely. I'm happy to help, and I think I've found exactly what we need." I told him about the Pinecrest Paintball Park. "They operate out of an old horse barn off King Street, out near Highway 10. It's farm country. No one around for miles."

"Paintball?"

"It's perfect—combines flying, teamwork, tactical manoeuvres and hand-eye coordination. An old rancher named Jerry owns it. His son converted the barn into a paintball arena when the old man retired. Tried to make a go of it but couldn't. Now the old man's sitting on a vacant barn and paintball equipment that he donates to charity events for the tax write-off. He was receptive to a contract. All he needs is a signature."

"How much of a commitment?"

"Six months."

"And the cost?"

"I'm willing to pick up the cost. After you get a feel for it, if you think the training is good enough, I hope you'll reconsider offering your covey's assistance when the time comes."

"That's most generous of you, Jackson. Sounds like we have a deal."

"Great. I'll set it up and send you the details. How about we all meet out there tomorrow night? No point in putting it off. Say . . . nine o'clock?"

I rented an SUV and drove out to meet Jerry in the afternoon. The barn loomed large in the distance long before I turned down the gravel driveway off Pinecrest Street. Jerry met me at the barn door and toured me around the place. His son had done a respectable job designing the space. It consisted of two levels: the main barn floor and an open upper loft. Down the centre of the main floor, stacked hay bales were wired in place to create the walls of a maze with dead ends and blind corners. Tarps were draped over the top of the bales in some areas and hung on metal rods in others ready to be swung into place to provide cover or an escape route. Jerry's insurers required him to run through the safety equipment, and afterwards, we fired off some paintballs. I was happy to see that Jerry hadn't exaggerated about the condition of the equipment.

After the paperwork was signed, I paid him in cash and he showed me the lockbox on the power pole outside the barn, where he kept the keys.

That night, another ATM clip came in. Sandra had pushed her sunglasses up into her hair again. I froze the frame. She looked beautiful with wind-tossed hair. It hurt to see her. It had been another sunny day in central California, and she squinted against the glare. Was I just imagining that she looked tired? They'd headed south after Morro Bay, but today's ATM was in Pebble Beach, so they had turned north again. Had she guessed by now that I watched these brief snippets of her life?

I sent the clip on to James. He phoned shortly after.

"Cole's making damn sure their pattern of travel is unpredictable, but I've noticed something else," he said.

"What's that?"

"Every stop they've made had multiple ATMs to choose from. That means we can eliminate any place along the route where there's only one cash machine."

"That still spreads us too thin to do any meaningful surveillance," I said. James strategically moved his surveillance people up and down the coast, but they'd yet to spot Cole's crew. Unfortunately, we only knew what three of them looked like. Who knew how many others Cole had in his employ?

"He'll make a mistake. We just have to catch it."

"Yeah. Let's hope it's soon." It had already been too long and with every day that passed, my doubt grew. More and more, I found myself waffling on James's conviction that Sandra had been kidnapped. Every time I saw a new picture of her, I wondered if she had made a conscious choice.

I told him about the headway I'd made with Avery. "They're not on board yet, but they will be. We're convening tomorrow after dark at a paintball park. It's in the middle of nowhere and we've got the place to ourselves. I'll show them some basic tactical strategies and get them thinking like a team." James knew what I was talking about. He'd been through the same training as I had, and then more with the military.

The next day I moored the *Symphony* in the south arm of the Fraser River. No point in remaining downtown when the covey favoured the southern suburbs. After night set in, I donned dark camouflage and lifted off from the unlit observation deck. I flew over wide stretches of unkempt scrub vegetation and farmers' fields and made my way to the big barn on Pinecrest.

Avery was the first to arrive. I recognized the distinctive purr of a Porsche engine and flew to the gravel parking lot to meet him. "Nice ride," I said, admiring the sleek lines of the black Carrera. "I have a Targa back in New Orleans."

"Ah . . . I'll bet you make better use of your sunroof down there. Is it a T-roof or a slide?"

"It's an older model—manual removal I'm sorry to say."

"Still, nothing quite like a Porsche to get the blood flowing."

"You got that right, but I thought you would have flown over."

"No. I haven't been able to fly since I was a teenager. It's not something I advertise, as I'm sure you can appreciate."

Yes, I certainly could—and he'd held off telling me until the last possible moment. "You can count on my discretion," I said, but my curiosity wasn't satisfied by a long shot. "That's an unusual condition, isn't it?"

"Yes. Shall we?" he said, and set off toward the barn.

Looked like I'd have to work harder if I wanted to get information out of Avery.

"The others will be flying in using the coordinates you provided."

By nine o'clock, everyone had arrived. We gathered outside the barn door at the west end of the building. Above it, loft doors provided access to the second floor. We flew a tour around the large structure. Retired farm implements poked out from under the tin-roofed lean-to that ran along the north side of the structure. On the east end, double doors on rail slides provided access at ground level. The south side was a blank slate. From thirty feet up, lights twinkled in the distance, too few and far away to cause concern.

We opened the second-floor loft doors and flew inside. Excited whispers broke out at the sight of the maze, and the Fliers broke off to explore the space. We regrouped in the suit-up area inside the main barn door.

Danny was the only one who'd played paintball before. He helped get everyone geared up for the game. After the others pulled on the padded jumpsuits, they collected protective face gear and joined Danny and me at the gun lockers. While Danny filled their hoppers with paintballs, I explained the game I'd chosen for our inaugural night.

"Tonight's all about getting used to flying in the gear and getting a feel for the gun and your environment. This is going to be a good old-fashioned game of hide-and-seek with one exception: everyone's hiding and everyone's seeking. The winner will be the one with the most kills, so keep track of them. You'll have ten minutes to find cover. When you hear the air horn, the game is live. If you get shot, stand down and return to the tent in the centre of the ground floor. When the air horn sounds twice, the game is over."

Avery agreed to observe the Fliers from the ground and I'd do the same from the air. We set them loose and I watched a mad game of scramble. Alex and Gabe immediately headed out the loft doors. Kate bounced off a sheet of canvas with a shout of alarm, but righted herself and disappeared into the maze. A paintball popped, followed by an anonymous giggle and a "Sorry."

After ten minutes I sounded the horn. Paintballs didn't start flying for an astonishing five minutes, but after the first burst of fire, Fliers started trickling down to the tent. Forty-five minutes later, Danny finally knocked Sydney out, and the game was over.

The second game went on for an hour, and Alex and Steve were the last two standing in that one. Afterwards, when we gathered, Avery had to beat down excited chatter to be heard. The games had been a big hit. The consensus was that they needed target practice and obstacle flight training. We laid out a schedule for four more sessions and called it a night.

I locked up and walked Avery back to his car. "I think this is going to work."

"I agree," Avery said. "They had fun tonight. It hardly seems like training."

"That's the beauty of it."

Avery stopped at the driver's door and turned. "Now that you've seen what you're working with, how long do you think it'll take to get us to where we need to be?"

"Too early to say. Some of them are already good marksmen and strategists. A few will pick up the skills with practice, others never will. The real test will be learning how to trust and utilize each other's strengths in a team situation."

"We should have started something like this a long time ago," he said.

"You've started now. That's what's important."

Avery thanked me, and we shook hands and departed.

Aboard the *Symphony*, another ATM file awaited. She was in Malibu looking relaxed, bored even. "What's going on, Sandra? If Cole is forcing your hand, why don't you show it?" She didn't answer, just turned away from the ATM, cash in hand, as usual.

Rather than bash my head against a wall, I turned my energies to the covey.

On the second night at the paintball park, I tacked up bull's-eye shooting targets along the south side of the barn for each of the Fliers. I started them at fifteen yards, and as their aim improved, moved them back, five yards at a time. It was clear to me that both Steve and Sydney had handled guns before. Alex and Danny were naturals, and Eden was holding her own.

The third night I set up an obstacle course and timed their runs, making them repeat the course until they made it through unscathed and on time. They were physically drained by the end of the night, but every one of them made it through. On the fourth night, I switched up the obstacle course and added bull's-eye and human-silhouette shooting targets strategically throughout.

After that, we decided to meet regularly, and I introduced teamwork into the games. First up were teams of two. I assigned the players and changed them out when they got too comfortable. We moved on to teams of three then four, and finally five. We reviewed offensive and defensive tactics, risk assessment and reconnaissance, and switched the games up to keep the Fliers interested and thinking.

All the while, I watched for their strengths, saw who thought on their feet, who utilized the resources at hand, who got creative, who learned quickly. Not surprisingly, Danny, Steve and Alex were at the top of the heap, but both Eden and Sydney showed promise. Eden was also a nurse, a fact I tucked in my back pocket, and as I got to know Alex, I learned that he had a handful of ex-law enforcement buddies in Seattle, another useful tip I tucked away.

Sandra was still moving north as the end of April approached. Cole hadn't made a mistake and we couldn't hone in on their coordinates. Sandra's ready cash meant they left no paper trail, and our only contact was the ATM footage and Cole's now weekly calls to his mother.

In early May, my frustration got the best of me. James phoned with yet another no-news update and we had a blowout.

"I know she's your sister, James, but she's stringing us along. How could she make this many withdrawals and not once give away that she's under duress?"

"Because she's strong, and she's careful, and who knows what horrors they've threatened her with. That she hasn't given herself away is probably what's keeping her alive."

"What's keeping her alive is that fucking bank card."

James showed up on the *Symphony* shortly after that argument. I was perfectly aware that he'd come to shore me up. As annoying as that was, I had to admit, his determination was admirable. I introduced him to Avery and the covey over a paintball game. He stayed for a week and then moved to a hotel. We weren't roommate material, and frustration with the search had clipped our tempers short. Only the not knowing kept us cordial, and kept us looking.

On the eleventh of May, the not knowing came to an end.

Sandra was still in California—Davenport this time—and looking beautiful as ever. She wore sunglasses and a dreamy smile. She looked content, as though she'd just rolled out of a hammock. And then Cole moved into the ATM's picture frame. I would have said he'd finally made a mistake, but he put his arm around her and looked right at the camera. It was no mistake.

James studied the clip for a long time, freezing the frames and going back and forth. I only needed to see it once.

"I'm done," I said, my chest in a vice. "I told you I'd keep looking for her as long as there was any doubt about her safety. There is no more doubt."

　　　　　　　　　　　　　　　　　　　　　　

"Damn it!" James leapt to his feet and paced to the end of the counter and back. "It can't be as simple as that. Why show his face now?"

"I don't know and I don't care."

"He must have known this would prompt you to close the account."

"You got that right. I'm not funding one more leg of their little holiday."

"Exactly. So what's his payoff?"

"You mean besides my humiliation? Maybe they were tired of being dogged by us and hiding out. They probably want to set up house and have babies."

"Oh my god . . . you're right!"

"Really, James? You're going to rub that in my face?"

"Think, Jackson! He hasn't slipped up once, so this was intentional, which means there's something in it for him. He wants us to stop looking for them."

"Terrific. He's going to get his wish, James. I'm finished. I'll kill the fucker if I ever get my hands on him, but I'm not wasting another minute chasing them, and I'm sure as hell not giving them another dime."

James ignored me and paced the length of the counter again. "Why does he want us to stop looking for them?"

I sighed in exasperation and headed to the fridge. "Beer?"

"Jesus." James froze midpace. "He's done with her. That's why he wants us off his ass. He's going to get rid of her." He looked at me with fear in his eyes—something I had never seen before.

It made me hesitate. "You think Cole would murder Sandra?" That was ludicrous. "Come on, James. Look at them."

He didn't answer. He returned to the laptop and replayed the video. I felt sad watching him. James had not wavered once in his belief that Sandra had been kidnapped. This despite dozens of ATM film clips of her in which she consistently presented a poised and calm facade. Did he really believe Cole would get rid of her? Or was this yet another way for him to deny what his sister was really up to? I set a beer down beside him.

"This looks bad, Jackson. I can't blame you for believing it."

"I feel a 'but' coming on."

James closed the laptop. "You've come this far, hang in for a while longer. I'll fund the account, but please don't close it."

"You're worried about her, I understand that completely. You're her brother. You love her, but step back. She's made her choice."

He curled his lip in a snarl. "She would never choose him."

"I wish that were true, James. I loved her too, but it's time to let go. She'll contact you when she's ready."

He jumped up. "You can't give up on her. Not now. "

"Cole is not going to hurt her."

"Are you willing to risk her life on that assumption?"

"You saw that smile on her face, right? What's it going to take to convince you that she's okay?"

"I want to hear her say it." He threw his hand in the air. "I want her to pick up a goddamn phone and talk to us."

"She's had three months to do that. She's chosen not to. Just how long are you going to wait?"

"As long as it takes."

"Well, looks like that could be a while."

"I can't give up on her. What she's doing . . . it's not her."

"Maybe she's changed."

"What if you're wrong about Cole, and she disappears?"

"I hope to god that's not the case, but look at them! They're happy. He has no reason to harm her."

"You're talking about Cole. The man who blackmailed you. The man who threatened you with the Tribunal. The man who hires thugs for protection. Because that man's capable of hurting a woman, especially if it serves to get back at you. And what then? Will you be able to live with yourself if we never hear from her again?"

I hung my head. He wasn't giving up.

"Wouldn't it be worth your while to stick around long enough to find the bastard and confront him?"

"Stop it, James. I know what you're trying to do." He sounded desperate and it was embarrassing. "Cole will surface eventually. When he does, I'll be ready for him."

James twisted the bottle of Corona in its sweat ring. "I know you think I'm wrong, and maybe I am, but for the first time since she disappeared, we're in a position to affect Cole's behaviour. If he wants us to back off, and we don't, he's going to react. He could make that mistake we've been waiting for."

I couldn't help but feel sorry for James. He'd grown on me in the past few months. He'd been close to Sandra, and her absence had hit him hard. When a marriage falls apart, you move on—plot your revenge perhaps—but you go your separate ways. You couldn't do that with family.

"I'll make you a deal, James. I'll keep the account open until the end of May—another three weeks. I'll continue to help search for her. I'll keep up appearances with Avery's covey. If we find them, giving Cole what he deserves will be my reward. But come the end of May, whether we've found them or not, I'm moving on. Deal?"

He didn't speak, just nodded and stared at the bottle of beer.

"Deal?" I repeated.

James slid his beer away, untouched. "Deal." He turned and left without another word.

I watched the ATM footage one more time, and then closed the laptop. James's analysis was usually spot-on, but this situation with Sandra had impaired his judgment. He refused to see what was right in front of his face. And seeing Cole with his arm draped so casually around my wife's shoulder, and her sleepy smile, made my blood boil. I thought about my father and what Bronwyn had done to him and felt his pain. Now I even understood why he'd kept those horrible photos. It was more than proof of his wife's betrayal—it was justification for crushing her and destroying Touchstone.

My mind turned to my pledge to be a better man than my father. I'd barely made a dent in that pledge, and now I was consumed with how good it would feel to wrap my hands around Cole's neck and choke the life out him. Had Dad been a better man before Bronwyn made a cuckold of him? Maybe Bronwyn gave Sandra some tips the day she contacted her. And just like Bronwyn, what Sandra had done was unforgivable.

Chapter Fourteen

As much as Sandra's betrayal hurt, knowing the truth freed me from the worry and the guilt. I relaxed for the first time in months. The paintball games grew more competitive and I jumped in, participating instead of standing on the sidelines. Alex joined me for a beer on the *Symphony* one afternoon, and we took her out for a cruise and a few laughs. The weather dried out and warmed up and I was beginning to think I might miss Vancouver when I left.

On the sixteenth, another ATM file came in. This time Cole was the one punching in the code and taking the money, but Sandra was right there with him. He had his arm around her waist and she rested her head against his shoulder. She wore sunglasses and a faraway smile. It was the smile that hurt the most. I sent it to James, who'd been keeping his distance, fully expecting him to call in his latest theory, but he didn't. He replied by email with his thanks. Maybe he was finally seeing the light.

When the phone rang at one thirty in the morning, I assumed it was him, but it wasn't.

"Sorry to wake you, Jackson, but something's come up."

It was Avery. "What is it?"

"A young woman I've never set eyes on before was just brought into Emerg. She's one of us."

"How do you know?"

"She has the second lens."

A second lens in a Flier's eye was the only physical manifestation of the gift. It's what enabled us to see in the dark. "What happened?"

"I don't know. She's unconscious, but her injuries suggest she fell from a height."

"Foul play?"

"I have no idea. That's why I called. I was hoping you could get out to the site of her accident right away and scope it out."

"Of course."

"Thanks, Jackson. I knew I could count on you. She was found in Sunset Park, close to Cliffside Avenue. That's in Summerset. Do you know where it is?"

"No, but I'll find it."

"Hurry, and be careful. Last I heard the police were still on the scene, but if rogue Fliers are involved, they might still be out there."

"Thanks for the heads-up. I'll report back when I know something."

I jumped out of bed and pulled on flying clothes. I checked the coordinates for the park. It was due south. I took off and followed the shoreline until I got close, and then headed inland. The police searchlights told me where she'd been found. I gave the lights a wide berth and used the treetops for cover as I probed the vicinity for other Fliers. I drifted down to a nearby footpath and found nothing along its route in either direction. If it was foul play, whoever was responsible for the woman's accident was long gone.

Once airborne again, I headed to the cliff at the edge of the park and flew the beach along its length. I passed the glow of the searchlights and continued until a tangle of bright yellow rope caught my eye. I drifted down to the sand and puzzled out what I'd found: roughly fifty feet of new nylon rope tied to a large rock, a hoodie that smelled of perfume, a pair of women's size eight shoes and, strangest of all, diving weights. What an incredibly odd find. And what were the chances that these things weren't somehow connected to the woman in the park? The site of her accident was only half a mile away as the crow flies.

Hundreds of footprints disturbed the sand around the rock. Most of them were in a straight line with the rock at its centre. I couldn't make any sense of it. I gathered the odd collection and headed back to the *Symphony* to call Avery.

"She's still unconscious and could be for a while," he said, in answer to my question. "It's easily a grade three concussion."

I told him what I'd found. "Nylon rope?" he said. "Is there any blood on it?"

"Just a minute." I pulled the coil over and took a closer look. "I'd have to say yes. What are you thinking?"

"She's got rope burns on both ankles."

"You think someone tied her to the rock?"

"Torture? Couldn't rule it out; she's pretty banged up. At least she wasn't sexually assaulted."

"Will she be all right?"

"Too early to tell. I'll keep you posted. And thanks, Jackson. I appreciate your help."

I dropped back into bed, and thoughts of Cole crept into my mind. I bolted upright. Could the woman be Sandra?

I dialled Avery. He was still at the hospital. His physical description of her dispelled my fear, but I never got back to sleep. The fear I'd felt that the woman could have been Sandra jarred me. After what she'd done, I shouldn't have cared, and it took far too long to push her memory back into the don't-give-a-shit column.

Avery's patient was in and out of consciousness the next day. He'd learned her name was Emelynn Taylor and that she lived on Cliffside Avenue. With Avery's blessing, I immediately passed those details on to Josh Walford, who went looking for information on her. He was able to provide a dossier, but it was incomplete in that it included no information on her father and no Flier affiliation for either her or her mother, who used the surname Aberfoyle.

I phoned Josh to quiz him on the missing details.

"The Toronto covey was surprised too," he said. "They sent out an investigator immediately, and confirmed that the mother isn't one of us."

"Then it's the father." The Flier gene was dominant—it had to come from one of her parents. "Who the hell is he?"

"I'm still working on that. The condo in Toronto and the house in Summerset are both in the mother's name and have been for more than ten years. Same with the utilities. Information older than that is archived and I can't get at it online. The mother self-identifies as single, not divorced or widowed, so I don't even know if the father's alive."

My next discussion with Avery added more confusion to the situation. "Her memory is spotty and at this point, I'm wondering about brain damage. She had absolutely no reaction to my *flash*, and I offered her numerous opportunities to respond."

That was troublesome. An eye flash was standard identification between Fliers. It was just one of the ways we used the second lens in our eyes. "She doesn't trust you."

"Maybe not, but I don't think it's that. It's like she doesn't see it, and I watched her closely. She had zero reaction to it."

The situation got more confusing with time. "She's lying to me," Avery said, at the end of her second day in the hospital. "And I can't keep her here much longer. She'll be discharged this time tomorrow. Did your contact find any more information about her family?"

"Not yet, but I did learn that she arrived from Toronto only a week ago. That house on Cliffside she's been living in has been vacant for a decade. Maybe I'll go over there and take a look around."

"Leave it for a couple of days. The police have stepped up patrols in her neighbourhood to address local concerns."

"Well, at least she won't slip away on us."

"She'd better not. We need to find out what happened to her. If this covey is under threat, I want to know about it. Gabe Aucoin has a contact with the police. He'll let me know when they step down their surveillance."

Three days later, Wells Fargo delivered another punch. Sandra and Cole had made it into Oregon at Crescent City. I steeled myself to open the file, but it didn't stop the pain of her betrayal from slicing through me. God how I wanted to get out of Vancouver. One more week, I thought. Just one more week and I could escape this torment. James sent a text to thank me for the file, and I wondered if he was getting any closer to accepting the truth of Sandra's decision.

Neither Avery nor James attended the next night's paintball game. James's absence was a relief. With less than a week to go in our arrangement, the last thing I wanted was pressure from him to stay the course. I got home late and pulled out the charts to begin plotting my cruise home. I'd make a holiday of it and take my time. Eden and Alex had family in Washington State; perhaps they'd want to accompany me to Seattle.

The next morning, Avery phoned. "I called Emelynn Taylor. Thought you'd be interested to know she's agreed to come to my office on Friday to have her sutures removed."

"That surprises me. I thought she'd steer clear of you."

"That's what I thought," he said. "It's curious, isn't it?"

"You think she knows you're the head of the covey here? Maybe she wants your protection."

"It's possible. But if that's the case, why didn't she go through proper channels when she came out here?"

"Are you going to talk to her about it?"

"I'll play it by ear. Why don't you come out and get a look at her? Tell me what you think."

I had to admit, I was curious about the woman. And what the hell, a distraction would be a welcome addition to my final few days in Vancouver. "I can do that," I said. "What time?"

When Friday rolled around, I watched for Emelynn from behind the cover of a window blind beside the door to Avery's waiting room. She arrived on foot with a slight limp favouring her left side. Otherwise, her demeanour gave nothing away. As she approached the door, I rushed to resume my seat on the far side of the room. Avery wanted me to have a few minutes alone with her before he called her into the exam room. When she finally opened the door, I waited until I felt her gaze on me before I looked up from the magazine.

"Good morning," she said, dipping her head so a mass of unruly hair fell over the scratches and yellow bruises on her face. She foolishly maintained eye contact, and I flashed her a greeting. She answered with a shy smile and dropped a tattered knapsack on the floor. Avery was right. She'd reacted like she hadn't seen it. How was that possible?

I studied her while she sorted through Avery's dated reading material. If she was nervous about my presence, she didn't show it. She had a pleasant face, young, which matched Josh's report. Twenty-one. Her body was well hidden under ill-fitting, off-brand clothes, so she probably didn't come from money. Just who was she? And what was she doing in Summerset without benefit of an introduction?

The door to the exam room opened and Avery stepped out. "Emelynn," he said, and then glanced briefly at me before ushering her behind closed doors.

Twenty minutes later, he escorted her out and closed the door behind her. "What do you think?"

"She didn't acknowledge my flash. It's like you said—she didn't seem to notice. Did you learn anything?"

"No. I kept the conversation light and nonthreatening. Asked her again what had happened, made light of it even, and she lied—again. Said she was in the wrong place at the wrong time. She's hiding something."

"I agree. There's something off about her. I think I should follow her and see where she goes."

"Yes. She's obviously not going to tell us. Let me know what you find."

I left immediately and caught sight of her at a bus stop around the corner. I turned in the opposite direction and hailed a cab. She boarded a bus, and I followed in the taxi. She got off on Deacon Street, turned down a side street and entered a boutique wine store. I paid the cabbie and wandered to the Starbucks on the far side of Deacon to keep an eye on her.

She emerged from the wine store with a bulge in her knapsack and headed in my direction. I eased behind a pillar as she passed and watched her go into a bookstore. She stayed inside a healthy fifteen minutes and then crossed the street and disappeared into a grocery store. I strolled past the bookstore and peered through the window. The clerk had her head down. I watched long enough to confirm that there was no one else in the store. I'd have to find out more about the clerk.

Emelynn came out of the grocery store with her knapsack stretched tight. I followed her to the end of Cliffside. She walked down a drive-way, unlocked the door to a small, tidy house and stepped inside. She hadn't looked back once. In fact, the entire time I'd followed her, she'd not looked over her shoulder a single time. This was not a woman concerned for her safety. Her behaviour was entirely inconsistent with having been brutally attacked only ten days ago.

Careful what you ask for, Jackson, I thought. It looked like I'd found something to fill my last days in Vancouver.

Who are you, Emelynn Taylor? And what are you doing here?

CHAPTER FIFTEEN

Avery was equally bewildered by Emelynn's behaviour, and we were in agreement that I should continue to follow her.

I rose with the sun, drove my rental car to Cliffside Avenue and waited. The paper was old news and the crossword finished long before I saw any activity. Shortly before ten o'clock, a tow truck with an old MGB on its flatbed pulled into her driveway. The driver unloaded the car and soon after, Emelynn opened her front door. She must have bought the car from Meyers Motors, the name painted on the door of the tow truck. The body language between the two of them spoke volumes. The driver reached out to touch her face; she pulled back. Apparently, he didn't know her as well as he thought he did. He stepped away and his focus shifted to the MGB. They circled the car in what looked like a show and tell. When they ran out of steam, she offered him her hand. I could feel his disappointment from fifty yards away.

After he left, she went inside and moments later returned with a bundle of cardboard that she stuffed in the car. I pulled out half a block behind her and followed her down Cliffside. She turned up to Deacon, drove a few blocks then took a quiet side street and parked in front of a mom-and-pop hardware store. She spoke briefly to the clerk just inside the door, and then they both walked out of view. I jumped out of the car and crossed the street to loiter in front of the real estate office next door.

The clerk reappeared at the front counter with Emelynn in tow and rang up her purchase: a coil of yellow nylon rope. My, my . . . this was getting interesting.

I returned to my car and continued to follow. She took her time with a coffee on the sidewalk patio at Starbucks and then drove by the recycling station before returning to visit the bookstore. The same bookstore clerk who'd been working the day before came out to admire her car. So they knew one another.

I trailed her the few blocks back to her home, got out of my car and ducked into the park to walk out the fatigue that had settled in my bones. A few yards down a deserted dirt trail, I pulled out my phone and dialled Avery. "You ready for this? The nylon rope I found on the beach belonged to Emelynn. She replaced it this morning."

"The rope was hers?" he said in a tone that echoed my own confusion. "That adds an unexpected twist to the mystery. Could her rope burns be self-inflicted?"

"Makes you wonder. She's sure not acting like someone who's recently been assaulted."

"When you found the rope, you said it had been secured to a rock?"

"That's right."

"Why would she tie herself to a rock on a beach in the middle of the night? She'd have had to exert considerable effort to inflict those rope burns."

"I'll bet that's why she wasn't wearing her hoodie," I said. "She'd worked up a sweat."

"And she was barefoot," Avery added. "She was running. She tied a rope to her ankle and ran until the rope caught her short."

"The pattern in the sand would support that theory. Maybe she's some type of masochist?"

"She doesn't recognize a flash, didn't know to contact the covey when she arrived, her mother, who raised her, isn't a Flier, and now this?"

"Avery, do you think it's possible she doesn't know what she is?"

"Impossible. She would have been losing gravity since puberty. She'd be dead by now."

"But it explains the diving weights. Maybe she's been weighting herself down."

"If that's true, Jackson, it's just a matter of time until someone finds out about her. She'll put us all at risk."

I'd circled back on the trail and was peering out from my cover in the trees. Emelynn's front door was in view. "Maybe it's time we confronted our mystery woman."

"I agree. I'll find a medical reason to coax her back to my office."

"You think that'll work? She's already lied to you more than once."

"What would you suggest?"

"I'll keep tabs on her. She's replaced the rope. She's bound to use it again, and as soon as she does, I'll confront her. She'll have no choice then." Besides, the woman had piqued my curiosity.

"Can you spare the time?" Avery asked.

"Sure." Working on this puzzle was better than speculating about the next ATM photo of my wife . . . and her lover. "I've got no big plans for a couple of days."

"All right. Let me know the moment you have answers."

I disconnected and checked my watch. It was half past one and I hadn't eaten since I left the marina at five thirty this morning. I kicked myself for not having grabbed something back at Starbucks. It was too late now. I returned to the car, slouched in my seat and adjusted my rear-view mirror for a better angle on Emelynn's driveway.

The chances I'd be spotted out here were slim. The homes on Emelynn's side of the street were buffered from prying eyes by a thick berm that grew along the ditch.

Emelynn's grey, gabled bungalow looked like both the oldest and the smallest house on the street. Because of the elevation, it wasn't obvious these were waterfront homes. Damn! Most of those homes also had beach access—I'd seen the staircases when I'd flown over on the night of Emelynn's accident. Would she leave the house by way of those stairs and slip right past me? I searched the glovebox for the obligatory rental-car map of the area. It looked like she'd have to hike more than a mile to get out by way of the beach. I convinced myself it was highly unlikely, especially in daylight hours, and settled in for the duration.

By the time six thirty rolled around, and she finally showed herself, my ass was numb. I reminded myself that I'd volunteered for this monotony, and turned the key. I followed her to the bookstore on Deacon, where she collected her girlfriend, and then we drove north for another twenty minutes. Shortly after we passed a *Welcome to Seaside* road sign, they parked and strolled into a restaurant with the uninspired name The Seafood House. After they'd been seated, I left them to find my own dinner. My choices were McDonald's or a cellophane-wrapped ham and cheese sandwich of questionable vintage from a Petro Canada gas station. McDonald's won.

So while Emelynn and her girlfriend dined on a three-course

seafood meal, I got to savour a lukewarm Big Mac. It took them two hours to finish eating, and by then I'd been in the car for fifteen hours. Fifteen fucking hours. What was I thinking volunteering for this? I'd likely worn a hole in my shoe from tapping my foot to ease the boredom. Made me wonder about the mental state of people who did surveillance for a living. James was a PI; he probably did lots of this type of shit.

The women surfaced at nine thirty and I dutifully followed. Emelynn dropped her friend outside an apartment building and then took a convoluted route back to Deacon Street. I kept half a block behind. She paused at the three-way stop and turned left onto Cliffside. A police cruiser followed behind her MGB, prompting me to turn in the opposite direction.

Shit! With darkness upon us, I couldn't let her out of my sight. I raced to the beach access I'd found earlier on the map, parked and jogged the trail to the seashore. It was rather disappointing as far as beaches went, more *National Geographic* than Club Med. I balanced my way across a wide expanse of unstable football-sized rocks until I was certain I couldn't be seen, then lifted off and skimmed across the water.

I skirted the lights that bled out to the beach from the houses spaced along the clifftop and made my way to Emelynn's back door. I stopped a few houses north of hers and watched her darkened windows. If she wasn't inside, she couldn't have gone far.

But she was there. Ten minutes later, I watched her step out onto her deck with a glass of wine in her hand. She gazed into the distance, unaware of my presence. Did she have night vision, I wondered, or was her gift damaged, like Avery's?

I took a chance and signalled her with a flash. Like before, she didn't react. I landed and picked my way across the rocks, getting closer, and tried again with the same results. Perhaps she was shielding herself with her *block*. Some Fliers' blocks were impenetrable.

She started down the steps, wine still in hand. I moved within thirty yards of her and studied her as she descended the stairs. She was completely at ease. Why did she feel so safe?

Christ! Adrenalin shot through me in a blaze of terror. What if she was one of the Tribunal Novem? They wouldn't seek out anyone's permission or protection. Had Avery and I drawn the wrong conclusions about her? Maybe she was at ease because we weren't a threat to her. Tribunal Fliers were the strongest of our kind.

I slammed my block into place at the exact same moment she turned her head and looked right at me. Surprise flitted across her face. I looked away. Fliers learned early never to trust the gaze of a stranger; the second lens in a Flier's eye could drop you to your knees, or worse. I took a few cautious steps and chanced another look. She stood still, staring like a deer caught in headlights. My mind blared a warning. Was it a trap?

Damn it! If she was Tribunal, I was already screwed—she'd already seen me; there was no turning back. I crossed my fingers that she had no reason to want to harm me, and set off with purpose, averting my eyes. The rocky terrain gave way to sand as I approached her stairs. With just a few feet between us, I caught her wide-eyed gaze, the Flier equivalent of a finger on the trigger, and my years of training kicked in automatically. I dropped my block and delivered a warning. She broke eye contact and stumbled, grasping the railing to steady herself. Immediately I knew I'd hit an innocent, and my remorse was instant. That jolt would have hurt like hell. Why hadn't she protected herself?

Her wine glass tipped and its contents spilled to the sand. She lost her balance and teetered into the railing. Shit! How badly had I hurt her? I rushed in and caught her gaze. "Are you all right?" She looked at me with terrified, unfocused eyes, and I made a split-second decision to contain the damage and put her under. This time without the pain.

I caught her just as she collapsed, and lowered her to the sand. Damn it! I checked her pulse. It was erratic; I couldn't leave her here. Who would have predicted this scenario?

"Looks like you're coming with me, Emelynn Taylor." I pulled her into a sitting position, slid one arm around her back and the other under her knees and lifted her. It had been a long time since I'd done a dead weight jump-start. I adjusted my grip, bent my knees and leapt. The moment my feet left the ground, gravity dissipated. I headed out over the water, got my bearings and made the trek to the marina. Traffic on the Fraser was quiet. The lights were lit below deck in the ship moored at the *Symphony's* stern. The occupants had retired for the night.

With caution, I approached the darkened observation deck of the *Symphony*. Gravity returned with my landing, and I quickly carried Emelynn under cover and settled her on one of the sofas. Then I dialled Avery.

"We have a complication," I said. After explaining what had happened, he insisted on coming out right away.

She was still unconscious when he pulled into the parking lot, thirty minutes later, and made his way down the dock. He checked her blood pressure and pulse. Her skin was pale and clammy. "This isn't good. Let's get her inside."

We put her in one of the aft cabins and he tucked a blanket around her. "I wish you hadn't jolted her."

"The effects of my jolt don't normally last more than two, three hours, tops."

Avery glanced at me across the bed. "She's still healing from a brain injury," he said, then turned his attention to adjusting her pillows. "Your first jolt would have been bad enough, but that second one? Who knows what damage has been done."

"The first one I regret—it was a mistake—but the second one wouldn't have hurt her, not physically."

"Under normal circumstances, maybe. At this point, let's just hope she survives it."

His words chilled me. We returned to the salon, but he checked on her frequently. Avery insisted on staying until she stabilized. Neither of us mentioned what we'd do if she didn't make it, but I, for one, had given it some unpleasant consideration.

"If she's a Flier, she's the worst one I've ever come across," I said.

"There's no doubt she's one of us. She has the second lens in her eyes. It would sure help if we knew who her father was?"

"Perhaps she wasn't born a Flier. She could have been gifted."

"Even so," Avery said, "she's wholly ignorant of our ways. Who would forfeit the gift and not ensure she knew how to manage it?"

"Maybe she stole it?"

"Not a chance. She's been lying to me, for sure, but it's not malicious. More like she's hiding something, being protective. Besides, to steal it, she'd have had to overpower one of us. There's no way she could have managed that."

"True, but there's something strange going on with that woman."

"I agree, and as soon as she's awake, we have to find out what."

It was close to two in the morning before Avery was satisfied that Emelynn's heart rate had stabilized, but she remained unconscious.

"How much longer?" I asked, trailing him to Emelynn's cabin.

"Hard to say." He removed the blood pressure cuff and tucked her arm back under the cover. "She's going to be frightened when she comes to. She might try to run."

"Yeah, it's what I'd do."

"Maybe she'll cooperate once she learns that we know what she's been up to," Avery said.

"Or she might not and go straight to the police."

Avery packed his cuff into his medical bag and removed his stethoscope from around his neck. "As improbable as it sounds, Jackson, I don't think she knows what she is. How she's survived this long is a miracle, but if she doesn't know what she is, then she's vulnerable and a danger to herself and to us."

"If that's the case, you're going to have your hands full."

"We can't let her go to the police."

"She'll come across like a raving lunatic," I said. "Don't worry about it."

"It's not her words I'm concerned about. What if she's able to demonstrate her gift? Do you think that's a chance we should take?"

"Of course not, but once you explain the situation to her, I'm sure you'll be able to talk some sense into her."

"Not until she comes to, and we can't move her."

"Well, she can't stay here." Though Avery didn't know it yet, I'd be leaving Vancouver in a scant few days.

Avery arched an eyebrow. "Need I remind you *why* she's here?"

I pursed my lips at the unnecessary jab. "I haven't forgotten." My gaze wandered to Emelynn's face. Her skin was still too pale, and she was deathly still. "All right. She can stay until she regains consciousness, but I can't commit to more than that. As you know, I have to be ready to pick up and go the moment I get word of our missing Flier."

"I understand." He closed his bag and turned to face me. "But perhaps I could impose on you a little longer. Whether or not she knows what she is, I'd like to see her contained when she awakens. At least until we have some answers."

"Contained?"

"Take the *Symphony* offshore. I doubt she can fly, and it'll remove the option of running. And if there are others involved, she'll be isolated from them. You can keep her safe and you'll have a better chance of finding out what she's up to."

"Me? What about you?"

"I'm afraid I get terribly seasick. Here at the dock, I'm fine, but out there? You'd have two useless Fliers on your hands."

"Oh, that's great!"

"It's just for another day or so, and I'd be grateful."

Damn. This was my reward for telling him I had no plans for the next few days. "A day or two. Max. And the moment I'm able to, I'm bringing her back here for you to deal with."

"Thank you. I hope she's not too much trouble. Would you like me to send Alex out to assist?"

"No. I can handle her, but put him on standby."

CHAPTER SIXTEEN

A mile and a half offshore, I found a good anchorage in a sandbar, far away from shipping traffic. Emelynn was still out of it when I checked on her. She'd better damn well recover quickly, I thought. She sure as hell wasn't going to delay my departure in three days' time.

It had been a long, tedious day. What I would have given for a few hours' sleep. Instead, I settled for a shower and a change of clothes.

Back in Emelynn's cabin, I took a seat beside the bed and put my feet up. She looked better, having curled onto her side, with more colour in her face.

A mass of hair trailed across the pillow. It was an unusual shade of, what? Brown? Or was that what auburn looked like? She was attractive, even if she was an unwelcome complication. I pulled a magazine into my lap and settled in for the duration.

I awoke with a start and caught my breath. It was daylight. My gaze darted to Emelynn. Thankfully, she was still asleep. I yawned and picked up the magazine I'd dropped. I'd just resumed skimming the pages when Emelynn's breathing changed. I kept perfectly still and lifted my gaze. Her eyes were open, scrutinizing the cabin.

"Welcome back," I said. "How are you feeling?"

She shifted away from me. "Who are you?"

"Someone you should have met a long time ago. My name's Jackson Delaney." I banked on my honesty disarming her.

"What do you want with me?"

"Nothing," I said, and she quickly looked away. She had every right to be frightened of my gaze. "I'm just trying to keep you safe." I dropped the magazine on the bedside table.

"Safe? You *kidnapped* me to keep me *safe*?"

"Safe," I repeated hoping the repetition would take her attention away from that other word, *kidnapped*.

"I didn't know I wasn't."

"I'm aware of that. That's why you're here."

"I don't understand."

"Yes, I'm sure you don't. There's a lot you don't understand, Emelynn. In fact, we have a lot to talk about—"

"How do you know my name? Where are we?"

I took a deep breath. "We're on my ship. I brought you here last night."

"Why?"

I held up my hand. The explanation would take some time, but we didn't have to do it here. "I'm sure you have a lot of questions, which I promise to answer. But right now, I'd like a coffee. What about you?" I stood and stretched my aching muscles.

"Coffee? That's your priority?" she said, with a flare of temper. "How about some answers?"

Yeah, so do we, I thought, and headed toward the door. "There's a head starboard." I motioned in its general direction. "Freshen up then meet me up top."

I left the cabin quickly and clambered up the stairs to the galley to brew a pot of coffee. I wished she hadn't mentioned kidnapping. The word dredged up thoughts of Sandra, thoughts I'd managed to snuff out these past few days. I texted Avery to let him know that Emelynn was awake and kicking.

The security monitors showed no sign of life in the hall below. I turned them off and took the tray of coffee up to the observation deck, where I resumed watching her movement on another monitor. She emerged from her cabin as I sipped my coffee. I'd taken the precaution of locking the doors, and she tried every one. She did the same on the main deck and had success with the door to the head that I'd neglected to secure. Her struggle to open the galley drawers told me she'd never been aboard a ship before. When she reached the bottom of the stairs to the observation deck, I turned off the monitor.

She stepped onto the deck and took in her surroundings, momentarily locking eyes with me. I motioned her over and she quickly looked away. She'd already learned her lesson about courting a stranger's gaze. She approached with caution. I studied her face and was rewarded the instant she recognized her rope and other belongings I'd left on display atop the coffee table in front of me.

She dropped into the seat opposite. I poured her coffee. "Cream?" I asked, and she finally dragged her gaze away from the table. She nodded yes. I poured the cream, and then pushed the cup toward her.

She took it and folded her legs under her. "What's all this stuff?"

Was she really going to try to deny ownership? "It's too late for that, Emelynn. Your reaction gave you away the moment you laid eyes on it." How long would she drag this on? I wondered, and rested my feet on the table.

"What do you want?"

"I told you. Nothing."

"So . . . you kidnapped me to return my things?"

Kidnapped again? At this rate, we'd be here all day. "You and I have something in common: something important." There was one surefire way to speed things up. I stood and crossed behind her, out from under the cover that protected the bow. I checked my surroundings. Daylight demonstrations were always dangerous. When I was certain I had Emelynn's attention, I lifted off and hovered three feet in the air. Her mouth dropped opened. Satisfied, I landed and returned to my place on the sofa. "I thought that would save us a lot of time and denial," I said, and picked up my coffee. My stunt had silenced her.

When she finally spoke, it seemed as though I'd made a break-through. "How did you know about me?"

"Dr. Coulter. He knew the minute he examined you at the hospital. Avery keeps an eye out for our kind."

She tilted her head. "Our *kind*?"

"Yes, Fliers."

"Fliers." She said it as if tasting the word for the first time. "Is that what I am, a Flier?"

"Well," I said, and a wry smile crept across my face as I glanced at her coil of rope. "Maybe not a very good one, but yes."

"What exactly is a Flier?"

So Avery was right. She had no idea what she was. "We're ordinary people who have an extraordinary gift: a talent, so to speak. It's as rare and inexplicable as clairvoyance or telepathy. The gift allows us to throw off gravity as easily as an overcoat."

"That's impossible," she said with a dismissive shake of her head.

I quirked an eyebrow. "It is possible. We're living proof."

"But how can that be? What you're suggesting contradicts Newton's law of gravity and who knows how many other scientific imperatives."

Damn. This was going to take some work. "Did you know that until 2005, scientists couldn't explain how bumblebees were able to fly? *Theoretically*, their stubby little wings made flight an aerodynamic impossibility."

"At least they *have* wings," she said. Her obstinate determination to cling to archaic beliefs needed to be shaken.

"My point is, bumblebee flight remained a mystery for hundreds of years. It's not unlike the puzzle of the Pyramids. *Theoretically*, the Pyramids shouldn't exist. Science tells us that it is impossible for the Egyptians to have constructed them with the tools and skills they had available at the time. Yet those tombs have stood for centuries thumbing their pointy noses at us.

"Nor can scientists quantify the power of positive thinking or the placebo effect and no one has ever definitively solved the mystery of the Bermuda Triangle. There are lots of things in this world that we don't understand, Emelynn, or that can't be explained by science. But that doesn't mean they don't exist. Science will catch up and figure it out some day."

She stared into her coffee. "How did Dr. Coulter know I was a Flier?" she asked, and I got the sense she had opened the door a crack.

"Your eyes. We have eyes that don't refract light in the usual manner. It's what allows us to see in the dark."

"So Dr. Coulter is also a Flier?"

"Well, he has night vision but he can't fly, which is highly unusual. He's also the reason you're here. He asked me to watch out for you. I was waiting in his office the day you went to get your stitches out. I've been keeping an eye on you since your accident, and believe me, babysitting you is not what I want to be doing with my time. Your being here was not part of my plan."

She listened with her brow pinched. "I only intervened because you left me no choice when you bought more rope yesterday. I didn't want you to kill yourself, which you seem doggedly intent on doing."

"You've been watching me?" she said, and her tone slammed the door closed. "You're the man I saw on the beach?" Her voice rose a decibel. "You're the one who was loitering at the foot of my stairs."

For Christ's sake. "You never saw me, and I certainly wasn't hanging around your stairs, but yes, I've been watching your movements. I'm sorry if that upsets you, but we needed to know more about you."

"You kidnapped me!"

Ah, damn. Back to that again? Her misplaced anger sparked my own. I leaned forward. "Yes! And you may not choose to believe me right now, but it's for your own good. We're trying to keep you safe."

"I *did* see you. The night before last. You were walking south, close to the water. You even looked up to the deck."

"It wasn't me. I wasn't on foot when I checked on you, so you can skip the accusation."

"Then who was it who left footprints at the foot of my stairs?"

Now she was just being petulant. "You live on a public beach. It could have been anyone."

Her glare turned into a frown and she finally settled back into the sofa. She picked at her cuticles, calm again. "How did you know what I was planning to do with the rope?" she asked.

At long last, we were getting somewhere. "The night of your accident, Avery phoned me with the few details he'd learned from the paramedics. I flew out there. It didn't take long to find your things on the beach. Rope burns on your ankles, rope on the beach. I put two and two together. It wasn't that difficult." She seemed to be back in listening mode. I refilled our mugs.

"So, what have you learned about me?" she asked, looking up at me with caution from under her brow.

Not enough, I thought. "Your name is Emelynn Taylor, your twenty-second birthday is next month, you have no siblings. We don't know anything about your father. You've been living with your mother, Laura Aberfoyle. You graduated from U of T with a BA last month and moved here a few weeks ago. The Flier community in the GTA has never heard of you or your mother."

"Well, you've certainly done some digging." She sounded indignant and I wondered if I'd lost her again. My stomach growled and my thoughts shifted to breakfast, or would it be lunch? She interrupted my thoughts. "You keep referring to *we*—who are the *we*?"

"Fliers. There aren't a lot of us so we keep track of one another, watch out for one another." She had to be as hungry as I was. We could talk over a meal. I stood. "Let's go below to the galley and get something to eat. I'm famished. I'll tell you more about Fliers over a meal and if you're up for it, you can fill in some blanks for me." She didn't immediately follow when I headed below, but I had faith she would eventually.

By the time I'd decided on pancakes and found the bacon, she'd joined me. She kept her distance, but watched intently as I approached the drawer she'd so comically tried to open earlier. "Yeah, about that—you have to lift up on the front of these drawers to pull them out. Keeps them from jumping open when the ship's underway."

I pulled out a bowl for the batter and two heavy skillets. Memories of Sandra bubbled to the surface. Pancakes were my special treat. Something I did on lazy mornings after long nights of spectacular love-making.

Thankfully, Emelynn saved me from going any further with that line of thought. "You're awfully confident that I won't find a way to escape."

"I'm not holding you here, Emelynn. You can leave any time you want." The bacon sizzled when it hit the skillet, its hickory scent a mouth-watering promise. "If there was any other way to manage this situation, I'd have found it." I started the batter and prepared the meal on autopilot, fighting thoughts of Sandra with the lure of the open sea only days away.

When the pancakes were done, I invited Emelynn back to the galley from the salon, where she'd wandered. "Sit," I said. We ate in silence. Afterwards, I cleared the dishes. Emelynn studied me as if I were an animal in a zoo and followed me to the sofa, sitting opposite.

Might as well get this rolling, I thought, and dove in. "Fliers are a tight-knit group. Someone should have known about you, but you weren't on anyone's radar either here or in Toronto. That's why we were so surprised to learn about you."

She cradled her torso. "How many of you are there?"

Did she think I wouldn't notice the pronoun? "*We* number in the thousands at best. Here in the Lower Mainland, including you, there are thirteen of us."

"I wouldn't be so quick to count me among your numbers," she said. "So far, I've learned that you've spied on me, dug up personal information about me and, oh yes, you kidnapped me. Those aren't exactly attributes of a group I want to belong to."

Kidnapped? Again? I laughed. I couldn't help it. I was tired and she'd set the obstinate bar to new heights. "Well, I see it quite differently. You were doing your best to kill yourself or bring yourself to the attention of someone who would do it for you. We took pity on you and brought you here to safety. Now I've fed you and I'm trying to teach you something about your rather unique situation." I thought the levity would help, but I was wrong.

"I don't think the police would agree with your assessment," she said with no hint of a smile.

And . . . back to square one. "You're right. They wouldn't. I shouldn't have been so flippant. I'm sorry. Maybe I could have handled things differently, but now that you're here, aren't you curious? Don't you want to know more about your gift and the people you share it with?" Avery had been right to isolate her.

She crossed her arms. I considered my options: facts hadn't worked, levity provoked threats and humility was getting me nowhere. "I can see that you and I have to build some trust—mend some fences, so to speak. Go on," I said, leaning forward. "Ask me a question."

"What's your name?"

"Jackson Delaney—I already told you that. Ask me something else."

"Prove it," she said.

Christ! She couldn't even believe that much. I pulled out my wallet and handed her my driver's licence.

"You're a long way from home."

"Yes, I am." But I'm going back soon, I thought, and held out my hand for the return of my licence.

"How did you learn about your condition?"

Man, this was going to take a while. "I was born this way, so I've always known about my *condition*, as you so oddly put it. My parents were both Fliers."

"They've passed away?"

"Yes, they're both gone now."

"I'm sorry."

I dipped my head in acknowledgement, a habit I'd developed in the months after my father died.

"Those of us who are born with the gift have night vision from the moment we're born. We've never known what it's like to be night blind. Flight comes later. Usually around puberty, so it differs for everyone, but by fifteen or sixteen, most born Fliers are fully functioning."

She shifted in her seat. "If you're not born a Flier, how else can you become one?"

That was a telling question. "You can be given the gift," I said, and paused, waiting for her affirmation. "Or you can steal it." Again, I paused. She offered nothing. "But, regardless of whether it's given or stolen, the person relinquishing the gift forfeits everything: the night vision, the ability to fly, sometimes even more than that."

She remained unfazed and I pressed on. "The process isn't predictable, so when the transition goes badly, it leaves the donor weak and vulnerable. About half the time, it kills them. Flier history is full of these cautionary tales so, as you can imagine, we don't take kindly to those who steal the gift. That's why it was important for us to know more about you."

Emelynn gave me nothing. Perhaps I needed to break this down for her. "Obviously, you weren't a born Flier—you're too old to be as inept as you are. Fortunately for you, neither your history nor our observations of your behaviour led us to believe you stole it. That leaves us to assume that someone gifted it to you. Am I right?"

She grazed her teeth over her lower lip. I remained silent and kept my frustration hidden and my fingers crossed. If that diatribe didn't get her to open up, I didn't know what would.

"Yes, I think so," she finally said, and I offered a silent thank you to whatever god pried her lips loose. "But I was quite young at the time. I don't remember it very clearly."

It didn't matter. At least she was talking. "Tell me what you do remember."

"I was twelve and living in that house you kidnapped me from. I was alone, playing on the beach . . ."

She stopped midsentence. No, no, no! "Go on," I said.

"I've never told anyone this before."

"That's good. It probably kept you safe. Go on," I repeated, but she didn't, so I coaxed her. "Do you remember how Dr. Coulter found you? Your belongings I recovered from the beach?" I leaned forward. "You're not safe out there anymore. I can help you."

It took her a moment to overcome her hesitation. "A woman named Jolene gave me 'the gift,' as you put it. The night vision showed up a few days later. That part has never changed. My dad died a few months after Jolene's visit and then my mother moved us to Toronto."

That didn't add up. "I don't understand. How could you have had the gift since you were twelve years old and still be so unskilled at flying?"

She quickly crossed her arms. "Well, unlike you, I didn't have my parents to show me the ropes, and I couldn't tell them." Her defences were back up. Not good. "Jolene was very clear that I keep it a secret."

"Hold up a minute. Where was Jolene?"

"I don't know," she said with a shrug.

"So what's your connection to her? Is she a family friend?"

"No. I'd never met her before that summer, and I haven't seen her since. Didn't really think about her again until high school when the floaty thing started to happen."

"*Floaty* thing?"

She corrected herself. "*Floating*," as if that made a difference. "Believe me, it wasn't a happy discovery." She described dangerous, increasingly frequent episodes when she'd lost gravity. "That's why I moved back here—why I've been practicing on the beach. I'm trying to learn how to control this thing. You have no idea how difficult it's been for me."

Difficult? That she was alive was nothing short of miraculous. "Well, that explains a lot."

"It does?"

"Yes, except for Jolene. Why would she gift you and then not put any support in place for your transition?" Though I didn't dare say it for fear Emelynn would clam up again, I wondered what role the Tribunal had played in Jolene's gifting. Did they even know about it? "No wonder you got into trouble—you're lucky you haven't killed yourself." And Jolene, a complete stranger. How odd. "I'll ask around and see what I can find on Jolene. Do you know her last name?"

"No. She would have been thirty-five or forty at the time. She was pretty with blonde wavy hair."

It wasn't much to go on, but I'd see if Josh could help. I pulled out my phone, but Emelynn distracted me.

"Why would a Flier choose to give the gift away?"

My knowledge of gifting was limited. "Most of the cases I've heard of involve Fliers who are suffering from a terminal illness. The gifting is always formally documented, so there isn't any question about intent. Like I said, there are repercussions to stealing the gift."

Surprise flitted across her face. She tucked her hands under her thighs. "So, where do we go from here? Will you take me home now?"

Home? Not a chance. Avery's maybe, but not until I was sure she understood the problem. "I could, but I don't think that's a good idea."

"Why not?"

"You're a Flier, Emelynn, and there are people out there who might figure that out. Given your antics, that isn't exactly a stretch. They would be more than happy to get their hands on you. Take my word for it—that would not be a pleasant experience."

She'd crossed her arms again. "Forgive my skepticism, but I find that a little hard to believe."

"Do you?" Really? This from the waif who didn't even know what she was. "It's happened before, many times." I repeated Sandra's cover story, and for the first time, I felt like it had an honourable purpose. "We still haven't found her and she's an exceptionally skilled Flier, not to mention intelligent and painfully careful. If they can get her, they can certainly get you."

"Jackson, I don't know what you want me to say. You don't look like a nutbar, but you did kidnap me. You've been spying on me and you kind of creeped me out last night. Granted, you haven't hurt me, at least not yet, but how do I know you're not one of those people you told me I should be so worried about?"

"Hurt you!" I jumped to my feet. Man, she was a test of my patience! "You'd know by now if I was your goddamn enemy. Why the hell did I let Avery talk me into taking you on?" Perhaps it was time for some reinforcements. "You—stay here."

Chapter Seventeen

Frustration fuelled my race up the stairs. Phone in hand, I called Alex. "It's Jackson. Has Avery filled you in on our mystery Flier?"

"He called this morning. Is she okay?"

"She's fine, but stubborn as hell. Can't wrap her mind around the fact that our kind exists. Even my hovering three feet in the air didn't convince her. She's not going to take my word alone. I know I'm asking you to risk a daytime flight, but do you think you can fly out here?"

Alex took my coordinates. "How about I bring Eden along?" he said. "She's off shift, and female influence might help."

"Couldn't hurt," I said.

While I waited for them to arrive, I texted Josh with the details Emelynn had given me about Jolene. I offered him a bonus for a fast turnaround. The intrigue surrounding Emelynn, though interesting, was turning into a complication with the potential to delay my exit plans.

My phone vibrated as I was tucking it away. Redmond. Terrific. I hovered my thumb over the decline option. He'd just phone back, I thought, and took his call.

"Hello, Redmond."

"Jackson. How are you holding up?"

"I've been better. I'm assuming you've seen the latest ATM clips?"

"I have. I'm sorry, son. I know how difficult this must be for you."

The "but" was loading, I could feel it. I paced to the bow. "I'm getting on with my life, Redmond. My marriage is over."

"If I didn't know Sandy better, I'd think the same."

"I think she's been pretty clear, and there's nothing any of us can do about it."

"You might be right, but you have to admit, this behaviour—not communicating with anyone—is wildly uncharacteristic of her."

"It is. But people change."

"Not like this. Sandy's my daughter, James's only sister. We won't stop searching until we find her."

"And I sincerely hope you do, but I can't continue fooling myself. She's made her choice."

"And what if it wasn't her choice?"

I raked my hand through my hair. "Damn it, Redmond!" He and James were deceiving themselves.

"It's not my intention to upset you, son. Watching Sandy in those ATM videos hurts me, too. I just wish you could see your way clear to sticking with James's plan awhile longer. They're in Oregon, getting closer every day. We'll know, one way or the other, very soon."

"Redmond, I—"

"Just think about it, son. That's all I ask."

"Don't get your hopes up. I've gotta go." I disconnected before he could plead any further, and dropped onto the sofa.

Alex and Eden landed a short time later. I shook off thoughts of Sandra and changed gears as I rose to greet them. A different challenge awaited below deck. At the aft stairs, I explained my progress with Emelynn so far, or lack thereof.

"She's right, you know," Eden said. "You did kidnap her. And then she wakes up in a strange place—a bedroom no less—with her kidnapper. She doesn't have much reason to trust you right now."

"Ouch! Cut the man some slack, babe," Alex said. "He probably saved her life."

"Yeah, well," Eden said, removing her hands from her hips. "She doesn't know that yet."

"It's the damndest thing, isn't it?" I said. "Having this gift and not knowing what it is?"

"I can't imagine," Eden said. "Let's go see if we can help her."

They followed me below. Emelynn stood against the portside wall with her arms crossed over her chest and her jaw set in stone.

"Eden Effrome, Alex Klause, this is Emelynn Taylor." Emelynn didn't move. "I've filled Eden and Alex in and they've agreed to help us out."

She immediately turned to Eden. "Did he tell you he kidnapped me?"

Eden shot me one of those *if looks could kill* expressions that women did so well.

"Yes," she said. "He filled us in."

"And you're okay with that?"

"You're putting us all in danger, Emelynn," Eden said. "I know you weren't aware of it at the time, but you are. I wish we'd been more subtle with you, but . . ." She half-turned to me. Her gaze only reached my knees, but I felt the sentiment. "With one Flier still missing, we couldn't take a chance. We don't have the manpower to go searching for two of you." Eden's tone was just the right mix of concern and warning, a skill she no doubt used every day as a nurse.

Emelynn jutted her chin. "How am I putting you all in danger?"

Alex answered. "You're connected to us now, Emelynn, whether you like it or not. If they find you, they'll look for others. They'll uncover Avery first. Those records are public. Once they find him, they'll find the rest of us. But they might find your family first. That wouldn't turn out well for them. The people we're talking about aren't nice."

Alex earned a reprimand from his wife for that remark, and she took over again. "We're not trying to scare you, Emelynn. Maybe we haven't gotten off to a good start, but we need you to understand the situation we're in. Your actions have serious repercussions on all of us."

Emelynn finally let her arms drop. "I think I need to sit," she said, and we moved to the sofas, a far less confrontational setting.

"Forgive my naïveté," Emelynn said, "but exactly who would want to steal this flying thing and why on earth would they want it?"

Alex looked over to me wide-eyed before answering. "Is it so hard to see the allure? The thrill, the power, to say nothing of the freedom?" He struggled for words.

Eden took over. "Secrecy is critical. Fliers are taught from an early age to be discreet about their gift, so it's unusual for an outsider to learn about us, let alone learn the particulars of how to steal the gift. But it happens."

I jumped in to reinforce what Alex had started. "Naturally, the Tribunal is a fairly effective deterrent; no one wants to be in their crosshairs." I then fed her the same line I'd fed the covey about the military and organized crime having us in their sights. "These aren't people the Tribunal Novem can just eliminate and be done with. They are powerful organizations that would love nothing more than to turn us into guinea pigs—see what we can do, and then try to bottle it."

"Oh, come on," Emelynn said, and I wondered if perhaps I'd gone too far, but then her expression softened.

Eden saw the opening and took it. "The gift isn't all doom and gloom, Emelynn. There's a reason it's referred to as a gift. Jackson asked us here to help explain our predicament, but we can also show you the upside to all this."

Eden looked from Alex to me. "I know it's daylight, but I think we should risk a demonstration. Emelynn needs to see what's at stake. We'll be careful." The dangerous daylight flight would be worth it if we got through to Emelynn. We nodded our agreement.

"Come on," Eden said. "We'll show you."

Once on the observation deck, Alex and I scanned the perimeter for prying eyes. Satisfied, Alex gave his wife the go-ahead, and she toed out of her shoes and soared into the air. I'd been impressed with Eden's agility in the paintball games, but this was far more expressive. I had to tear my gaze off her to catch Emelynn's reaction. Her mouth was open. Now we were getting somewhere.

Alex understood the need to be quick and took off the moment Eden landed, providing Emelynn with a good demonstration of power flying. When he landed, he pulled Eden into a passionate embrace. I turned to Emelynn.

A smile stretched across her face. "That was impressive," she said.

"There's a good possibility you'll be able to do this too," I said. "We don't know for sure, of course. Your development hasn't exactly been typical, but we can try. What do you say?" If she had any lingering doubts, I was certain they'd be extinguished once she experienced it herself.

"What do I say?" Emelynn looked at me as though I'd sprouted a second head. "I can't fly. I can't even lift off with fifty feet of rope and weights to launch. I think you're overestimating my skills a wee bit."

"I can help," I said. "Do you want to try?"

"How?" she asked. Skepticism clouded her face.

"If you let me . . . I can jump-start the process." I waited for her to figure it out, but she didn't. "I've done it before, Emelynn. How do you think I got you here?"

She frowned, but quickly rallied. "Okay, how do we do this?"

I held out my arm. "Come over here." She stepped forward, tentative, but game. "Turn around." I felt her hesitate. "You need to trust me. I'm going to put my arms around you and when I lift off, you'll lift with me. You don't need to do a thing. Are you ready?"

She took a deep breath. "All right," she said, and turned around, trusting me for the first time. Her hair smelled sweet. I smoothed the soft curls away from where they tickled my neck. She trembled when I folded my arms around her. Alex gave me the nod and I leapt free from gravity, rising above Eden and Alex, who remained vigilant.

"How are you doing?" I asked.

"G-Good. My gravity has gone."

"Amazing isn't it? If I let go of you now you would stay airborne. If you weren't a Flier, you'd drop straight down. But don't worry, I won't let go. Do you want to circle the ship?"

"Yes!" she said. I took it slow, knowing how brave she was being. She faltered once, and I descended a little knowing that height took practice to get used to. When we finished the circuit, I landed and held on until she was steady.

"That was incredible," she said. Eden and Alex beamed at her.

That was exactly what I'd been hoping for. Now all we had to do was make certain she realized that the dangers we'd mentioned earlier applied to her as well. "Would you like to learn to do that on your own?" I asked.

"Yes. Do you think I can?"

"I don't know, but I think we should try," I said. "The safest place for us to do that is right here, but not until after dark. There's less chance of someone seeing us then."

"We have to be so careful," Eden added. "We only fly in daylight when we have no other choice. Alex and I will help if you like. We aren't leaving until after dark anyway."

Emelynn agreed and we headed below, relieved to be done with the risky demonstration. She immediately started in on Alex and Eden with the twenty-questions routine. I poured a Coke and went to my computer. There was nothing yet from Josh, but I had a few of my own resources, including three popular secure message boards. I began searching for a thread with the name Jolene. All the while, I kept an ear to the conversation.

Emelynn addressed Eden and Alex's curiosity and repeated what she'd told me about Jolene. I was happy to hear her versions of events matched up, which meant she was either telling the truth or a very good liar.

Eden cautioned Emelynn about behaviour that would risk our exposure. I glanced over to check Emelynn's reaction. Her earlier exuberance had evaporated. With Eden's prompting, Emelynn divulged more of her past. It must have been terrifying for her to find herself inexplicably in the air, unable to control herself. And I'd been right about the dive weights. They were her rudimentary attempt to stay grounded.

"You must have a fairy godmother," Eden said. "I can't believe you've made it this long without mortal damage. And what if someone had found out about you? You'd have disappeared like the others."

"The others?" Emelynn asked.

"Yes, eighteen others—three from one family in San Diego," Eden said, and I was glad to hear the covey had paid attention.

I did one final search and then closed the computer. My gaze landed on Emelynn, who'd crossed her arms over her stomach.

"About two years ago—" Eden started.

I cut her off, sensing a retelling of the David Ashton nightmare. "How about we spare Emelynn the worst-case scenario?" I looked pointedly at Eden, who'd missed Emelynn's body language. I returned to the sofa. "I think she knows how important secrecy is to us."

Alex patted his wife's knee and said to me, "Sorry, man."

Emelynn changed our focus. "How did you two meet?" she asked Eden and Alex, and the conversation took a lighter direction.

Emelynn had an innocence about her I found endearing. Her life had been dangerously altered by a complete stranger, and yet she wasn't bitter. Even my treatment of her hadn't dampened her curiosity. Her face grew animated as she listened to Eden and Alex talk about their early days together in Seattle. She didn't even know them, and yet she looked happy for them. When the conversation let up, Eden volunteered to make lunch. I showed her around the galley and pulled out some cold cuts. I looked up to find Alex playing a game on his phone and Emelynn giving the bookcase the once-over. A moment of alarm hit as she tipped out one of Sandra's books. Damn! Some of those books had personal inscriptions to Sandra. I didn't need the covey learning of her connection to me at this late date. Emelynn pushed it back into place, and I breathed a sigh of relief.

I checked one more time for a response from Josh, and finding none, helped Eden with the heavy tray, and offered the sandwiches around.

"I'm not having any luck finding a Flier by the name of Jolene," I said. "It's a fairly unique name, which made me think it would be easy to find. I've put out some feelers so maybe something will come in later."

"You have a directory of Fliers?" Emelynn asked.

If only it were that easy. "Something like that." I took a sandwich and sat back.

Emelynn asked, "What's that thing you do with your eyes, Jackson? What you did to me on the beach last night?"

I nearly killed you that's what, I thought with remorse. "Most Fliers can do that to some extent, Emelynn, not just me." Alex raised an eyebrow, which I ignored. "You, however, being a Flier, shouldn't have been as susceptible as you were."

"So, what is it?" she asked, pressing on.

"It's complicated." How could I explain it? "Basically, it's a manipulation of both the adrenal glands and the nervous system. We use either our eyes or touch, or a combination of the two. What I did was cause an overload in your system. It results in a temporary loss of consciousness—no permanent damage. It's a useful skill."

"Useful skill?" She asked the question as if it left a bad taste in her mouth.

"Yes. Having the ability to immobilize someone is like having a built-in stun gun. It gives me an advantage."

"Good to know." Her derisive tone was unmistakable, but she had no idea how important an advantage was in our world, or how dangerous our world could be.

She climbed back on the twenty-questions treadmill to ask about the covey. I didn't begrudge her questions—hell, I'd have a lengthy list of them if I were in her position. I enlightened her on the concept of covey.

"Are you all members of the local covey?" she asked.

"Eden and Alex are, but I'm just visiting."

"Speaking of that," Alex interjected, "any word on Sandra?"

Damn. I'd hoped to avoid that topic. Keeping up James's ruse only twisted the knife.

"Is she the one you mentioned earlier who's gone missing?" Emelynn asked.

Terrific. I nodded impatiently and gave them my canned answer. "Not since last week. She's still headed north. Her cellphone's off. There's no new activity on her credit cards."

I thought that would satisfy them, but not Emelynn. "How do you know that Sandra is heading north?" she asked.

My sandwich lost its appeal. "I'm not comfortable talking about Sandra."

"Can't the police help?" Emelynn asked.

I pushed my fingers into my scalp. "Not so far, and please, Emelynn, I don't want to discuss Sandra."

"What about this *Tribunal* you mentioned. Can't they help?" Eden and Alex swung their heads in her direction.

"No!" I said, and jumped up. "They can't help." Christ! The woman never gave up.

"O . . . kay," Emelynn said, but I could see she wasn't done, and I didn't need her digging further into the situation surrounding Sandra.

"Emelynn," I said, raising my hand to silence her. "I know you are interested and curious, but you're going to have to believe me when I say that the less you know, the better. Let's just work on getting your flying skills up to par so you can take care of yourself."

Thankfully, Eden agreed. "He's right, Emelynn. Forget about Sandra."

We finished our meal in silence. It was becoming clear to me that I needed to talk in private with Eden and Alex. I'd promised Avery that I'd find out what Emelynn was up to. If they agreed with my assessment that she wasn't doing anything nefarious, then my job was done. We'd get her airborne tonight, and then I'd be free to go. How hard could it be? Fliers as young as thirteen could do it.

"Emelynn," I said, "why don't you go to your cabin and get some rest. It's going to be a long night."

She left without an argument, but Eden wasn't as obliging.

"Why'd you do that? She needs to trust us," Eden whispered. "You think she doesn't know we're talking about her now?"

"It was unavoidable. We do need to talk about her. I want to know if we're on the same track here."

"What track?" Alex asked.

"Is she telling us the truth?"

"No question," Eden said. "I don't think she could have fabricated those stories."

"I agree," Alex said.

"Okay, so we're in agreement. We get her up in the air, show her the ropes and then turn her over to Avery."

"'Turn her over?'" Eden repeated with a laugh. "She's not a criminal."

"And let's not get ahead of ourselves," Alex added. "We don't even know if she can fly."

That would be a terrible blow to any Flier. My thoughts turned to Avery. Perhaps he wasn't the only one.

Chapter Eighteen

W e were once again discussing Emelynn when she reappeared a few hours later.

"How are you doing?" I asked as she approached.

"Fine thanks. I slept." She had a soft crease on her cheek.

"Good. It'll be dark enough to start in another thirty minutes or so."

Eden turned in her seat. "We've been trying to figure out how to teach you the basics, and we think we've come up with a plan." She relayed the details, which included dealing with the elements, managing velocity and landing safely, but breaking from gravity was pivotal. Emelynn's brow furrowed at Eden's explanation.

I waded in with a different approach. "It's not a physical thing, it's psychological. Forget about your ropes and weights—they aren't remotely connected to the process. Jolene gave you an innate power and it resides deep inside you. You have to find that power and tap into it."

Alex added, "You need to train yourself to mentally throw off your gravity. Once you have it mastered, it takes only a moment of effort."

"I have no idea how to do what you're asking."

"Neither do we," Eden said, which was a big part of what we'd been discussing in Emelynn's absence. "We all learned to fly like we learned to walk so it's second nature to us. Trying to break it down into 'How-to' steps is tricky."

"If we don't get there right away, don't worry—I can always jump-start you like I did before," I said, but I reinforced how important it was for her to learn to do it on her own. Eden followed up with the concept of using a visual cue as a trigger. It was a lot for anyone to absorb.

Eden offered a reassuring smile. "We all had the benefit of years of preparation. No one expects you to master this in one night."

If Eden noticed my glare, she didn't acknowledge it. One night was exactly the time frame I'd had in mind.

Once up on the observation deck, I handed Emelynn one of Sandra's hair elastics to tie her hair back. Lovely as hers was, there was nothing more irritating than the sting of hair in the eyes when airborne.

We stood in a circle and one by one, demonstrated our individual liftoff styles.

Afterwards, Emelynn stared up at us with a frown on her face. "Now I suppose you think it's my turn."

"Come on, give it a shot," Alex said, cheering her on.

She rubbed her temples and adjusted her ponytail then took a deep breath and followed through the motions I'd demonstrated. Unfortunately, her feet remained planted. "So much for Jackson's approach." She shook out her limbs and tried once more, using Eden's method, but that one didn't work either. "Two down," she said, and looked up at Alex with a hopeful smile. She mimicked Alex's liftoff, but again had no luck.

She hung her head and I felt her disappointment. Maybe all her body needed was a taste of flight to get her going. It wasn't much of a bother to jump-start her until she got the hang of it. I drifted down to the deck. "Don't sweat it. It'll come, just give it some time. Meanwhile, let's get you up in the air. It's not like we don't have anything else to teach you."

I walked behind her. She fit perfectly under my chin. What was that fragrance? Oranges? "Ready?" She nodded and I bent my knees and lifted her free from gravity.

"Will you take me around the boat again?" she asked.

"Sure. Hold on." I strengthened my grip on her and, sensing she was more comfortable with the process this time, increased both my speed and height as we circled the boat.

I brought her around to face Eden and Alex. "Now remember," I said, "you're a Flier, so when I release you, you'll stay afloat. Here, hold my hand." I stretched out my right arm and she quickly grabbed my fingers in a death grip. Slowly I released her from my other arm. She wobbled, clutching my hand mercilessly. The sweetest smile bloomed on her face with the realization that she was weightless. It wasn't exactly the fledging I'd hoped for her, but I was happy to bear witness to this once-in-a-lifetime moment.

"We thought we'd start with Flying 101," I said. "You know how to swim, right?"

"Sure."

I tipped my head to Alex, who'd indicated earlier that he wanted to tackle this detail. He demonstrated a breaststroke that sent him gliding, and slowed by moving his hands into the "stop" position.

"A word of caution though," Alex said, returning to us. "Up here, away from gravity, motion is extremely sensitive. It doesn't take much effort to produce big results. Watch and see what I mean." This time he put enough muscle into the breaststroke to push himself into a horizontal position. He sped ahead and then torqued his body and used his momentum to come back to us.

Emelynn still had a firm hold of my hand. "You ready to give it a try?" I asked.

"Just don't let me fall."

"We won't," Eden said, reassuring her. "Alex and I will flank you and Jackson will position himself just ahead of you. We'll be your training wheels."

"Okay," she said, convincing no one.

The first time was bound to be scary, but there was no other way to get through it. "I'm going to release you now," I said, and extracted my hand then stifled a smile. Did we all look that unstable the first time, I wondered?

She found her balance and bravely proclaimed her readiness. We moved into position and I motioned her toward me. Her first attempt barely stirred the air, but it lit up her whole face. "That's a start," I said. "Now increase the effort."

Her second stroke was better and brought her to me. I reached my hands out to her shoulders to slow her down. "That's good, now a little more," I coaxed, backing up again.

She was getting a feel for it, and this time she pitched forward with her stroke and had real momentum behind her. Once again, I pressed my hands to her shoulders to slow her movement. She beamed with confidence, but a casual glance beneath her turned that confidence into fear in a heartbeat.

Immediately I recognized the danger and pulled her into my grip.

"I've got you." I signalled to Alex and Eden to head back to the *Symphony*. "Let's take a break." Emelynn's breathing was short and shallow. We landed on the deck, and she continued to tremble even after I released her.

How could I have forgotten? My own fear of heights had nearly killed me. I should have prepared her better. I didn't want to admit how much her panic had shaken me. If I hadn't grabbed her... "It takes some getting used to," I said. "The height, the movement, all of it."

Stone-faced, she turned away. I grabbed her shoulders and spun her back around. "Panic is not your friend up there. It makes you do crazy things, like pinwheel your arms. Big, rapid movements like that are dangerous."

She cowered under my glare, nodding like a frightened child. Damn. I'd been too harsh. Teaching her to fly could prove harder than I'd thought. I took a calming breath and led her to the sofas. She sat as far from us as she could, and stared up to the stars, distancing herself.

"The height got to her," I said in response to Eden's silent query.

"I'd forgotten how scary the height can be in the beginning," Eden said.

"We can't rush her," Alex said.

"She doesn't have the luxury of time," I said. "She won't be safe until she gets her gift under control."

Alex shook his head. "She's not going to have it figured out in one night, Jackson. No way."

As much as I didn't want to acknowledge it, he was right. There was far too much for her to learn in a couple of hours. Again, I marvelled that she'd managed to survive as long as she had on her own. And after what I'd done to her last night, I owed her. I could spare another day, two at most.

"Let's try again." I turned to Emelynn, who appeared lost in thought. "What do you say, Emelynn? You want to give it another try?"

After another jump-start, we moved back into position and carried on. We'd been at it for a few hours when, at one in the morning, Alex called it a night. I helped Emelynn land and held on to her while she steadied.

"Don't be alarmed," I said, feeling her sag against the force of her returning weight. "Until you get used to it, gravity will play tricks on you. It comes back with more force the longer you've gone without it. You'll be fine in a moment."

She looked embarrassed when she thanked me. We headed below.

"We need to keep working on the basics," Eden said, as I handed out bottled water. "Maybe add in some altitude changes."

"I agree," Alex said.

"Let's do some hovering, too. She's holding pretty steady when Jackson lets her go," Eden remarked.

There was no doubt that Emelynn was making progress, but slower than I'd hoped. Her naïveté had its charm, and that sweet wonder was compelling, but she felt like a complicated assembly required project late on Christmas Eve.

"I hate to bring this up," Emelynn said, drawing our attention, "but I have to go home. I need to check my phone, my email. And if I don't call my mother soon, she's going to worry about me."

Ah, hell. Her naïveté lost its charm real quick. Eden, Alex and I shared a knowing glance. Not only was it obvious to us that she didn't appreciate her own predicament—it was also obvious she didn't yet appreciate the danger her lack of skill posed to all of us.

"Yes, of course," I said, aiming to stem Emelynn's reckless yearnings without alienating her. "But it's too late tonight. We're too far from shore, and we don't have any way to get you off the ship right now."

Eden did her best to reinforce my argument. "Alex and I will be back tomorrow after dark. We'll go then. How's that?"

Emelynn's smile slipped. She shifted her gaze from me to Eden and then Alex.

I tried again, addressing her immediate concerns. "In the morning, we'll get your email set up on board and you can call your mom from my phone." Even to my ear, it sounded desperate. "Tomorrow night, we'll go to your house, you can pack a bag. Then we'll move offshore again so we can continue your training here on the ship, safely out of sight."

Emelynn squared her jaw and crossed her arms, not giving us an inch.

Eden and Alex gathered their things. "Wouldn't it be great if you managed a liftoff?" Eden said, forcing a smile. "You know, give Jackson a break." Her attempt at levity fell on its face.

I walked them to the stairs. "Don't forget about the car," I said, extracting the rental's keys and handing them to Alex. He'd agreed to take care of the car I'd ditched last night at the beach access north of Emelynn's house. I wished them a safe flight home and after they left, I considered my guest. The heads were stocked with toiletries, robes and towels, but we hadn't considered a visitor who arrived without luggage. I excused myself and went below to my stateroom. Sandra's neat array of lingerie stared up from the drawer I'd opened, oblivious to my contempt. I should have tossed the lot when I had the chance. I walked to my own dresser, pulled out a T-shirt and locked the door before heading back up the stairs.

"Something for you to sleep in," I said, handing it to Emelynn. She nodded her thanks.

I secured the exterior doors and led her below. At the bottom of the stairs, I pointed down the hall. "That's my stateroom. Just knock if you need anything." She wore a frown I couldn't interpret. I walked her to her cabin. "You've made a lot of progress today," I said, but my assurance didn't erase her frown. "Sleep well." I turned and walked to my stateroom. The soft close of her door followed.

What is going through Emelynn's head, I wondered as I stripped out of my clothes. Afterwards, I remembered Sandra's books. Shit. I yanked on a pair of pants and snuck back to the salon to pull the inscribed volumes, washing one more reminder of Sandra out of my life.

I dumped the books in the locker back in my stateroom and picked up my tablet, flipping it on to compose an email to Avery to update him on our progress with Emelynn.

I ran the cursor down the list of emails in my inbox and immediately opened the one from Josh with the subject line *Jolene*. It read,

Jolene Reynolds
Watercolour artist, Sun Meadow Cooperative, SF
Disappeared from SF/CA area
Known contact in Vanc area
Renowned for speed and undocumented special skills

The dates lined up with Emelynn's gifting. Looked like Emelynn was telling the truth, but who was Jolene Reynolds? And Josh needed to do better than *undocumented special skills*. I fired an email back to him.

I opened the one other email I needed to deal with: ATM footage of my ever-faithful wife, this time cavorting with Cole in Coos Bay. They'd been on a steady course north for more than three weeks now. The date stamp was eleven fifteen at night, yet Sandra kept her sunglasses in place. She wore a man's jacket. Cole's, I suspected, as he had an arm around her. She hadn't smiled this time. Maybe they'd had a lover's quarrel. Had she become disillusioned with him?

What I wouldn't give to see her come crawling back to me. Not that I'd forgive her, but rubbing her return in Cole's face would be delicious.

I shook myself free of the ridiculous notion. Sandra had far too much pride to come back to me. The closest I would ever come to getting some satisfaction would be ensuring Cole lost everything. A decade or two in prison ought to do it, but I knew the Tribunal wouldn't suffer a Flier imprisoned. No, I'd have to be more clever than that. Like my father, I'd bide my time for the perfect opportunity. I sent the file to James.

As far as I knew, there hadn't been a physical confrontation between my father and Richard. I wished I'd had the chance to ask Dad how he'd found the restraint, because I couldn't deny that I'd get immense pleasure from finding my beloved brother and beating the living shit out of him.

It struck me, as I turned off the tablet and set it aside, that I wasn't making much headway on being a better man than my father, at least as far as my personal life was concerned. Of course, it didn't help that my personal life was a sad echo of his.

My thoughts turned to Emelynn asleep in the aft cabin. Thankfully, my ill-conceived jolts hadn't done any permanent damage. A healthy glow had returned to her skin. And those eyes, man, they were a mesmerizing shade of green. A smile crossed my lips. Having Emelynn aboard put a kink in my plans, but there was one major benefit: she was a lovely kink.

Chapter Nineteen

Sunlight streaked across my bed. I took a quick shower and made it to the galley ahead of Emelynn. The email access I'd offered her needed to be set up, though I'd have to route her outgoing emails to Delaney's server until I could review them. The phone call I'd promised her, however, concerned me. She hadn't exactly convinced me that she understood her predicament, and a phone call could prove disastrous.

I brewed a pot of coffee and checked my emails. Finding nothing from Josh, I called him. He was confident he'd located Jolene's family but awaited confirmation. The Reynolds family lived on a ranch in California, north of San Francisco, and dripped old money. Their ancestry traced back to Scotland in the sixteenth century.

"Any idea what Jolene's 'undocumented special skills' might be?" I asked.

"I'm not having much luck on that front. The Reynolds family is a mystery, though I did find family roots in New York in the nineteenth century. And get this—I came across an 1860s reference to a ghost named Reynolds in Cortland County."

"Did you say ghost?" First Cole's Ghost and now this? *Soc au' lait*!

"I did. You can look it up. He was poisoned. Might be an ancestor."

"Are you suggesting Jolene Reynolds is a Ghost? A Flier Ghost?"

He snorted. "Nah, those are old wives' tales. I threw that in for fun. I'd like to think I'm not that out of touch."

"You had me worried there, Josh."

"Jolene Reynolds's family is attached to the San Fran covey. I know people there. If I can't find anything on my own, I'll make some discreet enquiries. If you're in a hurry though, I can contact her family directly. She's still missing. They'd probably talk."

"I'm not ready to open that door. At least not yet. But get me everything you can on the family. And I wonder if you could do something else for me?"

After some good-natured teasing, he agreed to send me any Flier-related ghost fables he stumbled across in his research. The legends had to originate somewhere, and a ghosting angle with a potential connection to Jolene, and therefore, Emelynn, intrigued me.

I'd begun setting up Emelynn's email access when she turned up. She looked better than she had yesterday—rested and bright. "Good morning," I said. "How'd you sleep?"

"Fine, thank you."

"Coffee's ready."

She filled a mug and took a seat in the salon. "What are you working on?" she asked.

I wasn't about to share that I was routing her outgoing email through the Delaney server, so chose something innocuous. "Seeing if there's any news." I immediately regretted my choice.

"Sandra news?" she asked. "Jolene news?"

I ignored her first question, and there was nothing to be gained in speculating on the second. "My San Francisco contacts may have a lead on Jolene's identity, but nothing solid yet." I'd tell her when I knew more.

"Are you hungry?" I asked, changing the subject.

"Sure. I could eat."

I double-checked the computer's security settings and signed off.

Over breakfast, she peppered me with questions about the *Symphony*. Afterwards, I offered her a tour, which initiated another barrage of questions. Emelynn's curiosity seemed genuine, and it felt as though we were building a tentative trust.

Back in the galley, I cleared our dishes and worked through how I would manage the phone call I'd promised her. I wasn't worried about the phone, it was untraceable, but she could still cause trouble if she raised an alarm. If she chose that path, I would have to incapacitate her. There was no other option. Then she really would become Avery's problem.

I felt her watching me as I wiped the counter. "I know we got off to a rocky start," I said, "but I hope you now understand why I brought you here. I also hope you know that you're safe here and we're not going to hurt you." I looked up to make sure she paid attention. "It's important, Emelynn. You need to learn how to fly and you need to learn quickly. The safest place for you to do that is right here." She frowned, which made it difficult to pick up whether she agreed with me or not.

"Do you trust me?" I asked.

She tilted her head, which did nothing to boost my confidence. "I'd like to, but if you don't mind, I think I'll hold off on that until I know you better. In the meantime, I'm willing to give you the benefit of the doubt."

Really? *She* was willing to give *me* the benefit of the doubt?

She looked away and a thoughtful frown pinched her face. When she turned back to me, her frown disappeared behind a confident smile. "You're worried about the phone call to my mother. The one you promised me last night. You're afraid I'll say something."

Damn right, I was. "I won't break my promise," I said. "You can call her. But I want you to make the call right here."

She put her hands on her hips. "Now who's the one with trust issues?" she said, and when she laughed, the tension in the air dissipated. Well now . . . chalk one up for Emelynn. The little troublemaker was enjoying this!

"Where's the phone?" she asked, holding out her palm.

There was too much at stake to let her think she'd softened me up. I maintained a serious demeanour. She reached for the phone the moment I produced it. I released it with a stern reminder. "You said you'd give me the benefit of the doubt. I'm counting on you to keep your word."

I folded my arms. She ignored me, turned her back and walked away. Cheeky! I twisted loose from gravity and shadowed her. She'd reached her mother's voice mail. With relief, I heard her leave a harmless message. I touched down directly behind her and took great pleasure in her yelp of surprise when she turned around.

"Jesus! You could have warned me."

"And spoil my fun?" I extended my hand for the phone. "Don't take it personally. I don't trust anyone—learned that the hard way." As soon as I said it, I knew I'd foolishly opened up a new line of enquiry. "Let's get underway," I said, hoping to staunch any curiosity I'd stirred.

It mostly worked, but then she dogged me as I went about my start-up routine, asking way too many questions. The last thing I needed was her thinking she could operate this ship on her own. "Why don't you put those dishes away?" I said.

She turned back to the galley without argument, and when I'd finished, she returned with the last of the coffee. We headed upstairs and I got the *Symphony* underway. Emelynn wandered aft and watched our wake. Her hair turned bronze in the sunlight. I'd never seen anything like it. She settled with her back to me, and I set a southeasterly course to the shallows near Sunset Park.

Ninety minutes later, I set anchor again, and Emelynn joined me below.

"Are we ready to go?" she asked.

"A few more hours," I said, wondering if she'd really forgotten. "We need to wait until dark." I checked the time and groaned. We had eight hours to kill and she was digging in for an interrogation. No matter how many one-word answers I supplied, she never lost interest. Eventually she wore me down, and I told her about New Orleans and losing Dad. We at least had that in common.

"He left me this ship," I said. "Dad really loved her. We had some great times here and now I've made her my home."

"Do you have sisters or brothers?"

"No!" It came out harsher than I'd intended, but she had no idea how raw a nerve she'd hit. I walked to the laptop and turned it on. "Let's get your email access functioning." When the guest user account popped up, I offered her my chair. "I'll leave you to it," I said, and escaped to the privacy of my stateroom.

I locked my door, pulled up the Delaney server on my tablet and signed in. Her first email arrived with a ding. She'd replied to Molly Connolly. It looked like that was the name of the bookstore clerk she'd gone to dinner with. Emelynn's reply held no threat so I sent it on. I lay on the bed and waited for the next one. It was addressed to her mother, and I was relieved to read her reassuring reply. Even if she didn't trust me, she was sticking to her bargain and giving me the benefit of the doubt.

I opened the security program and called up the video feed from the salon. Emelynn was practicing her liftoff. She didn't succeed, though her motivation to try was encouraging; she had a long way to go, and not a lot of time.

Josh hadn't reported in yet, and there was no word from James. Other than a few brief messages, James had gone quiet. I hadn't seen him since the night we made our deal. A part of me was curious to know if he'd made any progress, but not curious enough to call him. I hadn't changed my mind about extending my stay in Vancouver, and he'd only try to convince me otherwise.

With my return to New Orleans imminent, I'd been easing back into work mode. Ted Worley had sent me a construction contract to review, and I kept the security feed on the screen while I read it through. Emelynn moved to the bookcase and tipped out a number of volumes before returning to the sofa, where she paged through a magazine.

She couldn't have been more different from Sandra. Emelynn's edges were frayed, her hair, her clothes, her questions, whereas Sandra was polished. Emelynn was taller, younger. Braver. That Emelynn had survived her gifting was proof. She was a fighter. Sandra had simply walked away.

I managed to catch a few z's, and when I woke, I changed into warmer clothes and headed back up. Another hour or so and it would be dark enough to escort Emelynn home. I planned to push her hard tonight. None of us could slack off, especially not her.

Alex and Eden arrived a short time later. They were barely in the door when Emelynn started bubbling about going home.

I stomped all over her enthusiasm. This was not a night on the town. "Let's get this over with. I'll escort Emelynn to shore. Eden will come with us. Alex will stay here. You pack enough clothes for a few more days. We can do laundry here." She didn't seem the least bit discouraged by my directives. "We'll get you in and back out quickly, and then we'll head offshore away from prying eyes."

"Let's go then," she said, her effervescence intact.

I looked to Eden, who shrugged. I shook my head and we headed up top.

"You ready?" I asked, holding out my arms to Emelynn. Moments later, we were on our way. I soon regretted rushing her out the door—she hadn't tied her hair back. The blasted curls were everywhere.

Anxious to get this over with, I flew hard and fast. Eden stayed close. We approached from the safety of the deserted park and landed on the rocks in front of her place. "Brace yourself," I said, before I let her go. When Emelynn steadied, the three of us mounted the steps.

"You could have at least locked it when you snatched me," Emelynn said as she slid open the patio door.

She had no idea how trivial locks were in comparison to how close she'd come to dying that night. Still, I could make sure no one was inside. I pushed ahead of her. "Let me check it out."

The front room and her bedroom both had patio doors to the deck that ran the width of the house. A breakfast bar separated the front room from the galley kitchen, and down the hall, I found a tiny bathroom and two other small bedrooms, one of which served as an office.

I checked each room and headed out the heavy oak front door, the very one I'd been watching from my car only days ago. The garage was locked. I stepped out to the street and surveyed the few parked cars hidden by the wild berm along the road.

When I got back to the house, I encountered Emelynn dragging an oversized suitcase toward her bedroom. "You can't take that," I said. "It's almost as big as Eden and she'll have to fly with it."

"You fly carrying me," she quipped.

"You shed gravity. That won't."

Eden agreed. "I don't think I could do it, Emelynn. You'll have to pare down."

I left Eden with a "hurry-up" nod and went to the front room. The *Symphony's* lights twinkled in the distance. Ten minutes later they joined me, Emelynn carrying a much more suitably sized knapsack.

"Your hair," I said, looking pointedly at the offending curls.

"Sit down, relax," she said, scurrying off to find an elastic band.

"We can't stay." Eden joined me at the patio doors, and when Emelynn returned, Eden took Emelynn's bag and headed outside. I left Emelynn to lock the door and followed Eden.

When I arrived at the foot of the stairs, I heard a shriek from above. It took me a moment to realize it had come from Emelynn. Where was she? She screamed again and I caught sight of her spiriting skyward. Eden darted past me and I leapt up behind her. Eden reached her first, grabbed hold of her foot and yanked hard, tossing Emelynn back against my chest. I wrapped my arm around Emelynn's waist and landed us on the beach. What the hell had just happened?

"I'm sorry," Emelynn said. "That was embarrassing—"

Eden cut her off. "Is that what was happening to you before, in Toronto?" she asked, crossing her arms.

Emelynn tugged her jacket back into place. "Yes, but having weights in my pockets or a heavy book bag over my shoulder kept it in check."

"Weights wouldn't have stopped that," Eden said, raising her voice. "What were you thinking!"

"Shh," I whispered, afraid their voices would wake the neighbours.

"Are you kidding me?" Emelynn replied, matching Eden's angry tone. "You think I like doing that? It scares the crap out of me!"

I raised my hands to put a stop to their loud exchange.

"I'm sorry," Eden said, and backed away. "I know it's not your fault. You scared me. That's all."

Emelynn's expression softened. "I'm sorry for shouting." She turned her head to include me in her apology and repeated, "I'm sorry."

Obviously she was capable of lifting off—she just didn't know how to summon it. "We need to get out of here," I said. "Let's go."

When we landed back on the *Symphony*, Alex asked if we'd had any trouble. I rolled my eyes. "Not the kind you'd expect," I said. "You?" Alex shook his head.

"Why don't you go unpack your things, Emelynn." I motioned Eden to give her the knapsack. "We won't go too far tonight, but we do need to move farther away from your neighbours."

I caught a glint of anger in her eyes as she turned and then hurried down the stairs.

"You won't believe what happened," Eden said, and before she could elaborate within earshot of Emelynn, I herded them to the bow and then headed to the helm to steer the *Symphony* away from shore. Eden paced, dispelling her anxiety as she proceeded to tell Alex about Emelynn's mad dash. When Emelynn's cottage was but a speck on the horizon, I set anchor and suggested we return to the salon.

"You got anything to eat?" Alex asked.

"Check the freezer," I said.

Eden sidled up to me at the wheel. "Emelynn's a risk to herself and to us. She panicked up there tonight."

"I know."

"Can't say as I blame her," Eden said. "Honestly? I don't know how she's survived this long."

Soon after, Alex joined the discussion, and we tossed around some ideas to address Emelynn's situation.

Alex had chosen a pizza, and it was already out of the oven by the time Emelynn emerged. She spoke quietly with Alex and sat on the sofa with him and Eden. I approached them, helping myself to a slice from the pan on the table. It was later than I thought, and my stomach rumbled. I sank my teeth into the soft cheese and felt the noisy crunch of the crust.

Eden looked distant, completely wrapped up in her thoughts. Alex had his feet up, already finished his meal. I took another bite and shifted my focus to Emelynn.

"What?" she said, looking from Eden to Alex and then me.

Eden spoke. "We were talking about what happened to you earlier tonight. The risk of exposing us is only part of it. You could have killed yourself."

"I'm sorry," Emelynn said.

"You don't need to apologize," Alex said. "We just don't know how to help you deal with it."

I grabbed a napkin and wiped my fingers. "I think the unscripted flights will come to an end when you learn how to fly properly."

"The sooner that happens, the better," Emelynn said.

I nodded my agreement. "Given your impromptu side trip tonight," I said, "we think the most important thing for you to learn next is how to land."

Alex explained our strategy while Eden cleaned up, and then we headed up to the observation deck.

After I jump-started Emelynn, we hovered at the height of the canopy while Alex talked her through a landing. My thoughts drifted to tomorrow, the end of May. Was there any hope at all that Emelynn would be ready? I didn't want to hang around, but abandoning her didn't feel right either.

Alex's voice broke through my thoughts. "Don't forget, without gravity, every movement you make will cause an exaggerated reaction. All you need to do is raise your arms in a small sweeping motion. Jackson, you're on. Show her how it's done."

"Sure," I said, and rotated my arms in small upward circles until I gently touched down on the deck.

"Or," Alex said, "you can drop your upper body by bending at the knees. Eden, will you do the honours?"

Eden obliged and raised her arms above her head as she bent her knees to drift downward.

"You ready to try?" Alex asked Emelynn.

"Here goes," she said, as if she had nothing to lose, and she pulled off a beautiful landing on her first try.

Eden sagged with relief, mimicking my own feelings. "You did it," she said, smiling softly.

Emelynn beamed and it was infectious. "Let's do it again."

I lost track of the number of times I jump-started her. We were becoming comfortable in our routine. Each time she approached me she'd turn a dainty pirouette, lift her arms, and resettle them over mine. She probably didn't even know she sighed softly every time I lifted her.

She landed consistently, time and again, and by two in the morning, we felt confident she'd mastered it. Eden and Alex said goodbye and Emelynn and I headed down to the galley. I handed her a bottle of water from the fridge and escorted her to her cabin.

"You're doing great." I brushed the hair from her shoulder and let my hand linger there. Had she'd realized yet that she'd freed herself from dependence on me, at least for her landings? Tomorrow this time, she'd probably figure out her liftoff and be completely free of me. I'm not sure I liked losing an excuse to hold a woman in my arms.

"Do you have everything you need in there?" I asked.

"Yes, I'm good."

I bade her good night and returned to my stateroom.

Tomorrow was the last day of May. My agreement with James was over. I'd kept up my end of our bargain and could walk away, guilt free. The only lingering doubt came from the part of me that wondered if James's intuition might be right. But I couldn't dwell on it, and for James's sake, I hoped Sandra reconnected with her family soon.

I'd been putting off calling him fearing the guilt he'd no doubt try to lay on me again, but I couldn't put it off any longer. I dialled his number.

"Jackson," he said, answering on the first ring.

"How are you doing, James?"

"Holding it together. No new ATM footage?"

"Not since Coos Bay, night before last."

"You leaving tomorrow?"

"I've got some loose ends to deal with, but soon. Anything new on the search?"

"You've probably noticed Cole's not dicking around anymore. Now that he's moving straight north, I've been able to deploy the surveillance people more effectively. We're only missing him by hours now. Another week . . . ten days, and we'll have him."

"Ten days?"

"At the most. You thinking of changing your mind?"

"I'm tempted. Might be worth it just to get my hands on the bastard."

"Yeah, get in line."

"You know, Alex mentioned some law enforcement types he's pretty tight with down in Seattle. Think they could help?"

"Bloody right they could."

"Ten days? You're not nickel-and-diming me into another month, are you?"

"We're almost there, Jackson. Why don't you stick around and see this through."

Damn! Ten days? Could he have the happy couple in his net so soon? "I'm not going anywhere for a day or two. Let me think about it."

"If you pull out, I'd appreciate your keeping that account open for a few more weeks. I'll email you the funds to cover it."

"All right. I can do that. I'll be in touch."

I disconnected and crawled into bed. Ten days was tempting. I could almost feel Cole's greasy little neck in my hands. Perhaps I didn't need to rush Emelynn off the *Symphony* after all.

CHAPTER TWENTY

The possibility of finding Cole and Sandra haunted my sleep. At six in the morning, tired, but unable to turn off those thoughts, I climbed out of bed and weighed anchor to move the *Symphony* farther from shore.

We'd only travelled a few miles when Emelynn arrived on the observation deck with a quirky smile on her face.

"I made breakfast," she said, and handed me a banana.

Her enthusiasm felt like the perfect antidote to my sombre mood. In fact, a few more days of her company might be the answer to keeping tedium away while James honed in on Cole and Sandra. Despite the unending stream of questions, she was easy to look at. And lord knows she needed more time in the air. Yes, I'd enjoy that, I thought with a smile, knowing I'd made the decision.

After I cut the engines, we headed back to the salon. I left her to her emails and crashed on the sofa.

When I woke, I found Emelynn fast asleep on the sofa across from me. She lay on her back with both arms stretched over her head, leaving her midriff bare and the sofa blanket trailing on the floor. Her hair overflowed the sofa, tumbling over the edge, and sleep lent her face a guileless innocence. I sat up and eased my feet to the table. Emelynn's lips parted. I couldn't look away. She woke with a soft inhale and stretched sleepily. My groin stirred. Jesus, it had been months since a woman had that effect on me.

She rolled over and met my gaze. "I don't think I've thanked you yet," she said, and sat up.

"For what?"

"For last night. If you and Eden hadn't been there, who knows where I'd have ended up."

"It's not your fault."

"I know that, but I'm still sorry you're saddled with me."

Saddled? Now there was a thought. I shook it from my mind. "You're one of us, Emelynn. We stick together. I'd like to think you'd do the same for me if I needed your help." I decided to leave before my imagination got the best of me. "I'm going to take a shower." A cold shower, I thought, and made my exit.

The moment my door was closed, I powered up my tablet and sent James an email. "I'm in." I took a shower and then reviewed Emelynn's email to her mother before sending it on. Afterwards, I sent Alex an email asking him about his Flier contacts in Seattle.

When I returned up top, I found Emelynn making something to eat. I took it as a sign that she felt more comfortable on board.

"Good timing," she said, and offered me a plate.

I took a bite of the sandwich and mumbled my thanks as I wound my way to the sofa. I turned on the TV and found CNN. Before I finished eating, my phone buzzed. It was James. He was pleased I'd agreed to stay on, and he'd emailed me the funds to cover Sandra's withdrawals. Moments later, Alex sent me an email too lengthy to review on the phone.

I got up and turned on my laptop. Emelynn moved to the bookcase and tipped out a book. "What do you do for work?" she asked, resuming her inquisition.

I smiled to myself. She was on a roll again, but it wasn't an unreasonable question. "I took over my dad's business when he passed away."

"What kind of business?"

"Property development," I said.

"What's your role?"

"Making deals, mostly."

"You enjoy it?"

Funny, I'd not really given much thought to whether I enjoyed it or not. It was just what I did, what Dad did, all I knew, really. "Yeah, I guess. It keeps the *Symphony* afloat anyway."

Before she could dig further, I flipped the discussion to her. "You don't talk much about your mother. Tell me about her."

"Laura? We're not very close. She changed after my father died.

Became aloof, worked too much. And this gift didn't help. The secret felt like a wall between me and everyone else. I turned into that kid no one wanted to be seen with. Never could shake it, right through university. You get used to it though. I'm pretty good at being alone, now. And I survived." She actually smiled. "Lots of people have worse childhoods than mine."

Sounded like a lonely existence, but she was still young. And she was a looker. I doubted she'd be alone for long.

Emelynn settled in to read, and I turned my attention to Alex's email. He'd agreed to approach his buddies in Seattle to see if they'd be interested in helping out. My reply included James's contact information and the latest update on Sandra's whereabouts, along with a request to keep our discussions private.

When darkness set in, Alex and Eden arrived, and we headed for the observation deck to continue Emelynn's training. Now that I'd decided to stay a few extra days, there was no need to rush her. And as she hadn't yet cottoned on to the liftoff, I once again offered my assistance. The thin fabric of her faded jersey felt as soft as it looked.

At the first break, Alex informed us he'd have to leave early to accommodate an early morning work commitment.

"Of course," I said. "You've got to take care of business. We'll be okay on our own. She only needs one spotter anyway."

After he and Eden left, I turned to Emelynn. "You ready to put in some more time?"

"I know I need the practice," she said, "but I'm pooped."

I checked the time. We'd been out less than two hours. "You said it yourself—you need the practice," I said, chiding her. "Come on." I stood and offered my hand.

After another jump-start, she demonstrated her new skills. I felt her hesitation each time she tried some new combination and egged her on. And then the unthinkable happened: she lost her balance and tumbled out of control. I'd done the exact same thing as a kid. If I'd been closer, I could have stopped her before she began to flail, but her panic was full-blown by the time I reached her. My father wouldn't have let that happen.

I brought her back to the *Symphony* and set her down gently, dismissing her apology with one of my own. "No, that one's on me," I said. "You told me you were tired but I pushed you anyway. Don't beat yourself up. I should have been closer. Let's call it a night."

She didn't argue. Her shoulders slumped and I knew it was because her confidence had just taken a hit. Perhaps we both needed a good night's sleep. I escorted her to her cabin and tried to help her put it into perspective.

"We've all made those mistakes, Emelynn. Don't make more of it than it is. You did great tonight. You're learning quickly."

"Thanks. It doesn't feel that way right now though."

"You've made a lot of progress in three days. Just think how far along you'll be in a week." My words didn't seem to brighten her. "Good night, sleep well," I said, and turned down the hallway.

It was noon when I awoke to a grey, foggy day. Thoughts of Emelynn flitted through my mind. Would last night's panic attack set her back, I wondered? I made a call to Alex, who didn't answer, and then to Eden. Turns out Eden had been giving Emelynn's affinity for panic a lot of thought.

I put on the coffee and stared into the fridge looking for breakfast inspiration. With not much choice, I chopped the last of the fruit into a bowl and made a note to restock sometime soon.

A check of my inbox told me Ted Worley had made inroads in securing a parcel of land Delaney had on its acquisitions list. I provided my input and closed the computer shortly after Emelynn arrived.

She made hot cereal to accompany the fruit, and I waited until after we'd finished eating to raise the issue of the previous night.

"I spoke with Eden this morning," I said.

She frowned. "Oh? Did you tell her about my panic attack?"

"Eden reminded me we've seen that before. Remember? Back at your place, the night we went to get your stuff? We're thinking we need to address it. You know, see if we can help you deal with these panic attacks or, better yet, stop them from setting in. What do you think?"

She hesitated. "It scares me."

If only I could tell her how completely I understood, but revealing my own early fear of heights, and the disastrous results, would only add to her problem.

"Yeah, I know," I said. "But you've got to get a handle on this. Panic is absolutely deadly—you've already landed in the hospital once."

She reluctantly agreed. "You're right. Let's work on it tonight."

I admired her bravery. "All right then. Tonight."

We whiled away the early afternoon. Unwelcome thoughts of Sandra drifted through my mind. I stared out into the fog. We had about a sixty-foot ceiling from what I could tell. "You know," I said, "being socked in like this, we should be safe enough to get in some practice."

Emelynn looked up from the magazine she'd been thumbing through.

"You feel up to it?" I asked.

"I suppose," she said, with zero enthusiasm.

I'd take Emelynn's flagging confidence over thoughts of an unfaithful wife any day of the week. "After you," I said, ushering her ahead of me.

Chapter Twenty-One

Starting with a liftoff attempt was a bad idea. "Never mind," I said, sensing her frustration. It was just as easy to jump-start her. I called her into my arms and inhaled the scent of her freshly washed hair.

"You ready?" I asked. With her nod, I lifted us off and set her loose. "You're making progress, Emelynn, whether you notice or not. See how steady you are now when I release you? Just a few days ago you'd be rocking and rolling when I let you go."

"Yeah, I guess." It was nice to see a small smile on her face.

I set a slow pace and stayed within arm's reach, ready to slow her down or just offer a touch to reassure her I was near. We kept within sight of the *Symphony* and gradually she regained the ground she'd lost. She ran through her repertoire, testing her moves. I took to giving her a thumbs-up or a thumbs-down after each display. Soon, she had her hands on her hips demanding demonstrations of new moves, which she'd then grade with a show of fingers. The fog muffled our laughter.

When we finally headed below, we'd earned the rest.

"I haven't played like that in years," I said. "Sometimes I forget the simple pleasures of this wonderful gift. I guess I can thank you for giving me an excuse to indulge."

"My pleasure," she said with a sigh. "I wish I had the stamina to do that all day long."

My stomach reminded me that breakfast had worn off long ago. "Let's get a bite to eat," I said, making a beeline for the galley. We decided on pasta, and while I set a pot of water on to boil, Emelynn hunted through the fridge for the pesto that I assured her was in there.

With perfect timing, Alex and Eden arrived. Eden looked in the pot. "This looks great. Alex, help me set the table, would you?"

"Good thing you made lots," Alex said, wiggling his eyebrows. "It smells fantastic."

Over dinner, Emelynn shared the highlights of her antics in the fog. I kept her honest by adding the details she'd conveniently left out, like when she'd gotten too close and kicked me in the chest, or when she'd smacked herself in the head on a spin. Laughter filled the salon. It was the first meal I'd enjoyed around the table since Sandra left, and it felt like a new beginning. I resisted the urge to check in with James and see how close we were to ending Sandra's game.

The girls cleaned up, and afterwards, we piled up to the observation deck. Emelynn struggled again, unsuccessful in her liftoff. Frustration etched lines on her forehead, but she let it go after I got her in the air, where she showed off the new moves I'd taught her.

Afterwards, we landed to discuss the real work of the night—how to curb Emelynn's tendency to panic.

"She needs to be desensitized to the stimuli," Eden said. It was the same approach my father had taken with my own fear of heights, and it had worked.

"Or trained to work with it, when it happens," Alex offered.

Eden's face lit up with an idea. "I say we provoke a panic attack then talk her through it."

"It's risky," I said, remembering all too well the terrifying combination of height and panic. But I'd survived it. Emelynn would too. "Good thing there are three of us. She'll be safe enough."

"It's important," Eden said, addressing Emelynn, who didn't look pleased with the direction our discussion had taken.

I reinforced Eden's words. "It'll be the death of you if you don't get a handle on it."

With reluctance, Emelynn stepped out of earshot to let us work out the details, and when we had a plan worked out, she courageously allowed me to jump-start her, and we began the process.

I passed her off to Eden, who took her high above her comfort zone. Alex waited for Eden's signal then grasped Emelynn's ankles and sent her spinning. The three of us moved in close.

Alex called to her. "Spread eagle, Emelynn. Create resistance."

Her arms shot out first, and then her legs. I felt a twinge of pride. As she slowed and regained control, I saw a hopeful expression on her face. She looked around, seeking us out, but then she made the mistake of gazing below. Too late, I saw the panic in her eyes. Damn! She fell hard and fast, feet first, straight down. I dove after her and barely caught hold of a flailing arm just as her feet broke the surface of the water. Too fucking close. She held tight as I whipped us back to the *Symphony* at speed, and landed hard.

"Jesus!" I stormed away with balled fists. "What the hell were you thinking? You don't take on gravity when you're that high. You'll kill yourself." At that speed, from that height, she'd have broken her legs.

"You okay?" Eden asked her as she and Alex landed. Eden wrapped an arm around her and guided her to the sofa. Alex sat on the other side and offered comfort.

Shit. She was crying. Now I felt like an ass. I shook out my fists and approached with an apology. "I should have been better prepared," I said. "I just never imagined you'd use gravity, of all things—didn't even think you could." Most of us had to touch earth to regain gravity. "That's suicidal."

"Well, it's not like it was intentional!" Emelynn shouted, sobbing. "It's automatic. I couldn't stop it."

That was bullshit. I knelt down with my hands on her knees so she couldn't avoid my scrutiny. "It was a panic response: plain and simple. I know it wasn't intentional and it may feel like an automatic reaction, but you *can* stop it. You must. You already know how. You did it just this afternoon. It's in there," I said, tapping her forehead. "In your head."

Her nostrils flared, but I'd made my point. My own fear of heights and the resultant panic attacks had scarred me for years, and Emelynn was heading down that same path.

I stood and paced, talking through the problem. We could spare Emelynn those scars if we could successfully curb her panic. Eden and Alex conferred, and after we dismissed a number of options, we settled on teaching her how to invoke and control her gravity-fed plunge. If she could do that, then the panic might resolve itself. It would certainly be less life-threatening.

We returned to height, and I released her to Eden. Alex and I dropped down lower to act as her safety net if she couldn't stop herself.

Though I couldn't hear them, I watched carefully as Eden coached Emelynn. When Eden let her go, Emelynn fell backwards and then straight down. Absolutely amazing. How the hell did she do that?

Alex and I caught her, slowed her down and then returned her to Eden. "That was interesting," Eden said to Emelynn, when she'd steadied herself. "You take on gravity like it's an old friend."

"Yeah, and isn't that prophetic: the only flying skill that comes naturally to me is falling like a stone." Her wry humour drew our laughter and scattered the tension that stretched between us, but we were a long way from done.

She repeated the exercise. Dozens of times. She'd made good progress by the time we ended the lesson, but I knew from personal experience that panic wasn't something you banished in one night.

By the time we took a break, we'd all had enough. "Can I interest you in a glass of wine?" I asked, turning to Eden.

"That's the best invitation I've had all night." She took Alex's hand, and Emelynn and I followed them below.

I uncorked a bottle of red, and Eden helped me distribute the glasses. "Cheers," Alex said, offering a toast. "I think we reached a milestone today." He addressed Emelynn. "We still have to practice a few things, but you've got the basics under your belt. I think we're ready to let you loose."

Eden could barely contain herself. "We should fly tomorrow night," she said. "No more lessons, just flat-out fly."

Emelynn's face brightened. She probably wasn't as prepared as she should be, but she needed the experience, and I didn't want to dampen her spirits. "I agree," I said, raising my glass. "To tomorrow."

"You're going to love flying, Em. There's nothing quite like it." Alex said it with reverence in his voice. "It's what makes it all worthwhile. You'll see."

Their excitement buoyed our conversation. But soon enough, our glasses were empty and Eden and Alex departed.

Emelynn yawned and took her glass to the sink. "It's been an awfully long day."

I also felt the pull of my bed. "But a productive one," I said, and followed her to the galley.

Emelynn rinsed her glass. "I know I'm making headway," she said. "And you all are being so patient."

"I feel a 'but' coming on," I said, reaching across her to rinse my own glass.

"I just wish I was making as much headway with the liftoffs, that's all."

"I know." I laid my hands on her shoulders and offered my best advice. "Be patient. It'll come in its own time. Trust me." I let my hands linger, knowing as soon as she learned to lift off, I'd forfeit my liberty to touch her.

She offered a small but reassuring smile. "Let's go to bed." I turned her around and nudged her toward the stairs. "You'll be more enthusiastic after you've had your first flight."

She closed her cabin door, and I turned down the hall. Emelynn was being too hard on herself. She'd made remarkable progress, considering where she'd started from. Her affinity for taking on gravity spiked my curiosity. Was it one of Jolene's special skills?

I powered up my tablet and opened an email from Josh. He confirmed that the Reynolds in the San Francisco covey were Jolene's family. The family kept a low profile, but Josh was certain he'd learn more when he heard back from his contact in the covey. He'd also attached a copy of a nineteenth-century document he'd obtained from the National Archives of Scotland. It was a children's fairy tale, a ghost story, the moral of which appeared to be the importance of purity of thought and deed. Fear-based parenting—no better way to screw up your kids.

Interesting. A ghost story from when the family lived in New York, and now one from Scotland, where they originated. Coincidence? Maybe, but I was now more determined than ever to find out more.

James hadn't sent an update, and I'd not found the opportunity for a private discussion with Alex earlier. He'd probably be home by now. I dialled him.

"Hey, Alex. Just wondered if your Seattle contacts came through for us?"

"At five hundred a day plus expenses? They jumped all over it," Alex said. "We've got three of them for sure, maybe four. I'll send you their contact info."

"That's great. Can't thank you enough."

I took a shower and crawled between the sheets. Eight days left, maybe less. Sometime soon, I'd have to make certain James understood that I got first crack at Cole. With that happy thought, I succumbed to my exhaustion.

A loud bang startled me awake. Footfalls slapped against the floor in the hall and smacked up the stairs. It was still dark out. I leapt out of bed, yanked on my pants and raced for the hall.

Emelynn's cabin door swung on its hinges. I glanced inside. She was gone. I reached for the stair rail just as something upstairs thudded against the galley door to the back deck. I took the steps two at a time, but I was too late. The galley door hung open.

I called Emelynn's name as I rounded the aft steps to the observation deck, adrenalin fuelling my charge. She didn't answer. I caught a glimpse of a bare leg as it disappeared from the top step to the observation deck. What the fuck was happening?

I scurried up the steps behind her to the upper deck . . . and stopped dead in my tracks.

Emelynn leapt, launching herself off the *Symphony*. Her trajectory was a powerful eighty-degree line straight out. And she was fast! She let loose a triumphant shout that broke my trance, and I raced up behind her.

"Whoa there, Em . . . steady," I said, reaching for her. I watched for signs of panic. There were none. Utter joy stretched her face into a wide-ass smile.

"Well, look at you," I said, enjoying the moment. "I guess you figured it out."

"I guess I did," she said, her voice timid.

"Do you know how quickly you shot up here?" Had she heard me? I ducked down to meet her gaze. "You might want to take that speed down a notch next time."

She mumbled under her breath, and I helped her back to the deck.

"I should go back to bed," she said. She had a faraway look to her. Probably shell-shocked.

"I think that's best." I stayed close by her side until she was safely inside her cabin.

Back between my own sheets, I replayed her flight in my mind. Maybe it was just the angle, or an optical illusion, but it sure looked like she'd been flying at an extraordinary clip. Was I seeing the speed that Jolene was renowned for? Perhaps I'd find an opportunity to test that illusion tomorrow.

CHAPTER TWENTY-TWO

Fog billowed like sheets in the wind around the *Symphony*. I looked at the time again and debated whether or not to check on Emelynn. She'd never slept into the early afternoon before. I'd give her a while longer, I thought, and resumed my review of the latest Dixon Tower progress report.

A half hour later, Emelynn traipsed into the salon. She had an air of confidence about her I'd not seen before. I shut the file and stretched back in my chair.

"You slept in," I said.

She helped herself to a glass of OJ. "Yeah, looks like I did. Do you want some?"

I shook my head, snickering at her attempt to be coy knowing she had to be bursting inside. "So . . . how are you feeling today?"

"Pretty. Damn. Good," she said, allowing a smile to bloom.

There it was! "Yeah, I thought you might be." I trailed her to the sofa, anxious for an explanation. "What happened last night, Em? What was it that finally triggered a liftoff?" I sat close beside her.

She sat at the edge of the sofa and recounted a dream she'd had, pausing between thoughts as if she hadn't quite figured it out herself.

"I was flying but had this rock tied to my ankle . . . The rock dragged me down and I struggled against the weight of it . . . Somehow, I managed to cut the rope, which released the rock, and that's when I woke up."

"That's it?" I asked, unsure of what I'd expected but not imagining a dream, let alone one rehashing her painful experience on the beach.

"Yeah, that's it."

"Hmm." Disappointed, I flipped on CNN. Maybe I'd expected contact from Jolene, some celestial message from the great beyond. I settled back into the sofa. Emelynn sighed and settled in beside me, our thighs touching. I tried to focus on the news. Her new-found confidence looked good on her. Very good. If our lives weren't so complicated, I'd be tempted to make a move on her. Would she be interested, I wondered?

I chided myself for the notion and redirected my thoughts. "What would you like for breakfast?" I asked.

She practically jumped off the sofa. "How about I cook this morning," she offered.

She made a pretty good breakfast wrap. We ate in the salon, staring into the white nothingness beyond the windows.

"It's foggy out again. If you're up for it, we could get some practice in."

Emelynn swung her head around, her eyes wide. The frightened neophyte was back.

"What if I can't do it again?"

I reached for her hand and held it firmly, willing her to absorb my confidence in her. "It's inside you, Emelynn, and it's not going anywhere. You did it once—you'll be able to do it again."

She took a deep breath that didn't seem to help. "I guess I'm going to have to try it again, sooner or later."

She just needed to get it over with. I gathered our plates from the coffee table and started for the galley.

"Would you mind, Jackson . . ." I turned back to her. She stood, hesitating with her words. ". . . if I did this on my own? Just this one time. I'll be too nervous if you're up there watching me."

What? She was blowing me off? After we'd come this far together? "What if you need help?"

"I'll whistle if I lift off."

Shit! This could go wrong so many different ways. "I don't know, Em. You could fall and end up in the water."

"Please?"

I considered her plea. She wasn't blowing me off. It was fear I saw in her eyes. Fear that she'd fail. Fear that I'd be a witness to it. "Okay, but I'm not waiting for you to whistle. I'll give you a two-minute head start and then I'm coming up."

"Two minutes," she repeated, and bolted for the door.

I made a display of checking the time, but I had no intention of letting her fall overboard. "Go. Two minutes."

The moment she was out the door, I followed. She didn't notice me standing on the deck when she broke from gravity with a leap, and shot out like an arrow from a compound bow. Her speed hadn't been an illusion.

So much for her warning whistle. I leapt after her and heard her proclaim her independence with an exultant, "Yes!"

I flew flat out to reach her, finally grabbing her arm. "I thought you were going to whistle!"

She arched an eyebrow. "I thought you were going to give me two minutes!"

Neither of us had followed through, and she'd done it. She looked absolutely amazing, her face flushed red and her hair blowing wildly about her shoulders. A laugh crept up my throat at the sight of her trying desperately to contain her joy. Our laughter disappeared into the rolling fog.

"Come on," I said. "Let's have some fun."

She followed with enthusiasm, testing her agility and stamina. We dove toward the *Symphony* then banked sharply, twisting back around to tap her bow before soaring into the mist. She doubled back on me and pulled off a perfect pike which she ended in a roll, laughing all the way. I felt like a teenager again, streaking through the air in a cannonball tuck, hearing her squeal as I whizzed by within inches of her.

Though I challenged her many times, she didn't respond with the same speed I'd seen on her liftoff. We were both exhausted when we finally landed back on the observation deck and headed below.

"Do you realize I haven't had to correct you even once today?" I said. She'd truly shone out there.

"I hadn't, but you're right," she said.

It was not a trivial accomplishment. "I know it's early, but let's celebrate." There was no more perfect occasion. I poured us each a glass of wine and offered a toast. "Here's to independent flight."

She wandered over to the windows when my phone rang. The fog was beginning to lift. I watched her reflection while I spoke with Alex.

"Jin just confirmed," he said, naming one of his Seattle contacts. "Looks like you'll have four men at your disposal. I just sent you their information."

"When can they be ready?"

"They're clearing their schedules now. Let's get together tomorrow. I'd like to go over some maps with you and James."

"Sounds good. I'll set it up."

"Sure thing."

After I disconnected, I joined Emelynn in the salon. "Eden and Alex are bringing dinner." Alex's email arrived with a buzz of my phone. I forwarded his contacts' details on to Josh for his usual workup. Eden and Alex arrived an hour later.

"Wine before dinner?" Eden said, breezing past Alex, who'd dropped a large paper bag on the counter. "What's the occasion?"

Emelynn and I stood to greet them.

"Emelynn has something to celebrate," I said, crossing to the galley.

Eden and Alex turned their attention to Emelynn, who suddenly didn't know where to put her feet.

"I lifted off," she said, wringing her hands. "Twice."

Alex took two big strides, pulled her into a bear hug and spun her around. "Fan-fucking-tastic!"

When Alex put her down, Eden took his place and wrapped her in a rocking embrace. "Congratulations," she said. "How did it happen? I want every detail."

Arm-in-arm they walked to the galley, and Eden squeezed out of her the unremarkable dream of the rock and rope.

"Ask her what she was wearing," I said, and earned a playful swat from Emelynn. "Nightshirt. Nothing on underneath," I teased.

Eden shooed us away from the counter to make room for the food, and Emelynn set the table. Tantalizing garlic and ginger aromas mingled with the scent of deep-fried batter and filled the salon. Alex and I piled our plates high, and while we ate, we laughed and talked, sharing our days, sharing our stories. Throughout the meal, my attention was inexplicably drawn back to Emelynn, the quietest Flier at the table.

When we finally mounted the stairs to the observation deck, Eden, Alex and I held back and waited for Emelynn's debut. She nibbled her lip before closing her eyes with a heavy sigh. And then it happened. She lunged forward and roared into the night sky.

I was prepared, of course, having seen it before. Immediately, I launched and heard Alex and Eden right behind me. She'd already slowed when we caught up to her.

"She needs more practice slowing her ascent," I said, laughing at Eden and Alex's wide-eyed surprise. "But I think she's got the gist of it."

"Oh, you think!" Alex said, joining my laughter.

All Eden could manage was "Wow."

The moment the laughter subsided, Alex took the lead and guided Emelynn's first solo flight, a cautious route with gentle curves and low-angle slopes. I stayed in the rear with Emelynn in front of me and in my sights. She continuously tested herself, taking sharper angles, steeper dives, and looked back regularly to keep tabs on me. The smile never left her face.

When we landed, Emelynn's dyke burst, and a flood of observations and questions spilled out. We headed below to celebrate.

"Drink preferences?" I asked.

Alex responded with, "Surprise us."

I dropped ice into four tumblers and measured a shot of Drambuie and another of Laphroaig into each glass. Alex collected two of the drinks. Emelynn hadn't yet stopped babbling. I handed her a glass and motioned for her to take a breath. She clinked her glass against mine, took a cautious sip and then sputtered and coughed.

"It's a rusty nail," I said, and led her to the sofas, where she collapsed with a contented sigh. "I don't suppose I need to ask if you enjoyed tonight's flight."

"That was the best," she said, and I heartily agreed.

Emelynn must have tried talking to him during our flight because Alex cautioned her about sound travelling over water. She started in again on the questions, and he gave her a crash course in aerodynamics and drag reduction. Emelynn soaked it all up.

Early in the evening, Eden and Alex stood to leave. "I won't see you tomorrow, Emelynn," Eden said. "I'm working nights at the hospital for the next four shifts."

"I'm going to give you a few nights off, too," Alex said. "I like to work nights when Eden does, so we can have more time off together."

I glanced Emelynn's way. Would she be bothered by their absence, I wondered? "Looks like we're on our own for a few days," I said. If their absence bothered her, she hid it. Personally, I was pleased with the prospect.

Eden handed Emelynn a piece of paper with her phone number and email. I walked them to the door.

After they'd left, I turned on my laptop hoping for an update from James. What I got instead was a reality check: an ATM clip from Newport, Oregon. The first pleasant evening I'd had in weeks, and

Sandra had to ruin it. I looked over to Emelynn. She seemed safely preoccupied with the TV. I clicked on the file and watched my wife clutch at Cole's shirt. Once again, he'd made himself at home punching in the PIN while Sandra hid her face behind sunglasses, an unnecessary accessory given the time of night. I sent it on to James and signed out.

"It's all yours," I said to Emelynn, and took the heel of my drink outside to the foredeck. A cool breeze raised goosebumps on my arms. I wandered to the railing and stared down at the sea's gentle swell. If James wasn't just yanking my chain, very soon now I'd be able to put Sandra and Cole where they belonged, in my past. Though I knew James disagreed, Sandra had made her choice. I wouldn't be trying to change her mind; I no longer wanted to. But I did hope she wouldn't mind too much hanging out with Cole when he didn't look so pretty, because I had plans for his face that involved my fists.

I returned to the galley. Emelynn was on the sofa, and had pulled a blanket into her lap. "You want another drink?" I asked, dropping ice into my glass.

"Sure, I'm not driving," she said. "Why not?"

I handed her a drink and sat beside her. It pissed me off that after all this time, Sandra's ATM clips still had the power to ruin a perfectly fine evening. With a perfectly fine woman. A brave woman with a sense of adventure and an indomitable spirit. "I enjoyed myself tonight," I said. "I think you're going to be a strong Flier. You amaze me with the strides you've made in five days."

"Feels more like five months." She rattled the ice in her glass. "I guess I'd better head home soon. I'm sure you'd like your spare room back."

"Not really." I stared into my drink thinking how much I'd miss her annoying questions. "I'm kind of getting used to having you around." She responded to my smile with one of her own. Would she let me kiss her? "Here's to many more nights like tonight."

"Cheers." She raised her glass and then looked off into the distance, her attention sliding far away. What was she thinking about? Like me, she stood on the brink of a brand new life, with untold possibilities laid out before her. What would she do with that life?

I brushed the hair from her cheek, my fingers grazing the warmth of her skin. "Where'd you go?" I asked, startling her.

"Sorry," she said. "It's just . . . sometimes it's a little overwhelming."

I stretched my arm across the sofa behind her, fingering a lock of her hair. "I bet," I said. "It must have been tough on you growing up without your father, having to deal with this gift with no guidance. And now, to have this dumped on you—you've done well."

Her hair was thick in my hand, shimmering with copper. Sandra's would have felt limp in comparison, fine and straight, a pale shade of brown. Did she think about me when she lay in Cole's arms? How would Emelynn feel if I told her the whole story? Would she think less of me if she knew my wife had left me for my brother? I reached my hand under her chin and drew her to face me. She gasped in surprise but didn't pull away. I looked from the green of her eyes to the soft curve of her lips, rubbing my thumb along the contours, and then I gave in to my mood, leaned in and gently kissed her. She searched my face, but again, didn't pull away. With my next kiss, I tasted her.

Her lips were soft, her breath sweet on my cheek. Reluctantly, I pulled away. Months of unfulfilled passion stirred a painful erection, a situation I wasn't prepared to inflict on Emelynn. Not now, though I'd be damned if I could name why. Guilt, assuredly, but for what exactly? Taking advantage of a trusting young woman, or driving the final nail into the coffin of my marriage?

I took her hand in mine. "I wish you didn't have to go."

"I can come back another time. We could go flying," she said, a hopeful note in her voice.

We could do a whole lot of things, I thought, most of them involving her being naked. "I guess we'd better call it a night," I said, standing at an angle to hide the bulge in my jeans. "I'll take you home tomorrow."

"Thanks," she said, and took my outstretched hand.

At her cabin door, I pulled her close, careful not to press into her. I cradled her head and then gave an inch to my screaming libido and claimed her mouth one more time, delving my tongue inside and feasting on her. How easy it would be to take her now. Push into her cabin, throw her on the bed and plant myself between her legs.

I dragged myself away before I lost my self-respect and made good on my fantasy. "Sweet dreams," I said, and then left her there and strode to my stateroom, closing the door behind me. I relieved the pressure under a warm sluice of water. Such a sad fuck, I thought afterwards. Sandra flaunts her infidelity for the world to see and I'm beating off in the shower. Again.

If Emelynn was willing, why should I hold back? Sandra was

already beyond redemption. Forgiveness wasn't even on the table. The only way out was forward, and Emelynn was right in front of me.

Slumber played hide-and-seek until the early morning hours, when exhaustion finally won out. The sunrise brought a new perspective, and the bright day reflected my mood perfectly. I was done with the guilt.

I made coffee and phoned James.

"Alex wants to meet today," I said. "You available around noon?"

"Sure. Where?"

"How about the Flying Beaver over by the South Airport. There's a charter company nearby I want to check out."

"Okay. I'll see you there."

"I'll let Alex know," I said, and disconnected. I'd left the door to the lower level ajar and heard the click of Emelynn's door opening. The thought of her sent a flush to my face. I pulled two mugs from the cupboard and filled them.

"I heard you coming," I said, handing her one. I pressed my lips to her damp hair, reminding myself—no guilt. "How did you sleep?"

"Good. How about you?"

"It took me a while to fall asleep. I had someone on my mind," I said. God, it felt good to be moving forward. "I'll make breakfast today. How do bacon and eggs sound?"

"Like heaven," she said, and took a seat opposite the counter to watch me cook.

Emelynn cleaned up and I sent Alex an email with the details of our meeting. I joined her in the salon, savouring the last of my coffee.

"I guess you'd like me to take you home?"

"If you wouldn't mind," she said. "I need to touch base with some people, do some catching up around the cottage."

Cottage? That was quaint. I swirled the dregs in my mug wondering if she had her eyes on someone else. The young man from Meyers Motors perhaps? "Okay. You go ahead and pack. I'll meet you up top."

She disappeared below and I climbed the stairs to the observation deck and got us underway, setting course for the shallows close to her house. She joined me, all smiles, excited to be going home. When I'd anchored, I suggested taking her home in the *Symphony's* tender.

"Hmm," she said, staring at the Zodiac secured on a platform behind the galley. "Funny how you never offered to take me home in it before."

"Yeah," I said, grateful she hadn't pressed that point her first night aboard. "Funny that." I jumped over the rails to unlatch the Zodiac then raised it with the davit and lowered it over the side.

The trip to shore was quick. After she got out, I pulled the dingy up on the rocks and grabbed her knapsack. "I'll walk you up," I said. We teetered across the rocks, seeking out the flat sandstone and patches of sand, which were easier to navigate. We reached the foot of her stairs, and I did the gentlemanly thing, offering to check inside the house. She unlocked the patio door and told me to take my time, but I didn't see how; her cottage was tiny.

Regardless, I checked each room and then opened the front door, stepped off the porch and peered around a large neat yard. Roses bloomed in abundance in a nearby bed. She had no neighbours on the south and east, which abutted the park, and a dense hedge grew on the north side, separating her from her only neighbour.

I walked back inside and found Emelynn in her bedroom unpacking. "You know, Em, if I didn't know otherwise, I would have bet a Flier picked this location. It's perfect. With the exception of that one neighbour to the north, you can pretty much fly in and out of here unseen any night."

She stilled her hands and smiled, and I found myself wanting to know what she was thinking. I looked beyond her to the *Symphony* in the distance. Emelynn had only been on board her for a week. Somehow it felt longer. Strange how time played tricks on you when you weren't paying attention. It would seem quiet there without her. Too quiet.

I didn't want it to end yet. "I've got some things to do today, but how do you feel about going flying tonight?" I asked.

"I would have thought you'd be glad to have a night off."

"I've had too many nights off, and last night put me in the mood for flying. What do you say?"

She hesitated long enough to cause doubt. Finally, she said, "I'd like that, but I want to sleep in my own bed tonight."

"Sure," I said, relieved. "How about I pick you up after dark?"

"Sounds perfect."

Yes, I thought, and kissed her. "See you tonight." I let myself out and took the Zodiac back to the *Symphony*, where I weighed anchor and headed back to the marina in the south arm of the Fraser River. From there, I took a cab to the Flying Beaver to meet up with James.

He'd already claimed a table and sat staring out to the river. I ordered a beer and joined him. "I brought the charts," I said, dropping the rolls to the table. He looked up, startled. The charts covered the coastal area from Vancouver Island south to Portland.

James's beer was half empty. "Is Alex coming?"

"Said he'd be here," I said, and took a seat. The waiter tossed a coaster on the table and set a frosted glass of beer on it.

"You ready to order?" he asked.

"We're waiting for one more," I answered. He nodded and retreated to the bar.

I tasted the beer. "You and your dad know the players on the Tribunal, right?"

James snapped his head up. A dark glower clouded his face. "No. We don't."

Why did he have to be such a dick sometimes? "Stop jerking me around. It's just you and me here. I'm curious if they ever talk about Ghosts."

"Why? You worried about that film of Cole's?"

I inhaled an exasperated breath. "Just answer the question, would you?"

"No. They don't talk about Ghosts." He took a gulp of his beer. "Why are you asking?"

"The subject came up. A friend asked me to check out a new acquaintance. Did some digging and found two separate references to Ghosts. Fables, I suspect, but I figured if Ghosts do exist, the Tribunal would know. Maybe we're wrong about them. Ghosts, I mean."

James forced a laugh. "Don't waste your time. We've got enough to speculate about with Cole so close. Hey, there's Alex."

Alex slapped me on the back and shook James's hand as he took a seat. "I have some news. Avery presented your case to the covey. He's more comfortable knowing my contacts are reinforcing your efforts. The covey's agreed to help—on a volunteer basis, of course."

"We appreciate that," I said. "I'll call Avery with my thanks."

Though Alex had heard it before, James expanded upon our cover story about Sandra, shoring it up with Johnny Lorenzo's rap sheet and the trail of coastal ATM withdrawals. Alex listened intently, absorbing the details of James's surveillance and search strategy.

"Sandra was in Newport, Oregon, day before last," I said, and unfurled the appropriate map. "It's usually three to four days between withdrawals, which means they could be here, here or here," I said, pointing out the most likely locations. "And the past three times, they hit the ATM after eleven at night."

"You still don't know how many there are?" Alex asked.

"No," James said. "But two of Johnny's buddies haven't been seen in a while. They may be with them. I can get photos to your contacts in Seattle."

"If they're mooring at public docks, they aren't showing their faces. It's more likely they're anchoring offshore, and taking a tender in," I said.

We studied the Oregon and Washington coastlines over burgers, and by the time the waiter cleared our plates, we'd identified and divvied up the potential ATM locations they might use over the next few days. We still didn't have the manpower to cover every possible ATM 24/7, but with Alex's contacts added to James's surveillance people, we'd significantly improved our efforts. Fingers crossed it paid off, and soon.

"What's the plan when we find them?" Alex asked.

"First thing we do," I said, shooting James a pointed glance, "is find out if Sandra is with them by choice." James curled his lip. "If she is," I continued, "we deliver a message from her family, and let them be."

"But if she's being held against her will," James said with a frosty calm, "we paint whichever luckless town they wash up in with their blood, and take Sandra home."

CHAPTER TWENTY-THREE

Back aboard the *Symphony*, I went in search of the headsets I'd stashed months ago. Being able to easily talk with your flying partner improved the experience immensely, and I wanted that for Emelynn. I wanted her to experience everything this world of ours had to offer—and I wanted to test her speed. From what little I'd witnessed, it was extraordinary.

I anchored the *Symphony* in the shallows away from traffic about a mile south of Emelynn's house and flew out to meet her, landing in the sand at the foot of her stairs. She sat on the top step, waiting for me.

"Are you ready?" I asked, climbing the stairs.

"Can't wait," she said, grabbing the rail to stand. "I've been looking forward to this all day."

"Me too," I said, reaching the deck. She wore the black shoes I'd collected off the beach. "And I have something for you." I dropped one of the radio mics into her hand. She turned it in her fingers and raised a questioning eyebrow. "It's an earpiece with a microphone so we can talk to each other up there." I swept the hair away from the side of her face. "You fit it into your ear like this," I said, gently pushing it into place. "You'll need to adjust it so it's comfortable, and pull the mic out a little." She did as I suggested and wiggled it to fit. She'd adopted the dark clothing of a Flier, and it fit her snuggly. Nice change from the baggy clothes she'd worn the first time I saw her in Avery's office.

I dragged my gaze from her figure and looked around the deck. "Think you can manage a liftoff from here?" She answered with an enthusiastic bob of her head. I lifted off and hovered above, ready to catch her if she sprang too hard. She still had to think about the process, but she'd already gained control over her ascent, and joined me after a perfectly executed liftoff. I led the way over the tree canopy and south along the cliff at the edge of the park.

"Recognize that?" I said, as I pointed down at the spot where I'd found Emelynn's rope tied to the rock. I dipped below the cliff and circled the sandy beach. After the second pass, I searched the horizon.

"Let's check on the *Symphony*," I said. Leaving the ship unmanned always left me anxious. It was a straight shot to her bow and a good warm-up. I set the pace, and Emelynn kept up easily. We landed on the observation deck and went below. The anchor remained well set with plenty of scope. "Everything's good here. You ready to go again?"

She replaced the cap on a bottle of water she'd taken from the fridge and replied with enthusiasm. "Sure am."

I darted past her and leapt up the stairs, "Catch me if you can," I shouted, and tore off as fast as I could fly, steadily increasing my altitude. She closed in fast. I dove down and deked left to keep ahead of her, but the little imp cut me off and stole the lead, grinning from ear to ear.

"Having a hard time keeping up, old man?" she taunted over her shoulder, cresting at a height that would have sent her into a panic a few short days ago.

I flew hard, and each time I got close, she put out a little more speed to keep ahead. "Your momma flies better than you," I said, and heard her laughter echo in my ear. She upped the ante, using her arms and shoulders to bank her curves, and showed no fear when she flipped upside down.

"Come on . . . you gonna let the newbie get the best of you?" she called, keeping up the pace.

"Newbie's going to need a nap soon," I said, flying over her. She twisted to the right and dove straight down.

"Naps are for old men," she said, trailing laughter. I followed and poured on enough speed to tag her heel. She jerked away from me with a shriek, creating distance effortlessly then soaring high once more.

"Old men! Your momma would slap you for that remark. Newbie's getting cocky," I said, pushing hard behind her, but she gained further ground.

"You'll never catch me," she trilled, getting farther ahead. Then she got cocky and turned around. I thought her intent was to let me catch up, but when I got within inches of her, she whispered, "Come and get me," and then arched backwards and dove down, her arms in a point above her head. She did a 180 and flattened out ten feet from the water's surface. I followed, cutting the corner off her dive, and still couldn't catch up to her. It felt as if I were standing still, and I was flying flat out. She raced ahead of me, straight out of my league. I watched in awe. Test complete. Newbie was a phenom.

In no time at all, she was a dot on the horizon, and a little too far away for my comfort. "I'm losing track of you, Em. Let me catch up." I followed her trajectory. "Em," I repeated. "Slow down. I can't see you." I gazed left and right of her path, and couldn't spot her. "Emelynn!" Why wasn't she answering? Had I veered from her path? I flew higher, widening my field of vision. "Emelynn!" I called again, and still, she didn't answer.

Had her earpiece malfunctioned? Shit. Where was she? At the speed she was travelling, she could be out into the shipping channel by now. Would she know how to get back? Where the *Symphony* was anchored? "Answer me, damn it! Where are you?" I shouted, flying even higher, sprinting ahead.

Testing her speed was a huge, huge mistake. She wasn't ready. I shouldn't have pushed her. "Emelynn, please answer me." What if she'd panicked? I looked down. A swell heaved and waves rippled across the surface. Was she in the water? Could I have flown right over her?

I slowed and turned around, flying back the way I'd come. I kept my gaze on the water and prayed I was flying the right course. Fear clenched my stomach. How long since I'd seen her? Two minutes? Three? If she were in the water, how long could she fight the waves and swell? The cold? Each whitecap and rolling piece of driftwood looked like a call for help. I darted left and right, growing more desperate with each false alarm.

There was too much area to search. I flew back up and slowed my pace, taking in a wider sweep of the water below. Another minute passed. I swallowed the knot that inched into my throat. It was futile. "Where are you, Emelynn!"

The ripples from a splash of white water near the surface drew my eye. A flash of white moved just below the water. The belly of a fish? I moved lower. Another flash of white. The surface lay ten feet below me. I focused my attention on a three-foot circle, and caught a glimpse of a hand, pale below the dark water.

I dove with everything I had, piercing the surface at a low angle and gripping her forearm on my arc through the water. It took all of my momentum and the last of my strength to push through to the surface. But I had her. Once free of the water, I got my bearings and charged back toward the *Symphony*. Emelynn was unconscious and I didn't have the strength to pull her into my arms. Her head flopped backwards. Was she breathing?

The *Symphony* loomed in the distance, farther south than I had thought. I shot toward her and crash-landed, tumbling over Emelynn's body onto the deck. Recovering quickly, I rolled her onto her back. Please be alive. She wasn't breathing. I rose to my knees and started CPR, pumping her chest. Her mouth opened. She started to retch and I pulled her onto her side. Relief loosened the knot in my stomach. She coughed up more water than I would have thought possible, and curled into a ball, heaving up still more water between rasping breaths.

I called her name, but she didn't answer. "Emelynn?"

Her eyes remained tightly closed. Finally, she whispered, "I'm okay."

"Thank god." I pulled her against my chest and wrapped my arms around her, holding her tight. "I'm so sorry." I rocked her, clearing the hair that clung to her face. "I'm so sorry . . . so sorry." I kissed her head gently and cooed in her ear. "You flew so fast, I lost sight of you. I didn't think anyone could fly that fast. God, I'm so sorry. I couldn't find you."

She started to shiver and I came to my senses. Her skin was ice cold. I needed to get her below and out of her wet clothes, warm her up. I loosened my grip and looked at her face. She'd finally opened her eyes. They were bloodshot and her lips were blue. I stood and pulled her upright. I didn't have the strength to carry her in my arms so I bent and lifted her over my shoulder. I could hear her teeth chattering as I quickly descended to her cabin. I sat her on the edge of the bed and stepped into the head to start the shower.

I peeled her out of her clothes with as much dignity as I could manage and helped her into the shower. She flinched when the warm water hit her skin. I adjusted the temperature to cool it. She slid down the wall into a ball. I positioned the nozzle to spray over her and scooted out to get a towel. She hadn't moved when I returned. I reached in and raised the temperature.

I left her there, gathered her clothes and dumped them into the washing machine, along with my own. I donned a robe and returned to check on her, once again gently upping the shower temperature. Her eyes remained closed, but at least she was now able to withstand a normal temperature.

Back in my stateroom, I too stepped under a stream of water. I warmed quickly and washed the salt water from my hair. Someone had been watching over us tonight. I filled my lungs with the steam-laden air and released the tightness in my chest. Pure fucking luck. How else could I explain the impossible odds of finding her? I couldn't think about it without thinking of the other horrendous outcome that might have been. Twice now, I'd nearly killed that woman.

I pushed the emotion away and dried off. Back up top, I put another towel and robe in the dryer to heat for Emelynn and then poured a large brandy. I swallowed it in two gulps, feeling it warm my insides. Afterwards, I grabbed the towel and robe from the dryer and went to check on Emelynn.

She'd made progress; the scent of shampoo wafted out from the head. I left it ajar and returned to the bed to wait. I'd been such an idiot to let her get so far away from me. How would I ever regain her trust?

When the shower fell silent, I jumped up and opened the warmed towel. I held it ready then wrapped it around her shoulders and pulled her close. She'd stopped trembling and felt warm to my touch. Relieved, I kissed her forehead. "I put a housecoat out for you. I'll go make us a warm drink."

Upstairs, I poured us both a brandy, warmed them in the microwave and set them by the sofa. I turned Muddy Waters on low, inhaled deeply, and let the music soothe me. When Emelynn entered the salon, I embraced her, grateful she was alive. "I'm so sorry, Emelynn."

"It's not your fault," she said, seeking my gaze with those beautiful green eyes. "I never even asked, are you all right?"

"Don't worry about me," I said, leading her to the sofa. "I was in the water for only a second and I'm warm and dry now. Here, turn around." I positioned myself on the sofa with the armrest at my back, and pulled her against me, then reached for the sofa blanket and wrapped it around us. She snuggled into my chest.

"Brandy," I said, handing her a snifter from the end table.

Neither of us spoke. The miracle we'd just experienced precluded words, and I had no doubt it was a miracle. Could Emelynn be the window that god had opened in the face of Sandra's door? What was I waiting for? This beautiful, wild-haired mystery woman had been dropped into my lap and I hadn't yet claimed her. Why? Sandra had succumbed to temptation months ago, her vows irreparably broken.

Emelynn finished her drink and handed me the empty glass.

"Would you like another?" I asked.

"No, but thanks." She shifted her shoulders, sitting straighter so she could see my face. "Thank you, Jackson. For finding me, for getting me out of there."

"Shh," I said, lifting damp hair off her neck. She should be furious with me, not thanking me. A week ago I'd almost killed her with a jolt, and tonight I'd pushed her past her limits and she'd nearly drowned. And let's not forget all the near misses she'd suffered under my tutelage. Yet, here she was. The blanket had fallen to her waist and her robe gaped, exposing the curve of her breast. She studied my mouth then looked into my eyes and her lips parted. Her hunger was palpable, an invitation. The longing I recognized in her face sent a pulse to my shaft.

I reached inside her robe and grazed her waist. She gasped, her warm skin soft to my touch. I cupped her breast and felt her nipple harden under my thumb. Her breath came in sharp inhales. She closed her eyes and laid her head back against my shoulder, her ear close to my mouth. I pulled her earlobe between my teeth, only releasing it to taste her neck and then her freshly bared shoulder.

"Jackson," she whispered, "I need to tell you something." She turned her head to face me. "I've never done this before."

The needle scratched across the record in my head. I searched her face, hoping I'd misunderstood. "Never?" She slowly shook her head. "Ah, damn." Just how isolated had she been growing up? I couldn't do this. I shifted to move her off me, but she pressed my hand to her breast.

"I don't want to stop," she said.

My throbbing erection wasn't keen on the idea either. Had she been saving herself for someone special? If so, I wasn't that man. But . . . maybe she'd given up on finding him. Her hand pressed hard against my own, her breast beneath more than filled it, inviting.

"Are you sure about this?" I asked. She nodded her consent, and I could only hope she wouldn't regret it. My last experience with a virgin was in high school. It wasn't my proudest moment. "I'll be as gentle as I can," I said, and kissed my way to the small hollow at the base of her neck.

I rolled onto my side and studied her face. This was the tipping point. The line that could not be uncrossed. For both of us. She didn't waver. I stepped across the line and kissed her, opening her mouth with my tongue and tasting brandy. Her robe fell away with little effort.

She touched my chest, her hands tentative at first, and then she broke from my kiss and her gaze followed the trail of her hand. It had been too long since I'd felt a woman's touch. Did she know she was undoing me? I plunged my tongue into her mouth. My hips pressed into her of their own accord.

She pulled away. "You okay?" I asked.

"More than okay. You're just what I need tonight." A seductive smile crossed her face. She leaned in and licked my nipple, which sent sparks to my extremities. I cupped the back of her neck and let the sparks play out as she pressed her hands down the length of my body.

I gently pushed her away. "My turn." I kissed her throat, her collarbone and then wet her nipple with my tongue, pulling a small groan from the back of her throat.

Caught up in the passion, I'd almost forgotten what I was dealing with until I eased my hand between her thighs and she tensed. I slid my fingers back to her hard little button and caressed her gently, taking my time. She was ready the next time I slid into her.

"That's it," I whispered on a breath, coaxing her past the momentary hesitation. She relaxed for me and began grinding her hips against my palm, responding beautifully to my touch. It was time. I removed my hand and found the condom in the pocket of my robe. Emelynn interrupted my plan and wrapped her hand around my shaft. I shuddered at her touch and guided her hands, then stilled them before I lost my fragile control.

She watched me roll on the condom and I eased between her legs. Propped on one elbow, I glided my erection in gentle circles around her opening and gently pushed the tip inside her. It took all my restraint to not bury myself in her and make her part of me.

"You sure about this?" I asked one last time, praying she hadn't changed her mind.

"God, yes," she whispered. She moved her hands to my shoulders and I settled into the cradle of her hips, taking my weight on my forearms.

"This is going to hurt," I warned, pressing harder. I eased out and pressed in again and she dug her nails into my arms. I relieved the pressure. She urged me on and I pushed once more. "Relax, Em." I stilled until I felt her exhale, and then flexed my hips again, but her vaginal muscles were pressing hard to keep me out. I pulled back one more time.

"Easy now, breathe," I coaxed, and when she inhaled, I thrust sharply. She yelped and I felt the bite of her nails in my back.

God, she felt good. I didn't move, just held still and let her adjust to the sensation, a perfectly warm and wet sensation that quickly robbed me of my restraint. I pushed in farther and moaned a prayer. "Fuck." Not pounding into her might be the death of me, but I forced myself to hold steady and let her acclimatize.

When I sensed she was ready for more, I pulled back. She tensed. "No," she said.

No? She wrapped her heels behind me and thrust her hips. Ah—*no*, as in *don't stop*. I'd never been happier to oblige. I pushed back inside, deeper this time, and rocked into a rhythm, praying I could hold out until she was ready. Her hips met my thrusts, but her face betrayed the pain that should have been pleasure. She'd never come before I lost control.

"Look at me." She met my gaze and I latched on. "I can't hold on," I said, and flooded her central nervous system with endorphins, like only a Flier could do, ensuring her first experience would be one to remember. She threw her head back and her insides convulsed around me, undoing me. I pushed her knees forward and slammed into her as deep as I could go, once, twice, three times, and then I found my release and shuddered into her one last time.

Her contractions continued long after I'd finished. "You are magnificent," I said, smoothing my fingers up and down her arms. A blush warmed her cheeks.

"I really didn't know what to expect," she said, smiling. "But I sure liked the ending." How long would it be, I wondered, before she asked me about that ending and the rush of endorphins that I'd treated her to? Perhaps I'd keep the secret of a Flier's *rush* to myself for a while longer.

"It won't hurt as much next time," I said, already knowing there would be many more next times. I'd make certain of it, but not tonight. Discreetly, I removed the condom in a wad of tissue.

"Let's go to bed." I swung my legs to the floor and stood, offering Emelynn my hand. We gathered our robes and I led the way to her cabin, ever so grateful she didn't ask about my stateroom. Tomorrow I'd clear away the last lingering reminders of Sandra.

CHAPTER TWENTY-FOUR

I woke with the dawn. Emelynn lay on her back with her head turned away from me, one arm splayed in a nest of hair above her head. Guilt skated around the thrilling edge of waking next to a woman who wasn't my wife. It had been easier than I'd thought to slip the bonds of my marriage, and now it was done. I'd officially moved on. That reality saddened me. What I'd had with Sandra was irretrievably gone.

Emelynn twitched in her sleep. The arm above her head jerked into the air and she woke with a gasp, bolting upright. I lurched up beside her and pulled her, trembling, into my arms.

"You're okay," I said, and gently pulled her back to the bed cradling her against my chest. Her breath came in pants and sweat beaded her forehead. I drew her closer pressing my lips to her hair, banishing her nightmare—a nightmare about drowning, I had no doubt. Soon, I felt her relax. Her breathing calmed and she settled back into slumber.

The events of the previous night played out in my mind as I stared at the teak-panelled ceiling. It wasn't unusual for a Flier to possess an extraordinary skill; an impenetrable block, a deadly jolt or my own ability to render someone unconscious, but I'd never come across anyone with Emelynn's speed. I had no idea how I might help her manage it, but I was determined to try if she'd let me. When she learned how to use it safely, she'd be unstoppable, and combined with a steady aim and a half-decent jolt, she'd be untouchable. I hoped I'd be around to see it.

When I woke next, she was still in my arms. I gently disengaged and returned to my stateroom to don a pair of pants. I scanned the room with fresh eyes, and the sight of Sandra's remnants felt like an insult. I grabbed green garbage bags from the engine room and filled them. Underwear, lingerie, bathing suits and blouses. Jeans, sweaters, suits and dresses. Everything went. I rolled the clothes in balls and stuffed them in the bags, along with her toiletries, and dropped the bags on the floor of the locker. I'd get rid of them the next time I docked.

I dashed to the galley, my head clearer and feet lighter than they'd felt for weeks.

Emelynn was awake when I pushed back into her cabin. "Coffee?" I asked, offering a mug. She winced when she reached to prop her pillows behind her. She pulled the covers to hide her nakedness, and I stifled my amusement at her modesty.

"How are you?" I asked, approaching her side of the bed.

"I'm good."

I handed her a mug and she winced again reaching out to take it. I raised a skeptical eyebrow. "Really?"

"All right," she confessed. "That's a bit of a lie." She rolled her shoulder as I rounded the end of the bed. "My shoulder's sore. My knee too."

"I'm sorry," I said, "but I'm sure glad you're breathing." I climbed onto the bed and we toasted her health with our coffees.

Did she regret the other momentous event of last night? "How are you feeling about the rest of it . . . about us . . . about last night?"

"I'm still smiling," she said. "How about you? How are you feeling about us?"

"Me?" I said, and laughed. I reached under the covers to squeeze her thigh. "I'm on top of the world. If I didn't think you'd be too sore to enjoy it, I'd show you right now how good I feel about last night. In fact," I said, walking my fingers up her thigh, "I can hardly wait to feel good about us again real soon."

She slapped my hand away like an old pro, and dismissed my suggestion of a workout in the shower with a laugh. I drained my coffee and headed to my stateroom to shower. When I returned, she was standing with her back to me in the head's doorway, the robe cinched around her waist.

I watched her as I drew circles on my cheek with the electric razor. "I'm finished with the water now if you want to hop in the shower," I said, willing her to drop the robe. It fell from her shoulders as she stepped into the shower. I caught the briefest glimpse of her bare back and the tempting curve of her ass.

I took that image to the galley and folded her clothes, fresh from the dryer. I dropped them in her cabin and started breakfast. It wouldn't be pancakes. Emelynn and I would start a new routine. An omelette, I decided, with bacon, naturally. I ate too much of it, I knew, but the scent of hickory smoke sent me right back to New Orleans.

Emelynn arrived, thanked me for the clothes and poured us each another coffee. After we ate, she refused my help with the cleanup.

A quick check of my emails turned up Josh's dossiers on Alex's contacts. I forwarded them to James. There was nothing pressing from Delaney that required my attention, which meant I had the day free. I set the phone aside when Emelynn joined me and turned my attention to our newest challenge: taming her speed.

"I've been around Fliers all my life, but I've never seen anyone fly as fast as you last night."

"I'm sorry," she said. "I should never have done that."

"I'm not looking for an apology, Em. I'm just saying . . . you're working with some serious speed."

"Speed, perhaps, but not a lot of skill. It was careless of me to show off like that." She bit her lip when she looked down to her hands with an embarrassment that made me smile.

"No, it's impressive. It makes me wonder what other hidden talents you might have."

"Hopefully, the hidden-talent cache is empty," Emelynn said without a hint of humour. "And don't worry. I won't be flying that fast again."

It was a perfectly logical decision. A naive one, but I understood it. "Still, you do need to practice," I said, nudging her in the right direction. "How about this morning?"

"In broad daylight?" she asked. "Isn't that too risky?"

"We'll head offshore, far away from casual observers."

"I don't think so."

I disagreed. "You need to get back on the horse, Em."

"Come on, Jackson. Last night was a disaster. It wouldn't be getting back on the horse so much as it would be testing the temperature of the Pacific. Believe me, that is *not* something I intend to do again any time soon."

"That thinking is exactly why you need to get back in the air. You're going to be reluctant no matter when you do it. Better you do it sooner than later—before you ingrain false fears into your psyche."

She paused in thought and tucked her feet under her. "Maybe you're right," she said. She swallowed some tablets she'd pulled from her pocket and settled against the armrest.

At least she was considering it. Maybe when those painkillers kicked in she'd feel more optimistic. I set a course for an area outside commercial traffic lanes, and away from landfall. I didn't ask Emelynn to join me when I headed up top. She'd come when she was ready. A seagull screeched overhead. I scanned the horizon with the binoculars. Daytime flights were always risky but Emelynn was worth it, and we wouldn't be long. She was a fighter, even if she didn't know it, and she'd rally as soon as she felt the rush of flying again.

The *Symphony* traced a slow circle on autopilot while I waited on the sofa. A sailboat crossed the bow a half mile out and disappeared. Emelynn showed up an hour later. I didn't wait for her to change her mind. I crossed the deck and immediately lifted off to a hover, and extended my hand in invitation. After a moment's hesitation, she joined me. Our flight path bore a resemblance to the kiddie coaster ride at the fair: safe with just a hint of the big ride's potential. More than once I caught her smiling, but I didn't push.

When we landed, we headed to opposite sofas.

"Thanks, Jackson," she said. "I needed that."

Her cheeks were flushed again. "The fresh air?" I asked, teasing.

She smiled. "No, and don't look so smug."

It was impossible not to be pleased. The tension I'd seen in Emelynn's bearing just a few hours ago had melted away. She'd gotten over the first hurdle. I propped my feet on the table and looked over her shoulder to the bright white clouds high in the sky. A small swell rocked us like a mother's hand on a cradle.

She made herself comfortable, stretching flat out on the sofa, and closed her eyes. The sun found her hair and lit it up with sparks of red and gold. When she drifted off to sleep, I went below.

My phone vibrated. It was my soon to be ex-father-in-law. "Redmond, how are you?" I answered.

"Good, thank you. I phoned to convey my thanks. Sandy's mother and I are grateful you changed your mind."

"I haven't changed my mind. I've only agreed to continue helping James so I can treat Cole to a little payback when we find them."

Redmond's exasperated sigh travelled across the airwaves. "Just be careful, son. They'll be armed."

I thanked him for his concern and disconnected. It was interesting that Redmond hadn't discouraged me. Perhaps he'd like a little payback from Cole as well.

It was two hours before Emelynn appeared in the galley, sleepy-eyed. I closed my laptop and crossed the salon to fold her in my arms. Her hair smelled of the outdoors.

"Thanks for the blanket," she said.

"You looked so comfortable; I didn't want to disturb you."

"What time is it?" she asked.

I checked my watch. "Just after five." I suggested another short flight before we headed to an anchorage for the night, and she readily agreed. By the time we landed again, she'd regained the ground she'd lost last night. Soon, she'd be ready to test her speed again.

Later, while I steered our course to the shallows by her house, I thought about the woman who'd forfeited her gift for Emelynn. That afternoon, while Emelynn had slept, I'd done some digging. With no further leads on Jolene, I'd researched the gifting process. Most of what I knew had been confirmed. The Tribunal maintained tight controls on all giftings, and the process itself was known only to them. Yet Emelynn had fallen through the cracks, proving that the Tribunal's control wasn't absolute. And for Jolene to abandon Emelynn meant she hadn't survived. Jolene must have known that was a strong possibility, so why hadn't she told someone? Her gift was extraordinary—what caused her to give it up? Was she terminally ill? Mentally unstable? I was left with more questions than answers.

It was after eight by the time I got the *Symphony* anchored for the night. Emelynn stretched on the sofa with a yawn. I didn't want her to leave. "Would you like to stay here tonight?" I asked. "We can make dinner, watch a movie if you'd like."

"Sounds perfect," she said.

I uncorked a bottle of Cabernet Sauvignon and poured us each a glass. We decided on fajitas and Emelynn volunteered to manage the vegetables while I prepared the chicken.

The iron skillet jumped its hook. I bent down to retrieve it.

Emelynn looked up from her chopping. "May I ask you something?"

I stood back up and sighed.

"What is it that brought you here to BC?"

I turned to set the skillet on the burner. "Sandra's abduction." I wanted to tell her the truth about Sandra, but I didn't want to lose her. After we found Sandra and her lover, then I would tell her.

"Why here?"

I leaned back against the counter. She should have been a reporter. "Whoever took her still has her and they're headed this way." *Took her*—I tried not to choke on the lie.

"I don't mean to sound insensitive, but how can you be sure that she's still alive?"

"The people who abducted her are making sure that we know it."

"How?" she asked, pausing with her knife in the air.

I glanced toward my glass wondering how much alcohol I'd need to numb myself after deceiving her.

I then explained about the cash withdrawals, the time-stamped ATM photos and the police's conclusion that she wasn't being coerced. At least that last part wasn't a lie.

"But you don't believe that."

I swallowed hard. "Of course not." Nothing about Sandra's supposed abduction was what it seemed. I repeated the lie I'd told Avery and the rest of her covey, and emptied my glass in two gulps.

I reached for the bottle of wine and poured another glass. "After the police dropped the investigation, we made a deal with the bank. They now send us the photos and the particulars of her withdrawals."

She pondered my answer then dove back in. "What makes you believe they're headed this way?"

I explained about the pattern of withdrawals and the coastal locations that suggested they were travelling by boat. "That's why I had the *Symphony* brought here. I want to be close, ready to go when the time comes." Ready to make them both regret their treachery, but I kept that thought to myself. "We're tracking them and, eventually, we'll find the boat they're on and then we'll intercept them." Hmm, intercepting them with Emelynn on my arm would be a bonus and a very satisfying *fuck you* to both of them, wouldn't it?

"I hope you find them soon," she said, and positioned an onion under her knife.

"We will," I said, staring into the bottom of my empty glass. It seemed her interrogation was finally finished. Thank Christ. That I had to lie was bad enough, but to paint Sandra as the victim got under my skin like a dog tick.

I'd gotten over it by the time we'd finished eating and afterwards, we took our wine to the salon and found a second-rate mystery movie. Emelynn was far more interesting to me than the movie. I wanted to peel her out of her clothes and feel her bare skin beneath my hands. When she upended her glass, I took it from her and set it on the table. She combed her fingers through my hair and I leaned in and kissed her, gently at first, but I couldn't hide my need. I devoured her with my mouth and explored her curves with my hands.

"You are very good at this," she said, easing away.

I held her hand to my chest and pressed my forehead to hers. "I'm glad you think so, but it has nothing to do with me." I pulled back and looked her in the eyes. "Do you have any idea how you make me feel when I'm with you?" I brushed the hair from her cheek, feeling her soft skin beneath my thumb. "To know what you gave me last night and that I'm the only one who has ever been inside you like that? You are so beautiful and you don't even know it."

A blush painted her face. "I don't know how to respond to that," she said, turning away.

She was utterly guileless. I guided her hand down my chest and pressed it into the bulge in my jeans. "You don't need to say anything," I said, rippling with pleasure. "How about we continue this below?"

She frowned. "I'm sorry, Jackson, but I couldn't possibly do that again tonight."

A carnal smile spread across my face. I had much to teach her. "There are lots of other ways to deal with this," I said, grinding into her hand. "Trust me . . . you'll like it." I stood and pulled her to her feet, and then escorted her to her cabin.

When I'd stripped her of her clothes, I stood back to admire her. I'd not had that pleasure last night. She was self-conscious at first, and timid, but her natural curiosity won out. She fell apart under my tongue and after that, she became an eager pupil and obliterated any thoughts I might have had of Sandra and Cole.

Chapter Twenty-Five

I woke early and managed to slip out of bed without waking Eme-lynn. Upstairs, I made the morning brew and thumbed through a missed text and a phone call, both from James.

I stepped outside to return his call. "What's up?" I said, when he answered.

"Did you lose your phone?"

"Took the night off," I said. "What's so urgent?"

"No more nights off. We're too close."

James could be such an irritant at times. "Did you find them?"

"Not yet. I got the dossiers you sent on Alex's contacts."

"Good. They look like they can handle themselves."

"Yeah, on paper," he said. "I've asked Alex to set up a face-to-face. You interested in coming along?"

"Sure. When and where?"

"This afternoon in Salem, Oregon. I've chartered a plane out of the South Airport. Meet us there at ten."

Shit. That didn't leave me a lot of time. "All right. See you then."

"And Jackson—pack a bag. It'll be an overnighter."

The unexpected trip would scuttle my budding designs on Emelynn, but at least it felt like I was finally doing something more concrete in our efforts to find the lovebirds.

I fixed Emelynn a coffee and dropped it by her bed none too quietly then continued on to my shower. She was awake when I returned.

"Got your coffee I see." She rested against the headboard, one leg on top of the sheet that threatened to fall from her breasts. Man, I'd made a bad trade. "Sorry for the early start," I said, "but I've got some business to take care of today. How about I get you home?"

She pouted, which was endearing, and all too soon we were in the Zodiac. We traversed the rocky beach and started up her stairs. Emelynn didn't notice the sandy outline of a footprint on the bottom step. I kissed her goodbye and closed the patio door behind me on the way out. At the bottom of her stairs, I stopped to investigate. Whoever had left that print left impressions in the sand on both sides of the staircase.

I set off for the Zodiac mulling over the footprints. The beach was public, but still. It seemed odd. I remembered something else, too; her first day on the *Symphony*, Emelynn had accused me of hanging around her steps—*loitering* was the word she'd used. Clearly this wasn't the first time someone had gotten uncomfortably close. It was probably nothing, but I was glad I'd checked her house.

I cruised to the Fraser River and docked at the marina. On my way out, I booked a service for the *Symphony's* engines in preparation for my return to New Orleans, and then took a cab to the South Airport. James and Alex met me outside the terminal. Three hours later, the Cessna touched down in Salem.

Alex scanned the vehicles parked outside the terminal building. A shiny black Dodge Ram 350 with a painted-out grill pulled alongside us. The driver looked as though he'd gotten lost on his way to a Hells Angels' rally. He powered down the passenger window, leaned over and growled, "Climb in."

We dropped our bags in the truck bed. Alex took the front seat, James and I the back bench.

"You let your kids paint your ride?" Alex asked, grinning.

"They're better with a roller than you, my man," he retorted, his lips barely visible beneath a thick moustache and matching goatee.

"Tony. This is Jackson and James," Alex said, nodding to us each in turn as he made the introductions.

"Good to meet ya," Tony said, pulling the gearshift into drive. "We're set up a couple a miles down the road." He wore a biker's vest over a black T-shirt, and both arms were heavily tatted.

He pulled into a Comfort Inn parking lot and stopped around the side of the building. I got a better look at him after we got out. Tony swaggered to the side entrance wearing his five-ten, two-hundred-pound build like a dare. He used his key card to gain access, and we followed him to his room.

"Gar. Got company," he said, pushing inside.

Gary was watching a Cubs game and testing his balance, leaning back so his armchair was teetering on two legs. He stood to greet us.

He shook Alex's hand. "Good to see you, man," he said. Gary's nose was broad and flat but clearly hadn't started out that way. He was shorter and smaller than Tony and wore his short-sleeved shirt untucked from his jeans. Less swagger than Tony, but just as much of a don't-fuck-with-me vibe.

Alex, once again, made the introductions.

Over the course of the afternoon, and a couple of beers, we learned that Alex and Gary had known each other since high school. Alex met Tony when Alex was fresh out of trade school and Tony took his bike to Alex to be painted. Back then, Tony worked vice with the Seattle PD. He didn't elaborate on his current occupation.

Two others, not present, were Gary's contacts: Jin and Mark. They were scouting the coast north of Newport, Cole and Sandra's latest ATM stop. We would meet up with them in the morning.

We bent over maps studying the Oregon and Washington coasts. James showed them stills from the last two ATM clips, and the map where we'd plotted the California withdrawals. When the beers were gone, we checked into the hotel and found a nearby pub for burgers.

We agreed to meet at seven the next morning and headed to our rooms. A short while later, there was a tap at my door.

I walked down the hall and let James in. "What's up?" I closed the door behind him and followed him down the short hall into my room.

"I had a very interesting discussion with Alex this afternoon before you arrived at the airport," he said, taking the only chair. He leaned forward with his elbows on his knees. "Tell me about Emelynn Taylor."

Ah shit. "Emelynn? Nothing to tell." I reclined on the bed and laced my fingers behind my head. "Avery Coulter found her in his ER. I'm sure Alex filled you in." I couldn't hold it against Alex. James was bound to find out about her, but no one needed to know how far our relationship had gone, especially not James.

"She's staying on the *Symphony*," he said, straightening up and leaning back to look down his nose. "Seems kinda strange you hadn't mentioned her."

"*Was* staying, and I don't answer to you. She left as soon as she got her wings, and it's not like I had much choice in the matter. Avery asked for my help. We aren't exactly in a position to say no."

"Fair enough. So what's her story?" He feigned disinterest, reaching for the hotel pen and twisting its cap. Emelynn was none of his business and that's how it was going to stay.

"She was gifted by a woman named Jolene. No last name. That's all she knows."

"Parents?"

"Not Fliers, and she wasn't raised like one."

"Odd, isn't it?" he said, stealing a sideways glance at me.

"Very. But she's not our concern. Eden, Alex and I did our part. She's Avery's problem now."

He hollowed his cheeks thinking it over. Finally, he moved on. "What's your impression of Tony and Gary?"

"Eager, competent. What do you think?"

"Yeah. Same." He stood and headed for the door. "See you at seven," he said, and a moment later, I heard the door click closed. Just to be sure he'd left, I got up and walked down the hall to check, and then swung the safety catch into place.

Back on the bed, I pulled out my phone and dialled the number I'd programmed in for Emelynn.

"Hello," she answered.

Her voice sounded as though it were coming from the bottom of a well. I took a wild guess. "Are you in the bathtub?"

"How could you tell?"

"I can hear the echo," I said, laughing, "and you're splashing." I pictured her naked, lying in a bed of suds. "I'm taking the *Symphony* in for maintenance in Richmond, day after tomorrow. If you don't already have plans, maybe you could pick me up and we could do something together?"

"I'd like that," she said. Another splash had me wishing I could slide into the suds beside her.

"Any more news on Jolene?" she asked.

The Jolene question felt like one of those nagging loose ends that threatened to unravel with a tug and leave a gaping hole. Until I knew what lurked in that hole, I'd keep what I did know to myself. "No, I haven't heard anything back."

"What about Sandra?" she asked.

Sandra's name from Emelynn's lips reverberated in my gut like the strike of a gong. "No, nothing there either."

"You'll find her," she said.

Yes, and very soon. How would it feel, I wondered, facing Sandra after all this time? Would I see remorse in her face?

Emelynn interrupted my thoughts. "Are you all right?" she asked.

"Sure, I just don't like to think about it."

"Do you keep in touch with her family?"

If you only knew. "All the time," I replied.

"How can I reach you?" she asked, changing the subject. "Your phone number doesn't come up on call display."

"No, it wouldn't." I'd made certain of it. "It's a Louisiana number. I don't suppose you've got a pen or paper there with you in the tub?"

"You suppose correctly," she said, and suggested I text it to her so she wouldn't have to get out of the tub.

"You got it," I said, but I had no intention of sending it. One less complication. "Good night, Emelynn."

The next morning we piled into Tony's truck and drove west through a downpour to Lincoln City, on the coast. We met Jin and Mark at a place called Maxwell's. They wore the standard Flier uniform: black on black. It was early for ribs, but we'd only had coffee for breakfast. Jin was a slight, focused man of few words. Mark had an easy laugh and the crew-cut of an ex-military grunt. Once again, we reviewed the maps in detail. James told them his surveillance people would pull out when we had a bead on the vessel Sandra was travelling in. It was far too dangerous for the non-Gifted to be involved in the eventual confrontation.

Tony dropped James, Alex and me at the Salem airport, where we boarded the charter back to Vancouver. After we cleared customs, we parted ways.

It was late by the time I got back to the *Symphony*. The service manager had taped a note to the door telling me his crew would be by in the morning. I unlocked the door and dumped my bag by the stairs. With James outside my orbit, I felt the relief of emancipation. I liberated a beer from the fridge.

The celebration was premature. An incoming call from James dampened my spirits. "Miss me already?" I asked, answering.

"I thought you'd like to know that Cole's aware the *Symphony* isn't in its slip at the yacht club. Bronwyn mentioned it in their phone call tonight."

"Then Cole knows exactly where we are." The *Symphony's* mandatory Automatic Identification System transceiver, would pinpoint her position.

"No doubt. And if he wasn't sure before, now he'll know for certain that we're on to him. No other reason for the *Symphony* to be in Vancouver."

"You worried he'll give us the slip?"

"It might be better for Sandra if he did. Right now, we're on a collision course. This isn't going to turn out well for one of us. He knows that. We know that."

"Stop assuming she's a victim, James. Cole has a monumental ego. He's probably looking forward to a meet-up. What better way to rub Sandra in my face."

"Yeah. You keep telling yourself that."

"Listen, we're never going to agree on Sandra's motivation. But Cole knowing we're here won't change a thing, unless you're suggesting we quit looking for her."

His silence gave me pause.

"No," he finally said. "We'll stay the course, but how about we don't add fuel to the fire. He'll be tracking the *Symphony* now. Let's keep her in Canadian waters. Hell, if you're right, he'll come to us."

We hung up. I drained my beer and opened another. This bullshit had been going on too long. I headed to the foredeck and settled in a lounger to call Emelynn. The rain hadn't followed us past Oregon, but the night was cool.

"Emelynn, how was your day?"

"Productive. I learned how to start the lawn mower," she said with a laugh. The couple who'd been caretaking her home during her and her mother's ten-year absence were giving her pointers. I'd never run a lawnmower and knew nothing of deadheading roses or Whipper-snipping, but her enthusiasm made me want to. Before we hung up, she agreed to swing by the marina in the morning while the *Symphony* was being serviced. She'd be a pleasant reprieve after two days of plotting a course to find my cheating wife.

The marine techs arrived at eight in the morning. I showed them to the engine room and took my coffee and the laptop out to the aft deck, where I could keep watch for Emelynn. Ted Worley had dropped a large file in my inbox. It was the feasibility study of a project on the outskirts of Lake Charles that would garner Delaney & Son international attention. I lost myself in the details until an incoming call from Josh interrupted my review. "What do you know, Josh?"

"My contacts in the San Francisco covey tell me it was rumoured Jolene Reynolds had been unstable for years before she disappeared. Apparently, she'd lost a baby. It sent her over the proverbial edge."

"What'd you learn about her family?"

"They emigrated from Scotland in the nineteenth century. An Edward Reynolds purchased a ranch in California in 1893. It's just north of Bodega Bay. They raise cattle and operate an equestrian centre. Mother's name is Jeannette, father's name is Stuart, both still living. She has a brother named Mason. They rarely attend covey functions I don't expect to learn more without direct contact."

"I'm not ready for that. Not yet. Thanks for the intel. I'll be in touch." I hung up. Though I hadn't expected any mention of Ghosts, I admittedly felt disappointed. And though Jolene might have been unstable, she might also have had good reason for not telling her family about gifting Emelynn. An enquiry could prove dangerous—they might not be happy to learn a stranger possessed Jolene's gift.

I checked my watch. Emelynn should have been here by now. I stood and stretched, and then walked to the railing and looked down the dock. Sunlight bounced off the water. She must have been delayed. I packed up my laptop and dropped it inside. Below deck, the marine techs were well into the *Symphony's* maintenance. It would take the better part of the day to complete. I made sure they had what they needed, grabbed my sunglasses and went back outside. A warm breeze stirred the air.

I spotted Emelynn making her way toward me and charged down the steps to intercept her. She'd dressed casually in a jean jacket and capris. When she stepped into the *Symphony's* shadow, she raised her sunglasses.

"Good morning, beautiful," I said, and leaned in for a kiss. A fresh citrus scent clung to her. "Let's go for a walk along the dyke," I suggested. "I could use the exercise after being on board for so long." I pulled her hand into mine and headed toward the parking lot.

"Have you learned anything about Jolene?" she asked.

Already with the questions. "Nothing yet," I said, and preemptively answered what would surely be her next question. "And nothing else on Sandra either."

"I hope something turns up soon," she said, and thankfully dropped both subjects.

At the top of the ramp, we crossed to the parking lot and she led me to the MGB that I'd seen only from a distance before. Up close, it was in better shape than I'd expected.

"You like?" she asked.

"It's a classic," I said. "What's not to like?"

She told me about the car as we drove to the dyke and parked. It had belonged to her father. She'd discovered it in the garage where it had sat for ten years after his death. Turns out the young man from Meyers Motors was the mechanic who'd restored it for her. I was happy to learn he wasn't still sniffing around.

The warm day brought the dog walkers and bicyclists to the trail. Seagulls screeched above our heads as mothers pushed strollers past. We sauntered with no particular destination. It felt good to stretch my legs. We stopped at a fish-and-chip shack for a bite of lunch and then checked out the small shops along the water's edge. A pair of racing goggles caught Emelynn's attention.

"Great idea," I said, nodding my approval. She chuckled softly and shook her head. "What is it?" I asked, taking her hand. "What's so funny?"

"Not funny, at least not hee-haw funny," she said. "It's just so incredibly, oddly, normal. Here you and I are, having a perfectly normal day: walking along the dyke, shopping, eating lunch—just like everyone else." She stopped to scan the area for eavesdroppers, and then added, "Only there's nothing normal about us. That's what I'm finding so amusing."

It wasn't the first time I'd seen the gift through her eyes. It gave me pause. "I forget how new you are to this life." I pulled her close and pressed my lips to the top of her head. "One day this *will* be normal for you. Eventually, flying will seem as natural to you as breathing." I felt a surge of gratitude for whatever force had kept her safe to this point, and held her close.

I'd promised her dinner in exchange for her company, and took her to Steveston's Jetty. Over a plate of oysters, she told me about Molly Connolly, the bookstore clerk I'd been curious about. They'd been school chums before Emelynn moved east, and had reconnected in the bookstore after she returned to Summerset.

With a little prompting, I learned how she'd coped while growing up with Jolene's gift. It hadn't been easy, and she had few friends as a result, but she didn't weigh herself down with the negatives.

After dinner, she drove us back to her place. "Are you sure you can find your way back to the *Symphony* from here?" she asked, heading to her stereo.

"I'll be fine. Do you have any wine?"

"To the right of the fridge," she said. "Glasses are in the cupboard above."

The soft notes of acoustic guitar settled into the background. We took the wine out to the deck and leaned against the railing, gazing out across the water. The night air was cool, bringing with it the pungent scent of a low tide.

"I don't recognize the music. What is it?" I asked.

"One of my mother's CDs. *Guitar Music for Small Rooms*," she said.

It was the perfect choice. "Hmm."

"What?" she asked, tilting her head.

"Are you trying to seduce me?"

A coy smile teased her lips. "Maybe," she said, and took a sip of her wine. "Is it working?"

Emelynn, the seductress. I liked this side of her. I reached my hand to her face and traced my thumb along her jaw, then guided her free hand to the growing bulge in my jeans. "I think it's working just fine. What do you think?"

"I'd say you enjoy acoustic guitar."

Her smile melted under my lips. She stroked me like she knew what she was doing. She'd been a fast learner. I curled my hand under her curtain of hair and stroked her nape. She slipped an arm around my waist and stepped into me, pressing her lips to the base of my throat. She fit perfectly. The wine glasses occupying our hands no longer seemed like the stellar idea they had been just a moment before. I set mine on the railing and relieved Emelynn of hers.

"That's better," I said, and cupped her breast. Her nipple was already hard. She needed to be naked.

I pressed my forehead to hers. "Bedroom," I hissed, and caught her arm, turning her toward the door.

But my step faltered as I glimpsed a shiny disk in the arbutus tree adjacent to the deck. I stopped short and yanked Emelynn back and into a tight embrace. She tensed. I turned us full circle and spoke quietly. "Look over my right shoulder into the branches of the arbutus tree." Her head jerked up. I squeezed her. "Don't make it obvious."

I nuzzled her neck and whispered, "Do you see anything unusual?" Her gaze was too low. "At about the same height as your roof," I said, maintaining my amorous ruse.

"I see something reflective," she said. "Maybe about the size of a Red Bull can?"

"That's it. Have you ever noticed it before?"

"No. What is it?"

"I can't be sure, but if it's what I think it is, we have a problem."

CHAPTER TWENTY-SIX

Emelynn rushed into the house, with me on her heels. "Do you have binoculars?" I asked, guiding her ahead of me, away from the windows.

"No. What do you think it is?"

"It looks suspiciously like a camera."

"A camera?" she asked, furrowing her brow. "What would a camera be doing there?"

"Good question." And I could think of only one answer: someone knew about us. I paced the hall. Who? And how long had they been watching?

"I need to get a closer look. I'll be back in a few minutes." I left through the front door. I lifted a few inches off the ground and skimmed across the lawn, checking the surrounding trees for similar devices. Finding none, I flew up and examined the camera. It looked new—fresh from the box. The tree's trunk had been damaged, as had the bark where the camera was mounted. I opened the camera's SD slot and removed the card. Whatever was on it would tell us something.

Emelynn waited at the front door, holding it open. I rushed in and closed it. "Will your computer read this?" I asked, showing her the memory card.

She shrugged. "I have no idea. What did you find?"

We rushed to her computer on the dining room table. "It's a camera, but it doesn't look like it's been there for long." I powered on the laptop and scanned the media slots. "I think we're in luck," I said, inserting the card.

The file contained hundreds of images. I clicked on the first thumbnail. A crow in flight. "It's motion activated," I said, and browsed through the images. The camera captured a north-facing pie-shaped section that stretched up the beach to her neighbour's place and broadened out from Emelynn's deck to midtide. The *Symphony* would have been in range. Not good.

The camera was state-of-the-art. Expensive. "They're high-resolution photos. Whoever is taking these can blow up the detail of even the smallest pebble on that beach." I flipped back to the first image. "This was taken at six fifteen this morning. The camera isn't wired for remote transmission, so whoever is behind this either set it up, or changed the card, early this morning."

Emelynn stilled beside me. I let the images flow, most of them bird shots, and watched the time stamp. Emelynn didn't come into frame until eight seventeen. She'd been on the deck, barefoot in a long shirt.

She covered her mouth with her hand and whispered, "Oh, my god."

A series of photos followed her movement from the deck's railing to the lounger, and ended when she stepped back inside. I flipped to the last shot. Fuck! I pushed back in the chair.

"What is it?"

"These images are thermal infrared."

"What does that mean?"

"It means that whoever is behind this isn't fooling around. That camera is high-tech . . . professional." The images looked eerily similar to the blackmail footage from Cole. Had he found me? "It means someone spared no expense to set up 24/7 surveillance of this area."

Emelynn sat down, smoothing a tablecloth that wasn't there. "Could it simply be a wealthy bird-watching group studying migratory routes? Or maybe it's an environmental organization monitoring sea levels?"

"If either of those were the case, you and your neighbours along this beach would have been notified. It's too big an invasion of privacy for it to be legitimate." Could this be James's handiwork? I wondered.

"How long do you think it's been there?"

"Maybe a week. The thing is clean and the scars on the tree where it's been mounted are still fresh."

"Then Eden, you and I have all been photographed . . . flying."

Which meant we had to find whoever was responsible. I removed the card from Emelynn's computer. "I need to return this to the camera," I said, and headed outside.

Could Emelynn be the target? Maybe those footprints I'd seen in the sand at the foot of her stairs belonged to our spy. I slipped the card back into the camera and glanced over to Emelynn's kitchen window. I could think of one way to catch the culprit.

Back on the ground, I phoned Alex and gave him a quick rundown of the situation. "We need to set up countersurveillance. Can you get your hands on a camera?"

"I keep a spare at my shop. It's nothing special, but it'll work. When do you want it?"

"Right now. Bring it to Emelynn's place." I gave him the address as I walked back inside and closed the door.

"I can be there within the hour."

"Great," I said, and disconnected.

Emelynn sat curled in a ball on the sofa. She took my hand when I sat beside her. "Who was that?" she asked.

"Alex. I've asked him to bring over a security camera. If you don't mind, we'll set it up in your kitchen window. With any luck, we'll get a look at who's retrieving the memory cards from that camera. If we can ID them, we might be able to figure out what's going on. We should, at least, be able to tell if they're Fliers or not. You okay with that?"

"Sure, anything to help. Do you think that whoever's behind that camera has seen us flying to and from the *Symphony*?"

"Without knowing how long that camera's been there, I'm afraid that's a real possibility."

"Could it be connected to Sandra's disappearance?" she asked.

"It could be." Cole had been my first thought. I couldn't blame her for thinking the same.

She inhaled and squeezed my hand. "In that case, I think you'd better tell me the rest of the Sandra story."

I stared at the back of her hand and skimmed my thumb over the smooth skin of her knuckles. "How do you know her?" she asked, prompting me.

I hated the lie, but I'd dug this damn pit myself. Now I was stuck in it "She's a friend and one of my covey back in New Orleans. I wish you weren't so curious about her. But more than that . . ." I looked up to her face, her brow lined in worry. Nothing I could tell her would ease that worry. "I really believe the less you know, the better. If the people behind that camera are connected with Sandra, you'll be safer if you don't know anything about her."

"I don't mean to upset you," she said. "I just want to help."

"You can't at this point. I wish you could, but you're too inexperienced a Flier. When we find her, we'll need a team of our best to get her back."

"But I'm fast, Jackson. You said so yourself."

"Fast only helps if you can control it, Em, and you're too green right now." I squeezed her hand, hoping to soften my critique. "You are fast, the fastest I've ever seen, but your speed would be a detriment to us if we ended up having to pull you out of the Pacific."

Far from discouraging her, my words seemed to fuel her. "I'll keep practicing," she said. "Maybe I'll surprise you."

"Maybe you will," I said, and grinned, remembering her seduction on the deck earlier. "It wouldn't be the first time."

She answered my grin with one of her own. "Will you stay?"

"For a while. I asked Alex to come as soon as he got his hands on a camera. We'll set it up tonight if you don't mind."

"Of course not."

I reached my arm around her shoulder and pulled her close. She folded against me, her knees still bent. She jumped at the doorbell's soft chime. "Let me," I said, and rose to answer it.

"That it?" I asked, letting Alex in.

"Yup. Won't take long to set it up."

"Good. Their camera doesn't have a view of Emelynn's kitchen window. The kitchen's down the hall," I said, closing the door behind him.

He walked ahead of me. "How are you doing?" Alex said to Emelynn, who'd risen to greet him.

"I'd be better if there weren't a camera outside watching my every move."

"Yeah, we all would," he said, and then turned to me. "Where do we need to set this up?"

I pointed to the kitchen window and Alex got to work. With the help of some books for camouflage, we laid the camera in place and connected the transmitter to Emelynn's router. She stood on the far side of the breakfast bar and watched the operation with interest.

"It's not high-tech," I said, finishing up, "but it will take a photo of that damn tree every sixty seconds during daylight hours. I've set it up to send the images through your router to my computer, so don't turn off your router." I stood and walked over to where Emelynn watched over Alex crouched by the router.

Alex looked up at her. "Will you feel safe staying here? You could come stay with Eden and me. We have a spare room."

"Thanks, Alex," she said, "but I think we'd have a better shot at finding out who's behind that camera if I stayed here and kept up the impression that everything's normal. I don't want to scare them off, especially if they're watching to see when Jackson is going to make a move to go after Sandra."

Alex switched his attention to me. "Do you think that's what this is about?"

"I don't know. I can't connect those dots, but I can't rule it out yet either."

I reached for Emelynn's shoulder. "I think you staying here is a good idea, but only if you feel comfortable doing it. If you could carry on like nothing's up for the next twenty-four hours or so, we might get an ID."

She cradled her elbows and put on a brave face. "I can do that."

I gave her tense shoulder a reassuring squeeze. She wasn't comfortable, that much was obvious, but whoever was behind that camera had already been skulking around for a week and hadn't confronted her yet. We had to risk one more day. "Keep your doors and windows locked. Don't open up for anyone you don't recognize. I'll know the minute someone approaches that camera. Where's your phone?"

She fetched it from the coffee table and I input my cell. "That's my phone number. Call me any time. Until we know who's behind this, we need to keep a lid on it. Don't tell anyone about our discovery."

"Eden already knows," Alex said, standing and brushing his pants. "I phoned her before I left the shop."

"No one else then, okay?" I turned to Emelynn. "We don't know who's involved in this so let's not inadvertently warn them."

"Agreed," she said.

Alex nodded. "Well then, there's nothing else I can do here tonight. I'll update Eden when I get home." He addressed Emelynn again. "Call us any time if you change your mind."

She thanked him and walked him out.

I followed her down the hall, and when Alex disappeared from sight, I said, "I've got to head off too, if I'm going to make it back to the *Symphony* without a cab." Not that I wanted to fly back, but if I stayed, I wouldn't want to leave her bed until morning, and if our spy sensed my presence, he might not show his face. "Are you sure you're okay with this?"

"I'm not thrilled about it," she said. "But I think it's best."

She looked good wrapped in courage. I lifted her chin and kissed her. A soft sigh escaped her lips as I pulled away. It enticed me back and I kissed her properly. Thoroughly. And before I could change my mind and take her with me, I stepped back.

"Lock up behind me," I said, and tore myself away from her.

The cool air on my flight back to the *Symphony* took my mind off Emelynn's warm lips and soft curves.

The likelihood that James had installed the infrared camera was small. He hadn't even known about Emelynn until two days ago. So either Cole knew my whereabouts, or our activity around Emelynn's place had garnered attention. Either way, our own camera would soon catch the culprit.

I awoke with the dawn and flipped on the computer. The kitchen cam had already sent a stream of photos. A quick review showed nothing alarming. After a light breakfast, I opened Worley's report on the Lake Charles project and resumed my review while I kept an eye on the incoming photos. The day was shaping up to disappoint, already grey and colder than yesterday.

Just after nine, my work came to a grating halt. Another ATM clip landed in my inbox. This time from La Push, in Washington. James was right; they were getting close.

Once again, Sandra clung to Cole like she'd never clung to me, and wore sunglasses even though the time stamp pegged the shot at close to midnight. She was hiding from me now, just like she hid from the press. And so she should. Her behaviour was unbecoming to the point of embarrassing.

If Cole was behind the camera at Emelynn's, he'd get worse than a beating. Bastard!

I pushed away from the laptop, grabbed a jacket and headed down the dock to cool my head. At the marina gates, I took the footpath that followed the shore of the Fraser. Emelynn called while I sat on a bench overlooking the tidal flats.

"Everything all right?" I said, welcoming the interruption.

"Yeah. How's our camera working?"

"Good so far. I've been up since dawn monitoring the photos, and I've got to say I'm pretty tired of looking at that damn tree. Luckily, I do have some work to do so it's not a total waste of time."

"I'm going to go out, take a break."

Speaking of breaks, mine was over. "Sure. I'll call if anything interesting shows up."

"Thanks," she said. "Talk to you later."

I hung up and returned to the marina. Back on board, I forwarded the ATM footage to James, but not before torturing myself with a second viewing. The fact that her family was now funding their romp up the coast didn't take the sting out of it. But that was good. Sandra's betrayal added the fuel I needed to keep myself in James's game.

The kitchen cam supplied nothing more interesting than a squirrel all morning. I finished my preliminary notes on the Lake Charles project and fired them back to Worley. When I'd dealt with the rest of my inbox, I headed to the marina pub for a burger and beer.

Every sixty seconds my phone lit up with another photo. I must have looked like one of Pavlov's dogs, swiping at the small screen then taking a bite of my burger and a swig of beer at one-minute intervals. When the phone buzzed with a real phone call, I nearly dropped my beer.

"How's that camera working out?" Alex asked.

"Good. The photos are sharp. If our spy shows up in daylight, we'll get him."

"Damn straight we'll get the bastard. You need a break yet? I'm finishing up here soon."

"Terrific. This is bloody monotonous. Come on out. I'll have a cold beer ready for you."

On the way out of the pub, I picked up a six-pack and headed back to the *Symphony*.

Alex arrived a short time later. "Where'd Emelynn go?" he asked.

"Said the pressure was getting to her. She took off for the day."

Alex scanned through the earlier shots. "Eden and I were talking last night, trying to figure out who could be behind this. It's kinda strange, don't you think, that Emelynn doesn't know the woman who gifted her? Have you learned any more about her?"

"I've made some enquiries, but it's still a mystery."

"Any chance your enquiries may have prompted someone to come poking around?"

"It's a possibility, I suppose."

He could be right. Not only had Josh been hunting down intel on Jolene, but I'd also been scanning the secure message boards. Could Jolene's family be the culprits?

I couldn't blame the Reynoldses for wanting to know what happened to their daughter, but a camera was overkill. One conversation with Emelynn was all they'd need to know the gifting had been voluntary. And the family must have known Jolene had been despondent at the time. So if it was the Reynolds family, why go to these lengths? Unless there was more to Em's gift than her incredible speed.

Alex interrupted my thoughts. "I almost hope it's the family of the woman who gifted her, because if it's something else, like Emelynn exposing the gift, whether she was aware of it or not, we could be in for a whole lot more trouble."

"Could be amateurs," I offered.

"With that equipment? I'm thinking government. Didn't you suspect the military or organized crime might be sniffing around our kind?"

"Let's hope not," I said, feeling the bite on my ass from the lie I'd fed them weeks ago.

Emelynn called and we talked briefly, just before six in the evening.

I said to Alex, "Emelynn's home to change and then she's going out again. She'll be gone a couple of hours."

"Good. We can rest easy for a while."

"You interested in dinner, or is Eden expecting you?"

"No, Eden's on nights. If you're cooking, I'm happy to help you eat it. I'd better give Eden an update though."

He took his phone out to the deck and returned a short while later. "Eden says hi. She's convinced she's been filmed flying from Emelynn's deck. It's eating her up. I told her I'd stay until sunset, when our camera shuts down."

"Sunset's not until nine. How about I put on a couple of steaks?"

We ate on the aft deck with the laptop and a boring but steady stream of photos to keep us company.

"Say, what happened with you and Emelynn the other night? Eden tells me she had a close call."

How much had Emelynn told her? I wondered. "Yeah, too close. She got away on me."

"On you?" he said, raising his eyebrows. "How'd she do that?" He broke his gaze to stab at a piece of steak.

"I underestimated her. Let her get too far ahead of me."

"I heard it was a little more than an underestimate. That girl's got speed, or so I'm told."

So much for keeping *that* to myself. "Like you've never seen. Any of us would have lost her. If I'd known, I wouldn't have pushed her."

"Shouldn't surprise us, I guess, given how little we know about the woman who gifted her. Makes me wonder what other skills Emelynn might develop."

You and me both, I thought.

Alex cleared the table when we'd finished eating, and I stood to scrape the grill.

He returned with two more beers and set them on the table, gazing at the laptop's screen. "About fucking time! We got the bastard."

I came running. Alex backtracked to the first shot of our culprit. A hooded figure, large and definitely male. His face was covered with some sort of mask. "Not one of us," Alex said, observing the shot of the man climbing the tree.

I dialled Emelynn to warn her away.

"Not much to go on. Do you recognize anything?" Alex asked.

Emelynn's phone rang three times then went to voice mail. Shit.

"No, nothing familiar," I said.

Maybe Emelynn was on the phone. I dialled her again.

"That's it," Alex said. "He's out of the shot now. Where's Emelynn?"

"She's not answering." Her voice mail picked up again.

"Let me try," Alex said, and pulled out his own phone. After a minute of listening, he hung up. "Voice mail. It's too light outside to fly from here. What's the fastest way to get to her?"

"Go release the mooring lines. Quick. I can have us out far enough to fly in ten minutes." I climbed the stairs two at a time and fired up the engines. Alex scurried around the dock tossing the lines back on board.

He jumped onto the aft deck as I was pulling away and shouted up at me, "Go!"

Ships the size of the *Symphony* were built for comfort, not speed. Still, with the bow already pointed in the right direction, we made a swift departure. Before we'd cleared the mouth of the Fraser, I had the waypoint for the shallows outside Emelynn's place up on the chart.

"I can chance it from here," Alex said, when we were a hundred yards off shore.

"Go in across Sunset Park," I said, pointing it out on the navigation screen. "I'm headed to this area, out front of her place."

"I'll let you know what I find," Alex said, and then he tore off.

I kept the *Symphony's* throttles open and pushed on. Once again, I dialled Emelynn and once again, it went to voicemail.

It felt like an eternity before Alex checked in. "She's not here," he said, still catching his breath. "Her car's gone. It doesn't look like anyone's tried to get inside her place."

"Okay. I'm still fifteen minutes out."

"I'll head your way when I see you," Alex said.

By the time I arrived, dusk was upon us. I set anchor, and Alex landed on the deck. "Any sign of her?" I asked.

"No. Let's hope she just turned her phone off."

Neither of us voiced the fear that someone might have taken her. Time crawled while we took turns watching her place with the binoculars. We distracted ourselves with the ship's gadgets. Being mechanically inclined, Alex was keen to know how to set and weigh anchor. After that demonstration, I walked him through the Navtech system.

Eventually, the distraction wore thin. The wait became too much. I had to do something. "I'm going to go have a look around. You okay to stay here?"

"Sure."

I flew for shore and landed on a trail inside the park. The trail led to the cul-de-sac at the end of Cliffside Avenue, close to the foot of Emelynn's driveway. I studied the ground as I approached her house looking for signs of a struggle. There were none. The garage doors stood open, the one on the left held in place by an old stick. The jamb of her front door didn't have a scratch. Feeling somewhat relieved, I skimmed across the lawn toward the arbutus tree and rose to the height of the camera. I snapped off a leafy branch and draped it over the lens. I then flew the perimeter of the house and checked every window and the patio doors for signs of forced entry. Finding none, I took a seat on a lounger on her deck and called Alex.

"No change here. I'm going to stick around. She can't be too much longer."

It was almost eleven o'clock. My head spun the clock forward. How long should I wait? At what point do I make the call that she's been taken? Goddamnit, Emelynn! If you've turned your phone off... I couldn't finish the thought because I didn't want to think about the alternative.

I paced the deck for twenty minutes before I had my answer.

A car turned into her driveway. I flew up to peek above the roof and saw her MGB. My blood started a slow boil. I landed on her deck, flexing my fists.

The front door opened and closed. It was her. Unscathed. I turned my back to her, my relief mixed with anger so hot I wanted to throttle her.

The patio door slid open. "What are you doing here?" Emelynn whispered, grabbing my arm to pull me inside. "You scared ten years off me."

"Oh, *I've* scared *you*?" I said, narrowing my eyes as I pressed in. "Where's your goddamn phone!" She caught my anger and wisely stepped back. How could she be so careless? I threw my hands in the air. "I've been calling you for an hour and it's going to voice mail."

Her eyes went wide. Abruptly, she turned and rushed to her bedroom. I walked the length of floor inside her patio door.

"Oh hell," she mumbled, hurrying back with her phone in one hand, her purse in the other. "The battery's dead."

I stopped and stared at her.

"I'm sorry," she said, the picture of remorse.

I turned and paced one more circuit before I spoke. "I'm glad you're okay." I pulled out my phone and called Alex. "She's fine," I said.

"That's a relief. Was her phone turned off?" he asked.

"No, dead battery . . . We'll be there soon."

"I'll weigh anchor," he said, and disconnected.

"What's that all about?" Emelynn asked as I tucked my phone away.

"We got a couple of photos just before sunset. They're not much, but I want you to come take a look. Maybe you'll recognize him."

"Is he a Flier?"

"No, and he had his face covered, so there's not much to go on."

"How did you get past the camera?"

"I obstructed the lens. Are you ready to go?"

"Just give me a minute to change, okay?"

Emelynn scurried back to her bedroom. I inhaled deeply and exhaled the dregs of my anger.

She was dressed for flight when she returned. "Is that the *Symphony* out there?" she asked.

"Yes. It's out of the camera's view. Let's go." I motioned her ahead of me down the hall.

She grabbed her goggles and locked up, and we hurried into the park to lift off under cover. Once airborne, I flew back to the arbutus and dislodged the branch blocking the lens. I rejoined her. We flew south along the cliff's edge of the park, and then took a 90 degree turn straight out to the *Symphony*.

We landed on the observation deck and Alex stepped out to meet us. Emelynn jerked in surprise. "You had us worried," Alex said.

"I know—I'm sorry," she said. "I'm not usually this blonde."

He chuckled. "Let's go look at the photos."

I led the way below and headed to the cockpit.

"I've weighed anchor," Alex said, smiling as though he'd just flown solo for the first time.

As I piloted the *Symphony* away from shore, he and Emelynn settled at the laptop and Alex walked her through the photos.

"What's that all about?" I heard her ask.

"It's some kind of climbing spur," Alex said. "See here. He's jammed the spur into the side of the tree."

"I don't recognize him," she said. "But he's so nondescript. He could be half the men I know. I'm afraid I'm not much help."

"Neither are these photos," Alex said. "I sent them to Eden too, but I don't think we'll be able to ID anyone with them."

I called to Alex, "Help yourself to a beer. We'll be another ten minutes or so."

Alex headed for the fridge. "Do you want one?"

Emelynn declined, but Alex delivered one to me, and then he and Emelynn moved to the sofas.

"I don't think we'll get more photos of this guy until tomorrow or maybe the day after," Alex said.

I checked the time. "If he's on a thirty-six-hour cycle, then he'll make a collection day after tomorrow at dawn." The SD card's capacity was huge at half a terabyte.

I shut down the engines and joined them on the sofa. "We're in a holding pattern until he shows again."

"Yeah, meantime, Eden's worrying herself sick." Alex rubbed his temples. "At least she's off for a few days after tonight."

"Why don't we go flying?" I suggested. "It'll take our minds off it for a while."

"Speaking of which," Alex said, turning to Emelynn with a grin on his face, "I hear you have a new trick."

Emelynn whipped her head in my direction. "You told him?"

Her misplaced accusation took me by surprise.

"Actually," Alex said, "it was Eden who told me."

A flush crept into Emelynn's cheeks. "Oh, yeah, I guess I did mention it to her," she said, and then apologized.

Alex guzzled his beer. "Let's go." He reached for my bottle and walked our empties to the galley.

Emelynn stood with a mumble and smoothed her pants. "I'm really not comfortable with the show-pony thing."

Show pony? Hell, if I had that speed, I'd be prancing with my head held high. Luckily, I'd already replaced the earpieces we'd lost. "I've got something for us." I'd picked up a box of eight, enough for whatever team we put together to confront Cole. "Help yourself."

"Cool." Alex plucked one from the box and excused himself, walking toward the head.

Emelynn hadn't moved. "What is it?" I asked. When she didn't answer, I lifted her chin with my finger. She twitched and her eyes darted like a frightened child's. I knew then the earpiece had triggered a reminder of the last time she'd worn one.

I stared into her eyes. "That will never happen again."

Even with fear still written on her face, she reached for an earpiece. "No promises, Jackson. Like I said, I'm not ready yet."

"You might surprise yourself," I said, admiring her courage.

Alex rejoined us and we climbed to the observation deck. With no one around for miles, one after another, we took off and flew acrobatic circuits around the *Symphony.* Alex demonstrated his incredible skill, tumbling from terrific heights, always in tight control. In turn, I challenged him to outdo my backflips. We both kept a close eye on Emelynn, encouraging her to join in the fun. Did she know, I wondered, that before I'd met her, I rarely flew just for the hell of it? I reminded myself to thank her for that when we were alone again.

We slowed to catch our breath, and I flew over to Emelynn. "How are you doing?"

"Great," she said, without any of her usual enthusiasm.

"You're holding back—I can tell."

She crossed her arms. "I told you—I'm not ready to test my speed again, not yet."

"I think you should—just like I thought you should get back up in the air as soon after the accident as possible. Besides, there are two of us to back you up tonight."

She arched an eyebrow.

"Don't look at me like that. Maybe you think it's too soon for me to be challenging you, but you know as well as I do that you have to learn how to deal with your speed. The only way to do that is to use it. I'm not suggesting you commit suicide, just get back out there and test it. Get some more experience under your belt so you can master the speed, instead of the other way around."

She dropped her defensive posture. I'd finally gotten through. "All right, I'll try. But don't expect miracles," she said.

"That's more like it," I said with a wink. "We'll try to keep up." Alex had heard it all and didn't need my prompting to follow as I sped off to create the distance Emelynn needed to do her thing.

And do her thing, she did. Spectacularly. She had to be doing fifty miles an hour when she passed between us.

"In-fucking-credible!" Alex shouted. He looked at me with his mouth open.

"And *that's* why I lost her," I said, and the weight of my guilt fell away for my part in the episode that nearly killed her.

Emelynn's voice came over the mic. "Okay, show's over," she said, and turned back to join us. The corners of her mouth were turned up in a bashful smile.

Alex howled. "Wow! Emelynn, that's beyond impressive."

"It's embarrassing," Emelynn said, dipping her head.

"Nonsense," I said. If Alex hadn't been there, I would have wrapped her in my arms and made her earn that blush. "Let's keep going."

Emelynn pulled away. "Gladly," she said, and executed a perfect swan dive. Alex and I followed, and soon Emelynn forgot our presence and started really testing her speed. Alex and I looked at one another and shook our heads. She had no idea how rare her speed was. We watched in amazement as she drove herself, adjusting her body to reduce the drag and equalize the force of her movements. Each attempt looked more fluid than the last.

We returned to the *Symphony* when she'd finally had enough.

"Thank you," she said. "Both of you. I know I resisted at first, but that was fun. I feel much better now for having done it."

Alex patted her shoulder. "I'm sure the accident scared you, but Jackson was right. You needed to get back out there and test yourself." Alex pulled out his cellphone and yawned. "I'm glad I saw it for myself. That speed of yours—man—that's something." He glanced at his phone. "It's after two. I've got to go."

I shook his hand. "If I catch an interesting photo, I'll call."

The moment he was out of sight, I pulled Emelynn close. "I've wanted to do this all night," I said, and tasted her lips, cool from the night air, and soft as satin. When I pulled away, she had a curious smile on her face.

"So I'm guessing you didn't tell Alex about the happy ending to our swim the other night?"

"Of course not. That's no one's business but ours." Evidently, she hadn't told Eden either. That pleased me—less pressure all around. "Will you stay tonight?"

She gave me her seductress grin. "I'd like that."

Down in the galley, I asked her if she wanted wine.

"I wouldn't say no to a glass of white."

Her choice was a surprise. "White? I thought you preferred red." I checked the fridge and came up empty. Way to impress the women, Delaney.

"I'm ambidextrous."

"Good to know, but I'm out of white." I knew I should have stocked up. "Will red do?" I asked, pulling out a Corona for myself.

"Sure," she said.

I put on some tunes and went below to pull a bottle from the rack. "You like Malbec, right?" I asked, returning to the galley.

"Indeed. It's my current favourite red."

At least I remembered that much, I thought, and retrieved the corkscrew.

She'd set out a wine glass, and was leaning against the counter. "I almost hate to say it for fear of jinxing it, but I feel pretty good about tonight's progress."

"You should; you're doing great." I popped the cork and poured her a glass. "Cheers," I said, tapping her glass with my beer bottle. I relaxed against the counter across from her.

More than great, and we'd only explored flight so far. If her extraordinary speed was any indication of the strength of her gift, then her jolts and the sparks at the lower end of that spectrum could also be extraordinary. She might turn out to be an asset when we found Cole after all. How would she feel about that? I know how I'd feel. I'd like nothing more than to confront Cole and my lovely wife with Emelynn by my side.

Emelynn interrupted my thoughts. "What are you thinking?"

"Ah, it's nothing." I remembered my Corona and tipped it back. "Next time we're flying, I'd like to teach you how to jump-start someone into flight."

"Why's that?"

"In case you ever need to help an injured or unconscious Flier... Say, rescue one from the Pacific?" I stared down my nose at her.

She rolled her eyes. "Oh, I get it."

"Kidding aside, it's something all Fliers should know how to do. Like CPR." And it might come in particularly handy in a combat situation. I set the Corona down and crossed the floor to wrap her in my arms. The fresh scent of the night air still clung to her.

"Jump up," I said, boosting her to the counter. I nudged her knees open to stand close, and caressed her cheek, rubbing my thumb over her lips. She sighed and sucked my thumb into her mouth. My jeans grew uncomfortably tight as I watched, and imagined something else in her mouth. Perhaps we could work some more on her oral skills tonight. I wrapped a hand around the back of her head. She tasted of Malbec and a promise.

My mind slipped away, and all I could think was that she wore too many clothes. I slid my hand under her hoodie. Her skin felt hot through the thin fabric of the tank top she wore underneath. I unhooked her bra. Everything had to go. I yanked the hoodie up over her head, tossed it aside, and then loosened that damn tank top and pushed it and the bra up over the swell of her breasts. Ah, magnificent. I felt the weight of them and then I felt her hand at the back of my head, pushing my mouth to her nipple. She completely undid me. I flicked it with my tongue then closed my lips around it, which earned me a sigh. I did to her nipple what she'd done with my thumb and got a purr in response.

It wasn't enough. I wanted her moaning my name. "Let's take this below," I said, and kissed each breast then pulled her shirt back down. The little vixen reached her hand to my jeans and stroked my wood with a come-fuck-me smile on her face that I felt powerless to resist.

By the time we stumbled into her cabin, I'd removed half her clothes. I made short work of the rest when we got horizontal. Naked suited her. I feasted my eyes on her, and let my hands find all her secret places. Places she didn't even know she had. My lips caressed her curves and my tongue worshipped her. She melted and then blew apart under my touch. Watching her come made my balls ache. Tonight, she was going to feel me inside her again. She needed it too. Her first time had been painful. This time would be pure pleasure.

I wrapped myself in a condom before she had time to blink, and then rolled on top of her, spreading her knees with my hips. Immediately, I pushed inside her. Her eyes widened. I pushed again, burying myself. I felt her relief as she exhaled. Another hurdle jumped.

"The second time is so much better than the first," I said, and slowly pumped my hips. She felt incredible, and she rose to greet my thrusts. This time, she would come without my rush. I kept up the rhythm until I was on the brink, and had to still to regain my control. Emelynn didn't like that much. She pushed against me, trying to restart my rhythm, but I needed another minute.

"Roll on top," I said, when I was back in control. With my hands on her hips, I guided her motion. "Slowly," I warned, still close to the edge. The bounce of her breasts didn't help. "Slowly," I warned again, knowing my control was tenuous. I pressed against her clit with my thumb to help her along. When her orgasm hit, it was so much sweeter than before. She milked me like I hadn't felt in years, and I gave her all I had. We fed each other, my spasms feeding hers for what felt like forever.

Finally, she folded over on me, and I rolled her to the side.

What a fucking ride. Laughter rose up my chest. Only her second time doing the horizontal mambo and she'd already mastered being on top. I turned on my side and caught a glimpse of that wide-eyed, beautiful face, naive and full of innocence. She'd learned to fuck like she'd learned to fly. The laughter I'd been trying to suppress burst out.

"I never would have thought you had it in you, Em. You surprise the hell out of me and might I say, that was fantastic."

She paid me with a beautiful smile. I tucked her under my arm and pulled up the comforter, and before sleep tugged me away, I wondered if she'd agree to make the trip back to New Orleans with me.

CHAPTER TWENTY-SEVEN

I woke with a start. What the—

"Good morning," Emelynn said, leaning down to kiss me. My attention dropped to the gap in her robe.

Ah, yes. Now I remembered. "Hey," I said. She'd brought coffee. My stomach clenched. Shit. I hadn't locked my stateroom last night. Would she have gone in there and found some last trace of Sandra? I sat up and rubbed the sleep from my face. I contemplated the mug before I reached for it. Guess I'd find out if the coffee turned out to be poisoned.

But her demeanour held no trace of deceit. We enjoyed our coffee in bed but didn't linger. I'd promised Ted Worley I'd phone in on a conference call, and on top of that, the wind was up and I could feel the swell building. I needed to get Emelynn home before it got any worse.

"I'll meet you upstairs," I said, pecking her cheek. Everything seemed to be in place in my stateroom. If she'd been inside, I couldn't tell. I showered and dressed and locked the door when I headed to the galley. I poured another cup of coffee and fired up the laptop.

Emelynn joined me in time to review the photos that had come in. They held no surprises. And with such a large capacity on the camera's SD card, our spy wouldn't switch it out for another twenty-four hours.

The worsening weather made for a rocky trip to shore in the Zodiac. We fumbled out of the small boat and huddled against the wind, picking our way to Emelynn's stretch of beach. She hurried up the stairs to her deck, paying the depressions in the sand no mind. I stalled, taking a closer look. Someone had been sniffing around . . . again.

Once inside, I checked over the kitchen cam, and then went outside to investigate around the arbutus. I don't know what I expected to find. A dropped wallet with ID would have been nice, but our spy had left nothing but fresh gouges in the tree trunk.

"No new clues out there," I said, returning to the house.

She bounced up from her seat at the dining room table, where her laptop sat open. "I'm going to be out most of today," she said. "And Eden's coming by tonight."

"All right. I'll call if anything comes up." I kissed her goodbye. "Keep your phone charged and with you—please."

She assured me she would, and I left her at the patio door, motioning with my finger for her to lock it.

After a rough trip back to the *Symphony*, I piloted her to the marina on the Fraser.

The online conference call stretched on for two hours. Afterwards, Ted Worley phoned me. "It's shaping up nicely," he said, referring to the Lake Charles project. "And Acquisitions just secured the property in Baton Rouge. If you want to be involved, I can put it on the back burner until you return."

"No need. I won't be here much longer. Make sure Legal clears it, and then get Permitting on it."

"Will do. Look forward to seeing you."

I stood and walked out to the foredeck to stretch my legs. Sandra and Cole had been in La Push last night. If they wanted to, they could be in Vancouver tonight. I slapped together a sandwich and called James.

"You got the latest ATM clip?" I asked.

"Yeah. They're close."

"You got a handle on their boat yet?"

"Gary got a hit with Sandra's photo. A woman working the fuel dock thinks they're on a tug called *MayBell*."

"And you were going to tell me this when?"

"It's hearsay right now. The moment I have confirmation, I'll call."

"I'll be waiting," I said, and disconnected. Was he trying to keep me out of the loop? The camera scenario had me on edge, and until I could rule James out, I couldn't trust him. It was time for me to shore up my presence with the team. I started with Gary. Within the hour, I'd touched base with everyone on the payroll. If James was thinking he'd do an end run around me, I'd put a stop to it. Neither he nor anyone else would keep me away from Cole when we found him. I owned a piece of his hide and I planned to take it.

Later that night, I poured myself a celebratory drink, albeit bittersweet. Sandra's belongings were finally gone. I'd cleared out my locker and dumped the green garbage bags into the marina's bin. But it hadn't gotten rid of her. Her touch was everywhere, as were my memories of her. If only I could tie those off in a green garbage bag. Instead, I drowned them in bourbon.

My phone woke me, buzzing against the teak like a jackhammer. I managed to grab it without opening my eyes and held it to my ear. "Yeah . . ."

"He's here."

"Emelynn?" I held the phone away from head and cracked open my eyelids to see the time. It was barely 6:00 a.m.

Emelynn whispered, "The man, he's in the tree—right now."

Shit! "Where are you?" I threw off the covers, raced across the stateroom and bounded down the hall.

"I'm in the bedroom now, but I saw him."

I took the stairs two at a time. "You need to get out of there."

"I'm getting dressed right now," she said.

I flipped on the computer. "Pull yourself together, get in your car and leave. Act casual, like it's just any other day. Don't forget your phone."

"Okay," she said. "I'm hanging up now."

"Call me when you can." I scanned through the photos on the laptop. He was bent over in the first picture. In the next one, he wore the mask again and stood at the base of the tree. The third photo showed him midclimb. In the most recent shot, he was changing the SD card. He'd taken off his gloves. I saw no jewellery.

Damn it! We needed a better picture and we were running out of time—he'd been in and out in seven minutes last visit. When the next photo came in, he was already halfway down the trunk. Shit! The next shot had him on the ground, but he'd pulled back his hood. I centred on his face and enlarged the photo. It wasn't good enough.

I drummed my fingers, hoping against hope there'd be another shot. The next photo was a gift. He'd removed his mask, and had turned toward Emelynn's kitchen window. Gotcha, you son of a bitch!

He was Caucasian with two deep *Vs* in his hairline. He wasn't anyone I knew. I fired off the photos to Alex and dialled his number.

I'd woken him. "Check your email. We got a shot of our spy." I heard Eden's sleepy voice in the background.

"Hold on a sec," he said, and then a minute later, "Okay I've got them. No, don't know him." His voice faded as he spoke to his wife. "Eden, you recognize this guy?"

I heard her say, "Oh my god," but the rest of their conversation was lost to me.

When Alex came back on the line, he said, "Eden recognizes him. Says he was in her Emerg two days ago."

"Who is he?"

"She doesn't know, but she's going to find out. The hospital will have his ID in the system. I'll check out whatever address he's given."

"It's probably bogus, but if it looks legit, don't go in alone. We'll do it together."

"I'll call you," he said, and disconnected.

I headed below and got dressed.

Twenty minutes later, Emelynn checked in. She was safely away and at a coffee shop. I gave her the good news. "We got a great photo, Em. He got careless, took off his mask at the foot of the tree. We got a clear shot of his face."

"Oh, thank god. That's great," she said, and I could hear the relief in her voice. "Do you recognize him?"

"I don't, but I sent the photo to Alex, and Eden recognized him."

"Eden? Who is he?"

"She doesn't know, but he came into her Emerg, night before last. She's already headed to the hospital to dig up his name and address. They're probably fakes, but it's worth a shot."

"What happens now?"

"Alex will check out the guy's address, see if it's real or not."

"And if it's real?"

"Well then, we'll have to have a little chat with him. Find out what he's up to. See if anyone else is involved."

"I don't know whether to be relieved or not."

"Get yourself a coffee, read the paper. I'll call as soon as I know anything."

Alex called within the hour. "We got the fucker," he said. "The clown used his real address."

"You there now?"

"Yup. Saw him pull into the underground a minute ago. Magnolia and Tenth. How soon can you get here?"

"I've got a cab waiting. I'll head there now."

I hung up and dialled Emelynn. "I think we got him."

She sounded out of breath. "What does that mean?"

"It looks like the idiot used his real address."

"How do you know for sure that it's him?"

"Alex has been watching the address Eden gave him for the past hour. The guy in the photo just showed up. I'm heading over there now."

"Be careful, Jackson."

"Always am. Go on home. I'll be in touch as soon as I can."

I hung up and jogged the length of the dock to the parking lot and the waiting cab.

The address was in Summerset, a few miles from Emelynn's place. I spotted Alex's motorcycle, paid the fare and got out. Alex stood on the corner, looking toward a condo that sat midblock. As I approached, I checked the time. 9:20 a.m. Vehicle traffic was light. Across the street, an elderly man walked a dachshund.

"That it?" I asked, nodding toward the building.

Alex said, "Yup. He's been inside half an hour."

"What's the security look like?"

"Main entrance is a glass door. It's locked. Gets you as far as the mailboxes. The second door is also glass, and that one gets you to the elevator. There's a camera aimed at the front door, and another one aimed at the elevator."

"How about the parking garage?"

"It's secured with a roll-up grate. Access is from the back lane."

"Camera?"

"Not that I could see."

"Good. Let's go find the emergency override." All automatic garage doors had one.

We spotted the cord that disconnected the door from its mechanism dangling from the track two feet inside the grated door. A few of the garbage dumpsters that lined the back lane weren't locked, and it didn't take long to find a discarded clothes hanger that suited our purposes. Alex watched for traffic while I hovered a few feet off the ground outside the ten-foot-high rolling door and fed the hanger in through the grate. It took two tries to hook the plastic pull-tab on the end of the cord and release the door. Alex lifted it and we slipped inside.

The door from the garage to the building's interior was locked, but there were no cameras. "You got his phone number?"

"Sure," Alex said, pulling out a piece of paper.

"What's he drive?"

Alex glanced around and pointed. "That."

I dialled the number. A man answered. "You own the silver Prius in number 16 downstairs?"

"Yeah, why?"

"Sorry to tell you, but it looks like someone's broken into it."

"Ah, shit!" the man said. "I'll be right down."

I disconnected. "Our escort is on his way," I said. "Let me handle him. You get the door."

We stood on either side of the door, Alex on the hinged side. When it opened, I looked our spy in the face and swiftly jolted him unconscious. We dragged him inside and found his keys.

"He'll be out for a couple hours," I said. "Should be enough time to have a good look around and see what he's been up to. Give me a hand, would you?"

We each took an arm, propped him between us and took the elevator back up to his unit on the fourth floor.

We didn't need his keys; his door wasn't locked. We shut it behind us and a woman's voice called out. "How bad is it, honey?" We stopped midstep.

Alex and I glanced at one another. Not being prepared for a second person had been an amateur oversight. "Take him," I said to Alex, and darted toward the voice.

I found her in the kitchen with her back to me. A scream died in her throat. I left her on the floor and did a quick check of the rest of the condo.

"That's everyone," I called back to Alex. He'd already propped the man up on the sofa.

"Give me a hand," Alex shouted from the kitchen. We got the woman off the floor and leaned her up on the sofa beside our spy.

"That's him all right," I said, standing back to get a good look. He was probably mid-forties, as was the woman. They appeared reasonably fit. My jolt would leave them with headaches, but no permanent damage.

"Take a look at this," Alex said, standing in front of a wall in the dining room. A desktop computer, piles of paper and file folders cluttered the dining room table behind him.

Two maps were pinned to the wall, one of the entire province, and another isolating a chunk of the south coast. That chunk included

Emelynn's beach. Each map had colour-coded pins with date tags. Most disturbing of all, taped up beside the maps were photos of Fliers, in flight, and there was no doubt that two of the photos were of Eden.

Alex ripped Eden's photos off the wall. "How'd he find us?"

I stepped close and examined the remaining photos. "He's been looking for a while, judging by these. See the dates." The oldest ones were from the mid-eighties.

"Avery may recognize some of these Fliers," Alex said, and turned toward the mound of paper on the table. He folded the photos of Eden and stuffed them in his pocket. I powered up the computer.

"The guy's some kind of bird specialist. Look at this stuff." He picked up a pile of journals and flipped through them. "*Avian Science, Journal of Field Ornithology, World Birdwatch, Science Daily*. There are dozens of them."

"His computer's password protected." I flicked through the stack of file folders. It looked like research on the areas where he'd identified sightings. Stapled research papers, some on yellowed paper, some newer, formed another pile. I picked the one off the top. "*The Integrative Taxonomy of a New Bird Species*, by Robert C. Wright," I read. "That's this asshole. He wrote this," I said, flipping the top page. "It's us. He's writing about us."

Alex peered down at the paper. The son of a bitch had summarized the data he'd collected and turned it into a research paper.

I jerked my head up as movement toward the door caught my eye. Alex saw it too, and froze. A broad-shouldered man with short-cropped hair stood at the mouth of the hall as though he had every right to be there. Not locking the door—another amateur oversight.

"Which one of you is Alex Klause?" he asked, looking down his nose from across the room. His movements were smooth and deliberate, like a precision machine.

I hesitated, despite having the physical advantage. The man was one of us, no question, but something told me size didn't factor into this scenario. He was dressed for flight and didn't seem the least bit fazed by the slumped forms on the sofa.

Alex spoke. "I'm Alex."

"I'm Edward Kosikov. We spoke on the phone a few days ago." Edward turned his attention to me and jutted his chin. "And who might you be?"

I ignored him. "Alex. Want to tell me who your friend is?"

A second figure stepped out from behind the man. A slight woman with dark hair and dark eyes. Also one of us. Also not fazed by the presence of two unconscious people.

Alex cleared his throat. "Mr. Kosikov is with the Tribunal Novem."

I glared at Alex. He'd called in the Tribunal? Without telling me? Fucking hell!

Alex looked back to Mr. Kosikov. "Ah . . . I think we got our wires crossed. I told you I'd call you if we needed help."

Edward looked pointedly around the room, his gaze lingering on Wright and the woman on the sofa. "Then why haven't you called?"

"We've got this," I said, feeling the new player out. "By the time those two wake up, we'll know exactly what they're up to."

Edward swivelled his head in my direction and arched an eyebrow. "I'll ask again, what's your name?"

"Jackson Delaney. And I'll say again, we've got this."

Ignoring us, Edward and the woman strolled forward. I stood my ground. Edward walked behind me and the two of them turned to examine the maps and the corresponding photos taped to the wall. Alex scooted to the side of the table.

"I'll get started," the woman said, and returned to the hall. I looked over at Alex and shook my head. She came back with a box in each hand.

"You may go," Edward said, his back to me, still studying the pins on the map. His arrogance was astounding. The woman began collecting the papers and packing them away in the boxes.

"We're not done here," I said, testing the man's resolve.

He turned around and looked up a few inches to catch my gaze. "Yes. You are."

I searched his face. It wasn't arrogance I found there. It was confidence.

Knowing when to fold my hand was something else I'd learned from my father. I tipped my head to the bastard. "Very well."

"We've already removed their camera from the property on Cliffside. Leave the way you came in. We'll clean this up and that will be the end of it."

He spoke as if the cleanup involved a mop and pail.

I stepped around him and joined Alex, who waited by the door. All I'd needed were Wright's contacts, and now, thanks to him, my best resource was gone! We exited via the parking garage and didn't speak to each other until we were standing beside his bike.

"What the hell were you thinking?"

He reached into his pocket and retrieved the photos of Eden. "There is no one more important to me than this woman, and he had photos of her. Worse, he knew where she worked. You'd do the same if it were your wife."

My wife? I snorted and shook my head. How little he knew. How little any of them knew.

Alex ignored my sneer and slipped Eden's photos back into his pocket. He rested his hand on the back of his bike. "Can I give you a lift to the marina?"

CHAPTER TWENTY-EIGHT

Back on board the *Symphony*, I poured myself a bourbon. Liquor hadn't passed my lips before noon since my father died. Today felt like a suitable occasion. I set the drink beside the laptop and entered Robert C. Wright into the search engine. I found him on LinkedIn and Facebook. On both sites, he indicated Summerset as his home but revealed no other personal information. I flipped through his contacts. None of the names jumped out at me, but that would have been too easy. I'd have to do more digging. I copied the information for safekeeping and closed the laptop.

Afterwards, I fired up the engines and headed to the shallows out front of Emelynn's. I took the Zodiac to shore and lumbered up the beach. There were no footprints in the sand. I supposed that Wright had been the one lurking about, but I'd never know for certain. I walked up the stairs and stood on Emelynn's deck, looking toward the empty spot where the camera had been mounted. The Tribunal were definitely thorough.

Emelynn wasn't in view. I took a seat on a lounger and dialled her number. "I'm out on your deck—want to let me in?"

"Sure, just give me a sec," she said, her voice groggy. Moments later, the patio door opened and she stepped out wearing a robe. I'd woken her. At least one of us had gotten back to bed after our early morning wake-up call.

"Hey." She took my offered hand and made a valiant effort to rub warmth into it. A breeze fluttered the leaves of the arbutus and brought with it the pungent scent of the low tide.

"It's over," I said. "I can't believe the guy used his real address, considering the trouble and expense he'd gone to in setting up the camera. It just doesn't make sense. I had him pegged for a professional. Guess he never thought we'd make the connection."

"What about the camera?" she asked, squinting up to the tree.

"Gone."

"That was fast."

"Yeah, we had some unexpected help," I said.

"Oh?"

"Apparently, Alex warned the Tribunal three days ago. They had a cleanup crew in the wings just waiting for a positive ID . . . so it's all taken care of." I tried not to sound bitter.

"Taken care of?" she asked, her face clouded with confusion.

"Yeah." I didn't bother hiding my scowl. "They swoop in, remove the problem and then we pretend it never happened."

"Why didn't Alex tell you about involving the Tribunal?"

"He should have. He didn't know they'd pounce like they did. Alex thought he was organizing backup in case we needed it."

Emelynn wrapped her arms around her torso. "What will the Tribunal do with the man?"

"The man *and* a woman. They took them both, and neither one will be coming back."

Emelynn's hands flew to cover her gasp. She had no idea what the Tribunal was capable of. What their presence really meant.

"As bad as that is, it's not the worst of it. The Tribunal's not in the habit of sharing information, so no matter what else they might be able to get out of the guy, we'll never know more than what we learned before they showed up, including who else might have been involved."

"What did you learn before they showed up?"

"He'd been researching us, though I'm almost certain he didn't know what we were. I read some of the stuff he'd written. He thought he was on the verge of a major scientific discovery, like he'd found some modern-day version of a lost Amazon tribe."

"Based on what?"

I told her about the photos and the corresponding pins on the maps. "Half of the pins were concentrated along the beach near your cottage."

"Here? This beach?" she asked, her brow furrowed.

I looked out at the *Symphony* on the horizon. "It'll all be gone by now: the photos, the map, everything."

She settled into the lounger beside me and pulled her knees to her chest in quiet contemplation.

Some time later, she stood. "I'm cold, Jackson," she said, extending her hand. "Come inside. I'll make us something warm to drink."

I took her hand and followed her inside to the sofa. Emelynn continued on to the kitchen. She'd been right all along. Our spy had been a birder. Or that's what he wanted us to think. I stared out the patio door to the ocean beyond. How had he gotten the photos of Fliers? Had he taken them himself, or were others involved? Did anyone else know what he'd been researching?

When Emelynn returned, she was dressed. She motioned to the mug on the coffee table in front of me. How long had that been sitting there? The lukewarm hot chocolate brought me out of my reverie.

Moments later, a soft thump outside on the deck drew our attention. Alex stared through the glass at us, and a moment later, Eden landed beside him. A daylight flight was risky enough, but with the Tribunal hanging around it was reckless.

No sooner had Emelynn slid open the patio door, than Eden flung herself at her and held on as if she were the dearly departed.

Alex closed the door and sidestepped the women. "Jackson," he said, then quickly shifted his gaze. "Em."

Eden loosened her grip on Emelynn and held her at arm's length. "Are you all right?" she asked.

Despite Emelynn's reassurances, Eden broke into tears and pulled her back into a bear hug. She sobbed, "He was after *me*, Em. I've never even *seen* the man before. He just showed up in the ER. You know how careful I am. Why me?" She straightened her arms again. Deep lines etched her brow.

Emelynn said, "You were just unlucky, Eden. He set a trap and you're the one he caught. It could have been any of us." Emelynn extracted herself. "Who is he?" she asked. "Where's he from?"

"He's local—said he'd fallen from a ladder, but there was nothing broken or contused." Emelynn offered Eden a tissue. "Now I know it was just an act," Eden said, dabbing her eyes. "I keep trying to figure out how he found me, but I'm drawing a blank."

She blew her nose and swallowed, and then looked at me. "I'm so sorry, Jackson."

Eden was taking it way too hard. I stood and gave her a reassuring hug. "It's over now." I bent down to her meet her gaze. "You have nothing to be sorry about. You were the victim here." She looked more fragile than I'd ever seen her before.

"I feel like I've put you all through hell," she said, looking to the floor.

"We're covey, Eden. We protect one another," I said. "It's what we do."

Alex moved toward the kitchen. I followed and took a seat at the counter. "Em, I'm going to disconnect this, okay?" Alex indicated the camera hidden on the windowsill.

"Sure," she replied, and she took Eden's hand to guide her to the sofa. "Here, sit down."

I left the women to shore each other up and turned in my seat toward Alex, who'd disconnected the camera and was pulling the wires.

"I wish you'd given me a heads-up earlier about the Tribunal," I said.

"Sorry, man," Alex replied, keeping his attention on the wires. "I know how you feel about them, but I couldn't take a chance. Not with Eden."

I frowned. Take a chance with Eden? What was he talking about?

"You know . . . because Eden was here," he said, circling his fingers to indicate Em's place. "The night before you found the camera, she was here—wearing her scrubs—with her stethoscope. Anyone would have been able to see she was a nurse just on or off shift."

That was an interesting angle. "And you thought he'd be able to find her, based on that?"

"He *did* find her based on that, in less than twenty-four hours, so don't tell me I overreacted."

True enough, I thought, but how did our spy manage that? "She could have been any medical professional. How could he have searched all the local clinics and hospitals, all the wards and all those shifts and found Eden so quickly? He'd have had to have incredible access, and that's even before you figure in the legwork involved." No. I shook my head. "Something doesn't add up. Think about it. He must have had more information."

Emelynn stood and walked to her computer, which sat in its usual place on the dining room table. What started off as a casual flip through some papers beside the computer quickly turned into a frantic search.

"What is it?" I asked.

Ignoring me, she darted into the kitchen, bumped Alex out of her way and dug through her trash. She stood and stilled. "He was here," she whispered.

Eden tilted her head. "Who? Where?"

"The note you gave me?" Emelynn said. "The one with your phone number and email address?"

"Yes?" Eden said, furrowing her brow.

"It's gone. It was here . . . right beside the computer. I sent you an email and it was right there." Emelynn pointed at the laptop.

Eden's face lit up with comprehension.

"He was right here. In my house. He found you because I left that stupid piece of paper out." Emelynn pressed her fingers to her temples.

Alex and I exchanged glances. "Did you notice anything else?"

"My computer. It was open. I usually leave it closed. That's why I noticed. But things have been so crazy around here . . ."

"What about the guy who cuts your lawn?" Eden asked. "He has a key."

"Charles? God no. We've known him for years. He's harmless."

"What about doors or windows?" I asked. "Did you notice anything unlocked or left open?"

She paused. "No, nothing that I noticed."

Alex and I burst into action. I took the north side, he took the south. We checked every door and window in the small house.

"You find anything?" Alex asked when we met at the front door.

"Nothing."

We returned to the front room. "There are no signs of forced entry," I said. Emelynn had taken a seat on the sofa, hugging her knees. "I knew these guys were professional. I knew it!" Wright was more than a birder on the hunt for a new species, and there was no way he pulled this off by himself.

"I hope the Tribunal knows what the hell they're doing." I clenched my fists. If only Alex hadn't called them.

"Jackson, man," Alex said, sitting on the stool I'd vacated. "The Tribunal doesn't do half measures. You know that." Eden moved to stand behind him, her arm around his shoulder.

"I hope so," I said.

Emelynn turned to me and asked, "Won't Eden or Alex get the chance to hear what the guy has to say?"

Was she not listening? "No. No questions; no answers; no witnesses. It's the way of the Tribunal."

"Well, go ask them now," she said, dropping her feet to the floor. "Surely they'll understand our concern."

Alex cleared his throat. "Emelynn, the Tribunal doesn't take questions. After they arrived on the scene, Jackson and I were . . . dismissed." He reached to his shoulder and covered Eden's hand. "I'm not sorry I contacted them, not with all the other unsolved disappearances. I'm just sorry we'll never know the rest of the story."

I snapped my head toward him. "That's precisely why I don't want them involved in Sandra's situation." It was imperative I drive that point home so we didn't have a repeat when we went after Cole. "You get that, right?"

"Sure. Sandra's your business. I know that." Alex's expression conveyed sincerity and apology in equal measure. "The Tribunal won't hear about it from me. You and your covey can handle it any way you feel best. You can trust me."

"Good," I said. "Because what happened here is not the same thing we're dealing with in Sandra's case. Her abductors haven't hurt her, and they won't; they're using her to get to her money."

"You can count on us. We'll help you when the time comes. The covey's already agreed to that."

Satisfied that I'd gotten through to him, I dropped to the sofa.

Emelynn sat on the opposite end. "I'd appreciate it if you wouldn't jump down my throat when I ask this next question," she said, "but I need to know. How can we be so sure this is over?"

Alex and Eden looked to one another and then to me. How could I make Emelynn understand? "Remember how I incapacitated you on the beach?" She nodded. "Well, multiply that threefold then add some extra special effects. The Tribunal's Fliers are the strongest of our kind. They told us they would take out the threat and they will. It's the reason they exist—it's all they do. Then they'll cover their tracks."

The matter was out of our hands, "unless we wanted to be the Tribunal's next targets," as Alex put it. Nothing we could say or do would alter the day's events.

We jumped at Alex's suggestion of a change of scenery, and within the hour, we were seated at a Thai restaurant on the other side of Sunset Park.

We emptied a couple bottles of a local Cabernet Sauvignon, ate a fine meal and talked around the edges of the Tribunal and Robert C. Wright. Still, I couldn't get my mind off the man. Was Wright a puppet or a player? And if he was a puppet, who was pulling his strings? The Reynolds? Cole? James?

Late into the night, we drifted into the cover of a small park and said our goodbyes. Alex and Eden flew home and I escorted Emelynn to her deck.

"Will you stay?" she asked.

I pulled her close. As tempting as she was, I wouldn't rest until I had some answers. "Thanks, but I need to get back to the *Symphony*. I can't leave her unattended at anchor." Reluctantly, I kissed her goodbye and flew off.

I steered the *Symphony* back to the marina, locked up and settled in front of the laptop. First up was an email to Josh, asking for everything he could get me on Robert C. Wright. Next, I did some digging of my own.

By the early morning hours, I'd made a cursory pass through all the names in the birding groups Wright was a member of. Again, no name jumped out at me, but I had somewhere to start tomorrow. I turned off the computer and went to bed.

Chapter Twenty-Nine

My cellphone buzzed, waking me just after nine in the morning. "Good news," Gary said. "Johnny Lorenzo took a leak off the *MayBell* a few minutes ago. Jin identified him."

"About fucking time! Finally. We've got them."

"By the balls. Jin and Mark will stay on them, spell each other off and find out how many others are on board."

"Where are they now?"

"In the Juan de Fuca Strait, headed east."

"Thanks for the call, Gary. Keep in touch."

I hung up. After all this time. I could almost feel Cole's greasy neck in my grip.

I leapt out of bed and hummed my way through a quick shower. I dressed and headed up top to meet a brilliant day. With a coffee in hand, I signed on to Facebook to resume my research on Robert C. Wright.

It didn't take long. His profile was gone. I checked LinkedIn with the same result. He was being systematically erased. Looked like the Tribunal had gotten Wright's password, which meant whatever else I found on him would be only what the Tribunal wanted to be found.

Damn it! It was fucking good thinking that I'd copied Wright's contacts when I did. I closed the laptop, strode to the foredeck and dialled Josh. "What'd you dig up on Wright?" I asked.

"I'll have a dossier for you in a few hours, but I gotta tell you, there's not a hell of a lot. The man doesn't have a big cyber footprint."

And it was getting smaller by the minute. "I'm sending you a list of his contacts. I want to know who these people are."

"I'll get right on it."

After we disconnected, I sent him the list. Determining whether Jolene's family, Cole or James had been involved in the camera incident was once again out of my hands, at least for a few hours.

My thoughts turned to Emelynn. I should have stayed with her last night. Getting a leg over would have been a lot more satisfying than researching Wright. Perhaps I could make up for my error. I grabbed my sunglasses and headed down the dock.

Two hours later, I set anchor in the shallows off Emelynn's beach and took the Zodiac to shore. I found her lounging on the beach in her housecoat, her back against a bleached-out log. I sat beside her. "I see you're having a leisurely morning," I said, and leaned in to steal a kiss. Her hair had that slept-in look to it that stirred arousing memories of her in my bed.

She cradled an empty mug. "There's more coffee. Would you like me to get you a cup?"

"I'll come with you." I stood and offered my hand. We walked to the stairs and back up to the deck. "I thought you might like to join me for lunch on the *Symphony* today."

She stopped and looked back, a smile on her face. "That sounds like a wonderful idea. Help yourself to coffee and I'll get dressed."

I found a coffee mug and settled in the front room. An instruction pamphlet for a GPS lay on her coffee table. I was flipping through it when my phone vibrated. It was the Wright dossier from Josh. I opened the attachment and scrolled through the basics of vital stats: occupation, work history, credit record.

I called to Emelynn, "Do you have any plans for the rest of the day?"

Wright's driver's licence was clean and he had no criminal record.

"No plans," she said, her voice muffled.

"Good, then we won't have to . . . rush." I looked up from the phone, sure my mouth gaped. It couldn't be helped. Emelynn had stepped out of her bedroom wearing a pale-blue dress that hugged her curves and showed off toned legs. I couldn't wait to peel her out of it. "Wow, you look great. I should invite you to lunch more often."

She strolled over and gave me a kiss that told me she'd be more than happy to oblige. I offered her cleavage an appreciative glance and smiled into those lush green eyes. I slipped the phone in my pocket. Wright's dossier could wait.

Back aboard the *Symphony*, I slid our lunch into the oven and caught a glimpse of Emelynn caressing the tulips I'd dropped in a vase on the table. The florist had chosen well. With a bit of luck, my last-minute shopping trip would pay dividends after lunch. She studied the place settings, while I popped the cork on a bottle of Prosecco, and mixed mimosas.

"Shall we?" I asked, handing her a glass and gesturing to the aft stairs.

She paid me with a beautiful smile. "We shall," she said, and we headed up. She stood by the railing gazing back toward the beach. "You are full of surprises today."

"Only today?" I asked, and smoothed my hand down her thick mane of hair. It took all my restraint to keep my hands off the zipper of her dress. The temptation teased me for the thirty minutes it took our lunch to heat. Why hadn't I gone with the cold lunch option?

Back in the galley, I served up a salad with the quiche and shrugged off her compliments. "Don't be too impressed; I didn't make it myself."

After we'd eaten, I poured two more mimosas, and we took them back up top. A warm breeze stirred the air. Emelynn strolled the circumference of the deck, finally returning to the rail to gaze out to the home she called a cottage. The sunlight picked out the copper in her hair as she tipped back her flute. I took her empty glass and set it beside my own on the deck, and then pulled her toward me, her back against my chest. I inhaled her sweet citrus scent. She melted into me as I brushed her hair aside and trailed kisses down her neck to her shoulder.

Her trust in me was an aphrodisiac. Emboldened, I slid the straps of her dress off her shoulders, and when she didn't protest, I slid the zipper down and peeled down the top of her dress, baring her breasts. I loved that she was game to follow my lead, and of that I was sure. She sighed as her breathing deepened, giving away her heightening lust.

A breeze licked her exposed flesh, drawing goosebumps along her arms and hardening her nipples nicely. She shuddered under my touch, but when she tried to turn around, I thought I'd try something new.

"Bend forward," I said, pressing her into the railing. With my other hand, I undid my belt and the weight of it took care of my shorts. I flipped Emelynn's skirt up over her ass and the little temptress shimmied to help me pull her panties down. She peered over her shoulder with her bottom lip between her teeth. "Spread your legs," I said, and nearly lost control watching her comply. Her backside, presented like this, would test the vows of the devout. She jerked at the touch of my hand against the inside of her thigh, and gasped when my fingers found her warm opening. It took all my self-control to take her slowly. I didn't want to rush through this. I wanted her to remember today, and remember it fondly so she'd beg for a replay.

But my dick had other plans. Urgent plans. I teased her clitoris with one hand and snaked the other one, the one that had been inside her, to her mouth. And when she curled her tongue around my fingers, tasting herself, I lost control and drove into her, taking my fill. I didn't let up until she came, clenching me long and hard, and then I lost myself in the wonder that was Emelynn.

I came hard and folded over her back. "God, that was good," I said, wrapping an arm around her waist. She was exactly what I needed, my antidote. When we'd regained our breath, I let her up and pulled her close. "Did you enjoy that?" I asked.

She murmured yes and kissed me. We gathered our clothes and headed below.

"You go shower," I said, turning to the galley. "I'll clean up lunch."

She disappeared below deck and I quickly stacked the dishes in the dishwasher. I flipped on the computer and waited for it to connect. As soon as my email was up I clicked on the Wright dossier that Josh had sent earlier and scanned the highlights. There was nothing to connect him to Cole, or anyone named Reynolds. Josh had nothing yet on Wright's contacts.

My phone buzzed to life with a call from James, but I could hear Emelynn starting back up the stairs. I sent him to voice mail and tucked the phone in my pocket as I came around the counter to greet Emelynn.

"Did you leave any hot water for me?" I asked, dropping a kiss on her head. "I'll be quick," I said, and dashed for the stairs.

Back in my stateroom, I texted James and told him I'd call in an hour. That would give me enough time to get Emelynn out of earshot before I called him back. I then jumped in the shower.

After a quick change of clothes, I bounded up the stairs. When I saw Emelynn, I abruptly slowed my pace. She stood in the galley with her arms wound tightly across her chest. "What's wrong?" I asked.

She shifted from one foot to the other and seemed to struggle to find her voice. "We didn't use a condom," she said.

Her words dropped like marbles on a tile floor. Shit! "You're right. I'm sorry." A pregnancy was the last thing I needed. I wrapped my arms around her, but she didn't return my embrace.

I pulled back. "Are you angry with me?"

A tight smile crossed her lips. "No, of course not," she said. "It takes two, right?"

If this was her trying to convince me, she was doing a lousy job of it, and I didn't have time for the drama. What was done was done. If there were consequences . . . well, we'd deal with them. Emelynn clammed up. It felt too much like the silent treatment I was all too familiar with, so when Emelynn trumped up an excuse for me to take her home, I didn't hesitate. So much for making today a fond memory.

I took her home in the Zodiac and returned to the *Symphony*. After I had her moored at the marina, I called James.

"Got your message," I said. "What's up?"

"Where've you been?"

"Took the *Symphony* out. Had my hands full. Do you have news?"

"Gary told you about Jin spotting Lorenzo on the *MayBell*?"

"He did. Do they know yet how many are with him?"

"Not yet, and no sign of Sandra, but it has to be them. They're in the strait, coming this way."

"If he's heading for the *Symphony*, they could be in Vancouver this evening."

"I don't think they'll risk a border crossing with the likes of Johnny Lorenzo on board."

"You thinking Seattle?"

"The entire seaboard, from Olympia to Bellingham, is ripe with ATMs. He'd have his pick of them at any port."

"Good thing we won't have to guess," I said. "I'm assuming Gary's men are keeping the *MayBell* in sight?"

"Yes, and as soon as we have a handle on how many of them we're dealing with, we'll make a plan."

"You pulling your men off now?"

"Yes. It's strictly Fliers from here on in. Who are you thinking we should lean on from Avery's covey?"

"Alex, for sure. Danny. Steve. Eden might be useful to have along for her medical training."

"Sounds good. We'll know their numbers soon. Keep your phone on."

"You too. I'll set up a training session. Might be our last chance before we confront Cole's crew. I'll text you the details."

One of the details I wouldn't be sharing was my intent to include Emelynn in our game. That is, if she was speaking to me after this afternoon. How would she handle the training? I wondered. Regardless,

I would make certain to observe James's reaction when he met her. He wouldn't be able to hide it if he recognized her, and that alone would tell me whether or not he'd had a hand in the camera on her property.

Later, I phoned Jerry and reserved the paintball barn.

At dinnertime, I called Emelynn and invited her to the paintball game. I wasn't getting the cold shoulder, but I wasn't entirely sure I was back in her good graces either. After some initial hesitation, she agreed.

"And Em," I said, "just so you have a heads-up, I'm going to use the opportunity to brief the covey on the incident with the camera."

She thanked me for the warning, but before I could hang up, she asked if I'd learned anything about Jolene.

Shit! The Jolene business had slipped from my radar. Perhaps it was time to throw her a bone, but a small one. "Ah . . . yes . . . there was something. A Flier by the name of Jolene disappeared from the San Francisco area around the time you received your gift. If I'm not mistaken, her name was Jolene Raymond."

I felt guilty for lying about the surname, especially because Emelynn was so relieved to hear the scrap of information. But I didn't want her researching on her own. Not if the Reynolds family were sniffing around. I'd come clean with Emelynn eventually, but I didn't need that complication right now.

The chime of her doorbell announced the delivery of her dinner and ended our call.

By noon the following day, I'd lined up the rest of the covey. With everyone in place, I called Avery.

"Jackson, good to hear from you," he said.

"You're sounding chipper. You up for some more training?"

"I'd been thinking we were due for another session. Do you have it set up yet?"

"Ten o'clock tonight," I said, and then briefed him on the camera incident. We'd kept him in the dark, but I felt confident he'd understand our reasoning. "I'd like to share the details tonight with the covey. They should know what's going on."

"I agree," he said, and was pleased that his tone held no animosity. "Send me the man's photo and I'll make sure everyone gets a copy."

When I texted James, I told him we were meeting at ten thirty. The man was punctual, and tonight I didn't want to be preoccupied with the covey when he laid eyes on Emelynn.

Chapter Thirty

Half the covey arrived ahead of me to the paintball park. We made small talk waiting for the others to show up. The bouncing beam of a lone vehicle's headlights drew our attention.

"That's Avery," I said, recognizing the distinctive purr of a Porsche. Avery stepped out, and then Emelynn emerged from the passenger side. Strange that neither one had mentioned that arrangement to me.

I excused myself and jogged over to greet them.

"Avery," I said, shaking his hand.

I grasped Emelynn's shoulder, gauging her mood. "Em, glad you made it." She tucked a stray curl behind her ear and nodded, leaving me in the dark. Gabe motioned Avery over and left me to introduce Emelynn to the others.

I escorted her to where Victoria was talking with Eden and Alex, only to learn that Emelynn had already met Victoria. Seems Avery had made the introduction at the Richmond Mall, which was interesting. Emelynn hadn't told me she'd met someone else from the covey.

A quick check of the time told me I had about fifteen minutes before James showed up. I hustled Emelynn along and introduced her to Kate and Deidra. They exchanged pleasantries and we continued to where Danny and Gabe were deep in conversation.

Gabe recognized her. "Nice to see you again, Emelynn," he said, extending his hand. She also knew Danny. He teased her about the day they'd met, again at the Richmond Mall, and I learned that Avery had called on a number of the covey a few days ago to teach her how to use her flash. So that's where Emelynn had gone to avoid being home under the watchful eye of the surveillance camera. The last two introductions were to Steve Elliott and Sydney Davenport, whom she hadn't yet met.

I leapt up on a discarded pallet and called out to get the group's attention as I looked about. "Has James arrived yet?"

"He said he'd be here," Alex said.

With less than ten minutes before he showed, I dove in. "Before we get to the game," I said, "I need to brief you on a recent incident." I explained what had happened since we'd discovered the camera and installed our countersurveillance equipment. After I mentioned that it was Eden who'd identified the man, all eyes shifted to her, and when I noted the Tribunal's involvement, the noise level picked up.

"Avery has the man's photo and he'll email it to you, or have you already?" I asked, looking to Avery.

"I'll send it tomorrow," he said.

"As far as we know, only three of us were exposed, so let me know if anyone else recognizes him. We've been assured that the matter has been dealt with, but this incident is a reminder. Everyone has a camera phone these days so be vigilant."

Any other covey would have unleashed outrage, or a barrage of questions, at least, but I got nothing more than an escalating noise level. A few members flocked to Eden to offer their support. The complacency in this covey was alarming.

I checked my watch. "It looks like we'll have the whole contingent tonight—that is, if James ever shows up." I scanned the yard to be sure he hadn't snuck in and then continued.

"You've all met Emelynn now. She's the only one who's never played paintball before, so let's go over the game for her benefit."

I outlined a six-man-team configuration the covey were familiar with and described the equipment and rules of the game.

"Avery is neutral so he won't be armed. He'll be in the centre of the barn under the canvas with the red cross marked on it. If you make it to Avery, he will put you back into the game by neutralizing your paint mark with his blue dauber. He can only void two paint marks at a time. If you have more than two paint marks, you're out, so you might as well take a seat in Avery's tent until the game is over.

"We've got the park to ourselves until dawn, so we'll get in a few games if we're lucky."

I looked over to Emelynn. "Any questions?"

"Not yet," she said, tucking in her chin.

"Great. Let's split into groups then. Who wants to lead?"

Danny stepped forward immediately. "I'll be green leader."

Alex stepped up to claim the red leader position.

"Great. Danny, you start first. Pick your teams."

I'd been about to step down off the pallet when, with perfect timing, James skulked around the end of the barn. "Hey, James, glad you made it," I called, motioning him over. "You're just in time. We're picking teams."

James drifted closer, acknowledging the Fliers one by one with a nod of his head. He studied them as if he were going to be tested later on minute details of their appearance. I watched his face, observing carefully the moment his gaze took in Emelynn. He cocked his head and hesitated for a telling second. He hadn't recognized her, I was sure of it, and the relief I felt knowing it surprised me. James hadn't been involved in the camera incident, which left Cole and Jolene's family as the most likely suspects.

The entire covey watched as James approached Emelynn. "James Moss," he said, extending his hand.

"Emelynn," she responded.

He held her hand long enough to raise a few eyebrows. I'd seen James employ this tactic before and couldn't decide if he used the prolonged contact to endear or intimidate. Personally, I thought it was off-putting.

"James, you're with me," Danny said, getting us back into training mode.

Alex called out next. "Eden, you're on my team."

They took turns, selecting their six-man teams. Emelynn and I both ended up with Alex.

We headed into the barn, where Gabe helped Avery hand out the gear and the coloured team vests. Eden seemed to have taken Em under her wing, and they headed to the area where we took practice shots and adjusted our scopes.

Avery shouted over the din. "I'm headed to the tent now. Take ten minutes to reacquaint yourselves with the space. The barn doors at the other end and the loft on this end are both open so you've got good access to the great outdoors. When I sound the horn once, you'll have five minutes until the next blast. At the second horn, it's game on. If you hear the air horn twice in short succession, the game is over and we'll meet back at the tent." He turned and headed off.

Nervous energy flitted through the group, and I hung back to observe Alex manage the team. He pulled them together, walked them through the arena and made them a part of the game planning. Once outside, he circled the exterior of the structure, ensuring the team was familiar with the outdoor playing field. His insight was spot-on in matching players' individual skills to the tactical positions he'd identified. He paired Emelynn with Eden, another smart move, and then the first horn blew.

We took our positions, mine being to guard the loft door, and after the second horn blew, I watched Emelynn to see how she handled herself. She hung back and kept a low profile, turning her head to check her surroundings. Eden shouldered her weapon and peeled off to take out a player. Eden's hit ratio got better with each game. I made a mental note to talk to her about waiting until she was closer to her target to raise her weapon.

I missed some of their action while defending the loft door, but picked up watching again when Eden gave Emelynn the nod to take out an encroaching player. Emelynn flew out and fired too soon and wide. The force of the shot sent her reeling, and if she hadn't nicked her opponent, she would have been out of the game. She was, however, using her speed to advantage.

Victoria poked her head out of the loft and I took her out with a single shot. She was one fine-looking woman but had neither the skill nor the mindset to be a soldier. I slid inside and observed Deidra, who was positioned by Avery's tent. She hid herself well, but hesitated when she should have pounced, letting two targets get by her.

The game ended when I picked off Danny, the last of his team still in the game. Avery blasted the horn and Fliers swarmed the barn, collecting around Avery's tent in a frenzied buzz of excitement.

Avery leapt onto a hay bale outside his tent. "We've got time for another game," he said. "Is everyone up for it?" The positive response spurred him on.

"Okay, come see me so I can void your paint marks. Then you can regroup. Alex, you're at the east end this time, Danny you're at the barn doors. You've got ten minutes. The game starts on the first horn blast." He stepped off the hay bale, pulled his blue dauber from his pocket and set to work.

I searched for James, and found him beyond the edge of the crowd, talking with Danny. Danny and Steve were two of the Fliers we'd discussed for Sandra's rescue team. I'd check in with James later and get his assessment.

Emelynn and Eden stood together, laughing. They had that special combination of good looks and confidence that turned heads, made people take notice. Come to think of it, they'd make a pretty good decoy if we needed it when we set our plan in action. Eden's medical training would certainly be an asset, and if Emelynn could control her speed as well as I'd seen tonight, then maybe I needed to seriously consider including them.

I found Alex and asked him to pair me with Emelynn for the next game. I wanted to push her and see how she responded. Afterwards, I sought her out. "Looks like you and I are the only two who didn't get hit," I said, draping a brotherly arm across her shoulder. I had my back to James and didn't need him getting the wrong impression.

Emelynn didn't shy away from me. Perhaps I'd misread her earlier.

When the game planning started, Alex once again assigned positions, putting Emelynn and me in the offensive leads. It was the best possible place for me to assess her skills.

As the team dispersed, I took Emelynn's elbow to lead her out of the loft and down under cover of the lean-to. "How do you think we should approach this?" I asked.

She liked Eden's tactic of taking a position at an unexpected distance. "But instead of high," she said, "how about we stay low and way out there?" She pointed to the field surrounding the barn.

"Okay," I said. "Let's go before someone sees us and figures out our strategy." We raced to the field and settled into a horizontal hover in the tall grass.

"I'll move left," she said, "you move right and we'll meet on the other side. We may have to do a few sweeps before we can move inside."

Not bad, I thought. The horn still hadn't sounded. I told her that I'd overheard a conversation inside between James and Gabe, and thought she'd hit them both.

"Did I?" she asked, a coy smile playing at the edge of her mouth.

I hid a grin and looked toward the barn. "Interesting that both of them said they didn't see who hit them. I still don't think they know." I swung my head back in her direction, making certain she saw the question on my face. "Did you play with your speed by any chance?"

"I might have," she said, once again with that coy smile. She'd definitely gotten over whatever had had her acting so strangely before.

The horn blared followed by a spattering of gunshots from inside the barn. Two of the other side's players swiftly exited the loft door, where Sydney alone stood guard. Emelynn elbowed me and sprinted off after them, plying her speed. She sighted her weapon too soon and shot twice, missing both opponents. She was going too fast to turn and shoot again, but she'd distracted them, and I was able to follow up and hit both players once more before they got to Sydney. Sydney's eyes widened as Emelynn whizzed by her at a speed I'm sure she hadn't witnessed before.

Emelynn slowed and drifted down behind her before flying a wide arc back to me. "Way to go, Em," I whispered as she approached. "They didn't have a chance to react before I got them twice more. They're out of the game." She brightened, pleased with herself. And because I didn't want to miss her in action, I convinced her that we were better as a team and shouldn't split up.

"Let's see who else we can find," I said, before she changed her mind. We went on the hunt, staying low and moving quietly around the perimeter of the barn. Two of the other team's players snuck under cover of the lean-to before we could get them, and Emelynn sped up. I grabbed her arm to stop her and leaned in to whisper, "Let's sit tight for a few minutes. See if they make a move." It didn't take long. They flew out at a forty-five-degree angle, one following closely behind the other. "We've got them," I said. "They're heading to the barn doors to take out Alex and Steve. Looks like they're going to sneak in behind them." I arched an eyebrow. "But they didn't see us—and they certainly won't be expecting your speed. You ready?"

She didn't hesitate and took off, letting her speed have free rein. Her first shot was wide, but she actually hit her target with the second shot. We were going to have to work on her aim. Alex heard the shots, and he and Steve quickly dispatched their opponents.

When Emelynn and I returned to our positions, we headed inside. I wanted to get a sense of how she'd do in a confined space before the game ended.

The moment I tucked inside the loft door, I took two hits. Damn! That's what I got for concentrating on Emelynn more than the game. I flew back out the loft door and drifted down to the ground, out of the game. Emelynn fled past the loft and carried on to the opposite end of the barn. I followed her.

Once inside, she used her flash to team up with Eden. Avery had taught her well. In short order, they coordinated their efforts and put the last opponent out of the game. The horn sounded twice. The game was over.

I headed toward Avery and helped him distribute sodas. "Emelynn's sure come a long way," I said.

He passed a Coke to Deidra. "Yes, she has. Thanks to you."

"And you. She used her flash tonight. Remarkable considering she didn't recognize a flash just two weeks ago. How strong's her block?"

Sydney approached. "Do you have a water in there?" Avery bent down to retrieve a bottle and handed it to her.

She walked away and Avery straightened. "Her block, like everything else about her, is extraordinary."

"Good thing she's a quick study."

"She is, but she's also young and vulnerable." Avery turned to face me. "I take my responsibility to her seriously. I'd hate to see her get hurt."

I paused. "As would I," I said, and had the distinct feeling we were no longer merely discussing Emelynn's training.

"Glad to hear we're on the same page," Avery said. He walked away to join Gabe and the soccer moms in an animated discussion, one of many surrounding me. The novelty of the training games hadn't worn off. Avery would be wise to continue them after James and I departed in a day or two.

Avery jumped back up on his hay bale and got our attention. "Looks like that's it for the night. Red team wins 2–0, which means green team buys the first round. Jackson will organize a night out this week. Good night, everyone," he said, and jumped off the bale.

Perhaps I could talk Emelynn into sticking around. I wouldn't mind a repeat of our afternoon on the *Symphony*. I found her and tapped her elbow as she turned away from Sydney. "I have to stay to lock up. Do you want to hang around for a while before you head out?"

"Only if you'll help me get home," she said. "I don't know if I can find my way from here."

"Yeah, sure," I said, and then turned away to attend to the paint guns. Alex and Eden stayed to help sort out the coveralls and masks, and Emelynn and I saw them out the door and waved goodbye.

We stepped back inside, and the moment the door closed, I dragged Emelynn into my arms and kissed her. She responded with enough heat to stir an erection, leaving no doubt she was game for another round in the sack. I was tempted to take her right there, but knowing she was primed made me think a little anticipation would make it even better later.

I held her at arm's length. "How would you like to do some more flying around in here?" I asked.

She pouted. "All this comfortable-looking hay and you want to fly?"

Her arousal was plain on her face. She wanted it all right, which only confirmed my decision. She'd have to wait.

I stepped away before I changed my mind. "*That*, little girl, can wait. *This*"—I said, gesturing around us—"we only have for another hour."

I flew up to the rafters, daring her to follow.

CHAPTER THIRTY-ONE

Emelynn's once jerky and unsure moves were now swift and confident. Her intoxicating speed belied her inexperience, leaving me awed each time she blew by me. Her left turns weren't as sharp as her rights, and I saw a split-second of hesitation each time she committed to a change of direction. That would come with time, but was she ready? Even if I couldn't yet share the nature of my conflict with Cole, would she lend her talents? Would she understand and forgive me . . . after the fact?

And did I dare risk it?

She wouldn't admit she was tired, but after she'd collided with a second hay bale, I suggested we wrap it up.

Outside, I had another brilliant idea. "Remember what I said about jump-starts being like CPR?" I said. She thought about it before nodding. "How about I show you how to do one?"

"Now?" she said, arching an eyebrow. "With you?"

"Why not?"

"You've got about sixty pounds on me for starters."

"More like seventy," I said, chuckling. She had to experience it for herself to know I'd weigh nothing once in the air. "But it's not like lifting dead weight. Come here. Get behind me," I said, pulling her against my back. "Put your arms around my waist." When she did, I fed her instructions. "Now think about your liftoff—that surge of energy you feel when you break free of gravity."

"Okay," she said in a tentative voice.

"You'll have to ramp up the energy a little as you lift me."

She tightened her grip. "You ready?"

"God, I hope so," I said, taking one final look around.

She widened her stance and adjusted her limbs as if she were preparing to lift a refrigerator. I held on tight as she heaved, and the next moment we were hurtling upward at a dizzying velocity. Experiencing that speed of hers, first-hand, exhilarated me, and I rode it out, laughing into the wind.

With reluctance, I helped slow us down and then freed her arms from my waist and pulled her around. "Not bad for a first attempt," I said. "Want to try that again?"

After a few more jumps, she had the technique mastered, and I made my decision. I would ask her to join us, and pray she'd forgive my deception. She would understand after she saw my wife with another man. I couldn't wait to be rid of the lie.

"Do you feel as confident with the jump-start as you look?" I asked.

"They aren't as difficult as I'd imagined," she said, grinning. "But I suspect you knew that."

"Come home with me," I said, tugging her close. "I want to ravage you in the privacy of the *Symphony*."

"Ravage?"

"Utterly."

"Mmm, I like the sound of that," she said.

She made me promise to escort her home in the morning, and then pulled out her new GPS insisting I input the *Symphony's* location in the event we got separated. That wouldn't happen, but this would be her longest flight to date and I'd anchored south of the Fraser River in an area she wasn't familiar with. She was understandably anxious. I wished I'd thought to bring earpieces along. I led the way, skirting the city lights until I had a straight shot for the *Symphony* over water.

We landed on the observation deck and headed down to the galley. "How about a drink?" I asked, selecting the rocks glasses.

"Sounds good," she said, pulling the elastic from her hair as she drifted toward the sofas.

I dropped ice into the glasses, selected my favourite Scotch and then sweetened it up into something memorable. And just to make sure my night went according to plan, I set some tunes playing.

"Rusty nail," I said, handing her a glass. She looked up at me, her lovely green eyes half hidden beneath her brow. My dick twitched at the seductive smile that spread across her face.

"You know, you don't need to feed me booze to have your way with me," she said, drawing her fingers across my wrist before taking the glass from my hand.

Oh . . . we were going to have fun tonight. "I'm glad to hear that," I said, moving away to take a seat on the sofa opposite. I rested my feet on the coffee table between us and savoured my drink, letting my gaze roam across her body—a body I planned to unwrap before our drinks were done.

I waited until she caught my eye, then latched on and pushed my rush into her, grazing her libido just long enough to pull a gasp from her. How long before she asked me about that tantalizing Flier perk? I wondered.

She rearranged her legs and settled into the sofa. With the glass cradled in her hand, she pointedly licked the rim, making me wish it was something else she was licking. She set her drink aside long enough to remove her hooded sweatshirt, and then reclaimed her glass and poked at the ice cubes.

All right. Game on, girl. I rested my glass on the sofa and, one by one, unfastened the buttons on my shirt before slowly stretching my torso, tugging my shirt-tail loose. I smoothed a palm down my chest and tucked my fingertips into the waistband of my jeans, drawing her attention to a growing bulge.

If her smile was any indication, she liked what she saw. She set her glass aside again, and this time it was her tank top she removed, revealing a sexy bra that barely contained her breasts. She was every man's wet dream sitting there with a promise of sex on her face, her clothes half off and a drink in her hand.

My turn. Her gaze never left me as I removed my shirt and flipped open the button on my jeans. I picked up my glass and savoured another sip. Over to you, sweet thing.

She took her time, enjoying her drink as well as our game. This time, when she set her drink down, she rose to her knees and removed her leggings, followed by her socks. She wore a thong and flashed me a glimpse of her ass before she settled back down and stretched her long legs out to the coffee table. I had a mind to frame that thong and hang it in my stateroom. She retrieved her glass, ruthlessly ending her turn.

Did she realize the security cameras were picking up our little strip-tease? From two different angles? I drank her in, enjoying the thought that she had very little left to remove. Finally, giving in, I set my drink aside and unzipped my jeans. When I stood, I pulled a condom from my pocket and let it fall to the sofa. Her gaze followed it. I waited for her attention before peeling out of my jeans. I tugged off my socks, adjusted my Jockeys so she could see exactly what she had coming, and sat back down. It was showtime and I was primed.

Happily, she didn't make me wait. She unhooked her bra and held it out before letting it drop to the floor. Her breasts were magnificent, her nipples hardened points. She picked up her glass and stirred the ice cubes with her finger, and then she touched the wet finger to her nipple, painting it with Scotch. My balls contracted as she repeated the dip-and-paint tease with her other nipple.

I'd be damned if I was going to come without being inside her. I upended my drink, removed my last piece of clothing, and reached for the condom. It was my turn to unhinge her. I seated myself and slowly unrolled the condom down my shaft. She shivered as I stroked myself.

"Get over here," I said, unable to withstand another moment without touching her.

She took her time, finishing her drink before sashaying to stand before me. I leaned forward and licked my tongue across the width of her stomach, holding her ass in my hands. She tugged at my hair as I pulled her thong down and slid my hand between her legs. Attagirl, wet and ready. I nudged her legs further apart and pushed my fingers inside her velvety softness, and then leaned in to taste her, teasing her clitoris with my tongue.

She moaned encouragement, which I didn't need, and fisted her hands in my hair.

"Don't stop," she whispered, and it wasn't until that plea left her lips that I knew just how much our little game had affected her. Moments later, under my careful ministrations, she came undone.

Damn! What a fucking turn-on. I grabbed her hips and pulled her down to straddle me. This time, she was the one with the moves, taking charge and adjusting her limbs. She plunged down, smoothly enveloping me in one move.

"Fuck," I groaned, and arched into her. This was paradise. She rose and plunged again, and then braced her hands on the sofa behind me as she moved into a steady rhythm, positioning her bouncing breasts mere inches from my face. She would be the death of me, I thought, and grasped one none too delicately. I sucked hard on her nipple, which tasted of Scotch, and her pace faltered.

Moments later, she cried out as a second orgasm rippled through her. Her insides clenched my cock and her pace faltered again. I was so goddamn close. "Don't stop," I said, urgently guiding her hips with my hands. Soon after, I reached my own release and bowed up into her.

Afterwards, she stayed put, clenching me inside her. I felt every nuance. I opened my eyes and revelled in her just-fucked expression. Gently this time, I reached up and cupped her breasts. My cock twitched provoking another round of clenching that made me want to stay inside her all night long.

"This keeps getting better and better," she said, kissing me before easing off and settling beside me. I cleaned up with a tissue and pulled her into my side. Emelynn was turning out to be a pleasant surprise. Once again, I toyed with the idea of travelling back to New Orleans with her. The possibility had the makings for a perfect sexcapade.

I rubbed her shoulder, which had grown cold. "Let's go shower," she said, sitting forward.

The sound of a soft thud on the deck above froze me in place. She looked at me with a question on her face. The sound of footsteps confirmed my fear.

I jumped up and shoved Emelynn toward the door to the lower deck. "Go to your cabin. Lock the door."

Whoever was here was a Flier, and not invited. No Flier in his right mind would dare arrive like this, unannounced. I raced back to the credenza and grabbed the handgun I'd stashed. When I turned around, Emelynn was gone. I flicked off the safety and leapt over the galley counter for cover, crouching with my gun aimed at the door, chest height. Emelynn's cabin door slammed shut below.

Chapter Thirty-Two

J ames blew past me and through to the salon with a nasty scowl on his face and fisted hands.

"What the fuck!" I jumped up from my crouched position behind the counter.

James swung around and stopped, his face frozen in a scowl. "I left you a message an hour ago. Do you not answer your goddamn phone?"

"I nearly killed you, for Christ's sake." I slammed the gun on the counter and emerged from behind the counter.

James stared an uncomfortably long time at my state of undress, and then he gazed around the salon. "Son of a bitch! You couldn't wait, could you?"

"You've got brass fucking balls coming in here like this." Spying my Jockeys beside the sofa, I marched over, scooped them up and yanked them on.

"Last I checked, you still had a wife."

"Wife? That's a laugh. She's acting like a fucking whore." I walked to the far side of the salon and turned off the music.

James took a few stiff steps toward the coffee table, squinting like a gunslinger. "We're this close to finding her and you're too busy keeping your dick wet to step up and help." His words came out through tight lips.

"You have no idea what's going on here."

James reached for the abandoned rocks glasses on the coffee table. "Yeah? Then what the fuck is this, Jackson?" I guessed his intention with the curl of his lip and twisted in time to avoid the hurtling glass. It crashed into the wall behind me. Asshole. When I turned back, he'd rounded the sofa and spied Emelynn's thong. Terrific!

He picked it up and presented it like a prize. "Whose are these?"

I had my hands on my hips and shook my head. I would not justify his invasion of my privacy with an answer.

"This is just great," he said. "You are one first-class fuck-up!"

I'd had enough of his looking down at me like I was dog shit on his shoe. I grabbed the first thing I could get my hands on and aimed for his head. He ducked and the TV remote smacked the wall by his shoulder and broke into pieces. "This isn't your concern, James! Stay out of it."

"Like hell it's not," he said, leaping across the back of the sofa, gunning for me. "You selfish bastard!"

The fucker lashed out and landed a punch. We were matched for height, but I had a few pounds on him. I recovered, feigned a left and hit him with a right undercut that sent him stumbling backwards.

He pitched forward, ready to go again. Fucking idiot. I sidestepped him and raised my hands. "Jesus Christ! Back off, James."

He straightened, bringing a hand to his jaw. "This is beneath even you—who is she?" he demanded, but didn't wait for an answer. "It's Emelynn, isn't it? Does she know about Sandra?"

Damn him to hell! And why the fuck did I care? It wasn't like Sandra was keeping a low profile. "Yes, it's Emelynn," I said, looking over his shoulder toward the closed door that led below. "And yes, she knows about Sandra."

James paced to the sofa and back again, and then turned and marched toward the downstairs door. I raced to stand in front of it, barring his way.

He resumed his snarl. "So, she's the Ghost you've been researching?"

I frowned. Like it was any of his business.

He exhaled in a huff and stared at the floor. "This is not good," he said. "She's going to distract you."

I raised an eyebrow. *That* was his concern? Talk about fucking overkill.

He looked me in the eye. "I knew something was up when I saw you watching her fly tonight."

Again, none of his business, I thought, and gave him a snarl of my own. "She is not going to distract me."

"You're already keeping secrets, Jackson. We can't afford to lose our focus now. We're too close."

"That won't happen." It took every ounce of control I had to rein in my temper and remember that Sandra was his sister. "We're going to find Sandra and take her home," I said, aiming to calm him.

"You'd better hope so." He shook his head in disgust and turned back, pacing behind the sofa. "Alex's contacts got close to the boat last night. They're sure it's the one they're holding her on. They followed it to a marina south of Seattle. They don't know how many men are on board, but they're watching it."

So that was the message on my phone he'd referred to. Hardly warranted a visit, but I suspected he'd been looking for an excuse to drop by unannounced.

James stopped pacing. "We'll learn any time now. You have to be ready."

"We *are* ready," I said. "You saw us tonight."

"You'd better put your team together and do it quickly. I'll phone the minute we know the numbers." With a final shake of his head, he turned and pushed through the salon door and raced up the stairs.

I turned on the security feed. When I was certain he'd left, I gathered our clothes, headed down to Emelynn's cabin and knocked on her door.

She opened it, her gaze skittering around behind me. I dropped our clothes on the bed and took her hand, pulling her down to sit beside me. Her attention narrowed in on the welt James had left on my face, the arrogant bastard. I hoped he had a matching one on his jaw.

"Did you hear that?" I asked.

"Some," she said. "Are you all right?" She touched a feather-light finger to the welt as if to erase it. She hadn't heard the worst of James's remarks or her touch wouldn't have been so gentle. I breathed easier.

"I'm fine," I said, taking her hand. "It was James. He's angry." I shook my head. "He's so focused on finding Sandra that he's not thinking straight, and he knows you were here."

She looked over to the door. "He's gone?" she asked.

"Yeah, he's gone. He thinks our relationship is going to distract me." I tucked a curl behind her ear, smiling at the memory of our most recent distraction. "You certainly are that, but I won't lose my focus."

"I don't understand. Why is James even involved?"

"He's with the New Orleans covey. We're working together."

She paused, considering my revelation with a frown. "This isn't what I'd call working together," she said, touching the welt on my face.

"It's just James. He's intense and he takes covey seriously. The sooner we find Sandra, the sooner he can get back stateside. James tells me our contacts are close to finding her. That means we have to be prepared to move quickly. I need my team ready to go."

"What's your plan?"

I told her about Sandra's ATM withdrawals. "Two or three men accompany her each time, leaving some of their men behind to guard the boat. Our plan is to grab her on the way to or from a bank machine, when we'll only have two or three men to deal with."

"Who's on your team?"

"There'll be six of us, including James and me. We're using Alex's Seattle contacts, so he'll be there, and I'm going to ask Danny to join us. I'd like Eden to come, in case Sandra needs medical attention, and Steve Elliott's my backup if any of the others can't make it."

I took both her hands in mine. "But Em, I want you with us. Your speed might be the edge we need." And her presence would be a little payback for James and his insulting stunt tonight, not to mention a kick in the balls for Cole.

"Me?" she said, furrowing her brow. "Just a few days ago you told me I was too inexperienced. You said I wasn't skilled enough with my speed to be any help to you at all."

"That was before I watched you in action earlier tonight. I misjudged you. You are ready. You're more than ready."

She shook her head. "I'd like to help, Jackson. Truly, I would, but I'm so far out of my depth here."

I squeezed her hands. "You and Eden will be our secret weapons. They may be expecting a rescue attempt, but they sure as hell won't be expecting women. At a minimum, you can distract them. And they won't have a clue about your speed, Emelynn. You might be able to do things we can't. Please say you'll help us."

She looked down at our hands, thinking about it. When she looked up, she asked, "What do I need to do?"

"Keep your passport with you. We might not use official channels, but it's best to have it anyway. Keep your cellphone charged and within reach. And bring street clothes—something attention getting—in case you need to act as a decoy. I'll organize a float plane to take us close to our target, but be prepared to fly home on your own."

She looked up. "Okay, count me in."

Yes! I threw my arms around her. "Thank you." She had no idea how much her presence would bolster me when I faced my wife decorating Cole's arm.

"Now get into the shower. You have to go home to get ready, and I have a team to organize."

I left her in her cabin, retrieved my robe from my stateroom and returned to the salon, where I'd left my phone. My first call was to Alex.

"Hey. Looks like the waiting is almost over. The ship carrying Sandra has been spotted close to Seattle. We're only a day or two away from launch."

"Okay. I won't start anything at the shop that I can't drop in a flash."

"Terrific. And Alex, Emelynn has agreed to join us."

"Emelynn? She's untrained."

"Yeah, but you've seen her speed. I don't know anyone who could catch her."

"True, but in case you hadn't noticed, a blind shooter would have better aim."

"Don't worry. I don't plan on putting a gun in her hand. She'll be on the sidelines, ready to turn on that speed if we need it."

"I don't know, Jackson. Even on the sidelines, she'll be a liability. Our attention will be split. We don't need that."

That was just the opening I'd been looking for. "Fair enough. So how about this: ask Eden to join us. They can back up each other, and you have to admit, she and Emelynn would make one hell of a distraction if we needed one. We'd have Emelynn's speed, and it goes without saying how valuable Eden's medical training would be."

"I can't ask Eden to take that risk."

"I'd only use her as a decoy. The people holding Sandra won't even know she's with us."

"Let me think about it. Who else have you lined up?"

"Danny, for sure. I'll call him next. With your four contacts and the four of us, I think we'll have enough muscle to take them down."

Emelynn opened the door and stepped into the salon, her hair damp from the shower.

"Sounds good," Alex said. "I'll see how Eden feels about coming along and let you know."

"I'd appreciate that. I'll be in touch," I said, and disconnected.

"That was Alex. He's all set. Are you ready to go?"

She'd already programmed her GPS to show her the way back to her cottage. I escorted her to the observation deck and kissed her good-bye. In a few short days, she'd know the truth. Hopefully, it wouldn't destroy what we had. I was counting on her company on my return to New Orleans to wash away the last remnants of Sandra. And lord knows she'd improve the scenery immensely.

Sleep played hard to get leaving me tired to face an overcast day. I trudged to the head, and then pulled on a pair of jeans and climbed the stairs hopeful a cup of coffee would help wake me.

While it brewed, I received a text from James. They'd counted five men aboard the *MayBell*.

My mouth was full of bagel when Alex called.

"Eden's agreed to join us," he said.

"That's great. Thank her for me. Looks like there are five men accompanying Sandra."

"We can work with that. They'll leave one or two behind to guard the boat anyway."

"That's right. I'll book the float plane today."

"Sounds good. We'll be ready."

After I'd organized the plane, I called James.

"We're all set," I said. "Everyone is lined up and we have a Turbo Beaver on standby in Richmond."

"Who's joining us?"

Call me petty, but I'd been waiting for that question. "Danny, Alex, Eden . . . and Emelynn," I said, grinning into the phone. To my heart's delight, he jumped all over it.

"Are you out of your fuckin' mind?"

I shouldn't have laughed, but if he thought I was going to play nice when I finally caught up to Cole and Sandra, he was mistaken. "You think that's inappropriate?"

"Seems trashy is quite appropriate for you these days, Jackson. But I was thinking more of our mission, and of how little your mistress offers the team."

"That's where you're wrong, James. She's the fastest Flier I've ever seen. And Cole won't be expecting women."

"You think I don't know what you're doing? You're transparent, Jackson. Do as you wish, but you'd better hope the women don't get in my way."

I hung up, comforted by the thought that James and his family would soon be ex-relatives I'd never have to deal with again. Soon, I'd be leaving Canada and taking the *Symphony* down the coast. If Emelynn agreed to come along, I could stretch the journey out. Maybe I'd call Graham to captain; maybe I'd even hire a cook. That would free Emelynn and me up to do the trip back to New Orleans in style.

And that tempting thought sent me out to restock dry goods for the trip ahead. The fresh food, however, would have to wait until we crossed into the States.

Minutes before midnight, my phone dinged. A film clip had come in from Wells Fargo in Tacoma. My wife making another withdrawal, no doubt. I clicked on the attachment and watched the now familiar scene play out. But this clip was different. I squinted at the small screen, certain that the man standing with Sandra was not Cole.

I sprang to the laptop and turned it on, tapping my fingers on the counter as it went through its start-up gyrations. I opened the attachment and ran it on full screen. Halfway through the late-night transaction, Sandra pushed sunglasses into her hair and blinked several times, as if she were trying to focus her vision. Her eyelids were half closed. Was she drunk? While she waited for the cash to spit out, she closed her eyes and rested her head on the chest of the man behind her. A huge man who looked an awful lot like Johnny Lorenzo wearing aviators and a new goatee. Her head wobbled on her shoulders as she reached for the cash and then Johnny's hand shot out and took it from her. He forcibly turned her around as if she were a small child, and retreated. The screen went blank.

I stared in disbelief. What the fuck was that? I hit replay and watched the whole thing again. Surely Sandra hadn't sunk that low. I pressed my fingertips to my forehead to stave off the pressure I felt building and played it one more time.

I slammed the laptop closed and staggered back to drop on the sofa. Was Sandra playing at a new game? There was no doubt she was inebriated, though that was out of character. But hell, what did I know about her character anymore?

Though it pained me to do it, I sent the clip to James.

It took less than five minutes for my phone to ring.

"You still think she's with them of her own volition?" he said.

"I don't know what to think." Unformed thoughts played pinball in my head.

"She's stoned out of her tree! She doesn't touch drugs and you know it."

"Then she's had too much to drink."

"Her pupils are dilated. That's not alcohol."

My head pounded and a sense of dread filled my chest. "What are you suggesting?"

"That she's being held prisoner with Johnny Lorenzo and his crew for company. They're drugging her."

"You're guessing."

"Am I? Or is it just easier for you to deny it because you can't admit you were wrong, and you've been wrong all along," James said with a caustic edge to his voice. "And now you're blinded by a lover."

"Don't pull that shit with me. My wife took a lover long before I did. I'm sorry if her choice turned out badly."

"What I saw in that ATM clip didn't look like a choice to me."

I yanked the phone away from my head and held it in a death grip. Blood pounded in my ears. I hurled the phone at the sofa opposite and stormed out to the foredeck. I grabbed the rails to steady myself. Heat crawled up my neck. Rage, like I'd never known, boiled up inside me. I had to get out of there.

I grabbed my jacket and ran up the dock. The path along the river's edge was unlit; the gravel crunched beneath my sprinting feet. When I'd passed the solitary bench overlooking the tidal flats, I flew into the darkness and out over the Fraser. I crossed over the river's muddy mouth into the Strait of Georgia, and kept going. Tankers and container ships bobbed on the water below.

Eventually, the rush of wind cooled my heated rage, and I felt like I could breathe again. I slowed my westward flight, swung a wide arc north and considered the question I could barely form: could I have been wrong about Sandra?

I knew I hadn't underestimated her fury the night she'd left. She'd made it clear her sympathies lay with Cole, not me. Should I have been more concerned about her absence in the early days? No, it's not like she hadn't shut me out before, after an argument. The last time, she'd trotted off to Spain and was gone for weeks. This time she'd quit a job I knew she'd loved; she'd obviously planned to be away for a while. No, she'd left me. It would take an act of willful stupidity to think otherwise.

Yet I couldn't get past the lump that formed in my chest when I thought about the latest ATM clip. Sandra with the likes of Johnny Lorenzo? Cole, I could see, but not Johnny.

Then again, it might be that Sandra's choice of companion wasn't as it seemed. Maybe it was a simple case of Cole being unavailable. Johnny and Cole were buddies; maybe Cole sent Johnny along for her protection.

Still, a sense of foreboding weighed on my conscience, eating away at the certainty of Sandra's betrayal I'd once taken for granted.

Land loomed on the horizon and I checked my bearing. Without realizing it, I'd flown to the coast where Emelynn's cottage sat. I put on the brakes and skidded to halt. Emelynn.

What had I done?

I turned away. Guilt was a shitty companion, and it rode me all the way back to the edge of the Fraser River. I slipped back down the dock to the *Symphony*, seeking her solace and a shot of bourbon.

Instead, I found James loitering on the foredeck with his arms draped over the rail and his gaze pointed at me.

"You're trespassing," I said, as I boarded.

The smug little bastard didn't react. He just straightened and folded his arms. "I have something you need to see, and I wanted to deliver it in person."

Ah, the perfect ending to a perfect evening. I ignored him and entered the salon through the starboard door, leaving him outside.

Never one to take a fucking hint, he stepped through the slider at the bow to join me.

I paused at the galley cupboard with my back to him. "You want a drink?"

"Not tonight." The leather on the bar stool creaked.

I got myself a glass and poured a shot, tasting it before I turned around.

"What is it, James?"

He pulled up something on his phone and slid it across the counter to me. I caught the phone and held it up, staring at a snapshot of Cole getting out of a car in front of the distinctive iron gallery of the Pickwick in New Orleans.

"Why are you showing me his ugly face?"

"One of my men took that photo a few hours ago. Cole's not on the *MayBell*."

I stared at him in disbelief. "Are you fucking kidding me?"

"Wish I were," he said, gesturing for the return of his phone.

"Damn it!" I slid it back down the counter. "Was your sister with him?"

"No."

I downed the drink and set the glass on the counter, twisting the tumbler with my fingertips. "Maybe something came up. He'll be back." I poured another shot. Took a gulp.

"Or he wants us to know he's not on board. And Sandra is. I think he's setting Johnny up and Johnny's too stupid to know it."

"How do you figure that?" I asked.

James spun his phone on the countertop. "Cole has carefully choreographed these withdrawals. He's never once made Sandra look coerced. Until now. So either Lorenzo's gone rogue, or Cole set him up knowing he couldn't pull it off without drawing attention."

"Whose? The police?" I shook my head. "Cole wouldn't let that happen. He knows Johnny'd turn on him with a smile. Cole's not stupid enough to take that risk."

James cocked his head. "It's not such a big risk if Johnny's dead when the police get to him."

I caught James's gaze and frowned. "You think the bastard played us?"

"I have no doubt. He's been running this show from day one. He knew exactly where the *Symphony* was and sailed as close to her as he dared. And then he baited us with that last ATM clip knowing we'd have no choice but to get Sandra out of there. He also knows we're not going to leave witnesses for the police to question."

"Or," I said, "he had to attend to some business back home and Lorenzo took advantage of his absence."

James slid from the bar stool and walked behind it. "That version doesn't explain Sandra's condition."

No, it didn't. And I didn't want to examine that consideration right now. I downed the second shot and poured another. "Does it really matter which version is accurate?"

James rested his forearms on the back of the stool and exhaled heavily. "Not to me, as long as we can be civil and work together because someone's going to view that film, and when they do, chances are good they'll call the police."

"That can't happen. With the police all over Cole, we'll never get to him, and I want his fucking head."

"Sandra needs to be our priority right now. We can take our time with Cole after we eliminate his crew."

"We? No. I own Cole's ass. You're welcome to Johnny."

"Oh, Johnny's gonna pay, I can guarantee that," James said, straightening.

"All right. You want to toast to that?" I said, holding up my glass.

"No, and lay off the booze," James said, nodding to the bottle. "I've seen your hangovers. You'll be useless in that condition."

Still an asshole, I thought. I stared at the amber liquid a moment longer, and then turned and dumped the shot in the sink. Unfortunately, he was right on more fronts than I cared to think about. "The pilot needs two hours' notice."

"Okay. We'll hit them tomorrow night. Let's get some sleep." He turned his back and strode to the door.

I called after him. "Emelynn stays on the team. Her speed is phenomenal. We may need it."

He stopped and spoke over his shoulder. "I've seen her fly. Bring her. Just keep her the hell away from me."

Damn straight I'd keep Emelynn away from him.

I lay in bed and stared at the ceiling. One more day. Tomorrow, Sandra would answer the questions that had haunted me for months. I tried not to think too much about whether I could live with her answers.

Chapter Thirty-Three

In the morning, after I'd sorted out the charter, I called Alex. "We're pulling Sandra out tonight. The plane's scheduled for a 4:00 p.m. departure."

"Got it. The van's fuelled and ready to go."

"All right. I'll make the calls. You'll collect them?"

"Tell them to be ready by 2:00. I'll meet you at the float-plane terminal."

Next, I called Danny, and then I brought up Emelynn's number. My finger hovered over the send button. I'd already lost Sandra, and the time had come when Emelynn might very well walk away as well.

I set the phone down and strolled to the aft deck and sat in the shade. Diesel fumes wafted across the marina. I toyed with the idea of telling Emelynn about Sandra before we took off, but it was a toss-up whether she'd understand, or bolt.

What the hell—a few more hours wouldn't make any difference.

I returned to the galley, prepared the *Symphony* for my absence and then retrieved my phone. This time I didn't hesitate. "It's time."

"My bag's packed," Emelynn said, and the sound of her voice plucked at my conscience.

"Can you be ready in twenty minutes?"

"I'm ready right now."

"Good. Alex will be by to pick you up. He'll take you to the float plane. I'll meet you there. I've got to go," I said, before I said something more. "See you soon, Em."

I called a cab, collected my overnight bag and headed up the dock.

James beat me to the terminal. I spotted him leaning with one shoulder against the side wall of the small building as he thumbed through screens on his phone.

"James," I said.

He looked up without moving his head. "Jackson. Where are the others?"

"They'll be here soon."

He returned his attention to his phone. "Dad's on his way to Seattle. He's waiting for my coordinates to meet up with us."

"Redmond? You think that's a good idea?"

He straightened up and crossed his arms. "Nope, but you try stopping him and let me know how that goes."

"Ah, shit." I rubbed my forehead and paced away from him. No one on the team knew Redmond Moss. Hell, we'd never even mentioned his name. Alex's contacts would be within their rights to stand down. Damn it! I turned back to James. "Keep him at a distance if you can, would you?"

James's gaze cut across my shoulder, behind me. I turned to see Alex and the rest of the team crossing the road. With forced smiles, we exchanged tense hellos. We certainly didn't look like the carefree tourists I'd described to the pilot hours earlier.

I outlined the scenario I'd set up. "We're heading to Lake Union to do some sightseeing. Is everyone ready?" They bobbed their heads in agreement, but I didn't see a single touristy smile.

We sailed through the security check, where the co-pilot collected us. He led us down the ramp to the waiting Turbo Beaver tied to the dock. The pilot was already on board. James immediately jumped in and took a seat behind him. Danny followed and sat beside James.

Eden looked back to Emelynn, and then she and Alex boarded and took the middle seats. Emelynn hugged her small knapsack tight to her stomach and squeaked a nervous laugh when she realized the co-pilot was waiting for her to surrender it. He passed the bag to the dock hand and helped her up the narrow steps to the back seat.

I leaned into the cockpit to confirm the next day's return-flight details with the pilot, and then jumped aboard and took the seat beside Emelynn.

Her gaze darted around the small space and sweat beaded on her forehead. "You okay?" I whispered.

"Yes," she said. I knew it was a lie. Eden reached between the seats and gave Emelynn's knee a reassuring pat. The comforting gesture tweaked my memory; Emelynn's father had died in a float-plane accident. No wonder she was anxious.

Alex twisted in his seat and winked at Emelynn, drawing a smile out of her. With James's attention on the Beaver's controls in the cockpit, I reached an arm around Emelynn and gave her a quick squeeze.

The engine noise precluded conversation, which suited me. I wasn't in the mood for small talk. The flight path took us westward first, over Vancouver Island, before turning south, adding more time to our journey—more time to wait and wonder and second-guess. Finally, the pilot banked and descended into Lake Union. He throttled down the engines after a smooth landing, and we taxied to the wharf, where a dock hand waited to secure the lines.

We exited the plane, collected our bags and walked up the ramp. After clearing customs, we gathered outside in the parking lot.

I turned to James. "Let's go pick up the rental van." We left the others behind and crossed to the Hertz booth. I'd already decided James would drive—it would keep some distance between him and Emelynn.

When we went back to get the others, I jumped out and motioned for Alex to take the front seat. Everyone else piled in the back. James followed Alex's directions and drove north on Third Avenue. It was after 7:00 p.m. and still bright out.

On our right, Lake Union glittered in the sun as we bore northwest along the shore. I nudged Emelynn and then tapped Danny and Eden to get their attention. "We're going to rendezvous with Alex's contacts, get a bite to eat and then coordinate our plans."

"Stell's Burgers—fantastic!" Eden said, giving the fast-food joint Alex had chosen an enthusiastic endorsement.

Emelynn retrieved her GPS from her bag and studied it as James drove. She didn't notice his gaze on her in the rear-view mirror. James's attention slid to me, watching him, and he quickly looked forward. Danny played air drum to an old Phil Collins song on the radio.

We found Stell's Burgers and cruised around behind it to the back parking lot. Alex spotted the black van Gary had said they'd be travelling in. We parked beside it, and then piled out and shook hands. Alex introduced Danny to Gary and Tony. I turned to introduce Eden and Emelynn and saw that they were halfway to the restaurant, headed to the restroom no doubt.

We gathered around the picnic table in the grass at the edge of the parking lot.

"You bring any hardware?" Gary asked.

"No. We flew charter. Too risky. You?"

"We're packing, but we're not planning on making that much noise."

"Did you get the first aid kit?"

"It's in the van"

"I'm going to grab a burger," Danny said. "You guys want anything?"

He took the orders, and trotted off with the C-note I handed him.

James addressed Gary. "The man we suspect kidnapped our covey mate was spotted in New Orleans."

"When?" Gary asked.

"Last night," James said. "I doubt he's returned."

"Good. One less man for us to worry about."

Tony unrolled a detailed map on the picnic table. We studied it with the help of Gary, who circled the area where the *MayBell* was last seen. He pointed to where Jin and Mark were holed up, and we discussed strategy.

I looked up at the sound of footsteps and saw Danny returning with Eden and Emelynn in tow. While Danny passed out burgers and fries, I prepped the team.

"Sandra is being held on a forty-five-foot dump of a ship named the *MayBell*. Gary has been following the *MayBell* the past three nights." I tapped my finger to the map. "She docked at the Stabbert shipyard late last night."

Gary said, "Unfortunately, Stabbert is less than twenty-five miles from the Puget Sound Naval Shipyard. The naval yard has eyes on the sky so that limits our movement."

Gary continued as he unwrapped his burger. "The *MayBell's* been operating with a five-man crew, but we couldn't watch them last night. We'll have to reassess once we spot them again. They're armed and at least three of them are Fliers." He fisted his burger and took a bite.

I outlined the strategy we'd discussed. "We'll start at Stabbert's shipyard and scout the shoreline north from there to pick her up again. Gary has two men stationed about three miles north of Stabbert," I said, pointing out their location on the map. "But they haven't spotted her yet. When we locate the *MayBell*, we'll keep her in our sights until she docks. If they follow the pattern they've set so far, they'll be hitting another ATM tonight, sometime after eleven o'clock."

"You gotta like those odds," Alex said, licking his fingers. "Five of them to eight of us, not counting our two distractions." He gave Eden a lecherous wink. She playfully rolled her eyes.

"Let's just hope they're not expecting us," I said. "I'd prefer to drop in on them unannounced, if you know what I mean."

I looked down at my wrapped burger, which didn't appeal to me in the least, and tossed it into the bin. Tony threw his garbage on top of it, and then rolled up the map.

"We'll be less conspicuous travelling in one vehicle," I said, standing. "Gary, you and Tony ride with us."

We piled back into the rental van with James behind the wheel and Alex riding shotgun, and continued north. No one spoke. Seemed we were all buttoned down, contemplating the night ahead.

I looked out over Salmon Bay as we crossed the Ballard Bridge, and checked my phone. Only a few hours now and I'd see my wife, have my answers.

Luckily, there was little traffic, and we arrived at the Stabbert shipyard before I could think too deeply about Sandra's situation.

Following Gary's directions, James drove straight past the security hut and turned left, not stopping until we were on the dock, safely hidden beside a corrugated steel building.

When James turned the engine off, dusk closed in, and the clank and groan of overhead cranes punctured the quiet.

"Eden, Em, stay here to guard the van," I said. "We'll be back as soon as we've located the *MayBell*, then we'll head north to rendezvous with Gary's men. Is everyone with me so far?" I asked, looking around to make eye contact with each of them.

"Danny," I said, pointing to a box under his seat, "hand out the earpieces, would you?" He opened the box and passed them out. "They're good for about a five-mile radius." Tony took one and looked over at Gary, who whistled his appreciation. "Gary, take two for your other men."

"There are a lot of us on this channel," I said, "so keep chatter to a minimum." Danny slid the side door open, and we jumped out and blended into the growing darkness.

Tony motioned for us to follow him, and we flew off over a cluttered work yard, skirting the overhead lights and using the shadows to search for the *MayBell*. We landed near a battered dock's edge, where half tires assured boats a cushioned landing.

Danny and Alex assessed the path ahead, nodded at one another and immediately took off. Gary tapped his mic, then pulled his earpiece out and adjusted it.

I held my hand up to the crew, and then turned my back and flew twenty yards off to do a com check. "*Jackson here. Answer me when I call your name.*"

Everyone answered in turn. "*Good,*" I said, and flew back to confirm our plan. "*We're splitting up. James and I are checking the slips. Gary and Tony are headed to the dry docks. Danny and Alex are already sussing out the outlying anchorages. We haven't found her yet.*"

Gary and Tony flew off to the right, James and I to the left. The dull grey bulk of the *MayBell* wouldn't be easy to spot; she would blend into the night unlike the stark white hull of a ship like the *Symphony*.

The slips were a ways to the south and lit well enough to keep us a good distance from them. James pointed to himself and then to the slips along the outer edge of the long dock. I nodded, and dropped down to the inside edge, keeping just above the water. I checked every slip, but the *MayBell* wasn't there.

My earpiece sparked to life. "*Please tell me that's one of you.*" It was Eden speaking in a whisper.

Shit. "*Not us,*" I said, looking around for James.

"*Nor us,*" Gary said.

"*It's not us,*" Alex said, his voice tight.

"*Damn,*" Eden said. "*We've got company.*"

Alex came on again, speaking quickly. "*There's a map in the glovebox. Tell whoever it is that you're lost.*"

I rounded the last slip and sped toward the end of the dock and spotted James. I flew out to join him. James shook his head. He hadn't spotted the ship either.

I heard a gasp from one of the girls and cupped the earpiece to catch the conversation.

Alex pounced. "*What's happening?*"

"*A complication,*" Eden replied.

I looked over to James. He glared back with his hands on his hips, but he could stuff his attitude. I cocked my head and took off in the direction where we'd left the rental van.

Eden squeaked out, "*That's no security guard.*"

Panic added volume to Alex's voice. "*Eden? Talk to me.*"

Damn it, I was still too far away to intercede. "*What's happening?*" I asked.

I heard one of the girls yell, "*Go!*" and then the distant screech of tires. The conversation that followed came from the bottom of a well. "*Left here,*" and that was followed by further directions: "*Turn right at the hut and don't stop.*" I slowed my flight. Emelynn and Eden had escaped whoever it was and were fleeing in the rental van. Which meant our ride was gone.

The radio fell silent. James drew up behind me as I reached the half-moon tires at the end of the dock. Gary and Tony were a short distance away, closing in fast. We stood like boys on the edge of the gym at prom.

I motioned to Alex, who was approaching fast. His voice broke through. "*Are you okay?*"

The pause before she answered felt very long. Finally, Eden said, "*Yeah, we're fine. It was a close call, but we made it out of there.*"

Emelynn's voice came on the line. "*Someone needs to go check on that security guard.*"

"*He was dressed like a Flier,*" Eden said in a quiet voice, as if she was talking to Emelynn, not the team, "*and he had his gun drawn.*" Why was Eden qualifying their actions?

"*But he didn't have a block up,*" Emelynn said.

Oh shit. Did we already have a body to dispose of? "*What did you do to him?*" I asked.

It was Eden who replied. "*Let's just say you don't want to get on Em's bad side.*"

Chapter Thirty-Four

I'll check on the guard," James said. "*Make sure he doesn't warn the wrong people.*" He immediately flew off, and I was left wondering what exactly Emelynn had done to the man.

Gary, who'd been thumbing his cellphone, said, "*The* MayBell *just passed our position at Golden Gardens Park.*"

"*Is Sandra on board?*" I asked.

"*Can't tell yet,*" Gary said. "*The same goons as last night are on deck.*"

"*Okay, Gary, ask your guys to stay with her. We're on our way. James, when you're done with Mr. Security, catch up with us. Danny, Alex, you're with me. We're heading up the coast to find Gary's men. Don't forget who's watching the skies. Fly close to the ground and keep your air times short. Eden, Em, start up the coast and let us know when you pass Golden Gardens Park.*"

Gary lifted off to take the lead. The rest of us followed. A crescent moon hung low in the eastern sky and the air felt cool. When shore lights forced us away from land, we flew within feet of the water's surface. It wasn't long before Gary gestured ahead, pointing to the frothy wake behind the distant stern of the *MayBell*. She was holding steady at about ten knots. Gary flew ahead to rendezvous with Jin and Mark. The rest of us kept astern of the tug.

Our earpieces sparked to life moments later when Eden announced they'd arrived at Golden Gardens Park.

"*Okay,*" I said. "*We're following the* MayBell *and she's not slowing down. Continue north and check back in another ten minutes.*"

James caught up without a word and stayed at a distance. With the *MayBell* an easy follow, I pulled out my phone and texted him. "What happened to the guard?"

"Looked like a jolt. He won't be talking."

A fatal jolt? From Emelynn? No wonder she'd sounded distraught. Yet one more piece of Jolene's extraordinary gift.

I texted, "Where's Redmond?"

James replied, "North of us, in Everett."

Everett was twenty-five miles away. Redmond wasn't a stupid man; he'd know the consequences of his interference. I'd have to trust twenty-five miles was enough distance to temper his impatience.

The *MayBell* continued her steady trek north. Eden's next check-in was south of Carkeek Park. "*You're ahead of us,*" I said. "*We're keeping pace with the* MayBell *so we won't be able to keep up with you. They might pull in at Richmond Beach. There are a few ATMs there, but I think the better bet is Edmonds; it's bigger with more options.*" I suggested she head there and find a safe location for a rendezvous.

"*Okay, we're on our way,*" Eden responded.

We continued on, keeping the *MayBell* a safe distance ahead. The lights of Richmond Beach approached, but the tug never slowed nor strayed from its northern trajectory.

Alex approached on my right, and we came to a hover. "It's Eden," he said, holding out his phone. "They're in Edmonds, out of range for the earpieces, but they've found a secluded place to meet up." He put her on speakerphone.

"What'd you find?" I asked.

"The north end of the boardwalk is heavily treed and almost deserted. It'll work."

I nodded my approval to Alex. "Hang tight," I said. "The *MayBell* just rounded Richmond Beach and is headed your way. Let's hope she pulls in there."

"We'll wait to hear from you," Eden said, and disconnected.

"*Did the rest of you hear that?*" I said.

"*Got it,*" Gary replied, followed by affirmatives from the others.

Twenty minutes later, the lights at the southern edge of Edmonds came into view. We headed away from shore to skirt the lights.

"*She's slowing,*" James said.

Mark interrupted. "*The Captain of the* MayBell *just radioed the Edmonds wharfinger.*"

"*Looks like she's headed for the public dock,*" Gary said. "*Mark, stay with her and keep us updated. We want to know when she docks, and see if you can get a head count.*"

"*Everyone else rendezvous at the van as soon as you can. James and I are on recon,*" I said, motioning James over. "*We'll be there soon.*"

I took off southeast, with James on my tail, and flew inland over the unlit edge of forested land south of the marina. We dropped down to the asphalt and set a brisk pace north, keeping to the shadows. Train tracks ran north-south, east of the marina, fenced off on both sides.

"*They'll have no choice but to head this way,*" James said, pointing north from the docks toward the parking lot. On our left sat the marina's pub, a well-lit single-storey structure. "*We'll position the women there. They can lure our targets into position.*"

I swung my head in James's direction. I'd not expected James to acknowledge Eden and Em, let alone involve them.

He ignored me and we continued north. "*The targets will have to exit over there,*" I said, indicating a walkway adjacent to the marina's entrance. "*And there's a perfect location for a set-up.*" I gestured to a squat cinder-block building sporting a public restroom sign. "*Gary said three of them are Fliers. We'll have to keep out of sight—make sure their attention is on Emelynn and Eden so they don't see us.*"

The back side of the building was unlit and adjacent to a treed strip of land that ran parallel to the railway fencing. James flew off and disappeared behind the structure. A moment later, the dim lightbulb over the men's entrance on the north side of the building winked out.

"*That'll help. They don't all have night vision,*" he said, rejoining me. We jogged north, through the parking lot. Dayton Street, the major east-west artery for traffic between the waterfront and downtown Edmonds, lay ahead. Most of the ATMs were situated on or near Dayton. "*They won't take Dayton. They'll take this road east, and cross over to Dayton on one of the smaller side streets.*"

I looked up the narrow road. "*If we miss our opportunity by the restrooms, those vacant lots on the right would do,*" I said. "*Let's find the others.*" With no one in sight, we lifted up and crossed back toward the water. We soon spotted the tree cover Eden had mentioned and dropped down, emerging at the north end of the boardwalk.

The others, with the exception of Mark, waited by the van. I kept my mic on to keep Mark in the loop. "*Let's go,*" I said, not wanting to loiter in numbers that would draw attention. James took the wheel again and Alex climbed in beside him. The rest of us piled into the back.

We headed south, back toward the marina. At the entrance to the marina complex, we drove over a speed bump and shortly after, I pointed out the cinder-block building. "*That's a public restroom.*" Both the north and east sides of the building were now perfectly dark. Farther along, I pointed out the bar adjacent to the marina. "*That's the Loft.*"

James drove to the south end of the marina's parking lot, turned and stopped. "*The MayBell will moor somewhere in that area,*" I said, gesturing to the public slips beside the pier. "*If they follow the pattern they've used in the past, two or three of the men will take Sandra to an ATM between eleven and midnight. The banks are all located in a two-block area around Dayton Street, north of here. They'll come down that pier, pass by the bar and take the path that goes past the public restroom. The Amtrak fencing you can see over there will funnel them through this parking lot.*"

James restarted the van, and headed north again, back the way we'd come. "*They won't risk taking her along Dayton because it's too busy, too bright,*" I said, as the van wobbled back over the speed bump. "*Once they're past the restrooms, they'll have to continue through this park area,*" I said, gesturing to our right, "*then across the Amtrak rail.*"

We continued to the first intersection and turned east before crossing the tracks. James took up the commentary. "*They'll continue up this road, past these empty lots and up to the corner.*" James pulled over and parked. "*We can't be sure what route they'll take beyond this point.*"

"*Our best bet is to snatch her before she gets to that corner,*" I said, pointing ahead of us to the far end of the narrow road. "*We need to make our move at some point between the pub and these empty lots, preferably without an audience.*"

James pulled out. We continued east to the next corner, and then turned north on Edmonds Way. We hit Dayton and turned right. Two blocks along, I pointed out a U.S. Bank, and in quick succession a Bank of Washington and a Horizon Bank. They all had ATMs. We continued east on Dayton another five minutes until it morphed into Main Street. James slowed down and turned left into Pine Ridge Park. He parked the van in the deserted shadows and turned off the ignition.

Mark's voice came over the earpiece. "*They're docked, but not for the night. They've taken a two-hour slip. I haven't got a head count yet.*"

Gary responded, "*Stay on it, Mark, and keep us posted.*"

I checked my watch. It was time. I took a deep breath. *"Eden, Em, we need you on the ground close to the targets. Go to the Loft and change into your street clothes. You'll guide them into position for us. Okay?"* They bobbed their heads.

"Gary, Tony, we'll meet up with Mark to watch the MayBell *and follow Sandra from the air, when they make their move. Alex, James, Jin, Danny—meet up behind the public restrooms, keep out of sight and wait until we tell you they're on the move. You'll position yourselves in the air in front of them.*

"When they get into range, we'll extract Sandra and take out the targets. We'll have the advantage of surprise, and with four of you in front and another four of us behind, we'll also have the advantage of numbers." I gazed around the van, measuring the level of tension. *"Those are damn good odds,"* I said, hoping to knock it down a notch. Eden and Em didn't loosen up, but the men slapped hands with hoots of approval. That was better.

"When Sandra's secure, we'll splinter off. If the targets are disabled, and I sincerely hope that'll be the case, they won't be following us, but if any of you pick up a tail, call for backup.

"We'll meet back here at the van. The keys will be in the ashtray." I caught James's eye and he nodded. *"If you can't make it back to the van, then get yourself to Lake Union. The float plane is scheduled to take us back tomorrow at noon. If you miss that flight, get yourself home and I'll reimburse your expenses."*

I checked the time again. *"It's after ten. Time to get into position. Any questions?"* No one spoke up. I then asked Mark, who was still watching the *MayBell,* if he'd heard and understood the plan.

"Yeah, sounds good, but I think our odds just got worse," he said. *"It looks like the* MayBell *picked up a man in Stabbert's yard. I count six of them and I haven't seen the woman yet."*

"Damn it. Let's hope the increase in numbers doesn't change the rest of their routine." I slid open the side door of the van and hopped out. *"Gary, Tony—we're out of here."* I poked my head back in the door. *"Be safe,"* I said, and looked pointedly at Emelynn in the back seat. *"I'll see you back here soon."*

Everyone piled out of the van. I caught up with Gary and Tony, who were already inside the park's treeline. We lifted off and broke through the tree canopy and veered north, dodging the lights on our way back to the water. We then headed south, giving the *MayBell* a wide berth. When we had her in our sights, we took up positions in the upper canopy of the nearby trees. Mark crouched in the shadows below.

Eden's voice came over the earpiece. *"Em and I are on the ground and headed to the pub."* I couldn't see them from my vantage point, but silently urged them to hurry.

James checked in next. *"James here. We're in position."* Good. That meant he, Alex, Jin and Danny were ready.

Fifteen more minutes passed with no activity from the *MayBell*. It was impossible to stop running Plan B scenarios through my head. But the odds of a successful extraction at sea, on the small confines of a boat, and where they'd be free to use weapons, didn't appeal. I changed position to get a line of sight on James's crew, but they were well hidden.

"Eden here. We're in the pub and all set."

Finally, we were ready. I inhaled a deep breath and returned to watching the *MayBell*. Now we just had to wait for Lorenzo to make his move. A move that would be one of his last.

Minutes passed. I tapped my watch. Gary whistled. I looked his way and he directed my attention to the tug. Two men had emerged onto the aft deck. Soon a larger man stepped out of the wheelhouse with a slender figure by his side. I leaned forward desperate for confirmation that the woman beside Johnny was my wife, but she remained hidden in his shadow. The other two men stepped off the boat onto the dock, and one of them offered a steadying hand to the slender figure. It seemed an awkward extraction with Johnny unwilling to move out of the way.

And then finally, she stepped off the boat and looked up. For one brief moment, I saw her face. My heart slammed behind my rib cage, and I grabbed a branch to steady myself.

"I can see Sandra," I said. Even from this distance, she looked beautiful. Johnny remained by her side as they made their way up the dock. Another image—one of Cole with his arm around her—played out in my mind.

Don't, I thought, and pushed the image away. *"They're leaving the boat,"* I said. *"Eden, Em, head outside and stay in front of the pub until you see them."*

I met Gary's gaze and then Tony's. We were ready to move.

Mark spoke from his position below us. *"Five of them left the boat."*

I whipped my head around to confirm the number.

"I see three with the woman and two others a few paces behind," Mark said.

　　　　　　　　　　　　　　　　　　　　　　　　　JP MCLEAN

That was two more than we'd hoped for.

Gary cut in. "*Jin, you better get back here. We're going to need you.*"

"*On my way,*" Jin replied.

I flitted higher to get a better look. The group gathered where the pier met the boardwalk and their muffled voices drifted up. The last two men to exit the tug turned right, away from the Loft. "*The two stragglers have split off from the main group and are headed south toward the boardwalk.*" And though I hated to, I added, "*We need to cover them.*"

Gary directed his men. "*Jin, Mark, Tony: follow them but don't engage unless they try to join up with the others.*"

Shit! Though I knew there was no avoiding it, our numbers had dropped from eight to five in a big hurry. And if the stragglers didn't run back to join the coming fight, we'd have to find them later, and dispose of them.

Gary and I stayed in position, watching the group's progress below. The two who had turned south had three shadows high in the air trailing them. The others were moving as predicted, with one man out in front of the couple and the other in the rear.

I provided an update. "*Three men and a woman just left the pier and are now on the boardwalk. They're heading your way, Eden.*" Sandra was indiscernible from the hulk of a man beside her.

"*We see them,*" Eden said.

"*Good. Position yourselves in front of them and let them get close.*"

I motioned to Gary. We lifted up and floated out of sight at the edge of far-reaching branches that lined the path. When Emelynn came into view, I paused. Her dark flying clothes were gone, replaced by cropped pants that cupped her ass and invited appreciation. She'd taken down her hair and it hung in thick curls down her bare back. Vitality clung to her like an aura.

Eden had also changed, and she looked sexy as hell in stiletto boots and a bare midriff. They made one hell of a good decoy, I thought, and congratulated myself for bringing them along. And even better, their drunken play-acting would draw attention away from the rest of us.

"*Okay, good. Keep them close,*" I said. "*We need to move them across the tracks and into the park.*"

Gary and I drifted along behind them, hidden in the tree cover. Their unintelligible drunken banter wafted up to us, and Gary smiled his appreciation and gave me the thumbs-up.

"*That's right,*" I said. "*A little farther then start slowing them down.*"

They'd crossed into the park but were still twenty yards from the restrooms. We held our position and I gazed ahead. James lay atop the restroom building, out of sight.

Muted conversation spilled out of the Loft along with two couples. They headed away from us, toward the docks.

Below, the girls continued their drunken ruse. Eden reached over and pushed Emelynn's shoulder. "No way," she said with a slur, and staggered backwards.

"Yes way," Emelynn said, and they broke out in laughter as if they hadn't a care in the world.

Together, they blocked the path, causing Sandra's crew to stop. The man in the lead hesitated momentarily and then swung out around them. "Excuse me, ladies," he said, and beetled past.

"*Perfect. Better than we could have hoped for*," I said. Five more yards and we'd be in the restroom's shadow, hidden from the public's view. "*Now keep them separated and move forward, slowly.*"

Emelynn wrapped her arm around Eden and they stumbled forward, lurching toward the squat building. They were acing it. Gary and I hung in the air, behind and to their right. The men faced forward. Sandra was on Johnny's left, and I still hadn't managed to see more than a glimpse of her.

And then Emelynn got it into her head to turn around. I sucked in a breath and stilled. The two women in my life, face to face. The animation drained out from Emelynn's face. Her gaze slid from Sandra to the hulk beside her, and then as quickly as she'd dropped out of character, she snapped back in.

"So sorry," she said, slurring her words. She took a tentative step backwards, and then another, slowing their pace. They were at the corner of the building. Her arm remained bound around Eden. "My friend went and got herself a promotion today," she said. "We're celebrating." Her gaze wandered back to Sandra. And then she stumbled.

Shit! Gary and I blew our cover and closed in, but Emelynn caught herself and straightened. She abruptly turned around and took a jerky step forward, steadied by Eden.

One of the kidnappers remained in front of the girls, Lorenzo and Sandra were right behind them, with a third man at the back. Gary and I remained exposed. Up ahead, James's crew were now all on the restroom roof, visible to anyone who cared to look.

Gary and I glanced about. The surrounding area was clear. Gary pointed to himself and then the man in the back. I pointed to myself and then Johnny. A sadistic grin curled Gary's lips. I looked ahead to James's crew and gave him the thumbs-up.

"James, you're with me. We've got dibs on the filth holding Sandra." The man in the rear spun around, but Gary was already on him.

I heard Gary say, *"You gonna run, you fucking coward?"* a moment before Alex and Danny dove off the restroom roof, and then I lost track of them.

James shot forward, straight to Sandra on Johnny's left side. I moved in on Johnny's right. Johnny's confusion didn't last long. He lifted Sandra off the ground and swung her by the waist in James's direction. Her legs clipped James, knocking him on his ass, but it left Johnny's right side open. I blasted him with a jolt that should have knocked him senseless. Instead, he curled his lip in a growl and punched out, landing a solid right to my shoulder without ever losing his grip on Sandra. I staggered back, stunned. Did the goon have a metal plate in his head?

He shot glances between James and me, using Sandra like a shield, blocking every attempt James made to get to him. I watched their dance for an opening and took a chance. I leapt up and swung out, connecting with his ear. His head barely moved, but his fist snapped out with incredible speed. I bowed in half, narrowly missing a gut punch, and landed in a crouch.

That's when I got my first good look at Sandra's face. Her beautiful blue eyes were unfocused; her face held not an ounce of emotion. I swayed and dropped my hands to the ground to steady myself. White noise quieted the grunts and slaps of fists on flesh around me. What had they done to her?

Rage blinded me. I rose up and threw all my weight behind my fists, releasing a torrent of roundhouse hits that connected with muscle and bone. Pain registered in my fists and shot up my arms, but I felt cut off from it. I'd kill him for what he'd done. The huge bastard staggered back. I lunged for him, too late to see the fist that hit me. Next thing I knew, I was on the ground unable to breathe. How I'd gotten there, I didn't know. A shot rang out. And then another.

I blinked hard against the darkness that skirted my vision and forced air back into my aching chest. I had to get to Sandra.

When I opened my eyes, James's face hovered above me. "Come on," he said, offering me his hand.

"Where's Sandra?"

"She's close. We've got to get out of here."

I let him help me up and steady me, and looked around for Sandra. It had been a long time since I'd had the wind knocked out of me. The big bastard had nearly knocked me out.

"Can you make it to the restroom roof?"

I nodded and followed him to the flat roof's back edge, where we'd be unseen from the ground.

"Sit," he said, and I didn't argue. James cupped his ear. "We've got Sandra," he said. "Let's go. Disperse."

I felt for my earpiece, but it was gone. A headache bloomed. "I didn't see what happened."

"You hit your head pretty hard," James said. I reached to the back of my scalp and my fingers came away covered in blood.

"I heard gunshots."

"Johnny had a gun. Hit you upside of the head with it, and then shot wild. I made sure he didn't get a second shot." James removed a gun from his waistband and moved it to the small of his back.

"Where'd you get that?"

"The Stabbert guard had a gun. And he wasn't with Stabbert. He had no ID." Now I knew why James had jumped at the chance to check on Emelynn's security guard.

James duck-walked to the other side of the roof and scanned the scene of the fight. He spoke to the team, too quietly for me to hear.

He scooted back to me. "Lorenzo and the other two are dead."

"We've still got three more to deal with," I said. Sirens sounded in the distance.

"Let's get Sandra to safety first," he said.

Sandra. The memory of her vacant face paralyzed me. James had been right. Sandra had been drugged and held against her will. And I hadn't believed it. I'd given up on her. Worse, I'd dragged Emelynn into this mess. How would I ever explain it to her?

"Come on, let's go," James said, once again offering me his hand.

Regrettably, I needed it, and wobbled to my feet.

"Can you fly?"

"Yeah, I'm good."

"Okay. Follow me."

He took off, and though unsteady, I trailed behind. Cruisers with lights flashing passed below, sirens wailing. We dropped down on a grassy boulevard at the edge of the parking lot north of the Loft.

"What are we doing here? Where's Sandra?" I asked, wary of the flashing lights that felt entirely too close. Sirens compounded the mother of a headache that hammered at my skull.

"Small detour. Rest a minute. I'll be back," James said, and took off at a crouch toward a large maple tree thirty yards distant.

He couldn't have picked a worse time to take a leak. I sank to my haunches and squeezed my eyes closed. I needed to get to Sandra. Apologize. Beg for her understanding.

A minute later, James called to me. "Jackson, over here."

I opened my eyes to see him on his knees waving urgently. I rose as fast as my pounding head allowed, and approached with caution. After a few steps, I saw a form lying on the ground beside him.

Sandra! I raced in and fell to my knees beside her. She rolled her head in my direction and reached for me. I'd betrayed this woman completely, and she was reaching for me. I took her hand and cupped her cheek. Could she ever forgive me?

"Take her," James said.

Without another thought, I lifted her and cradled her in my arms. She pressed her hand to my chest and crushed my heart.

"Get her out of here," James said, nudging me with a gentle push.

I leapt up, skirted the tree's canopy and darted away from the lights and sirens. I flew a wide arc north, and then headed back inland racing to the safety of the van. Sandra shivered in my arms, never once dropping the hand she held over my heart.

The side door of the van slid open and Alex and Eden spilled out.

"Set her here," Eden said, lifting the armrest of the bucket seat. Eden jumped back in and crouched on her other side.

"Don't leave me," Sandra whispered, fisting my shirt.

"I'm right here. I'm not going to leave you."

"Take her other hand," Eden said, crouching between the centre seats. She pressed her fingertips to the inside of Sandra's wrist. Then, done with her pulse, Eden lifted Sandra's eyelids, one at a time.

"Sandra, my name's Eden. I'm a nurse. What drug have you taken?" Eden took Sandra's arm and pushed up her sleeve, examining the skin.

"I don't know," Sandra said, and her head lolled to the side.

"Check that arm for a needle puncture," Eden said to me.

I pushed up her other sleeve and traced my finger along the soft, white skin. "I don't see anything."

"Was it a pill?" Eden said, tugging Sandra's sleeve back down.

"What did it look like?" I asked.

"Never see it," Sandra said, her voice slurring.

"Keep her awake." Eden slipped out of the van, put her phone to her ear and stepped away.

I looked down at Sandra's face, pale and drawn, and smoothed her hair. She pressed into my hand.

"I knew you'd come," she said. "I waited . . . so long."

Her words stabbed through my chest. I couldn't breathe. "I'm so sorry."

"Jackson!" Alex called. I spun around. Eden dashed for cover at the back of the van. Out front, from behind the treeline, two men approached. Fliers. At twenty yards, the man in front removed his hood. Redmond, and he'd brought his own backup. I squared my shoulders.

"It's okay. He's her father. James must have called him," I said. Alex shot me a heated glare. Eden poked her head around the back of the van, her phone to her ear.

"Jackson," Redmond said, caution slowing his stride. But the moment he laid eyes on Sandra, he rushed in and brushed me aside.

"Sandy, honey, open your eyes." He shook her shoulders. "Look at me."

"Dad?" She squinted up at him and her brows drew together. A tear rolled down her face.

Redmond pulled her forward in an embrace. "Thank god. You're going to be okay, honey. We'll take care of you. I'm taking you home."

"Home?" she said.

Redmond released her with a kiss to her head and set her back in the seat. "New Orleans. Your mother has been so worried."

"Louisiana?"

"Yes, honey. We've got your old room ready."

What the fuck? I leaned into Redmond's ear and growled, "She's coming home with me."

He twisted his head and scowled. "I think she'll be more comfortable with us."

"Please, Dad," Sandra said. "Take me to the *Symphony*."

He looked at his daughter. She reached for his hand. "Please."

Eden approached with Alex at her side. "My name's Eden Effrome. I'm a nurse. Your daughter needs to be kept awake until the effects of whatever drug they've given her wear off. Ideally, she should have blood drawn so we know what's in her system."

"Can you do that here?" Redmond asked.

"No, but a doctor I know is organizing it right now. I'm just waiting for a call."

"Thank you, Eden," I said, intervening. "Excuse us a minute." I tapped Redmond's elbow and stepped away. He reluctantly followed.

When we were out of earshot, I turned to him. "You heard Sandra. She wants to go to the *Symphony*. With me."

"You think she's going to feel the same way when she learns you gave up on her?"

"You're conveniently forgetting a few details, Redmond."

"I'm not forgetting what's important." He stormed away from me, his hands on his hips.

He returned with a look of determination in his eyes. "The police have already found three bodies. When this is done, there will be six. Seven if the one at Stabbert dies."

Thank you, James. "They won't find any more bodies, you can be sure of that."

"They shouldn't have found the three they did. But regardless, the police are going to cast a wide net. How do you think it's going to look if you're a no-show for your own charter tomorrow?"

"I'll cancel it."

"Both the charter and that van's rental can be traced back to you, and the mileage on the van will put you in this vicinity. If you're not at the airport tomorrow as expected, smiling like a tourist for their cameras, they may start asking questions. Is that a risk you want to take given the shape that Sandy's in right now?"

"Damn it!" I spun away from him. The bastard had a noose around my neck and knew it.

He called to me. "Nathan and I will take care of Sandra."

I marched back to him and stopped a foot from his face. "You'll take her to the *Symphony*, or you won't take her at all."

His nostrils flared. He paused. "Agreed. We'll take her to the *Symphony*."

"Don't fuck with me, Redmond."

"Likewise . . . son."

Chapter Thirty-Five

Letting Redmond take Sandra was one of the hardest things I'd ever done. In her weakened state, he could poison her against me before I had a chance to explain myself. Fuck! James, the little shit, had obviously been keeping his father well-informed. Had James told him about Emelynn as well?

Emelynn. Damn. I dropped my head in my hands. She'd be here any minute. How would I ever explain Sandra to her? Or her to Sandra?

I jerked at the touch of a hand on my shoulder. "Let me clean that," Eden said. "Keep your head down."

I'd forgotten about the laceration to my scalp. Eden snapped on a pair of latex gloves and wiped at the wound with wet gauze. "You and Sandra are close," she started, but she didn't get the chance to follow up because James landed, with Emelynn collapsed in his arms.

Eden and I jumped out of the van as he laid her on the grass. The left side of her torso was covered in blood.

"What the hell happened?" I asked.

Eden shouted to Alex, "Bring me the first aid kit." She squatted beside Emelynn and lifted her shirt. A small round hole on Emelynn's abdomen oozed blood with the beat of her pulse.

James cast off Emelynn's bag and knelt beside her. "Lorenzo's shot went wide. It must have hit her."

I glared at him. "Lorenzo's shot? You sure about that?"

He stiffened and returned my glare. "My shot is in Lorenzo's chest, so yeah. I'm sure."

"Roll her over," Eden said, and James hauled Emelynn onto her side. She moaned in protest. "That's good. Conscious is good." It didn't sound good to me.

Ragged edges ringed the wound on her back. "Looks like it went through," James said. Blood dripped onto the grass.

"We need to get pressure on it. Hold her there." Eden rifled through the first aid kit and tore open a large gauze pack. She pressed the sterile pad to the wound on Em's back.

Emelynn let out a sickening moan. "You're hurting her," I said, and dropped down opposite James.

"Of course it hurts!" Eden hissed. "She's been shot, but if we don't get that bleeding stopped, she'll die. Here," she said, and grabbed my hand. "Hold this in place with as much pressure as you can."

The moment my hand was in place, Eden jumped to Emelynn's other side. She ripped more gauze from the pack and pressed the material to the wound on her abdomen. Emelynn writhed, groaning in pain.

"James, take this one. Press hard."

James pressed his palm to Emelynn's abdomen and she cried out, curling into him. James and I were close enough to butt heads. I clenched my jaw and squeezed my eyes closed to keep from drilling my fist into his skull.

Eden's clipped voice derailed my thoughts. "She's conscious, lungs sound clear, breathing okay. Entry wound is left lower quadrant. Exit is left posterior flank." She stood beside me with the phone to her ear.

"James, Avery's asking if you know what hit her."

"A 0.38 calibre. Close range."

Eden repeated it, and bobbed her head, listening to Avery. "Got it. I'll call again in a few minutes." Eden hung up. "If the bullet hit a kidney, we won't be able to stop the bleeding. She'll need surgery. Keep the pressure on. We'll give it another five minutes and check."

Sometime during those five minutes, remorse crawled into my soul and set up camp. I'd gotten Emelynn into this, and now her life was on the line. This was my fault.

Alex, who'd been keeping watch, moved in close, his hand covering the mic on his earpiece. "Gary and Danny are on their way. The two stragglers and the one they left behind on the boat are all down and on the tug. Jin and Mark are taking the *MayBell* offshore right now. They'll get rid of them."

"It's time," Eden said, and knelt beside me. "Let me have a look."

The blood-saturated gauze came off with my hand. This time the wound didn't drip. Eden applied fresh gauze. "It looks good. Lay her down."

James eased her onto her back and stood. He pulled his earpiece from his pocket and fit it into his ear. I heard him address Gary as he stepped back.

Eden took James's place by Emelynn's side. She lifted the edge of the gauze and let out a deep breath. The small hole had stopped oozing blood.

"All right," Eden said, resting on her heels. "We may have gotten lucky. I'm going to need a hand getting a pressure dressing on her, and then we're going to have to pray the bleeding stays controlled."

"We have to get her to a doctor," Alex said.

"Yes," Eden agreed, rifling through the first aid kit.

"A hospital's out of the question," James said. "I'll talk to Avery. See if he knows someone."

After I helped Eden with the pressure dressing, I fished Emelynn's hoodie from her bag and we put it on her.

James handed Eden his phone. "Avery wants to speak with you." She took it and stepped away.

Danny and Gary emerged from the woods and jogged over.

"How's Emelynn?" Danny asked, his eyebrows knit together.

"The bleeding's stopped for now," I said. "But we need to get her to a doctor." I turned to James. "Did Avery come through with a name?"

"I've got an address in Bellingham. It's ninety minutes north." He addressed Gary. "Can you deal with a detour?"

"I've got all night," Gary said.

"Help me get her into the van," I said, and together, Danny and I lifted Emelynn onto the back bench seat and laid her down. She whimpered but never opened her eyes.

Eden returned James's phone. "The doctor's expecting us," Eden said. "Let's go."

She crawled into the back with Emelynn and took her hand. It should have been me, but I couldn't do it. I was the one who'd put her there.

I walked to the front and took the seat beside James, who'd already started the engine. Everyone else jumped in and we pulled out and headed to the I5.

We talked in hushed tones during the drive north. Silence stole our conversation each time a groan sounded from the back seat, and not even Gary's play-by-play of how they'd dealt with the last three kidnappers could keep my remorse at bay.

When we arrived at the doctor's house, she met us in the attached garage in yoga gear and a ponytail. She closed the overhead door behind us.

We piled out and she climbed in. She and Eden spoke in quiet tones, and a few moments later, the doctor backed out.

"Let's get her inside," she said.

Danny and Alex were closest and sprang into action. I stepped away to give them room, and somehow ended up excluded from the protective huddle that moved Emelynn inside the house. If I'd owned up to our relationship earlier, I could be there to help her. But I hadn't . . . and I had no right.

An hour later, we got back in the van, without James or Gary; they'd remained behind with Emelynn. Leaving her there felt wrong— like I'd abandoned her; I hadn't even said goodbye. And it burned my ass that James insisted on staying behind, but I had no ammunition for an argument.

Alex drove back to Lake Union. We pulled into a Holiday Inn, and soon dispersed to our rooms. The rest of them no doubt slept. But I could only wait out the night wondering if Redmond was pumping Sandra full of hate, if Emelynn had survived, and how the hell I'd ever look myself in the face in the morning.

My father had been right about Sandra. She was too good for me. I didn't deserve her. If she never forgave me, it would be my own fault. But I wouldn't give her up without a fight. As much as it pained me to realize it, taking Emelynn to my bed had been all about soothing my battered ego. I'd accused my father of something similar. The difference being that he hadn't been married when he'd done it. I'd made conscious decisions to live my life differently than my father, and yet here I was, slogging through the same muck, filthier than he'd ever been.

James never showed up at the hotel. He didn't even return my calls or texts.

But Redmond did. His tone was clipped when he confirmed they'd made it back safely. At least he'd kept his word about delivering Sandra to the *Symphony*.

Though I was certain it would disappoint Redmond, I wasn't arrested when we arrived at the float-plane terminal for the charter home. In fact, the trip would have been entirely uneventful if it weren't for Eden's telling me that James had accompanied Emelynn to Avery's in the early morning hours.

How convenient for James. He had all the time he needed to pump them both full of poison and lies and paint me to be the lowlife mothers warned their daughters about. James wouldn't be happy until he'd destroyed anything that might have existed between Emelynn and me.

But then again, I'd already done that.

Chapter Thirty-Six

After we cleared customs in Vancouver, we gathered in the parking lot beside Alex's van.

Danny turned to me with a sombre expression. "Are you heading back to New Orleans?"

"Yeah, soon." I said, and looked away. Guilt and remorse weighed me down. I shifted my bag to my other shoulder.

Alex offered a genuine smile. "Let's get together for a drink before you go?"

I nodded, unable to bring myself to lie to his face after what they'd done for me. For Sandra.

"I can't tell you how much I appreciate your help," I said, looking Danny, Alex and Eden in the eye. "And I'm very sorry about Emelynn. That should have never happened."

"Not your fault, man," Alex said, naively excusing me.

"Avery says she's going to be fine," Eden said. "Call him. Go and see her. I think she'd like that."

Again, I nodded, cringing a little more inside.

"You sure you don't want a lift?" Alex said, repeating an offer he'd made earlier.

"Thanks, but no. I've got some things I need to take care of before I head home. Thanks again."

I shook hands with the guys, and Eden offered a hug that I stiffly returned. I suspected she'd later regret that hug.

I watched their van turn out of the parking lot, and then I walked back to the terminal and hailed a cab to take me to the marina.

A part of me was relieved to see the *Symphony* safe in her slip, but the walk up the dock felt like a death march into enemy territory.

Redmond looked up when I entered the salon. He'd left the Gucci suit and brogues at home and looked every inch a Flier. He was in good shape for an old man.

"Where's Sandra?" I said, dropping my bag at the entrance.

"She's resting. Finally." There was no mistaking the ice in his voice as he set his book on the coffee table.

I raised an eyebrow. "Oh?"

Redmond stood and crossed his arms. He fixed me with the steely glare of a tiger eyeing its prey. "Where are my daughter's things?"

Yeah . . . knew this was coming. I put my hands on my hips and stood my ground. I didn't need to explain myself.

Redmond's face contorted in rage and he exploded. "Her things, goddamnit! Where are her clothes?" He sidestepped the coffee table and swung his hands in the direction of the bookcase. "Her books? Her bloody toothbrush!" Redmond's face was the exact same shade of red my father's got when he couldn't bend my will.

I gazed at the floor, shaking my head. I refused to feed his tirade.

"She was hysterical when we arrived," Redmond shouted. "Tore through this place like a hurricane looking for some small token of the life she used to have."

Yeah? And what about the life I used to have? I was so done with his crap. I dropped my hands from my hips. "I'm sorry for that. But they're just things. They're replaceable."

"Is that how you see it? How do you think Sandy felt when she stripped off her filthy clothes expecting to find something of her own to wear? Something to erase the memory of Johnny watching her put those clothes on. Something that didn't carry the stench of that tugboat?"

"I'm not having this discussion with you, Redmond. This is between my wife and me. Where is she?"

"You gave up on her. You're not fit to be her husband."

Bastard! "You don't get to make that call," I said, and stormed for the staircase to the lower staterooms.

"Alexandra!" I called, racing down the stairs. I charged down the hall and pushed open the door to our stateroom.

She sat on her side of the bed with her back to the headboard, her knees to her chest. She swivelled her head toward me in slow motion. Dark shadows circled sunken eyes and her hair looked like a bad wig, as if she'd fallen asleep when it was wet and uncombed. She wore one of my Saints jerseys and a pair of lounge pants that would surely fall off her if she stood up. She was absolutely gorgeous.

A deep V formed between her eyebrows. "Dad's right. You gave up on me," she said, and her voice hitched.

I closed the door and approached the bed, sitting as close as I dared. Tears rimmed her eyes, threatening to fall.

"Not intentionally. I thought you left me for Cole."

I'm not sure how long we talked. Hours, I suppose. Redmond's footsteps were a constant warning that he lurked nearby.

Sandra told me about the night she'd stormed out. The last night I'd seen her. Cole must have been watching. He'd texted her. Asked her to meet him.

She couldn't tell me why she'd agreed. Perhaps she didn't know herself, but she drank the herbal tea he'd offered. And when he told her what he'd planned, she remembered telling him to go to hell. The rest of that night remained a blank.

I crawled up the bed to sit beside her and draped an arm around her shoulders. We relived the painful weeks we'd spent apart. I recounted our efforts to find her, and she told me what she remembered of her journey up the coast. But her memory had holes in it I could sail the *Symphony* through.

Regardless, one question above all, had to be asked. I picked at the fraying cuff of the old jersey she wore. "Did Cole or any of the other men force themselves on you?"

She stared off into the distance, frowning in concentration. Her arms remained locked around her knees and she began rocking herself. Finally, she spoke. "I'd remember something like that, wouldn't I?" Her words were mixed with tears and anxiety lined her face. I wanted Cole's head on a spike.

I decided to spare her learning about Emelynn; she wasn't strong enough yet.

"I am going to take care of Cole, Sandra. I promise. He'll never touch you again."

She clutched at my arm, her eyes wide in alarm. "You mustn't."

I pulled my head back and studied her face. This was not up for discussion. "Cole is going to pay for what he did to you . . . to *us*."

"No! You can't."

I frowned. Was this some kind of Stockholm reaction?

"Tell me why," I asked.

"The film he gave us. The one with the Ghost. It's real."

Oh crap. We were back to that? "Sandra, please. We've been through this."

"I didn't make it clear before because of the risk. I'm telling you now. *Ghosts are real.* I know it for a fact, and if anything happens to Cole, that film will be released to the Tribunal. They'll find out what your father did. You can't take Cole down without taking yourself down with him. I don't want that." She entwined her fingers with mine and looked up at me, pleading. "I need you."

Her mental state was worse than I'd thought. "All right," I said, and patted her arm in reassurance. "Let's get some rest." We settled on top of the covers. I pulled her close and pressed a kiss to her head and held her until she drifted off. When her breathing deepened, I pulled my arm free and slipped from the room to let her sleep.

Adding to an already bad night was James, who had joined his father in the salon. They were dressed like twins and sat facing one another on the sofas with their forearms draped over their knees: bookends. Two against one, as always. Redmond straightened when he saw me, and his expression hardened.

"Sandra's resting," I said, to Redmond's unforgiving glower.

Undeterred, Redmond swung into full lawyer mode. "Diana's arriving tomorrow morning," he announced. "She's bringing an addiction specialist, Dr. Sinclair."

"Sandra's mother and the doctor are both welcome," I said, and then to James, "What did we learn from Avery about the drugs in Sandra's system?"

He had his back to me and didn't turn around when he answered. "It's lorazepam. High doses. Probably in liquid form."

I crossed to my computer and fired it up. Lorazepam. A sleep aid and anti-anxiety med, as I recalled. "Side effects?"

James replied. "Confusion, memory loss."

"And highly addictive," Redmond added. "Your brother set Sandra up for a long, complicated withdrawal. Six months, or so I'm told. And she may never recover her memories."

I turned on Redmond and stomped to within an inch of him. James lurched to his feet. Redmond recoiled ever so slightly. "Don't you ever call that disgusting piece of shit my brother. I hold Lake Borgne's pond scum in higher regard than Cole Des Roche." Redmond had the decency to dip his head. I returned to my computer and searched for lorazepam. The results were not comforting. I closed the laptop. Both men remained standing, their hands loose on their hips.

"Sandra's memories are vague, at best," I said. "She has very little recollection of her time on the *MayBell* or her interactions with Cole or Johnny Lorenzo."

"Oh, she remembers Johnny Lorenzo," Redmond said, shaking his head.

"What the hell are you talking about?"

"He liked to watch her dress every few weeks when he brought her clean clothes."

Sick pervert. Was that all he'd done? "Sandra told you that?"

Redmond's steely glare returned. "That animal terrorized my daughter."

I curled my fingers around the counter's edge and sucked in air to cool my temper. Sandra had told her father, but she hadn't said a word to me. I was still on the outside. "Lorenzo is dead. He'll never hurt her again," I said. "The only one left is Cole, and he's mine."

"Cole?" Redmond's anger vibrated like a base chord. "Fuck Cole. He's in New Orleans. Your wife is right here, just like you asked." His finger stabbed at the floor like he was punching a hole. "If you ever loved her, then prove it. She needs you to be present or be gone. And I don't care, one way or the other."

The fact that I'd never heard Redmond utter "fuck" before gave me pause, but it didn't derail me.

"I have no intention of abandoning my wife, but Cole will pay for what he's done." I scooped up my laptop. "The minute Sandra's stable, I'm going after him," I said, and turned for the stairs.

I climbed onto the bedspread beside Sandra and watched her fitful sleep. Guilt pinched my soul each time she opened her eyes in a blind panic. She'd flail her arms and kick at me if I was too close. I lost count of the number of times I comforted her. I moved a chair to the bedside and dozed, never getting more than thirty minutes' sleep before the next bout.

The sound of running water woke me. Sandra was in the shower and it was barely 4:00 a.m. I headed up top to brew a pot of coffee and found James asleep on one of the sofas in the salon.

He opened his eyes as I stepped into the galley.

"Where's your dad?" I asked, filling the pot from the tap.

"Below."

"I never got a chance to thank you for looking after Emelynn," I said. James didn't say a word as I turned my back and measured the coffee. I closed the bin, pushed start and faced him.

"How is she?"

James rubbed his face and swung his legs off the sofa, sitting up. "I will answer that question once, and only once, and then I don't want to hear her name come out of your mouth again. Emelynn will be fine in a month or so. It was a clean shot. In and out."

"Anyone ever tell you that you're an arrogant prick?"

He shrugged. "Call me what you want. My sister has been hurt enough, thanks to you, and she has a long recovery ahead of her. Your concern needs to be with her, not your mistress."

"Don't you dare turn Emelynn into a tawdry affair. She doesn't deserve that."

"You slept with her. That makes her your mistress. You chose her over Sandra." James stood and stretched his shoulders back.

"It was a lot more complicated than that. And you seem to be forgetting that you and I both searched for Sandra."

"But I'm not the one who gave up on her."

I felt my eyes falter from his steady gaze. "I didn't know. If I did . . . well, I'd have done things differently."

"If you loved her like she deserves, like a husband should, you wouldn't need to *know*, because you'd never have doubted her. On faith alone, you'd have led a charge through hell to find her."

Sandra opened the door to the salon. "James!" she squealed, and ran right past me and into his arms. He closed his eyes and held her tight, cradling her head. She clung to him like a burr. Maybe there was a thread of truth to what James said, but how could I love Sandra like a husband should when she kept me on the outside and chose her brother over me every time? I reached for coffee mugs as they embraced and exchanged reassurances. I delivered the coffee and took a seat. Sandra sat beside James, gazing up at him as if he was her hero. It should have been me she sat beside, me she leaned on. An hour later, they were still side by side when Redmond joined us.

At our prompting, Sandra filled in more details of her ordeal. She'd cooperated with Cole in the beginning, knowing that we'd be looking for her. Sandra didn't notice the scathing look that James shot me. They were in California by the time she'd decided that cooperating wasn't helping. She couldn't remember where, or when, but the first time she'd put up resistance, she found herself drugged. From then on, she was locked in her cabin, unsure of which meal would hold the drugs that would ensure she'd be docile for another bank withdrawal.

Later that morning, Sandra's mother, Diana, arrived with Dr. Sinclair. Diana was a petite woman who had an air about her that commanded compliance. She was the polar opposite of my mother, who was about as assertive as the pudding she'd made. My mother put everyone else's needs ahead of her own. Diana made certain that her priorities became everyone else's. Redmond and James were happy to kowtow, but I found little charm in her manipulations. Sandra normally butted heads with her, but from the moment Diana arrived on board the *Symphony*, her behaviour was all soft cooing edges and coddling.

Diana introduced Dr. Sinclair, who was dressed in a tweed jacket and loafers as if Diana had dragged him out of a university lecture hall. They sat on the sofa, Diana on one side of Sandra and Dr. Sinclair on the other. Redmond and James sat opposite and I stood behind them. Diana's face appeared frozen as Sandra answered the doctor's questions. We provided timeline context when Sandra couldn't, but as the questions became more personal, Sandra faltered.

"I'd like to examine my patient in private. Is there somewhere we could go?"

Sandra's gaze widened and darted to her mother.

The doctor didn't miss it. "You and your mother, of course," he said, and patted Sandra's hand. I escorted the bespectacled doctor, Sandra and Diana to our stateroom.

When the doctor returned to the salon, he told us that he would closely monitor her withdrawal, which would take several months. He spoke softly, almost in apology, as if he were explaining a delinquent child's behaviour. During that time, we could expect her to be confused and anxious and quite possibly agitated. "We'll step down the dosage cautiously, but until the Ativan is completely out of her system, she is to consume absolutely no alcohol," he said. "She'll also do better in familiar surroundings."

Diana left to pick up some things for Sandra and the doctor agreed to return the following day. After they left, I went below and made some phone calls.

Later that evening, I told Sandra's family that Graham was flying up, and he would arrange to take the *Symphony* home to New Orleans. Fortunately, Sandra's passport was still in the on-board safe. We would fly out as soon as Dr. Sinclair thought she was ready. Diana insisted we stay with them in New Orleans until the *Symphony* was back in her home berth at the Southern Yacht Club. For Sandra's sake, I agreed.

Three days later, we boarded the flight to New Orleans. Sandra, though still pale, looked lovely in a tan linen dress and matching shoes. Her soft, chestnut-coloured hair hung shiny and smooth down her back. Makeup hid the dark shadows beneath her eyes so that no one would ever guess the hell she'd been through. The first-class seat dwarfed her.

At thirty thousand feet, I stared past her and gazed out the window. Sandra wore her favourite perfume, and once again the reassuring and familiar scent of vanilla surrounded her. A bright blue sky with white clouds below completed the illusion of a perfect day.

The next week would be busy as we settled back into life in New Orleans. I'd already touched base with Jimmy and explained that Sandra and I had reconciled. He sounded genuinely happy for us, though I suspected he'd keep the drawn-up divorce papers in his safe for a while.

I reached over and clutched Sandra's hand. She smiled up at me, and then turned her head to the window. Two nights ago, I'd asked Dr. Sinclair in private if Sandra had been sexually assaulted. He'd acknowledged the possibility, but had no answers for me. He suggested a test for sexually transmitted diseases would be prudent. It was one more insult. One more nail in Cole's coffin, and it cleared my conscience of his inevitable demise. I decided right then that I'd take the secret of Emelynn to my grave to spare Sandra any more pain.

After we passed through customs, Sandra donned her trademark wide-brimmed hat and dark, oversized sunglasses. Her elegance and grace in the aftermath of her ordeal spoke of an underlying strength that I prayed would get her through the next few months.

We stepped outside, and the humidity closed in like an unwelcome embrace. The mid-eighties temperature seared us for the fifteen yards between the airport and the waiting limo before the air-con came to the rescue. That I'd forgotten how oppressive the heat and humidity could be told me I'd been away far too long.

Diana fussed over Sandra after we arrived at their home. Sandra excused herself a short time later, and I knew it was because she felt suffocated.

James arrived in time for a dinner of shrimp and rice. When we'd finished eating, Sandra placed her napkin on the table.

"God, I miss wine," she said. "I'd give anything for a glass of crisp, cold Chardonnay right now." Diana and Redmond exchanged worried glances. Sandra's laugh tinkled, and it was lovely to see her smile. "You know, you don't have to abstain because of me. But watch out when I'm off the Ativan—I'm going to drink every last bottle in your cellar."

I grasped her hand and gave it a squeeze. She excused herself and retired to our room, and I took Redmond up on his offer of a drink in his den. He poured three bourbons, neat. James stood like a sentry by the window. I dropped into the soft leather sofa and Redmond took a seat opposite in a tufted club chair. They had something on their minds. Emelynn, no doubt.

"I find myself in a bind," Redmond started. "And it has to do with Cole Des Roche."

I chuffed. "You don't need to worry about Cole. I'll be taking care of him in the very near future."

James didn't take his gaze from the window.

Redmond stared at his glass, swirling the golden liquid. "Sandy told me about her discussion with you. I know she told you about Ghosts. That they exist."

"Yeah," I said. "It's a side effect of lorazepam. Dr. Sinclair told us she would be confused for a while. Once it's out of her system, she'll see things clearly again."

Redmond took a swallow and resumed swirling. "Sandy's not confused about Ghosts. They do exist, and your father hired one to ruin Cole's family."

I paused and cast a glance at James. He didn't seem to be breathing. I looked back at Redmond. Were they putting me on? "Have you been dipping into Sandra's Ativan, Redmond? What the hell are you saying?"

He steadied a sober gaze at me. "Fliers who are Ghosts live amongst us. The Tribunal knows this, and they won't tolerate knowledge of it outside their own circle. And now that you know, you are also at risk."

I looked from Redmond to James, who stayed focused on the view beyond the window.

"How do you know this?"

"That's not something I can share."

I raised an eyebrow. Convenient.

"So," Redmond continued, "the bind I find myself in is that I want desperately to take Cole's life as compensation for his crime, yet I know that if he dies an untimely death, two things will happen. One: the film he put together of the Ghost your father hired will be delivered to the Tribunal, in which case they will most assuredly kill you for his crime. And two: Cole warned Sandy that if anything happened to him, the Tribunal would learn that she'd been kidnapped, in which case they might decide that she's too weak to trust with the secret they so desperately want to hide."

I stared into my glass. Somewhere in the room, a clock ticked. "That's an awful lot to swallow," I said, and looked up from my glass. "Why should I believe you?"

"I have no reason to lie, quite the opposite actually. I'd like nothing more than to see Cole pay the ultimate price for his arrogance. But I love Sandy more than revenge, and I'd like to think you do too. As much as I don't appreciate your behaviour surrounding Sandy's disappearance, she still loves you. Your death would hurt her at a very vulnerable point in her recovery. And Cole placing Sandy in the Tribunal's crosshairs is a risk I'm simply not willing to take."

"You knew all along. That's why you were so anxious to have me roll over for Cole."

"I had hoped I'd never have to tell you," Redmond said. "It's a dangerous burden."

"You seem to know an awful lot about the Tribunal. Just how well do you know them?"

Redmond emptied his glass. "Far better than would be my preference."

James turned from the window. He'd adopted the same sober stare as his father. "Can we trust you to stay away from Cole?"

As incredible as it sounded, I believed them. They were far too stone-faced to be putting me on. And here I thought this little tête-à-tête was going to be about Emelynn. "All right. But only if you promise the same. Because if anyone goes after Cole, it's going to be me."

"Agreed," James said, and the three of us shook on it.

Sandra and I spent two suffocating weeks with Diana and Redmond. They hovered like unemployed servants desperate for work. The one thing that tied us together was our love and concern for Sandra.

Each day I escaped their scrutiny to spend a few hours at Delaney. Ted Worley had done an admirable job in my absence, but steel prices continued to climb and Carl Prudhomme of Industrial Rod and Steel in Lafayette was playing hardball on the Dixon Tower Project. I could see now it had been a mistake to deal "fairly" with the likes of his ilk. I should have listened to my father. Prudhomme had less integrity than a crack dealer in a schoolyard.

I invited Desmond Cross, my father's old Flier associate, to a private meeting. Desmond hadn't been inside the building since my father died. He didn't need the money—my father had already made him a wealthy man—but he was happy for the *busywork*, as he called it. And he was just the type of degenerate who not only would find something useful to convince Prudhomme of the value of fair pricing, but also enjoy the sport of it.

Dr. Sinclair paid regular visits, and though Sandra's nightmares continued, her sleep patterns showed improvement. Sinclair liked to remind us that we were still in the *early days*.

When we returned to the *Symphony*, Sandra brought countless bags of the clothing, toiletries and bric-a-brac she and her mother had pulled together. Within days, the ship once again embraced her presence: books, framed photographs and an overflowing makeup counter in our ensuite head.

Weeks later, she still hadn't left the ship, which confirmed Dr. Sinclair's declaration that she had a long recovery ahead of her.

Late in July, more than a month after our return to New Orleans, I lied to my wife and told her I was meeting my old friend, Kyle Murphy, for drinks downtown. She wasn't keen on his visiting the *Symphony*, so readily kissed me goodbye. I lingered over her kiss, which was the only intimacy she'd been able to share since her rescue.

I drove my Porsche to the Pickwick and parked so I had a view of the entrance. The savoury scent of barbecue wafted in through the open window. Cole had been making a habit of dining here on Friday nights. He came out with a blonde on his arm and jumped into a limo. I followed them to the Four Points, where they registered for a room on the third floor.

I nursed a drink in the bar for half an hour, and then bid good night to the guard at the door, stepped out onto Bourbon Street and turned left. It was quieter around the corner on Toulouse. I walked to the end of the hotel and tucked into the building's shadow. When it was safe to do so, I flew up to the iron gallery that ringed most of the third floor.

I dialled Cole, hopeful his dick would flag at the sight of my name on his call display. He didn't answer. I texted him. *I'm outside. Gallery. You can come out, or I can come in. Your choice.*

The thumping and fumbling that ensued from inside his room put a smile on my face. I leaned back against the ornate ironwork and waited. A moment later, he strode out in his Jockeys, pretending he wasn't shitting his pants.

"What the fuck do you want, *brother*," he said. "I'm busy."

I looked him up and down. The blonde was going to be disappointed tonight. "You may think you hold all the cards . . . *brother* . . . but I can assure you, you don't."

His smile would have pleased Satan. He smacked his fists to his chest. "I'm still here. That tells me I've got a royal flush, and you're full of shit. As usual."

I pushed off the rail. "I learned about patience from our father. He dealt with your mother in his own sweet time. Took him years, but he didn't mind the wait. Made your family's fall all the more sweet."

He narrowed his eyes. "So, you admit it."

I shrugged. "Here's the thing . . . you only *think* you have something on our father, but what I have on you is irrefutable."

"You think you scare me, Jackson. You don't. I go down, you go down and so does Sandy. Now get the fuck out of my sight." He turned his back to me but halted at the sound of my voice—his hand on the doorknob.

"Our father has markers on everyone you know, and many more you don't. His influence is rooted deep in the darkest corners of this world. Corners you've only heard whispers of. Guess who controls that influence now, *brother*? From here on out, I suggest you count every day you wake up breathing as a bonus day. As I said, I'm a patient man, Cole. Sleep well."

I didn't look back. I strode the length of the gallery and around the corner to the darkened side, then leapt down to the sidewalk and returned to the Porsche.

I fired it up and drove east toward the Bayou Wildlife Refuge on Lake Borgne. When I reached the gravel service road, I cut the headlights and continued on until I found the path to the bayou I'd been searching for. I turned off the engine and frog song filled the air. The muggy air was thick with the stench of the bayou. I opened the door and stepped out, looking up to the stars that dotted the sky.

The Porsche locked with a chirp, and I headed down the trail to the lake. The bayou stretched before me. I leapt free from gravity and stretched for the sky. The wind brushed my hair and for the first time in weeks, I allowed my mind to wander to Emelynn. She was the one who'd encouraged me to fly for the hell of it. That's what I wanted to do now. I pictured her laughing green eyes and the quick smile that was never far from her lips. She'd be through the worst of her recovery by now.

I thought of the woman who'd gifted her, Jolene Reynolds, and wondered if her ancestors were the source of those ghosting fables. And now that I knew Ghosts weren't fables, I wondered if she'd been one. And what about Emelynn?

Many times I'd been tempted to call her, but I never had. I had no right. I'd hurt her and there was nothing I could do that would make it up to her. Better that I make it a clean break.

I flew down to the lake's surface, dipping my fingers into the warm water. A month from now would mark a year since my father passed. I'd been so afraid then. Afraid I'd turn out just like him. I'd been blinded by my arrogance, ashamed of the reputation he'd inflicted on us with his underhanded dealings. I'd thought I was better than him.

I wasn't. He'd turned the development business into a game, and then mastered it. There was much I could still learn from him.

When Sandra disappeared, I betrayed her—not once, by thinking she'd taken my brother to her bed, but twice, by taking Emelynn to mine. I'd thought I was better than Sandra.

I wasn't. Fate had given me a second chance with my wife that I didn't deserve. I wouldn't waste it.

Cole would pay for what he'd done. Not tonight. Maybe not this year. But in time, he'd pay.

And when he did, I'd do Dad proud.

THANK YOU

Thank you for reading *Lover Betrayed*. If you enjoyed it, please tell a friend or consider posting a short review where you purchased it. Reviews help other readers discover the books and are much appreciated.

—JP McLean

EXCERPT FROM BOOK 1

SECRET SKY

Lover Betrayed is Jackson Delaney's story, but Emelynn Taylor has her own version of events. How does Emelynn interpret Jackson's actions? How did she end up with a stranger's gift? And what happened to her after Jackson abandoned her?

Read on for an excerpt . . .

Can you tell me your name?"

"*Emelynn.*" I closed my eyes to dampen the cresting wave of nausea.

"She's nonresponsive."

No, I'm not. I forced my eyes open. The man's face was a blur. "*My name's Emelynn,*" I repeated but, oddly, I couldn't hear my voice.

"Did you find any ID?"

Nearby, a siren wailed. Had it rained? The damp air smelled of worms and wet earth. I lost the fight with my eyelids.

"No, and no sign of her shoes or transportation either. Are you ready to move her?"

"Yes, she's immobilized and secure. On three . . ."

The world tilted at a dangerous angle. Flashing lights throbbed, breaching my shrouded eyes.

"Female, early twenties, BP's ninety-eight over fifty . . ." The man's voice trailed off as I melted into the pleasant reprieve of a quiet darkness.

I liked the soft, fuzzy quality of the darkness. I felt comfortable there, but loud voices and harsh lights dragged me back and dumped me into a boisterous room. The clatter hurt my ears. I desperately wanted to shush these people, but that would be rude. A hazy face pressed in, but my eyes wouldn't focus. The man behind the face flicked a sharp light in my eye. So . . . inconsiderate.

"Can you tell me what day it is?" he asked, as if I were an idiot.

It's . . . hmm . . . What day was it? And why couldn't I move? An overwhelming desire to curl up and go back to sleep tugged at me. The man finally let me close my eyes. I pulled against whatever held me in its grip, but I didn't have the strength to fight it.

"Let's get a CT scan, spine and head, stat, and run a panel in case we have to go in."

Even though my eyes were closed, the room was too bright—and noisy. A cacophony of electronic beeps, bells and sharp voices assaulted my ears. I wanted to ask everyone to leave me alone, but my voice wouldn't come. They jostled me and I dipped into that blissful darkness again—the one that pushed away all the noise.

The darkness soothed me until the man with the snap-on gloves interrupted the calm again, his sharp light piercing my eye like a knitting needle. "Can you tell me in what city you live?"

Did he think I didn't know? I almost said Toronto, but that wasn't right, was it? Didn't I just move to Summerset . . . or was that a dream? Why was I so confused? God, my head hurt.

"Any change?" he asked.

Was he talking to me?

"No. She's still hypotensive, but stable."

I guess not.

"Pupils are equal and reactive," he said, and then he sighed. "It's been six hours. Do we know who she is yet?"

My name's Emelynn," I said in defeat, knowing he couldn't hear me.

"No, the police searched the park. No purse, no ID."

"What was she doing in the park at that hour?" someone asked.

"The police haven't ruled out that she might have been dumped there, but she was wearing workout gear so she could have been hit while jogging."

"It would have been late for a jog in the park, wouldn't it?"

"Maybe she works shifts?"

Listening to the conversation exhausted me. Before I could figure out what it meant, the darkness claimed me again. If only they'd let me stay there, but they were relentless with their light.

This time when the stabbing light woke me, the thought that perhaps I was dying flitted through my mind. Was I supposed to go toward the light? Maybe I wasn't doing it right.

When the light retreated again, I slept fitfully and had the oddest dream. It was the dead of night. A powerful storm was gathering strength. Gusting winds blew across the crests of angry waves, creating whitecaps that seemed to glow in the dark. Towering cedars and firs rained needles as they bowed to the wind. The great, crooked trunks of old arbutus trees groaned and twisted, spewing glossy leaves into the breeze.

And I had a bird's-eye view of it all.

Home was here in the dream, somewhere. I sensed it calling out to me, drawing me toward its warmth and safety. I knew the small cottage so well but couldn't find it. The storm would stop if I could just get inside, but the wind blew me out over the treetops, farther and farther away. And then I was falling . . . falling . . . falling through the night sky, careening out of control, crashing through the tree canopy until that blissful darkness put an end to the terrible fall.

The pointy light woke me. "Can you tell me your name?" The man peeled back my eyelids and flicked that damn light.

"Emelynn," I said, relieved to hear the sound of my voice. But the relief was short-lived. My head exploded in agony when I turned away from the light.

As the pain hit a crescendo, I heard him remark "I'm losing her" and I surrendered to the peaceful darkness where pain didn't reach me.

"Emelynn," the man said, the next time he woke me with the flicking light. "Emelynn, don't struggle—we've immobilized your head. Do you know where you are?"

I squinted, straining to bring the face behind the glasses into focus. "The hospital?"

"Good. That's good, Emelynn. I'm Dr. Coulter. You've had an accident."

"What accident?" Car accident? I don't have a car. No, wait, I think I do have a car. Why was this so hard?

"You don't remember?" He pressed his lips into a thin line and furrowed his brow.

I tried, but the dream was all I could think of. "Did I fall?"

"We don't know. We were hoping you could tell us."

"My head hurts."

"You have a concussion. I can't give you anything for it yet. Can you tell me what you were doing in Sunset Park last night?"

"I live there," I said, but that wasn't right either. Why was I so mixed up? Sleep once again tugged at me.

He seemed to share my confusion. "We'll talk again later."

I folded into the darkness, and when it faded, it revealed an airport scene that looked vaguely familiar. I drifted toward a young couple with a little girl and watched as the man leaned in to kiss the woman.

"I love you," he said, pulling away.

My heart stopped when I saw the man's face.

He turned to the little girl and mussed her hair. "Be good for your mother. I'll only be gone a few days."

Oh, god, no. I knew what this was. I had to stop him. "No! Don't go!"

He put his big tackle box on the luggage cart beside the bag that I knew held his fishing rods. "I'll be back Tuesday. Don't forget about those peanut butter cookies you promised me." He smiled down at the girl, then turned and walked out to the float plane tied to the dock.

"No!" I cried, as he ducked into the plane, oblivious to my presence. "Please," I begged. Then someone called my name.

"Emelynn. Emelynn, that's right, look at me. I'm over here." A woman in scrubs moved her face into my line of vision. I blinked up at her.

"It was a dream, that's all, dear. You have a concussion. Your head is braced. Try not to fight it. You were thrashing in your sleep." She adjusted the blankets and checked the IV.

Pain returned with my awakening and ramped up quickly. It wasn't just my head anymore. My entire left side was on fire. A moan escaped my throat.

"I'll get Dr. Coulter," the nurse said, hurrying from the room.

Time crawled while I played a miserable little game of Which Body Part Hurts Most. There was no clear winner.

Dr. Coulter arrived at a gallop. He and the nurse succinctly exchanged statistics at a rapid-fire clip. BP? One oh six over sixty. Urine? Clear. Orientation? Improving. With a clipboard in hand, he checked a number of beeping machines.

"Can you tell me your name?" He put the clipboard down with a clatter and pulled that damn penlight out of his breast pocket.

"Emelynn," I said, as he held my eyelid captive.

"Good," he said, distracted by his light-flicking exam. "Do you have a last name, Emelynn?"

"Taylor," I responded with trepidation. What kind of trouble had I gotten myself into?

He repeated the light exam with my other eye. "Very good," he said, and then he finally saw me, not just my eyes.

"Where do you live?" he asked.

"Cliffside Avenue."

He smiled warmly. "Glad to hear you've moved out of the park."

"Excuse me?" My head throbbed in time with the beat of my heart.

"During one of our earlier discussions, you said you lived in Sunset Park. I'm just happy to see that your memory is coming back. What do you remember about your accident?"

"Accident?" I mulled over his question, holding out for some clues. He wasn't offering any and my dreams were all mixed up with reality. Had I dreamt that I'd fallen through the trees or was that real? My head kept pounding. I drew my right hand up and followed the path of the tube sticking out of the back of it up to a dripping IV bag.

"Late Monday or early Tuesday?" he continued, bringing my attention back to his question.

"I'm sorry, I don't remember," I said, distracted now. "How long have I been here?"

"You came in on a 911 call at"—he checked the notes on the clipboard—"oh-one-thirty on Tuesday."

I tried to process the information.

"That's one thirty in the morning. You were found in Sunset Park. Do you remember why you were in the park at that hour?"

"The park is right beside my house." I tried to recall the details that would make sense of this scenario, but they escaped me, and the pain made concentration difficult. "I don't remember."

"Okay. Let's give it a few more hours. Memory loss isn't uncommon with this type of brain injury. It may be temporary."

"*May* be?"

"It's still early. We need to give it more time."

"It feels like I've been here for days."

"I'm sure it does. We've been waking you on the hour since you arrived. It's standard procedure for concussions. Unfortunately, your blood pressure is still too low and you've been unconscious more than not during your stay here in the ICU, so we're not done yet. How's your pain?" he asked. "On a scale of one to ten."

"Nine hundred," I said, closing my eyes. "What happened to me?"

"I don't know, but it was particularly hard on your left side." I heard him pick up the clipboard again. "You've got ten stitches in the back of your head plus seven or eight in your left ankle, and a whole host of contusions and abrasions, including some nasty-looking road rash on your face, but I don't think it'll scar." He flipped up a sheet of paper. "There's no evidence of sexual assault, but you sustained an injury to your kidneys. The blood has already cleared from your urine, so we'll remove the catheter in the next few hours."

I heard him set the clipboard down on the table again, and I opened my eyes when he took my hand. "I can give you something for the pain, but I'm afraid it won't help much," he said. "It's important that we're able to rouse you at regular intervals for the next six hours. Do you think you can hang in there?"

"Do I have a choice?"

He gave me a crooked smile. "I'll order your meds and check on you in a few hours."

The nurse returned with a needle and stuck it into the IV line. "I'll wake you in an hour."

A thick fog rolled in around me. I dreamt again, but not of the family at the airport or the terrifying fall through the tree canopy.

. . . I was nine or ten years old and beachcombing with my father. He had that tool in his hand, the one he used to break open fist-sized geodes searching for the crystals hidden inside. When I got close, he called to me and turned over a flat piece of shale. He laughed as I shrieked and ran away from the tiny crabs that scrambled to find fresh cover.

My heart quickened as the nurse woke me and the memory faded. She assured me it had been an hour. When she left, the thick fog came back, pulling me under.

. . . A blonde-haired woman in a wide-brimmed hat whispered my name. She held her hands palms out, inviting me to a game of patty cake, and I lifted my hands to mirror hers. She spoke in a quiet voice, repeating a haunting refrain while keeping watch over her shoulder, and when shadows approached, she vanished.

The nurse woke me again. I had dipped in and out of fog so often that my perception was all mixed up, making it difficult to sort out what was real and what wasn't. "What time is it?" I asked.

"Just after six in the morning," she said, pumping up the blood pressure cuff. "Wednesday." She paused to listen to her stethoscope. "You're in the ICU, and I'm happy to report that your blood pressure is improving." The Velcro made a ripping noise as she removed the cuff.

"Good morning, Emelynn," Dr. Coulter said, as he crossed behind the nurse to retrieve the clipboard. "Your vitals are looking better. How's your pain level?"

"It hasn't improved with time," I said, forcing a smile.

"Have you remembered any more details about your accident?" His expression was hopeful.

"No," I said. The lie came easily; I was good at lying. I'd been hiding my secrets for a long time.

Dr. Coulter raised his chin and glared down his nose. "Well, keep trying. You're out of the danger zone, so I'll give you something more for the pain now. Maybe you'll remember more after you've rested." He frowned in disappointment as he left my room.

He didn't believe me, but he didn't press me either, which was a good thing: I could fill the room with what I was withholding. Because unfortunately, I now remembered all of it. Every last detail.

Acknowledgements

Lover Betrayed was originally published as *The Gift: Betrayal.* The title change is a result of overwhelming feedback from the books' readership. My gratitude goes to Elinor Florence, who was instrumental and supportive throughout the rebranding process.

Writing *Lover Betrayed* was unlike any other writing project I've undertaken. It's a retelling of *Secret Sky* from another character's perspective. Jackson Delaney is Emelynn Taylor's love interest in *Secret Sky*. The scenes where these two characters engage and the dialogue between them are lifted directly from *Secret Sky*. From these bones, Jackson's story emerges.

It's been a challenge to craft a new story around an existing one, but thankfully I've not had to do it alone. My thanks go to John and Denis for their critical early input. Next up was my editor extraordinaire, Nina Munteanu, who is also a writing coach and author (https://ninamunteanu.me). Her razor-sharp instincts honed Jackson's character and sculpted the story to better fit the bones. Thank you, Nina. An intrepid team of beta readers then took on the challenge. Thank you Jean, Sue, Kathy, Eleanor, Cathy and Gee for your thoughts, your time and your enthusiasm. Your feedback is invaluable. And finally, my thanks go to Rachel Small of Rachel Small Editing (www.rachelsmallediting.com). Rachel is the best copy editor a writer could ask for. She polished *Lover Betrayed* to a sparkly shine with a command of the English language that puts mine to shame.

I would also like to give a shout-out to the owners and staff at Abraxas Books on Denman Island. They've supported my writing from the beginning. Thank you.

Thanks to the design team at JD&J Designs for *Lover Betrayed's* enticing book cover design.

And as always, my thanks and gratitude to my husband, parents and family, who make this journey so much more worthwhile.

All errors in the research and writing of this novel are entirely my own.

GLOSSARY OF TERMS

Covey: A group of Fliers who are geographically connected. Older coveys were and still are connected by family rather than location. All Fliers belong to a home covey and are expected to check in with coveys in areas they are visiting. Coveys are a source of information and are trained to protect their Fliers.

Crystal: All Ghosts need a crystal to achieve ghosted form. The two exceptions to this are Emelynn Taylor and the woman who gifted her, Jolene Reynolds.

Flash: Fliers can use the second lens in their eye to produce a flicker of light within the eye that other Fliers recognize.

Flier: A human either born or gifted with a mutated gene that allows him or her to shed gravity and take flight. The gene can also manifest with additional facets, such as memory reading and telekinesis. The mutation produces a second lens in the eye.

Founding families: The nine founding coveys are comprised of the oldest and strongest families within the Flier community. Centuries ago, these family coveys founded the Tribunal Novem to police the Flier ranks.

Ghost: A Flier with the ability to dissipate into molecules too small for the human eye to see. Ghosts are rare. The process of turning into this form is called ghosting. All members of the Tribunal Novem are Ghosts.

The Gift: The mutated gene that allows a Flier to shed gravity. The mutation produces a second lens in the eye. The gene can also manifest with additional facets, such as memory reading and telekinesis.

Gifting: The process of transferring the gift, in whole or in part, from one Flier to someone else. The receiver can be any human. The process strips the donor of the element gifted. When the entire gift is given, the process weakens the gift-giver and is fatal half the time. Giftings are strictly controlled by the Tribunal Novem. A Flier who has been gifted is considered a second-class Flier.

Jolt: Fliers can use the second lens in their eye to produce a wave of energy along a spectrum from sparks, which are like static shocks, to jolts, which are painful and can even be fatal. The degree of energy produced depends upon the Flier's particular gift and varies from weak to strong. A fatal jolt causes a brain bleed (hemorrhage or aneurysm), which is medically classified as a stroke.

The Redeemers: A group of Fliers who feel they have been wronged, or are not represented, by the Tribunal Novem. Their goal is to replace the Tribunal Novem. They are led by Carson Manse.

Rush: Fliers can use the second lens in their eye to produce a stimulative energy that falls within the low-end of the spectrum of energy they are able to produce. It's sexual in nature and used to heighten sexual arousal. Referred to as the/his/her rush.

Spark: Fliers can use the second lens in their eye to produce a wave of energy along a spectrum from sparks, which are like static shocks, to jolts, which are painful and can even be fatal. The degree of energy produced depends upon the Flier's particular gift and varies from weak to strong.

The Tribunal Novem: Judge, jury and executioner in the Flier world. They are comprised of one representative from each of the nine founding coveys. They are always Ghosts. Their identities are not known within the Flier community. The Tribunal's leadership rotates every five years. At any given time, five Tribunal members provide day-to-day investigation and enforcement.

DISCUSSION QUESTIONS

Spoiler alert: These questions contain spoilers that will ruin the story for those who haven't yet read the book.

1. When Jackson's wife leaves him without a word, do you think he gave up on her too soon?

2. When parents dislike a child's choice of spouse, can the marriage still thrive? How?

3. Does Sandra shoulder any of the blame for the way her family treated Jackson? If so, what could she have done to improve their treatment of him?

4. Though the reader never meets Jackson Delaney's father, Matthew, does the author draw a clear enough picture of him?

5. The Des Roche family hires ex-cons to protect their company's construction sites. Is this wise? Why or why not?

6. Do you think Jackson was doing Emelynn a kindness when he abruptly ended their affair?

7. Do you think Lover Betrayed is an apt title for this book? What are the betrayals depicted in this book?

8. If you were casting this book, who would you choose for the role of Cole? For Sandra?

9. The author chose to explore the father/son relationship in this book. Do you think she did this effectively? How did Jackson's character change in terms of his relationship with his father from the start of the book until the last line?

10. Lover Betrayed is Jackson Delaney's perspective on events that unfold in *Secret Sky*, the first book in The Gift Legacy series. The author wanted to highlight how gender and culture inform our understanding of words and body language and often result in vastly different and sometimes conflicting interpretations. If you've read both books, did you see where the misunderstandings occurred? Do you think your own gender influences which perspective you think is correct?

11. If you could ask the author one question, what would it be? Would your organization or group like to arrange an author appearance in person or online? If so, please contact the author at jpmclean @jpmcleanauthor.com.

A printable version of these discussion
questions is available at jpmcleanauthor.com/extras.

About the Author

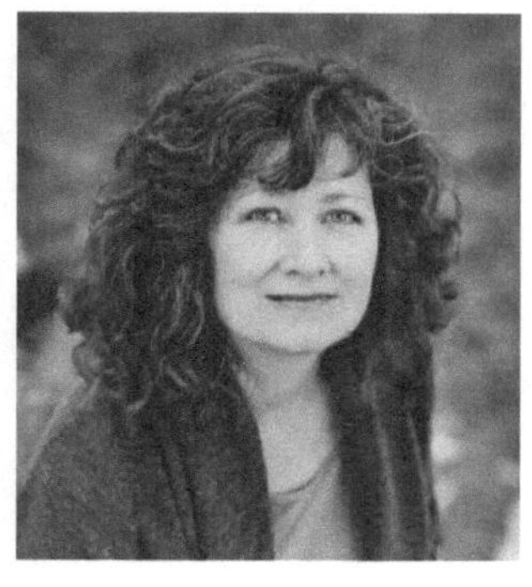

JP (Jo-Anne) McLean writes addictive supernatural fiction. She is an Eric Hoffer award winner, a two-time silver medalist in the Wishing Shelf Book Awards, a finalist in the Chanticleer International Book Awards and the Independent Author Network Awards. She is a B.R.A.G. medallion honoree and four-time Literary Titan Gold Award winner. Reviewers call her books *addictive, smart,* and *fun.*

JP holds a Bachelor of Commerce degree from the University of British Columbia's Sauder School of Business, is a certified scuba diver, an exploratory chef, and an avid gardener.

Raised in Toronto, Ontario, JP now lives with her husband on Denman Island, which is nestled between the coast of British Columbia and Vancouver Island. When she's not writing, you'll find her cooking dishes that look nothing like the recipe photos or arguing with weeds in the garden. She enjoys hearing from readers. Contact her via her website, jpmcleanauthor.com, or through social media.

 Sign up for her newsletter ~ jpmcleanauthor.com

 Find her on Goodreads ~ goodreads.com/jpmclean

 Like her on Facebook ~ facebook.com/JPMcLeanBooks

 Follow her on Twitter ~ @jpmcleanauthor